Alexander stiffened as if he had turned to stone, then reached out and hauled her close. "Do you think to move me with your talk of honor and knighthood? That is gone from me forever, and you helped make it so. I was willing to overlook your part in it, except to make you the object of ransom, but so help me, my lady, if you do not stop this foolishness and try to escape again, I will . . . I will . . ."

He was breathing hard and so was she, her lithe and shapely body pressed against him with no more barrier than two layers of wet clothing.

"What?" she demanded, arching her back to get as far away from him as she could. Still defiant, still bold. "What will you do? Kill me?"

He shook his head, and in the darkness of the night—with her in his arms—the longing he had tried to bury since he had first set eyes on her exploded within him. "I do not want your death, my lady. I would have you alive. And I would have this."

He captured her mouth in a fiery kiss.

MARGARET MOORE

All My Desire

AVON BOOKS
An Imprint of HarperCollinsPublishers

This is a work of fiction. Names, characters, places, and incidents are products of the author's imagination or are used fictitiously and are not to be construed as real. Any resemblance to actual events, locales, organizations, or persons, living or dead, is entirely coincidental.

AVON BOOKS
An Imprint of HarperCollins*Publishers*
10 East 53rd Street
New York, New York 10022-5299

Copyright © 2002 by Margaret Wilkins
ISBN: 0-380-82053-6
www.avonromance.com

First Avon Books paperback printing: October 2002

All My Desire

Chapter 1

In the early light of a July dawn, two men came down a wooded slope. Despite the risk of slipping on the mud and damp leaves beneath his feet, the short, slender one fairly skipped, as if he really wanted to dance as they made their way toward a village and the castle guarding it. The other—tall, muscular and firm of purpose—strode forward with a more lithe and lethal grace.

Both wore much mended tunics and breeches of brown wool. On their feet were leather boots that were far from new. Despite the genial summer breeze, they sported dark cloaks and hoods, as if expecting rain to fall from the white puffs of clouds drifting overhead.

Ahead, the great stone fortress seemed to rise out of the very precipice upon which it stood, making the houses of the villagers look like supplicants huddled around it. To the east of the castle, small boats clustered about the pier and along the willow-shrouded

1

bank of a wide river, which led to the sea some miles away. To the west, farms lay scattered along a narrow road leading further back into the wood. Even at this early hour, smoke curled up from the thatched cottages, and people went about the business of feeding their pigs and milking their cows. Chickens scratched in the dirt, geese squawked in their pens, a dog barked, and somewhere, a baby cried.

The tall man paid little heed to these sights and sounds. His envious eyes stayed trained on Bellevoire, the fortress that should have been his. The thick wall seemed impregnable, and its many merlons would hide a hundred archers. A series of round towers formed part of the outer wall, high places for keeping watch on the surrounding land and river. Other, smaller towers bespoke an inner wall and hinted at the size of the courtyard contained therein.

"You are sure about this?" his Gascon companion whispered. "In the broad light of day you wish to do this thing?"

He spoke as if he feared the very beeches, oaks and chestnuts spied upon them, or the little stream to their right, tumbling over rocks on its way down the hill, babbled a report of their presence to some unseen foe.

His lean, hawklike face taut with resolve, Alexander DeFrouchette glanced at his friend. "Calm yourself, Denis. The market crowd will make excellent cover for what we are here to do."

"It is easy for you, who has the blood of a frozen fish, to be calm," Denis replied, lightly leaping over a fallen tree branch as he hurried to keep up with Alexander's long-legged progress. "Me, I am no warrior—and I have never abducted a woman in my life."

"I have never abducted a woman, either," Alexander noted as he sidestepped a large rock, "but this is necessary, so it will be done."

His movement startled a pheasant nesting in the nearby underbrush. The bird flew upward in a flutter of wings into Alexander's face. With a soldier's curse, he reared back.

Arms akimbo, Denis grinned. "Perhaps you have not the blood of frozen fish after all."

Alexander made a noise that was a cross between a dismissive sniff and a disgusted grunt and continued down the hill toward the road that led to the village of Bellevoire, named for the castle towering over it. "You *are* sure Lady Allis will come to the marketplace today?"

Trotting after him, Denis nodded. "Unless she is ill, Lady Allis always comes to the village on market day with her husband. The tavern keeper was most certain. They like to spend time in the village and meet with the people, he says."

Alexander scowled. "To be admired and fawned over, no doubt."

"Sir Connor and his wife are very popular," Denis murmured, delicately clearing his throat before adding, "unlike your father."

"I do not care what these Saxon peasants thought of him."

"The tavern keeper also says that Lady Allis is a great beauty."

"It doesn't matter to me what she looks like. It is enough to know that she betrayed my father and married the man who killed him, and now she can provide a way to retrieve some of what her husband owes me," Alexander replied.

The last part of his statement was true; as for the first, he did harbor some slight curiosity about the woman who had so fascinated his father, but there was no need to tell Denis that.

"Of course I realize that her features are not important to you," Denis replied as if Alexander had accused him of being stupid. "Still, by her beauty we shall know her."

"We shall know her because she will be with *him*."

"It was years ago that you saw Connor of Llanstephan, now Connor of Bellevoire. Are you certain you will recognize him?"

Alexander's gaze again strayed to the castle of Bellevoire, the home of the usurper. "I will."

Indeed, he would never forget his first sight of the tall, dark-haired man who'd ridden among the Crusaders passing through his village in France. The finely attired and well-equipped knight had been singing in a deep, rich baritone, as cheerful as if he'd had not a care in the world.

It had been said they were on their way to join Richard the Lionhearted in Marseilles. Whoever they were, Alexander had thought, every one of that merry band had seemed part of a chosen company of God's favorites, bound upon a glorious adventure.

How he had longed to ride with them! Away from the women who either sneered at his mother or ignored her completely. Away from the men who came creeping into their cottage at night and made him leave. Away from the boys who called him terrible names and never let him share in their games.

Away from the only life he had ever known to one that *had* to be better.

He hadn't guessed then that he was looking at the man who would one day kill his father and be rewarded with all of Rennick DeFrouchette's possessions.

Denis slid a wary glance at Alexander.

Alexander intercepted his look. "A wise man does not ruin the thing he plans to trade. I will take good care of my prize."

"I do not doubt you, but what of the others in this with us? I don't trust the Norseman and his crew, or Lord Oswald's son."

The stream widened to a little pool. Thirsty, Alexander squatted and cupped his hands to drink the clear, cold water. When he was finished, he straightened and shook his hands to dry them while Denis drank. "The Norsemen are necessary to get the lady to the hiding place Lord Oswald is providing. As for Lord Oswald's son, Osburn represents his father, so we must accept him as one of our party whether we want to or not."

"Maybe we can keep him drunk," Denis proposed hopefully.

Alexander's only answer was a disdainful nod. He did not think much of Lord Oswald's vain, overdressed sot of a son and would have preferred never to have met him. Unfortunately, it was a condition of his mission that he endure the sot's company.

They reached the last line of trees bordering a curve in the road leading to the village. Alexander was pleased to find the lay of the land exactly as Lord Oswald had described. Travelers on either side of the curve were not visible to each other, and it was from here they could surreptitiously join the crowd going to market.

He scanned the road. At present, only a shepherd ambled along behind a few sheep. If they were to be inconspicuous, they would have to wait until there were more people. Still, it was early yet.

Denis ran another wary gaze over his friend. "Even in those clothes, I am not sure that you will pass for a peasant, Alexander. Everything about you proclaims that you are a man who fights with sword and lance and mace for his living. You can dress in rags, but you cannot hide those shoulders. Indeed, the very way you walk proclaims you are a warrior."

"This is a fine time to say so."

"Seeing that shepherd made me realize it. I am used to the way you look. Those in the village will not be."

"I cannot change my body."

"Maybe you could slouch?"

"I am *not* going to slouch into Bellevoire."

Denis sighed. "I should have known better than to suggest anything like humility to you."

Alexander shot him a look.

"Well, you are not a humble man and justly so, with your skill at arms. But if you do not round those shoulders of yours, you will stand out like an oak among wildflowers. However, if you wish to take that chance . . ." Denis concluded his statement with a shrug.

"If you are afraid, you can go back and wait with the horses."

"If I am afraid, it is because one of us should be.

Merde! We are about to walk into a lord's village and kidnap his wife, and here you are as calm as ... as ... that tree." Denis gestured at a slim birch. "Sending you alone into that lions' den would be fine thanks to the man who saved my life. Besides, you need me for the plan. I am to be the bait, or whatever you wish to call it, am I not?"

Alexander gripped the hilt of the sword beneath his cloak, for in truth, he was not calm; he was more tense than he had ever been in his life, with one memorable exception, for much depended on what happened this day. However, he did not want Denis to know how uneasy he was. "I could come up with another plan."

The Gascon put his hand over his heart and assumed the look of a martyr about to be led to his tortured end. "*Non!* I will go with you, though it means my death."

"You won't die," Alexander replied dryly. "If I have cause to believe we will fail today, we will leave and try another tactic."

When or what he did not know, but one way or another, he wouldn't leave this land without the wife of Sir Connor.

"However, Denis, since you are so concerned, I'll slouch—a little."

They both fell silent at the sound of jingling and clanging from the road. Looking through the trees, they spied a man driving a cart with pots and other iron items hanging outside it, moving toward the village. The tinker was a short, stocky fellow who looked half asleep.

They watched him drive by, then Denis squatted

on his haunches, a position he was able to assume for a long time. Just looking at him made Alexander's knees ache.

"Did you not say that you are the image of your father?" Denis asked, even more worried than before, it seemed. "If the likeness is pronounced, the villagers might guess who you are, and then they will wonder why you have come, and they might inform this Sir Connor—"

"Denis, why else do you think I am wearing this cursed hood?" Alexander growled, his friend's Cassandra-like croaking increasing his tension. "I know the risks of what we're about to do, and I've considered the things that could go wrong. Now either be quiet or go back to the horses."

Denis didn't speak for the next several moments, the quiet proving more disconcerting than Denis's fearful warnings. "Give me the sack," Alexander said at last, breaking the silence.

Denis rose and handed over the large cloth bag he had tucked through his belt. Usually such sacks were used to carry fleeces for measuring after they were cut from sheep and rolled. "You think she will fit in this?" he asked as he returned to sitting on his haunches.

"She should, unless she weighs over two hundred pounds. That's how much a wool sack like this will hold," Alexander replied, sticking the sack through his belt at the back. He had his sword hanging on his left; on his right, a rag with which to gag the lady and some lengths of rope to bind her; and now the sack. He felt like the tinker's cart.

Denis laughed softly, and as always when he laughed, his brown eyes became narrow slits in his face and dimples appeared in his cheeks, making him look like a mischievous boy. "I am sure she does not weigh that much."

"She'd better not, for I have a long way to carry her."

Finally a group of people approached the curve— a family bound for market, by the look of them. A thin, grizzled farmer and his plump wife with a basket over her arm led the way. Behind them came a young woman who had to be the woman's daughter, they were so alike. Any man who courted her would know exactly how she would look in twenty years. She, too, carried a basket, which she occasionally swung at a lad walking beside her. They were having some kind of argument, but not loud enough to attract their parents' notice.

He could see another wagon bearing a load of hay about half a mile back and behind that, what seemed to be another family. Soon enough, they could saunter out onto the road without attracting undue notice and join the general crowd going to the village.

He waited until the second family passed by. "Now," he whispered, and they slipped out of the trees and strolled along the rutted road as if they had been there all the time.

Soon they were in the bustling marketplace of Bellevoire, which was an even more sizable and prosperous town than Alexander had expected. Several of the buildings were stone, like the castle; others were half timbered and plastered with lime, making a sharp contrast between the exposed wood and the rest of the structure. Several had more than one story, too, later additions that hinted at increased revenue for the owners. In many of these, the bottom level had large windows with shutters that became stalls when the shutters were removed. Along with the permanent buildings around the green, which also included a large establishment that had to be a tavern and a smithy, there were several wagons serving as temporary stalls. In and around these, well-fed peasants wandered, the women with reed baskets in their hands for their purchases. Children chased each other, and dogs nosed interesting bits of refuse.

Keeping his head lowered and his shoulders rounded as Denis had suggested, Alexander peered out from beneath his hood. Pretending to be interested in the merchandise on display in the stalls or wagons, he was really surveying the merchants.

He also noted several soldiers among the crowd, no doubt from the castle. As he and Denis paused a moment beneath the overhang of one of the two-storied buildings, he contemplated leaving until he realized that the soldiers seemed no more watchful than the gossiping women clustered around the well.

Sir Connor must feel very secure.

That thought renewed his purpose, and Alexander gestured for Denis to follow him. They left the shadow of the overhang and wandered about the green.

Finally he saw a peddler who would suit his purpose. The man's goods were set up in the perfect place, in front of an alley between two of the taller buildings. On a small trestle table in front of his covered cart were ribbons and the sorts of little baubles women liked to purchase. The man himself looked on edge, and his red, bulbous nose told Alexander that not only was he a man who drank much, and often, but he was also very thirsty already although it was not even close to midday.

Alexander went on a little way, then halted near the entrance to the tavern and out of the way of the people walking by.

"The ribbon peddler is the man we want," he murmured as Denis joined him. He nodded ever so slightly at the merchant they had passed. He reached into his thin purse and pulled out three silver coins. "Get him as much wine as this will buy, Denis."

His countenance serious and sure, Denis nodded. "*Oui, mon ami.* He will be able to make merry for some time with this."

"That's just what I am counting on," Alexander said as he gave his friend the money.

In the lord's chamber in the southern tower of Bellevoire, Lady Isabelle's brow knit with concern as she sat upon a delicately carved chair and regarded her sister Allis, who was still abed. Feminine articles were scattered upon a dressing table nearby, while a pair of scuffed black boots lay beside a battered wooden chest bossed with brass studs. A gray woolen tunic had been hastily tossed over it. A colorful tapestry of bright red, greens and blues depicting a Christmas feast covered the north wall.

The morning sunlight came in through the high, narrow windows that faced south. It lit their faces, alike enough to pronounce that they were related, although Lady Allis was considered the more beautiful. Isabelle, it was said, was pretty and vivacious but lacked the cool poise of her older sister. It was generally accepted that this was why there were, as yet, no serious suitors for the younger sister of the wife of Sir Connor of Bellevoire.

"Are you certain you don't want me to stay with you?" Isabelle asked, her hands folded on her lap as she leaned forward intently. "It is no trouble."

Under a satin coverlet of green as pale as the first leaves of spring, Allis leaned back against a bevy of goosedown pillows. Her hair, a thick mass of blond lighter in color than Isabelle's, tumbled about her shoulders and over her white silken shift. Her eyes were clear and her color good, for she was not ill.

She was with child at last, after three years of marriage.

"I'll be fine in a little while," Allis assured her. "It is nothing more than morning sickness."

Isabelle smiled, then folded back the long, silk-lined cuffs of her berry red samite gown, trying not to show that she was still worried in spite of Allis's confidence. After all this time, she wanted everything to go well. She knew Allis did, too, of course, but it was different when one merely looked on.

"You are as bad as Connor, you know," Allis said, her eyes shining with love as she spoke of her husband in a way that made Isabelle want to sigh.

"He fusses over me far too much," Allis continued, a look on her face that was annoyed and yet pleased, too. "Although he agrees that it is too soon to announce my state, people are going to suspect the reason why if he keeps acting as he does."

Isabelle rose from the chair, picked up her

brother-in-law's tunic from on top of the chest and began to fold it. "He can't help fussing. He loves you."

Allis drew her knees up and wrapped her arms about them. "As I love him. I know he's anxious because it has taken so long, but I tell you, my secret will not be a secret for long the way he's carrying on. And if anything were to happen, his disappointment would be enough to bear without everyone in the village and castle offering me their condolences."

Feeling guilty for sharing her fears even a little, Isabelle opened the lid of the bossed chest and laid the folded tunic inside. Her long, thick braid, with its end encased in a bronze tip, fell over her shoulder, and she deftly tossed it back as she faced Allis again. "What should I tell people if they ask where you are this morning? They will miss you in the market."

"Just say I am a little unwell. Something I ate, perhaps. You'll think of something. You always do. Besides, somebody I trust must go with Connor. I've asked him to get me a blue ribbon to go with my new gown, and you know you can't really leave such things to a man."

Isabelle regarded her sister with apparent gravity, her hands clasped like a dutiful servant. "Is there anything else you'd like me to order your husband to buy for you?" she inquired.

Allis grinned, for she knew full well that Isabelle's manner and question were not meant to be taken seriously. "Well, since you ask, perhaps one to go with my green gown with the round neckline, too, if they are reasonably priced." She tilted her head and mused a moment, likewise seemingly serious. "You know, this is a very good idea. The merchants might think they could cheat a man, but you can simply put on that innocent face and get a far better price."

"What, this face?" Isabelle asked, widening her eyes, raising the corners of her lips in what was almost a jester's grin and fluttering her lashes as if she had a piece of dirt in her eye.

"Exactly," Allis confirmed with a nod of her head. "If you look at them like that, they'll probably *give* you the ribbons."

Isabelle straightened a few of the items on the dressing table, putting away a brooch in its sandalwood box, moving a candleholder further back. "I will gladly go alone," she offered as she glanced at her sister. "Then Connor could stay with you."

Allis shook her head. "It will only take a few moments from his day and it's good for the people to see their overlord in such a casual way. It makes them more likely to come to him with their troubles, and prevents strife."

"You're sure?" This time, Isabelle was serious as she faced her sister.

"Very." Allis smiled with that secret wistfulness that tugged at Isabelle's heart and made her yearn for a love of her own. "I want everyone to be as happy as I am."

"I fear that is impossible," Isabelle replied with a laugh. Her tone, however, was a little strained as she tried to shake off the sudden sense of despondency that thinking of love and marriage always brought. Her suitors had been lackluster at best. There had been the unfortunate Percival, who had cared for her far more than she had for him before he died. Sir Auberan de Beaumartre had also harbored a passion she had not reciprocated, and the foolish young man had gotten involved in a conspiracy against King Richard that had resulted in his banishment.

Isabelle had admired Connor's good looks and deep, melodious Welsh voice. Yet as she had come to understand the deep feelings her sister had for the once-impoverished Welshman, she had also realized that he did not stir any similar depth of emotion in her. He was handsome and worthy of admiration, but he did not inspire passion.

In her heart of hearts, she knew that was what she was really waiting for: a man who could rouse her passion as well as her admiration.

"You will fall in love one day, Isabelle," Allis assured her.

"Well, if no suitable potential groom appears, I shall simply travel from town to town with my innocent face," she said, clasping her hands together like a fervent penitent. Batting her lashes, she finished in an anxious simper, "Is there anybody here in want of a wife?"

Her eyes sparkling with merriment, Allis waggled her finger. "They might say yes, and then where would you be?"

"Betrothed," Isabelle answered with a curtsey, moving her skirt with a graceful air as she bent her knees. She straightened, and the folds of the gown fell back in place. "However, since I do not wish to be *merely* betrothed, I am content to wait."

Which was true. She would rather be alone than miserably wed.

"Good! I want my sister to be as happily married as I am, and that means you must not settle for just anyone."

Isabelle tucked her hands into her cuffs as if she were a novice in a nunnery and bowed. "Amen," she intoned.

Allis shook her head. "You, sister, are incorrigible! Now, you had best hurry along. I daresay Connor's down in the hall tapping his toe and anxious to be gone, thinking dark thoughts about chattering females."

"Very well." Isabelle's turn was almost a twirl as she pivoted on her heel. Her bright red dress, as vibrant as holly berries against the snow, swirled about her long and slender legs. "Off I go to buy some ribbons."

She paused at the door and gave her sister a saucy look before she waved a farewell. "And who knows? Perhaps I shall meet a marriageable man while I'm at it!"

Chapter 2

The handsome, dark-haired lord of Bellevoire tapped his right toe as he stood beside the empty hearth in the great hall. The oak beams holding up the slate roof were twenty feet above the floor of the huge chamber, and every inch of stonework was decorated with carving.

It was not an intimate space, but it was rarely empty. At present, servants of both sexes talked and laughed. Women swept the old rushes that covered the stone floor to make way for new. Some men were taking down one of the tapestries to have the dirt and soot beaten from it. A few foot soldiers sat on a bench and leaned back against the wall, discussing the virtue of maces over battle-axes.

Isabelle smiled when Connor saw her approaching. She was sure that once they were at the market, he would allow himself to be distracted by village business and leave the purchasing of ribbons to her.

Today, her brother-in-law was dressed in his usual

plain clothing of thigh-length black tunic, white shirt and brown breeches that hugged his muscular thighs. His breeches were tucked in leather boots, and he wore a simple leather belt, without his sword. Unlike most nobles, he did not sport the Norman style of hair, cut round his head like a bowl. Connor had always worn his hair long, and there was nothing feminine about it. In the dim light of the hearth on a winter's night, or the bonfires of Midsummer's Eve, he looked almost savage. If there had ever been a time he'd stirred her blood, it was then—but not for long, for he was too merry a man to inspire dark, exciting fantasies, especially when he was married to her beloved sister.

Connor broke into a grin when she reached him. "Allis has told you what I am to buy and that you are to make sure I get the right color," he said with a knowing look.

"Yes."

"She has no trust in my taste," he replied with a woeful sigh as he held out his arm to escort her from the hall.

"She has no faith in your ability to select the right color," Isabelle corrected as she slipped her arm through his. "Most women would not expect the overlord of a castle to know about such things. Weapons and defenses and perhaps how to dance, but not ribbons and fabric and hairstyles. It is enough that you must pay for them."

"Aye, that I must," Connor replied as they strolled through the large oaken doors out into the warm air of the summer morning and down the steps to the cobblestoned courtyard. Servants bustled about here, too, filling buckets, carrying various items from the storehouse to the kitchen, which was attached to the hall by a corridor. Others were mucking out the stables. A troop of soldiers prepared to mount and ride out to patrol the perimeter of Bellevoire. There had been peace in the land for some time, but Norse marauders were not unknown. The wide river had long held an attraction for the seafaring brigands, and their shallow-hulled vessels could come even this far inland upon it. Men outside the law who preyed on travelers were also a concern, for any road that led to London tempted such bandits.

"Wouldn't you rather I chose them by myself?" Isabelle asked. "Then if they are not quite right, you cannot be blamed."

Connor gave her a grateful look. "I cannot tell you how much I appreciate your offer. If she wanted a sword or a dagger, I would feel confident, but ribbons . . ."

They continued across the drawbridge over the dry moat, their footfalls echoing slightly. Connor nodded a greeting to a few tradesmen who were bringing foodstuffs to the castle.

"The market is going to be crowded," he observed as they sauntered toward the green. "Bellevoire is growing every day, it seems."

So it was, ever since word had gone out that the greedy, cruel Baron DeFrouchette had been killed and his estate given to a new overlord. As it became apparent that Sir Connor was a much more just and much less greedy master, more people came to trade, and to stay.

Leaning on his arm, her body close to his, Isabelle slyly whispered into her brother-in-law's ear. "God willing, it will increase by one more come the spring."

"Be quiet about that," Connor laughingly commanded, also in a whisper. "I am having enough difficulty not shouting it from the battlements. Allis will have our heads if we spoil the grand surprise at the harvest feast."

"I'll try not to, and so must you. She says you are fussing over her so much, people will guess." She patted his arm sympathetically. "I am delighted, too, but we should try to do as she wishes."

"I will," he conceded with a genial bow.

Arriving at the green, they surveyed the crowd of people, dogs, horses, carts and hastily assembled stalls.

"Which is the merchant from London with the ribbons Allis likes?" Connor asked.

Isabelle withdrew her arm from his and looked around. "I think the one at the southern edge of the green," she said, nodding at the slightly familiar wagon. "Why don't you leave that to me? I shall select them and later you can go to the merchant to collect them, and pay."

"Excellent idea," Connor said, his relief at being spared the selection process evident.

She nodded toward a plump, bearded man well dressed in a long tunic of dark blue, with a wide leather belt about his ample waist. The fellow bustled toward them as if he were under attack. "Here comes the reeve all in a bother to speak to you, for I doubt Bartholomew has business with me. I suspect he more likely wishes to 'have a word' with you."

Her lips twitched, and so did Connor's. They didn't want to laugh, for Bartholomew was nearly upon them, and he took his duties very seriously. On the other hand, he began every single conversation with Connor with those words.

Red-faced, the reeve came to a panting halt. "If I might have a word, my lord."

Isabelle had to turn away to hide her smile. "If you'll excuse me, Connor," she managed to get out without laughing. She hurried away toward the cart at the other end of the market.

It was not difficult for her to make her way through the crowd. People tended to make way for the nobility, even if they were friendly nobility, and Isabelle was well liked.

Nevertheless, their deference made Isabelle feel very much alone, as it always did. She wasn't distanced from the villagers and the servants of the castle only by her rank. As the chatelaine's younger sister, she had no real place here, except as guest.

Still, her situation could be worse—much worse, she reminded herself. She was safe with her sister and brother-in-law. The village and estate were thriving, the weather fair, Allis with child. Their younger brother Edmond was visiting Connor's brother, Caradoc, at his estate in Wales, and by all accounts, enjoying himself. The troubles with DeFrouchette and his coconspirators seemed over for good. Connor had feared repercussions and revenge because Lord Oswald, the man who had planned the treachery, had escaped, his power broken and his money given to the crown. But after three years, they dared to hope he had fled far away, never to return.

As for her own future, surely she was too young to worry that she could never be as happy as Allis.

As Isabelle drew near the cart, a slender, brown-haired man she had never seen before appeared beside it as if by magic. He began to call out to passersby to see his wares, and when he saw her, a merry smile dimpled his cheeks. "Ah, my lady!" he cried with a Gascon accent. "You must come and see what I have, for I can tell you have great taste and a discerning eye! I assure you, my wares are of the finest quality, all the way from Marseilles."

If she had not been headed for him anyway, his smile alone would have drawn her to him.

His brown eyes were like those of a particularly friendly dog as she studied the selection, which seemed as good as the London man's. "I'm looking for something in pale blue." She picked one up. "This will do, I think. I am to pick out some ribbons, and Sir Connor will come by later to collect them and pay you for them—at the price *we* agree upon."

"Ah, the great overlord of Bellevoire himself!" the peddler cried as he put his hand over his heart and bowed. "I shall be honored."

"There will be no deceiving him about the amount he is to pay, for I shall inform him of the sum we agreed upon before he arrives."

The slender man's eyes widened with surprise, and his expression became doleful. "*Oui*, my lady, of course I shall not try to change the price. Indeed, if I did, then you would be angry with me, and that I could not bear."

Isabelle thought he could bear her anger very well if he thought he could get more money from Connor. Despite his smiles and dimples and his *joie de vivre*, something told her this man was not quite what he seemed, and even the most charming manner could hide a cheat.

A green ribbon caught her eye, and she moved toward it. "This is very pretty."

She lifted it up and let the morning light play upon it. It shimmered and danced, green seemingly tinged with gold.

"It is more beautiful next to your pretty face. I have even more lovely things in a box in my cart. Would you care to see?"

Since many merchants kept their best wares away from the general public, who could not afford them anyway, this did not surprise Isabelle. "Yes, please," she said, eager to see more of the wonderful ribbon.

He led her around the cart, and she found herself in an alley between two buildings. "I don't see another—"

A tall, broad-shouldered man dressed in a ragged cloak, his face shrouded in a hood, stepped out of the shadows.

"Good day, my lady," he said in a low, deep and shockingly familiar voice.

A shaft of fear pierced her, taking her very breath away.

She whirled around. The peddler blocked the entrance to the alley, and suddenly a strong hand clapped over her mouth while another went around her waist, pulling her back against a body as solid as the stones of the castle. Kicking and struggling like a trapped animal, she was dragged further back into the alley.

The hand of the man holding her shifted. She twisted her head, then bit down on the tender skin between his thumb and palm.

The man growled a curse. His hold loosened, but not enough for her to break away. He stuck his bleeding hand into his mouth while his arm held her firmly clasped against him. She managed to turn in his grasp, and she struck him as hard as she could. He didn't let go, but she knocked the hood back from his face—and stared, dumbstruck with horror and disbelief.

She was face-to-face with the living image of Rennick DeFrouchette. "Y-you're dead!" she stammered in a hoarse whisper.

Something struck her head. Pain radiated, and, as the hated face before her swam and dimmed, she desperately tried to call for help.

But no sound escaped her as she fell to the ground.

Panting, Alexander looked down at the young woman's crumpled body, and he tried to calm his racing heart. Given what he had seen and heard of well-bred young women, he had not anticipated a struggle of any kind. He had expected Lady Allis to be so shocked by the realization that she was about to be kidnapped that she would be virtually paralyzed with fear. Indeed, he had more than half expected her to swoon the moment she realized she was in danger. He had never, ever, thought she would fight back as energetically as she had.

"*Mon Dieu*," Denis whispered, the piece of wood he had used to strike her limp in his hand. "What a wildcat."

Alexander nodded.

"I know she was not to be harmed, but I had to hit her."

Alexander could not fault Denis as he crouched down and examined the bump on the side of the woman's head, but he didn't want her dead or in-

jured. He wanted her alive, and fit to be ransomed.
"I don't think she's badly hurt."

Indeed, he was rather sure she wasn't. He had
seen many a man injured while working or training,
and her wound looked superficial. Still, any injury
that rendered one unconscious could not be completely dismissed. "We can't be sure until she wakes
up."

"*Merde!*"

"You did what was necessary. Go keep watch,"
Alexander commanded quietly.

With a nod, Denis obeyed.

As his friend peered out of the alley, Alexander
pulled out the rag he had stuck into his belt. He knelt,
put it between her full lips to gag her, and tied it. His
hand hurt like the devil, but he ignored the pain.

After tying her wrists and ankles, he grabbed the
wool sack that had fallen to the ground in their unexpected struggle and began to work it over her
body, starting with her head.

She was indeed a lovely woman, with fine features, a shapely figure and the most beautiful blond
hair he had ever seen. No wonder his father had
waited for her hand even though that had left him
prey to her duplicity, and no wonder Sir Connor had
killed for her.

He would surely pay a great deal for her return,
as well.

She was younger than he had expected, though,
and with her eyes closed, she looked very sweet
and vulnerable—which was certainly far from the
lady's true nature. She had betrayed his father for
another, and together they had robbed Alexander of
Bellevoire.

As he pulled the sack down over her, he was sorely tempted to let his hands linger on the body clad in that fine, soft gown. He wanted to caress her rounded breasts. Run his hands over her trim waist. Stroke her slender thighs.

But he would have her awake, looking at him with those light blue eyes so like the summer sky. He wanted to see them filled not with fear and wonder but with passion and yearning.

Rarely had any woman inspired anything like the desire now surging in his blood, and the heat coursing through him proved nearly impossible to ignore.

Usually his encounters with women were swift and brief, by his design. He did not want any intimacy other than the most basic. Yet if he could be with this woman, he would take all night.

He forcefully reminded himself she was merely a thing to be ransomed. He would not fall prey to the lure of her, as his father had done.

After tying the sack, Alexander threw his hood back over his head, then hoisted the lady's limp body onto his shoulders. He hunched with the weight.

"Can you manage?" Denis asked as Alexander approached.

He shifted his burden to a more comfortable carry. "I worked for a mason in my youth, remember?"

He had toted stones much heavier than Lady Allis of Bellevoire. He had not begrudged the work because he'd wanted to become strong. Now he was very strong, and Lady Allis was no heavier to him than a sack of flour.

He peered into the busy market to make certain

no one was watching the alley, then stepped out and started to walk back the way they had come. He skirted the busier areas, taking care not to appear guilty of anything except carrying a sack full of wool. Since nobody was giving them a second glance, he decided he was safe.

They left the village without the lady waking, screaming or struggling. Part of Alexander was relieved; another part was concerned that Denis's blow had caused her more harm than he had supposed. Despite his growing worry over the lady's state, Alexander did not pause in his journey back to the hill and the place they had hidden their stolen horses. As long as they did not attract undo notice, he would not slacken his pace.

It wasn't until they slipped from the road and had to climb back up the hill that Alexander began to get winded. They reached the secluded glade far from any farmer's fields or pasture at last, however. A gray gelding of some value and a brown mare were tethered with long ropes Alexander had brought for that purpose, and they grazed near a small stream. Willow trees and alders helped hide them, as did tall reeds and long grass.

Denis threw himself onto the ground with all the loose-limbed ease of a man who knows how to fall without hurting himself while, with a grunt, Alexander laid down his burden. Muttering a curse, he put his callused hands on his back and stretched before he pulled out his sword. He began to cut the binding around the wool sack and then around his captive's ankles.

"What are you doing?" Denis demanded, sitting

bolt upright as Alexander began to pull the wool sack off. "Are you not still going to keep her in the sack or bound?"

"I don't know how well she can breathe," Alexander replied. "I can't sling her over the horse's rump as if she really were a sack of wool. If she woke up, she'd surely start squirming and then fall. I intend to keep her hands tied, but I don't want her harmed more than she is."

Denis said no more as Alexander removed the sack and took off the lady's gag. It didn't matter if she screamed here; there was no one nearby. He had made certain of that when he'd selected the place for hiding the horses.

The young woman's face was as still and peaceful as if she were sleeping in her own bed. Her chest rose and fell with her steady breathing. Wisps of hair had escaped from the blond braid making him think she would look just the same after sleeping in a bed. His bed. After they had made love. He imagined her body beneath him, warm and soft and welcoming.

A surge of even more powerful desire jolted him to the tips of his toes.

Forcing away the intense, untimely hunger, he went to the stream and splashed cold water over his face until his wayward desire was once more under control. Denis joined him to take a drink.

When Alexander turned back, he saw a flash of red—the skirt of his captive's gown disappearing into the trees.

Ignoring the pain in her head and her aching body, Isabelle stumbled through the trees. It was hard to keep her balance with her hands tied, and the shady ground was slick and muddy from the rain two days ago.

Her throat was dry, her breathing hoarse, but desperation drove her onward, especially when she heard her abductors chasing her.

With a cry, she tripped over a log and fell hard on her hands and knees. The rope cut into her wrists, yet she struggled to her feet, her skirts impeding her.

She could hear the heavy pounding of her pursuers' feet as they closed on her. Sobs choked her as she ran—until somebody caught hold of the back of her gown.

"Oh, no, my lady," that hateful, familiar voice said. "I do not let my prize slip from my grasp so easily."

She still tried to run, the strength of panic and determination humming along every nerve and sinew as he pulled her back and back and back.

Then he had her by the shoulders and turned her to face him. He was indeed the image of De-Frouchette, but younger and leaner, as if he had known deprivation, something DeFrouchette never had. His sapphire blue eyes were more intense, more searching. His body was fitter, harder, and his shoulder-length black hair was wild from the chase.

Her captor's dark brows lowered in a way very reminiscent of the hated Baron DeFrouchette. "It is no use, my lady. I have you, and I intend to keep you. If you try to run again, I will catch you. But if you do as you are told, you have nothing to fear. You are worth far more unharmed. Sir Connor owes me much, and your ransom will be some recompense."

Ransom. Small comfort, but she clung to it the way a man in danger of falling from a cliff clings to a tree branch.

"Who *are* you?" she demanded.

"I am the baron's son, Alexander DeFrouchette."

Based on his appearance, she could believe it, and yet . . . "It is well known that cowardly traitor had no sons."

To her utter surprise, Alexander DeFrouchette laughed, and a cold, mirthless laugh it was. "I know better than you the kind of man he was. But whatever he was, I am still his bastard son."

Baron DeFrouchette had been an immoral, lustful man, so this could well be true.

The slender peddler from the market appeared. Winded, he leaned against a chestnut tree for support. "Alexander, this is not the time for talking. We must go."

The son of Rennick DeFrouchette made a mocking bow, and the corners of his lips curled slightly. "You see, I must have the honor of your company for some time yet, my lady. Will you come with me peaceably?"

For some time yet? Her legs began to tremble, but she willed strength back to them. She was Isabelle, daughter of the earl of Montclair, and she would let no bastard son of a hated enemy see her fear. "I suppose you mean that expression for a smile, but I assure you, I find nothing amusing in your crime. Nor should you, for when you are caught—and you will be!—I will take great pleasure in seeing you hanged."

With a scowl, he reached out and grabbed the

binding between her wrists with his strong right hand. "Come," he commanded as he turned on his heel and pulled her.

She tried digging in her heels, but it was no use. He simply yanked harder on the rope binding and tugged her onward. Having caught his breath, his friend loped through the trees ahead of them, and by the time they returned to the glade, he had the horses untied.

There were no saddles, only bridles and a rope for a rein.

DeFrouchette stopped beside the gray horse. "Denis, hold her while I mount, then help me get her on the horse."

The Gascon did as he commanded, and Isabelle gave him a sneer for his troubles. She contemplated kicking him and running again, but if DeFrouchette was mounted, she would not get far.

Once seated on the back of the gelding, DeFrouchette leaned down and grabbed her under her arms, while the Gascon put his hands on her waist to hoist her onto the horse in front of him. She made herself as limp as possible to make it harder for them both, but, afraid they might drop her, she put her leg over the horse's back and sat. Her gown rode up, bunching up about her waist and thigh, exposing her limbs. She squirmed forward to get as far away from DeFrouchette as she could, while the Gascon eyed her legs with blatant approval.

She kicked him in the nose.

"*Merde!*" he cried in both anger and disbelief as he covered it with his hand, blood dripping out between his fingers. "She kicked me!"

"Don't try anything like that again," De-

Frouchette ordered in a voice that made her blood run cold. His left arm clamped about her waist like a band of iron, and he pulled her back against his chest. "I meant what I said about not hurting you, but I might change my mind."

Chapter 3

❧⟞◦⟝❧

As they galloped away from Bellevoire over what was little more than a wide path through the wood, Alexander struggled to control both his annoyance and his lust. Hearing of her loveliness and actually having her shapely body up against his were two very different things.

Every movement of the horse brought her body into contact with his, with only the gathered fabric of her gown between them. The fine fabric made him think of soft days and softer nights, of ease and comfort and riches such as he had never known—but that he might have known had his father not been killed before he had claimed him as his son.

Lord Oswald had described her as slyly clever. He should have said she had the heart of a warrior, the tongue of a fishwife and the pride of a queen. Then he would have been prepared to deal with his prize. Maybe.

As for her denunciation of his father, she had not

33

shocked or upset him. He knew, far better than she ever could, that Rennick DeFrouchette was not a good man.

She moved again, the sensation making him hard. "Be still!" he commanded, at war with both her and his own body.

"If you would not hold me so tight, perhaps I would," she retorted, panting like a woman in the throes of lovemaking. "I can hardly breathe."

He commanded himself to make no such comparisons in the future as he struggled to get his burning lust once again under control. He was no brigand to rape and pillage and steal. He wanted only what was justly his, some portion of what had been taken from him by his father's untimely death. "If I thought you would not try to escape again, I would loosen my hold. Will you give me your word you will not?"

She didn't answer. He hadn't really expected her to.

He glanced over his shoulder. Denis was no horseman, but he was keeping up, for the brown mare was very fast. He looked unhappy and afraid of falling, though. Fortunately, they had not much farther to go to rendezvous with the Norsemen.

Alexander saw no one else as they rode, and they encountered no soldiers on patrol. Obviously, Sir Connor had grown lax and was not expecting an attack. Had Alexander known how unprotected the land around Bellevoire was, he would have had Ingar bring his vessel further down the river.

At last they left the wood and rode over a ridge, and there, in the distance, on the other side of a large meadow, the curved prow of a Norse ship gently bobbed on the river behind the willow trees lining the bank. He could see it because he knew to look for it.

At about thirty feet long, it was not a particularly large ship. Normally, such a vessel was used for swift raids. This time, the ship and its crew had but one thing to do: take them and their prize out of England.

Alexander slowed his horse to a walk, which allowed Denis to come abreast of him. He wanted the Norsemen to see them clearly, so that they would be recognized as friends, not foes.

As he did, the lady stiffened and gasped with shocked surprise. Obviously, she had spotted the ship, rocking at its rest like a great beast.

"We could not stay near Bellevoire, of course," he said, his lips close to her ear, "so we must take you on a bit of a journey."

She smelled of roses, and it was all he could do not to press his lips to the curve of her jaw. His hips moved with the motion of the horse, bringing him again into contact with her. This time, though, he gave in to the temptation to feel the pleasure of arousal.

Her back as straight as if she had a lance up her gown, she inched away. "I might have guessed you would be allied with Norsemen," she replied. "You share their morals, after all."

Since they were nearly at Ingar's ship, there was no way she could escape, and they were safe from Sir Connor's troops, supposing he even knew where to look, so Alexander could afford to be amused by her fierce words. She was certainly not what he had expected, and as long as she realized who was master here, he might even find spending time with her . . . entertaining. "You know very little about me, my lady," he said, his voice low and intimate.

"I know enough."

"In the days to come, you may learn more."

"In the days to come, I shall amuse myself contemplating your slow and painful execution."

Perhaps "entertaining" was not quite the right word for the sort of conversation he would share with his "guest."

"Alexander," Denis said cautiously, "where are all the Norsemen?"

Looking over the lady's head, he scanned the ship. Ingar, the broad-shouldered, broad-chested blond fellow who commanded the vessel, stood in the bow near the great dragon's head, watching them approach. A few other Norsemen were also visible, sitting on chests that held their personal goods and any booty they divided, as well as doubling as rowing benches. But Denis was right; there should be more of them. "They're probably sleeping in the bottom of the vessel, napping in the summer's sun."

"I do not see Osburn, either."

Alexander sniffed. Lord Oswald's son was probably drunk, lounging with his back against the curved side of the ship. "That's not surprising. He's probably napping, too."

When they were nearly at the riverbank, Alexander pulled his horse to a stop and with some reluctance withdrew his arm from around the lady. He slipped off backward over the horse's rump, then, coming around to the side of the beast, reached up to help her down.

She twisted away. With an expression of utter revulsion, and in spite of her bound hands, she lifted her right leg over the saddle and jumped to the ground unaided.

Then she winced.

"What is it?"

She raised her angry blue eyes, and they seemed to fairly flash fire. Dressed in a muddy gown and with her hair disheveled, she looked like an indignant young goddess as she glared at him. "What does it matter to you?"

He pulled out his dagger, and fear flooded her eyes before she closed them, as if expecting a fatal blow. "I told you, you will not be harmed," he said as he sliced off the ropes binding her wrists.

"Really?" she replied, tilting her head skeptically as she rubbed her reddened skin. "I believe you will find a sizable lump on the back of my head and my wrists will be bruised for a week."

"I see there is nothing the matter with your tongue," he retorted. He glanced down at her ankle, noting that she was keeping her weight off it. "You will not be harmed if you do as I say. However, if you try to escape or refuse my help, I cannot guarantee that you will not," he said as he turned and smacked the horse's rump.

It bolted off. Denis dismounted and did likewise, and the mare ran off after the gelding.

The lady raised a brow. "Stolen, were they?"

"Yes. It was necessary," he replied as he faced her.

"I'm sure it's very easy for a man like you to justify whatever he does."

"Just as you have, my lady. I'm sure it is easy for

you to excuse the merry dance you led my father."
He glanced at his friend. "Denis, get aboard the
ship."

His friend immediately and obediently made his
way through the willow branches and down the
slippery bank. He waded toward the vessel, which
was about a yard out.

"I do not have to justify anything. Your father was
a traitor who died because he was trying to kill the
king," Isabelle declared, her fear growing and her effort to hide it becoming more desperate as she tried
to delay boarding.

With such a ship and such a crew, these men
could take her far away from Bellevoire, where Connor could not easily find her, provided he had even
realized she was missing. The sun was but halfway
down its course. He might not have noticed yet, or
he might have assumed she was visiting someone in
the village.

Her captor crossed his arms. "So it was claimed.
Since my father was dead, there could be no trial—
and a very convenient death it was for you and your
lover."

Lover? What lover? She had never had a lover.

"Oh, I know all about what you've done, my lady.
It is hardly a secret." All hint of mockery left De-
Frouchette's face, as well as his voice. "You and your
husband stole my birthright and Bellevoire, and
now your husband must pay."

Husband? God in heaven, he thought she was
Allis!

He had kidnapped the wrong person!

What should she do? Tell him of his error? But

what would he do then? Hold her for ransom still?
They could expect to be paid for Allis of Bellevoire,
but her younger sister? Connor and Allis would pay,
of that she was certain, but these brigands might not
be so sure, and might prefer the sure profit of selling
her into slavery. She could imagine the horrendous
fate that would await her then.

There was only one thing to do. She must let them
continue to believe she was Allis of Bellevoire, and
pray to God she was either rescued or was able to escape before they found out the truth. "How much
am I considered to be worth?"

"A few thousand marks in recompense will be
sufficient."

"A few *thousand*?" Connor didn't have that much
in coin.

DeFrouchette's lips curved into a mocking smile.
"Do you not think you are worth that much, my
lady? Lord Oswald certainly thinks so, and now that
I've met you, I cannot disagree."

Oswald! She might have known that blackguard
was behind this, waiting patiently for his chance to
have his vengeance on those who had destroyed his
ambitious, traitorous plans.

He must have hired this ship and this crew. He
had promised money to this scoundrel and his
friend and the Norsemen to kidnap her. That was always his way—to find someone with a grudge to do
his evil deeds for him.

Even worse, Oswald would know who she was.
"Where is your master? Waiting on the ship? I don't
see him."

"He is not my master."

He didn't say Oswald was aboard the ship, and she began to hope he was not there. That would buy her more time before they found out the truth.

"Alexander! What are you doing?" the Gascon called. "This is no time to be flirting with a woman!"

DeFrouchette shot a condemning glance at his friend. "I'm not—" Then sudden understanding, quickly followed by ire, flashed across DeFrouchette's angular face. "Enough of your delaying tactics, my lady," he growled.

Not nearly enough. And maybe Lord Oswald was on that ship.

She grabbed her skirt and took off toward the ridge as fast as she could run. Exhausted, she pushed her legs to their limit as she scrambled up the slope.

DeFrouchette caught up to her and grabbed her arm. As he yanked her to a stop, she thought he was going to wrench her arm from her shoulder. "That was a stupid thing to do," he snarled.

"Let me go!" she cried, pummeling him with all that remained of her strength. "Beast! Varlet! *Bastard!*"

He hauled her close, embracing her so that she couldn't hit him any more, his fiercely enraged face inches from hers. "You had better get this through that pretty head of yours, my lady. I have you and I will keep you until the ransom is paid. You can make this easy or difficult for yourself. It does not make any difference to me—but you will *never* escape from me."

With that, he picked her up and threw her over his shoulder, knocking the wind out of her.

Gasping, she had no more energy to try to free

herself as he clasped her legs tight and strode toward the ship. He skittered down the bank and waded through the water. She thought he was going to toss her over the side into the vessel like a sack full of rocks until she felt two large hands take hold of her.

Somebody—and it was most certainly not the slender Gascon—lifted her up and set her on the curved bottom of the ship. She grabbed the side to steady herself on the uneven deck, then looked up to see who had pulled her inside.

She found herself staring at a hulking, bearded Norseman whose blond hair hung in a tangled mass to his wide shoulders. He wore a silver band around his neck and a gold torc on his upper arm, and his tunic and breeches were of very fine wool sumptuously dyed in purple and red. His saffron yellow cloak, held by a large and ornate brooch of bronze, was thrown back over his shoulder. He was well armed, too, sporting an embossed swordbelt with a finely worked leather scabbard and a battle-ax stuck through it. As if this were not bad enough, his smoke gray eyes shone with greed and lust as he ran his gaze over her. It made her feel soiled, like an unwanted bold caress.

"By Thor's hammer," the Norseman cried, using the language of the sea traders that was a mixture of Norse, Norman and the language of the Celts. "Nobody told me this woman you wanted was so fine a creature, or I would have been easier to hire. Still, I'll wager she will bite and scratch and fight you with every kiss and caress."

As Isabelle's stomach turned with new revulsion, the Norseman looked past her to DeFrouchette, who had climbed over the side behind her. "I will give you a good price for her."

She would rather die than be that man's property!

She inched backward, away from him, and collided with DeFrouchette, who briefly put his hands on her shoulders to steady her.

At least DeFrouchette had said she wasn't to be harmed. But what *exactly* did he mean by that? Did that mean he wouldn't do anything else?

"She will be worth more to her husband," DeFrouchette replied.

The Norseman laughed—a low rumble, like an amused bear. "Well, you may be right."

She couldn't move forward, for the Norseman was there, and she couldn't move back, for DeFrouchette was there. Struggling against the terror building within her, she sidled sideways, toward the center of the ship, which was filled with oars, stores of food and skins holding wine or ale or water, various other bundles whose contents she couldn't guess, a furrowed sail and the yardarm lying beside what must be the ship's mast. At least five other Norsemen were in the vessel, staring at her as if she were on display at a marketplace.

God help her, maybe she was.

If there was one good thing, it was that Oswald was obviously not aboard that ship. Besides the huge blond man and the five other Norsemen watching her, there was only one other man sleeping in the stern of the vessel. He was far too thin to be Oswald.

"She is not for sale, Ingar," DeFrouchette repeated. "She is for trading, and until she is traded, she is to be treated as an honored guest."

She knew better than to believe a man of that ilk, but his words relieved her nonetheless. Between that and the realization that Oswald was not there to reveal who she was, her fear lessened a little.

Ingar shrugged, as if to say, "That is your loss, then."

DeFrouchette's stern gaze flashed over the other Norsemen watching. "Any man who forgets that will rue it."

Any man? Did that include him?

He glanced at her sharply. "Sit down and make yourself comfortable for the voyage, my lady," he commanded.

"Where?"

"Anywhere." His lips curved up. "There will be no escape, for there is nowhere to run."

"If I had known before that I was your *honored guest*, I might not have been so keen to flee," she lied, feeling a very small measure of triumph at the look that crossed his face.

Although she would have tried to escape anyway—and she still meant to even if she was as trapped as if she were imprisoned in a dungeon—she wanted to confuse him and make him wonder if he had erred.

She could not slip over the side now, though, so she reluctantly joined the Gascon, who was seated with his legs crossed as easily as another man sat in a tavern. Later, when it was dark and the ship was moving too quickly to be brought to a sudden halt, she would slip over the side and swim to shore.

DeFrouchette addressed the blond Norseman. "Where is the rest of your crew?"

Ingar pointed to the woods a short distance away. Isabelle followed his gesture, to see more fierce-looking Norsemen coming toward the ship, carrying dead sheep slung on poles between them. "Men must eat," he said.

Surely this raid would tell Connor where she had been taken . . . unless he would think this marauding had nothing to do with her abduction at all and was simply a random act of thievery.

DeFrouchette raised a brow. "All that for twenty men?"

"For later, too. Oswald does not pay enough. We take great risks coming so far inland."

"And you have taken a greater risk with this unnecessary raid. Why not just make a signal fire?" DeFrouchette demanded sarcastically.

"We will be long gone before anybody realizes these sheep are missing."

"We had better be."

"Well, well, well, what have we here?" someone called out from the stern of the vessel in the lazy drawl of a Norman nobleman.

Isabelle looked over her shoulder to see the slim man rising in the stern, his hands against the sides of the vessel.

She was shocked to realize he was not a Norseman, but there was no mistaking his accent, or the fact that he was dressed in the height of Norman fashion. His hair was nearly as blond as hers, cut round his head and the ends curled under, as smooth and glossy as a woman's—or a very vain man's. The vanity became more obvious as she ran a young woman's knowledgeable gaze over his clothing, which was a little rumpled. He wore a peacock blue brocade tunic with an embroidered white shirt beneath. His hose were likewise blue and clung to slender legs that lacked the muscle of a man used to riding or even walking far. His black boots shone and were gilded in a swirling pattern, like his swordbelt. A red jewel sparkled in the hilt of his sword. His dress, his manner and his voice all made her wonder what he was doing on this ship, for she could hardly imagine a man more different from a Norseman, or DeFrouchette, either.

The fellow seemed unsteady on his feet as he staggered toward them, as if he had just woken up and needed something to support him. Then she saw the wineskin in his hand and realized that he was drunk.

"Gentlemen, gentlemen," he exclaimed, waving the wineskin as he came to a swaying halt on the rocking vessel. "Are you a pair of squabbling children?"

DeFrouchette and the Norseman exchanged glances, like two confederates caught in a lie.

Who on earth *was* this man, that two such warriors would stay silent as he jeered at them?

The man turned his attention to her. He paid no heed at all to the Gascon.

"Is this the beauteous Lady Allis I have heard so much about?" he asked with a sodden, insolent grin. He put his index finger to his lip and shook his head. "Surely this disheveled creature with the shrew's tongue cannot be the fine, the splendid Lady Allis who has caused so much trouble? *You* are the woman men fight over?"

Whoever he was, he was aiding in her abduction and was therefore outside the law. "Yes, I am the Lady Allis," she said, getting to her feet with all the dignity she could command. "Who are *you*? A minstrel seeking employment, perhaps, to judge by your garments. If so, sirrah, I do not think a band of Norsemen are likely to appreciate your merry tunes."

The man stopped smiling and drew himself upright. "I am Osburn. You may recall my father, my lady. Lord Oswald."

No wonder DeFrouchette and Ingar deferred to him.

She bowed slightly and gave Osburn a smile she reserved for peddlers who tried to cheat her. "Of course I recall him, especially the day his treachery was discovered. It was a very memorable time."

Osburn waved the wineskin in a dismissive gesture. "A terrible misunderstanding," he slurred. "Terrible and most unfortunate for my poor father, who has been stripped of his lands and titles. That is why you must spend some time with us." Osburn leered at her. "You understand, my dear? We must repay you and your husband for what he has done to us, as well as enable him to repay us for what was taken away."

"I find your logic as disgusting as your methods, and I pray God you will all be caught and hanged."

DeFrouchette glared at Osburn, and she could almost feel his heated rage. "We should get underway, my lord, as soon as Ingar's men are aboard."

"Why, of course we should!" Osburn cried genially, as if he had already forgotten what she had said. "The sooner we are gone, the sooner I am back with my mistress, who is much finer company than a shipful of men." He ran an impertinent gaze over Isabelle. "I am not yet so desperate that this bedraggled creature will tempt me."

DeFrouchette stepped forward. "It was agreed that she would be treated as a guest."

"I am very friendly to my guests."

His expression fiercely stern, DeFrouchette took another step toward Osburn. Alexander didn't speak, and he didn't have to. Osburn flushed and backed away, and she could breathe again.

"Out of the way!" one of the returning Norsemen cried as he and his fellow tossed the first of the dead sheep, pole and all, over the side of the ship.

DeFrouchette moved quickly; Osburn was not so fast, and he nearly got clouted by the pole.

"God's blood, be careful, oaf!" he muttered as he stumbled back toward where he had been sleeping in the stern.

If she had been in a mood to find anything amusing, she would have found their scramble to get out of the way mildly funny. As it was, she hugged herself and fought back fear and rage and despair, more determined than ever to get away from this ship, its crew, that drunken sot and the man who was like Hades, lord of Hell, made flesh.

Chapter 4

In the great hall of Bellevoire, the flickering torch-light illuminated a group of anxious maidservants huddled near the kitchen corridor. The evening meal had been served, but the tables had not yet been taken down. The food left behind by the soldiers, who had set out to search for the missing sister of their mistress, was still to be cleared away.

"No sign of her at all, they say," Efe noted, twisting her apron in her middle-aged hands. "Like she up and vanished."

The younger, prettier Leoma tossed her head, leaned in closer and said, her voice likewise hushed, "Run off, I think. With a *man*. She's been moping around so much these past few weeks, it has to be that."

The elderly Gleda, who had served in Bellevoire during the time of DeFrouchette and had apparently been frowning ever since, sniffed skeptically. "What *man*? Have any of you ever seen her make eyes at a *man*? As for moping, I ain't noticed it. She's happy here." She eyed Mildred, the girl of fifteen who served as Isabelle's maid. "Ain't she?"

Chewing her thin lower lip, Mildred glanced about uneasily as she nervously tucked a lock of black hair behind her ear. "Aye, she's happy and she's never said anything to me about a man."

Leoma didn't believe it for an instant. "Yes, she has! Who is he?"

"No, no, it's not like that," Mildred protested, holding up her hands. "It's just that once, she told me it was a pity the baron was so evil, because he was not a bad-featured fellow."

The women all drew back, hissing like snakes in a pit, except for Gleda.

"Well, he wasn't," she asserted. "Not a good master, but he was handsome, in a dark sort of way. It didn't surprise me to hear she'd offered to marry him."

Leoma shook her head. "Not *him*. She always liked Sir Connor a little too much, if you ask me. Maybe she run off because of him. Girls with broken hearts do strange things."

"I don't think it was anything like that," Efe murmured, drawing their attention. "I think she was . . . taken."

"Like by magic? Spirited away by the faeries?" Gleda demanded, her hands on her ample hips.

Efe shook her head. "According to Bartholomew, a Frenchman got one of the merchants drunk, so drunk he wasn't minding his cart. Lady Isabelle was looking for ribbons, which this fellow sold, and the last time anybody saw her, she was standing near a strange young man at that cart. I think *he* took her."

"How'd he get her out of the village? The cart's still there."

Efe shrugged.

"Maybe he's her lover," Leoma suggested.

Gleda frowned even more, and Mildred was clearly not convinced.

"Well, *somebody* wanted that merchant out of the way," Efe offered, "and they did it. Maybe they lured her somewhere and . . ."

Efe colored as she fell silent. The other women looked ill, and Mildred started to cry.

Full of remorse, Efe patted the girl on the back. "There, there, now, don't take on. They'll find her. After all, there was no blood, neither."

Her comforting words only made Mildred cry louder.

"If only somebody'd noticed she was missing sooner," Gleda muttered.

"Don't be saying that where Sir Connor will hear," Efe cautioned as she continued to pat Mildred. "He feels terrible enough as it is. Searched high and low when he couldn't find her, questioned everybody, called out the guard and even got Bartholomew on the run looking for her. He hasn't had a bite to eat, either, between organizing the search and trying to comfort his poor wife. I thought she was going to faint dead away when he came to tell her."

"D-did you see *his* face?" Mildred asked, sniffling and wiping her eyes with the edge of her sleeve. "He looked like he'd rather be dead than have to tell her something like that. But Lady Isabelle was right in the village and in the market, too, so it's not his fault."

"Hush!" Gleda commanded, nodding at the steps from the lord's chamber. "Here comes my poor lady, white as a sheet. Stop your crying, Mildred, and we'd all better be about our business. There's nothing more we can do anyway."

But they didn't move, because at that moment, Sir Connor came striding through the door. They watched as his wife's face lit up even more than it usually did when he returned, all of them just as hopeful that Isabelle had been found, alive and well.

They also saw him grimly shake his head.

Her knees drawn up to her chest and her arms wrapped about them, Isabelle sat huddled in the center of the Norse ship. The Gascon sat a little ways off, still cross-legged and comfortable, eating some bread and cheese. She was very hungry, but she was certainly not going to ask anything of him, or anyone else on this cursed ship.

The Norse crew chewed on salted fish and drank from skins as they rowed without speaking. Their oars also made very little noise as they rose and dipped. It was no wonder they had proceeded as far inland as they had without being seen. In addition to the silence of their passage, the walls of the villages along the river were set back in case of spring flooding, and tonight the river was barely lit by a sliver of a moon.

Her lip curled with disgust as she regarded Osburn snoring softly in the bow, his wineskin cradled to his bosom like a lover. He was a vain fool who probably did nothing more than drink, wench and complain about his servants. She suspected he was never without a wineskin nearby, as some men were rarely without a sword.

She glanced back at the stern. Ingar held the steering board to guide the vessel. He must have the eyes of a cat; no lanterns were lit, and yet they stayed in the center of the river. Wrapped in a cloak against the chill night air, DeFrouchette stood beside him like a great, black bird of prey.

Connor was a powerfully built man, too, but there was always a lightness about him, no matter how terrible the times, as if he radiated honor and chivalry. If this DeFrouchette radiated anything, it was a brooding, bitter anger that had been festering for years.

The Gascon rose, then sat down beside her, crossed his legs and held out a loaf of coarse brown bread. "Will you eat, my lady?" he asked in a whisper. "I am sure you must be hungry. It is not the finest of fare, and I know you are used to better, but it is the best we have to offer."

She was tempted to shake her head and refuse. However, if she was going to escape, she would need the strength to do it. "Thank you," she said, likewise whispering as she accepted the bread and took a bite.

It was good, and she was glad she had agreed.

She slid her companion a glance. "Do you know where we are going, or is that to be kept a secret from me?"

He frowned. "I do not know exactly."

She couldn't tell if he was lying. "I assume Lord Oswald will be there to greet me?"

"*Non*, he will not."

She nearly sighed with relief, except that she realized the Gascon might wonder why she would be relieved about anything—and, indeed, why should she be? She was still in great jeopardy.

Her gaze drifted back to DeFrouchette. He seemed almost a part of the ship, swaying with its motion.

"You do not have to fear him, my lady," the Gascon said. "He has never hurt a woman in his life, and he means it when he says you are to be treated well."

She gave the man a skeptical frown. "How many others has he abducted?"

"You are the first."

"Then whatever he has done before may not influence how he treats me."

"He is a good man."

"Who takes women from their homes."

"For ransom," the Gascon protested, as if that absolved him of wrongdoing. "Do not knights take their fellows for ransom?"

"In battle or tournaments. But your master isn't a knight, and neither am I."

"No, no, he is not. Nor is he my master. We are friends, and my friend was to be a knight."

"He is hardly worthy to be a chivalrous knight if he steals a woman from her husband."

"He failed because his father was killed, my lady." The Gascon inched even closer and lowered his voice more. "His father had promised to name him his heir, and see him knighted if he learned the arts of war. So despite many trials, he did. He was on his way to England to show his father when he heard the man was dead—killed by another who was given all that might have been his. Imagine how it would be if you had one goal in your life and worked and suffered for it and then—poof!" The Gascon brushed his palms together, then spread his hands. "Gone, and through no fault of your own."

"That hardly gives him leave to kidnap me," Isabelle said, refusing to feel any sympathy for thwarted ambitions.

"Perhaps not, but then suppose a man seeks you out and says, 'If you do what I ask, I will see that the French king makes you a *chevalier*—a knight—and gives you an estate in Normandy. If you do this simple thing, you will be rich, too.' What then would you say, my lady?" He waved his hand in an exaggerated gesture of refusal. "*Merci*, but *non*. I cannot accept the dearest wish of my heart. I must not act against the man who killed my father and stole what was to be mine, not even if it will restore to me what was lost."

This was not the first time she had heard someone tell of Oswald offering revenge and retribution. He had tried to use Connor's grudge against King Richard to turn Connor into a traitor. However, there was one very significant difference between Connor and this DeFrouchette. "If your friend is an honorable man and so worthy to be a knight, he should have refused."

"Obviously, my dear Lady Allis, he is not," Osburn declared, sitting heavily beside her.

She had been so intent on her conversation with the Gascon that she had not noticed Osburn awaken, or come toward them.

"Speak softly, Norman," Ingar growled from the stern, "or you will wake the whole countryside."

Osburn sniffed, but when he addressed the Gascon, he did so in a whisper. "Go away, Dennis. I wish to talk to the lady."

The Gascon looked about to refuse, but then he shrugged and rose. "*Den-ee*," he muttered. "My name is De*nis*."

Isabelle got to her feet. "If you will excuse me."

She had no idea where she was going, except away from him. She would rather be back in the stern with DeFrouchette than have this man stinking of wine near her.

"No, I do not excuse you," Osburn said, roughly pulling her down beside him. "Come, come, my lady, if you can talk to *Dennis* here in such a confidential manner, you can speak with me. I'll share my wine."

"I don't want any wine."

Osburn leaned close, and his breath was nearly enough to make her gag.

"I was wrong," he said after taking another gulp of wine. "You *are* beautiful, even more beautiful than my father said." He shifted closer. "No need to be so nervous. I want to be friends."

Isabelle regarded him with all the scorn she felt as he laid his hand on her shoulder. "You must be mad if you think I could be anything but your enemy."

"Some men like women who put up a bit of a fight," Osburn murmured as he dropped the wineskin and turned toward her. "It's exciting knowing that a woman doesn't really want you. It will make it all the sweeter when—"

He yelped as he was lifted upward, so that he was suspended in the air, his feet dangling, barely touching the deck. Like a dog with a rat in its teeth, DeFrouchette shook him by the collar.

Isabelle scrambled to her feet. She sidled backward and to the left away from De Frouchette and Osburn; Ingar stood on the right side of the stern. The Norsemen nearby continued to row, but they watched the confrontation with avid interest.

"She is not here for your pleasure," DeFrouchette snarled. "Leave her alone, or you will have to answer to me."

"Put me down," Osburn gasped, his face reddening, his arms flailing helplessly as he tried to free himself, "or you will have to answer to my father."

DeFrouchette shook him again. "Not until I have your word you will not touch the lady again."

"I-I promise!"

With a scowl, DeFrouchette let him go. Osburn staggered upright and straightened his rumpled clothes as if trying to restore his lost dignity. "For a bastard, you have a lot of gall."

"So do you, for a man who takes few risks," DeFrouchette answered, his voice low but stern and harsh. "The woman is mine, not yours. I went to Bellevoire and got her. Your father paid for this ship and this crew. What have you done, except get drunk and sleep?"

Osburn put his hands on his hips. "I command here, DeFrouchette, not you. You are in my father's service, and since I am his son, you will obey me!"

"I am not in your father's service, nor am I in yours. I have made a bargain with him, and thus far, I have done what I swore to do."

"I represent my father!"

"Quiet!" Ingar ordered from the stern.

"You be quiet!" Osburn cried. He waved at the dark country all around them. "There's nobody around. Do you see any lights? Hear any dogs barking?"

The man was a drunken fool, Alexander thought as anger boiled within. A spoiled sot, a brat foisted upon him, and he had no right to go within ten feet of—

"Where is she?" Alexander demanded as he realized Lady Allis was nowhere to be seen. She had been back near Ingar only moments ago, obviously getting as far away from that sot as she could—but where was she now?

"Ingar, she was in the stern, near you," he said, striding toward the back of the ship.

"I was not watching her. I have enough to do to guide the ship and with you arguing fit to call down the Valkyries—"

"Oh my God!" Osburn wailed like a helpless child. "We've lost her!"

"Not yet, we haven't." A sound reached his ears, a splash different from the ones made by the oars. "Damn the woman, she's gone over the side."

"Rest oars!" Ingar ordered as Alexander scanned the dark river and banks behind them.

The Norsemen stopped rowing, leaning on their oars so that they would act as brakes, but they could not stop the ship immediately.

Osburn stumbled toward Alexander at the gunwale. "Can you see her? Where is she?"

There was real panic in his voice, and Alexander knew it was not concern for the lady's life that caused it.

"I'll find her," he vowed as he wrenched off his boots and threw them on the deck. He tore off his tunic and tossed it aside.

"You cannot just jump into the river!" Denis

protested, hurrying to his side. "You will drown!"

The ship, already on an angle from the extra weight, rocked more, making the Norsemen sitting on the side curse. Denis quickly moved back toward the center.

Alexander put his hands on the gunwale. "I can swim."

Denis didn't know of the days Alexander had spent by the miller's pond in his childhood, catching frogs to supplement the meager fare his mother could provide.

Alexander dropped into the frigid river, which was deeper than he expected. The cold water hit him like a slap, nearly paralyzing him, but he got his legs to move and rose to the surface, gasping for air. Fighting the cold as he treaded the water, he pressed his lips together to keep them from chattering and listened again.

There! He could hear her wading toward the bank.

With long, strong strokes his body cleaved the water as he headed toward the sound. He stopped once more to look and listen, and was rewarded with a brief flash of white on the bank. Her gown was red, but she was probably wearing a shift beneath and had gathered up the sodden skirts to run. A few moment's later, soaked and shivering in the chill night air, he scrambled up the slippery slope after her.

Once more he looked and listened, holding his breath. He saw a stand of trees not far off. If he were in her place, he would make for that.

With strides as swift as his swimming, and searching for another flash of white, he ran toward the trees.

He nearly cried out with triumph when he saw the telltale white. Picking up speed, but mindful that he was on unfamiliar ground, he reached the trees. Now he could hear her raspy panting and stumbling footfalls as she tried to run.

Thank God she was obviously too tired to run fast. That might be the difference between catching her and having her elude him.

For an instant, he actually considered letting her go. She had displayed courage and fortitude, and he admired that.

But if he let her go, he would have no prize to ransom.

He heard a thud and a cry. She must have tripped and fallen, and he was silently thankful.

There she was, clambering to her feet.

She was not wearing the red gown. She wore only her thin white shift, now muddy and soiled. Her sodden hair hung limply to her waist.

He grabbed for her but missed. Afraid she was going to escape him again, he threw himself at her, tackling her and falling with her onto the soft, muddy ground. She gasped and squirmed, but not with the power and energy she had demonstrated before.

His arms around her, his hips pressed against hers, she lay beneath him with only the damp silk of her shift between them. Her puckered nipples pressed against his naked chest and her body moved beneath him like a wanton lover as she struggled.

Although he knew that was not so, his desire awoke nonetheless, and his already boiling blood grew heated with a different flame. An impulse pri-

mal and possessive surged through him and he bent
his head to cover her mouth with his.

He half expected her to bite or scratch, but she did
nothing. She suddenly lay still and let him kiss her.
She yielded to him—or at least stopped fighting him.

She tasted of wine and wealth, of all the things he
wanted and didn't have. She smelled of flowers and
a life of prosperity and gentility he could only dream
about. She was everything that he had ever yearned
for, all the promises his father had made and not
kept, here in his arms.

He loosened his hold with his right hand so that
he could caress her. Her skin was more silken than
her shift, softer than goose down, more wonderful
than velvet. "You're so beautiful," he whispered, the
words drawn out of him as he brushed his hand
over her breasts.

She sucked in her breath and trembled.

"I will warm you, my lady," he murmured as he
leaned down to kiss her again.

She shifted, and he felt her hand meander lower.
Her fingers grazed his thigh, then moved between
his legs. Closing his eyes, he held his breath, delight-
ing in her light and gentle touch.

God's wounds, she wanted him, too. Why, he
didn't know or care. All he knew was that he craved
this woman as he never had another.

She pinched his inner thigh.

He cried out at the sudden, intense pain and,
wincing, rose and tugged her to her feet.

Trembling violently, her lips blue, she raised her
quivering hand as if she would strike him.

He caught hold of her wrist and forced her hand

down, which took more strength than he would have guessed.

"It will take more than that to get away from me."

"Then I will do more, any chance I get."

"Including trying to drown yourself?"

"I wasn't trying to drown myself. I was trying to get away from *you*."

"Where's your gown?"

"The bottom of the river, where I would have been if I hadn't got it off."

"Where you might have been anyway," he growled. "But you are captured again, my lady, so come along and stop this useless nonsense."

She stood her ground, and, although she could hardly speak for shivering, she managed nonetheless. "It will not be useless if it works." She crossed her arms and straightened her shoulders. "You claim that you were deserving of a knighthood before your father's death. Prove that you have the honor of a knight, if not the title, and leave me here. Tell the others you couldn't find me. They won't blame you, and I will never tell anyone who took me."

"I will not leave you here, benighted and freezing and wet," he said just as firmly, willing his own body not to shiver in the cold. "And I will not give up my prize so easily."

"Then it is just as well your father died before you could be knighted, for you do not deserve that honor."

He stiffened as if he had turned to stone, then reached out and hauled her close, so that he could see her face despite the darkness. "Listen to me, my lady, and listen well. Do not ever again presume to tell me how an honorable person behaves. You played my father like he was a lovesick lad and betrayed him. You were his promised wife, by your own word, and you let another man love you." He put his other arm around her, so that he held her to him in a strong embrace. "Do you think to move me with your talk of honor and knighthood? That is gone from me forever, and you helped make it so. I was willing to overlook your part in it, except to make you the object of the ransom, but so help me, my lady, if you do not stop this foolishness and try to escape again, I will . . . I will . . ."

"What?" she demanded, arching her back to get as far away from him as she could, still defiant, still bold. "What will you do? Kill me?"

He shook his head, and in the darkness of the night, with her in his arms, longing exploded within him. "I do not want your death, my lady. I would have you alive. Very much alive."

He captured her mouth in another fiery kiss. Need and passion combined with his anger to create an even fiercer hunger.

With a curse that would have made a soldier blush, she shoved him back and turned to run again.

With a curse of his own, he caught her by the waist, the blood still throbbing through his body, hotter than a smith's forge.

"Kiss me again and I'll kill you!" she cried, her shout rousing the birds in the nearby tree. "Touch me again and I'll . . . I'll strangle you!"

"Do not tempt me to see if you could succeed, my lady," he said, his voice a harsh rasp. "Or perhaps I should let you try."

He resisted the urge to cup her breast in response to her challenge although he could easily imagine the soft weight of her, warm in his palm, his thumb brushing across her pebbled nipple. Instead, he stroked her cheek.

"Well?" he asked softly as she stood motionless. "I have touched you again. Why don't you try to strangle me?"

"I have reconsidered."

Her placid tone astonished him. "Have you finally given up?" he asked, not willing to believe that was true.

"I will not give you the satisfaction of a struggle."

"Then you have surrendered."

She gave him a look of utter scorn. "To you? Never."

Wherever she got her astonishing courage, he had had enough of Lady Allis— her words, her haughty manner, her reminders of his detested parent, even the desire she inspired—and they had lingered too long in this place as it was.

His hand grasping her right arm, he started back toward the ship, all but dragging her. When she stumbled and nearly fell, he tugged her close, then put his arm beneath her knees and lifted her into his arms. She was trembling, either from cold or fear or both, and surely she could have no strength left—

Kicking, she pushed hard against him.

Was there no end to the ways she could try his patience? "I can go faster carrying you, my lady," he said grimly, ignoring her kicks and slaps. "It will be this way, or over my shoulder, as I did before. You choose."

Held captive in his arms, shivering and exhausted, Isabelle wanted to tell him to go to the devil. But in truth, she was freezing and at the end of her strength. She could not walk another step, and although she would rather take her chances of dying from exposure, he was not going to leave her. She had no choice but to let him carry her back to that ship.

In silent acceptance of the inevitable, she put her arm around his neck to steady herself and tried not to notice how the warmth from his body warmed her, too. She would not think of that heated kiss even if she had sensed more of yearning in him than domination or control. Alexander DeFrouchette was her enemy, and there could be no forgiveness for what he had done.

Chapter 5

❧

"**O**h, thank God! Thank God you've got her! She's not dead, is she?" Osburn cried from the bow of the ship when he spotted Alexander trudging toward the river, his prize limp in his arms.

She had been like that since they had left the stand of trees, her arm lightly about his neck, her head against his chest. The slow rising and falling of her breasts made him wonder if she had fallen asleep from sheer fatigue.

He tried not to notice how good she felt in his arms, as if she belonged there. That was surely as false a notion as her apparent surrender when she lay beneath him, when she had been lulling him into carelessness.

And how she had! The sensation of her lips against his had immediately made his plan, the ship, the ransom—everything except her—recede from his mind. She was everything he had ever yearned for, and everything he could ever desire.

She was the most beautiful woman in the world, and when she seemed to be responding, or at least no longer fighting, he had never known such pleasure and excitement.

All a sham, of course. His mind could not blame her; indeed, he could almost admire the strategy. But despite the pleasure, in his heart he wished he had never touched her. It would have been better not to have a taste of the forbidden fruit of a noblewoman's lips and body beneath him—especially hers. He already had enough cause to envy Sir Connor.

As for what she was doing now, if she was not really asleep, he wouldn't be surprised to discover she was merely resting while planning another escape. What her plot might be, or when she might act upon it he couldn't begin to fathom, but he would never underestimate her again.

Either way, he was pleased to note that she was no longer trembling, and he felt warmer, too.

"Why don't you answer?" Osburn called out. "Is she dead or not?"

"She is not dead," he answered, speaking only as loudly as he thought necessary for Osburn to hear him. There seemed to be no habitation around them, but surely it was not wise to shout.

The lady's arm tightened about his neck, and she slowly raised her head, perhaps in answer to Osburn's questions, or because he had awakened her. "I can walk the rest of the way. Put me down."

It was not a request but a command, and he immediately tightened his hold on her. "No. If you do not like your method of conveyance, my lady, you have only yourself to blame, for this is the only way I can be certain you won't run again."

Her voice dropped to a low whisper, intimate in the darkness. "Allow me a little dignity in front of Osburn and those Vikings."

"You did not stand upon your dignity when you went over the side of the Norseman's ship."

Her voice became softer yet. "Please."

It had been a very long time since a woman had whispered in his ear. The last had been his mother, telling him again and again who his father was and how great a man and how they must be prepared for his return, which would surely be soon. That he must try very hard to be worthy. Even as the months and years had passed, every night it was the same deluded litany.

This woman, unlike his mother, was proud. He could admire that pride, for he had seen what a lack of it could do. If he were in her place, might he not appreciate any consideration that allowed him to retain some self-respect?

But he was reluctant to do as she asked. She certainly couldn't run if he was carrying her.

Yet surely she must be too weary to try to escape again, and so tired that he could catch her again if she did.

He halted and let her slide to the ground, trying to ignore the pleasure of her body brushing against his. He fought not to notice the sensation of her shift riding up, knowing her long, slim legs must be exposed. He steeled himself against the sensation of her breasts moving slowly down his naked chest. He pressed his lips together to prevent himself from kissing her again.

She was an object of trade and nothing more. She could never be anything more. He would not throw away the plan and all it was to accomplish because of a wayward, fleeting desire, no matter how powerful it seemed. Desire did not last, and it left only anguish in its wake.

When she was steady on the ground, she lifted her brilliant eyes and gazed at him steadily. "Thank you."

Her simple words struck at the wall around his lonely heart. But they could not do more than dent it, for it was of ancient making and strengthened by a bitterness no woman's words softly spoken could overcome. "For your own safety, I want your promise as the wife of Connor of Bellevoire that you will not try to escape again."

Wrapping her arms about her body, she nodded. "You have my word as the wife of Connor of Bellevoire that I will never try to escape from you again."

"What are you waiting for?" Osburn demanded from his place in the bow. "Get her aboard."

"You are summoned," she said evenly.

She made it sound as if he were Osburn's lackey.

Scowling, he followed her as she carefully waded out into the river toward the ship floating a few feet from the bank. The Norsemen's oars were still in the water, holding it as steady as possible. Ingar waited at the side of the ship, and another man held the tiller. Not surprisingly, Ingar looked furiously angry.

Once she was at the side, Alexander came behind her to lift her into the ship, but she gave him a warning look over her slender shoulder.

"I will not have you put your hands on me again."

Her words were like another slap, one of many she had given him this day. But this one hurt the most, and it mended whatever breech in his self-defense her whispered request had made.

Ingar snorted with disgust. "Lift your arms, woman," he ordered.

She obeyed, and with no sharp retort. Ingar hauled her, dripping, onto the deck, paying no heed to her once she was on board.

"You, into the ship," he said just as brusquely to Alexander.

As Alexander clambered inside, aided by two of Ingar's crew, the Norseman jerked his thumb at Osburn. "This one has probably roused the entire countryside with his lamenting and shouting. I did not come here to be killed." He glared at Isabelle. "No woman is worth this much trouble," he grumbled before he strode to the stern and grabbed the tiller from the other man.

Now that the lady was aboard, Alexander expected Osburn to approach her. He didn't. He simply sank down in the bow and lifted his ever-present wineskin to his lips.

The lady made her way to the center of the ship, where Denis was standing with a blanket at the ready. With a few quiet words, he offered it to her. She accepted it, enshrouding herself before sitting with her back to the mastfish, a T-shaped support for the mast when it was raised.

Ingar gave the order for his men to commence rowing. Alexander moved swiftly out of their way, joining Denis a few paces from the lady.

Ingar set a brisk pace. Obviously well trained, his men rowed with swift, silent strokes, sending the ship shooting down the river like an arrow from a bow.

Denis plopped himself down and offered Alexander another rough woolen blanket that, like the Norsemen, smelled of salted fish and ale. The blanket around his shoulders, Alexander pulled on his boots and noted that Denis had brought his swordbelt and tunics there, too.

"*Merde*, I thought you had lost your senses, Alexander, jumping over the side like that!" Denis quietly exclaimed as they both leaned back against the yard and furrowed sail. "I swear I have aged ten years."

Alexander felt he had aged more than that. This venture, which had sounded so simple when Lord Oswald had proposed it, was turning out to be far more complicated than he had ever dreamed.

Rather like the lady.

"I had to get her back," he replied. "It's a damn good thing she didn't drown."

"*Oui*, of course," Denis agreed.

Alexander lowered his voice to a whisper that the grunting, sweating Norsemen couldn't hear. "I'm going to keep watch tonight. I don't trust Osburn, or these Norsemen. I wouldn't put it past them to kill us and sell her, if they thought they could get away with it."

"But Lord Oswald has paid them well, I'm sure."

"I hope he has paid them enough."

Denis gravely nodded. "With the amount of wine he has drunk, Osburn will probably pass out, but I think you are wise about the Norsemen, especially now that they have seen her . . . like that."

"Yes, I think Ingar was very serious about her worth as a slave."

"And he is right. *Mon Dieu!* Such beauty and such

spirit! I swear, my friend, that if she were to produce a sword and try to take command of the ship, I would not be shocked."

Alexander sighed as he moved his belt and scabbard close beside him. "Neither would I, although she has given me her word she will not try to escape again."

Denis's eyes widened, and he sat up straighter. "Truly? Her word?"

"Yes."

"Then maybe she will not. Normans hold their honor very dear, or so I have been told."

"I suppose."

Denis hugged his knees. "Why do you not rest now, and I will let you take the second watch? You must be very tired after chasing her all over the riverbank."

Alexander gratefully slid lower, so that his head was resting against the furled sail as he closed his eyes. "Thank you, Denis."

Something pushed against Alexander's back. He was on his feet in an instant, his scabbard in his left hand and the hilt of his sword in his right. The weapon was half out of the scabbard before he was even fully awake.

Several of the Norsemen were staring at him, as surprised as he was, in the breaking daylight.

"There is no need for alarm. We are just in the way," Denis quickly explained from where he stood off to the steering board side. "They want to raise the mast and set the sail."

"Oh." His heartbeat still as rapid as a wren's wings in flight, Alexander shoved his sword back into the scabbard, then joined his friend. His prize huddled near the prow, cloaked in the blanket, watching the Norsemen set about their task. Also in the bow were two of the Norsemen. They held a stay attached to the top of the mast, ready to help haul it upright. They were so close to her that she was as good as guarded.

Loose and tousled, her hair made him think that she, too, had just awakened. Her eyes were a little puffy from sleep, yet they shone with a sharp awareness of where she was and what had happened to her.

She met his gaze with undisguised hostility, but all Alexander could think about was the fact that beneath that blanket she was very nearly naked, clad only in that gossamer-thin silk shift that hid so very little, especially when it was damp. Aided by the memory of the kiss last night, his desire burst instantly, vibrantly to life.

Trying to subdue his unwanted craving, he forced his attention to Osburn, who lay near her, the wineskin at his feet. It looked as if he slept where he'd fallen.

"Oui," Denis said as he straddled one of the vacated sea chests. "He has not moved. A drooling man, even one so delightfully attired, is not a pretty sight, is it?"

Alexander gave his friend a sardonic little smile of agreement as he sat astride the sea chest to his friend's right. "You didn't wake me to take the second watch."

"You were sleeping as peacefully as a newborn babe, and I said to myself, 'Denis, he has earned a good rest, and you can sleep later.' *She* did not awaken until the Norsemen ordered her out of the way, too. Otherwise, nobody went near her." Denis's dimples appeared. "They were whispering about her all night, though. They think that although she is beautiful and they wouldn't mind making love with her, they agree with Ingar. She is not worth the fight she will surely put up."

"I didn't know you could understand them."

Denis grinned. "I understand enough of the words and the way they said them."

Alexander turned his attention to the activity on the ship, and how far they had come from Bellevoire. They had left the river, and, although they were close to shore, they were definitely at sea, which explained why Ingar was setting the sail.

Four of the brawnier Norsemen put the mast into the slot for it in the keel. Aided by the two pulling on the shroud, they levered the mast upward hand over hand, walking toward the slot until it settled into place with a thud. The raised mast swayed a moment, but the mastfish kept it from tipping backward, and an oaken block was slid into place to hold the other side of it steady. Then, the yard and furrowed sail were attached and the sail unfurled, the white square catching the quickening breeze. Except for the lines at the bottom of their sail, there was no other rigging. It was a simple, if heavy task, done with quick efficiency by Ingar's men.

Finished, they sprawled on the deck between their sea chests and fell asleep at once—except for the two who scowled at Alexander and Denis, clearly not pleased by the other men's temporary possession of their sea chests. Alexander and Denis quickly rose and went back to the center of the ship, where they sat down. The lady, Alexander noticed, stayed where she was.

"Ingar says we should arrive after midday if the wind holds," Denis remarked as he reached for a wineskin. He offered it to Alexander. "It's water, not wine. I think Osburn has finished all of that."

"I don't suppose Ingar mentioned exactly where this fortress is?" Alexander asked as he took a drink. The water was not very cold, and it tasted leathery, but he was glad to wet his throat.

He had accepted Lord Oswald's word that the place where they would hold the lady was safe, secure and secluded, but after yesterday, he was not nearly so willing to take the man's promises at face value.

"No, only that it is somewhere in Glamorgan, in the south part of Wales that Prince John used to rule." Denis shook his head. "The wilds of Wales."

"He wanted her far from home so that her husband couldn't find her."

"Then he has chosen well," Denis agreed.

"How did you sleep, Norman?"

Alexander and Denis both looked up to see Ingar towering over them. Grinning, he swept his cloak out behind him and crouched opposite them.

"Well enough," Alexander replied. He decided to take this opportunity to ask some questions, since Ingar seemed in a jovial humor. "Is the location of this fortress of Lord Oswald's truly a secret?"

"You have not seen it, or who guards it, or you would not wonder," Ingar replied. "It is not much of a fortress, yet he has hired Brabancons for a garrison, so I expect that anybody who does discover it does not live to tell about it."

Alexander tensed and Denis stared. The Brabancons were the fiercest mercenaries in Europe, men
infamous for their greed and cruelty. They would
kill anyone—man, woman or child—who stood in
their way. They were so notoriously vicious that
both Richard and his father had banned them from
England.

Lord Oswald was Richard's enemy, so it should
come as no shock that he would use such men, yet
the hiring of Brabancons was something Alexander
had not expected.

"He pays for the best men for the job," Ingar said,
obviously amused by Alexander's reaction to the
news of the mercenaries. He reached out for the
wineskin and took a gulp. Wiping his lips, he
belched, then said, "You and I are proof of that, ya? I
am the best captain of the best crew in the western
seas and you are skilled at stealing."

Annoyed, Alexander rose. "I am *not* a thief."

His gray eyes twinkling with a sly certainty that
angered Alexander even more, Ingar straightened so
that they were eye to eye. "Not an ordinary one, of
course. I should have said *kidnapper.*"

"I was destined for knighthood and it was for that
I trained."

Crossing his arms and genuinely puzzled, Ingar
raised a thick blond brow. "Why would you waste
your time and skill with that? Chivalry is for boys
playing at war, not men who can really fight."

"I don't expect a Norseman to understand."

"That does not mean he cannot fight," Denis said,
leaping to his feet as well as his friend's defense. "He
once held off an entire village all by himself."

Ingar looked so impressed, Alexander decided he

wouldn't clarify that the villagers had, for the most part, been armed with sticks—except for the butcher with the cleaver.

"I thought he would be good," the Norseman said. "I would gladly welcome such a man into my crew, Norman, if you wish to fight to good purpose."

"I have no desire to plunder and pillage."

Ingar threw back his head and laughed. "Of course you do. All men do, if they can. Most cannot, though." He ran a canny eye over Alexander. "You would be a wealthy man if you join me."

"I have been promised a knighthood and money after we collect the ransom."

The sly, knowing look lingered in Ingar's eyes. "You abduct a woman for ransom and yet you are too good to sail with me?"

Alexander's jaw clenched. "This is different," he muttered, telling himself it was so.

"He never said he was too good to sail with you," Denis protested.

Ingar, however, was clearly not offended, for he smiled as he regarded the Gascon. "There is no need to defend him. It is his loss if he will not join me." He put his hands on his lower back and stretched like a cat after a long nap. "This wind will speed our progress. Now I will sleep until midday, when we should be near Oswald's fortress. There are some treacherous rocks that guard the bay, and while Lars is good with the steering board, I am better."

With that, he went back toward the stern, said something to the man holding the tiller, wrapped his cloak around himself and lay down.

"A strange fellow, that Norseman," Denis remarked as they settled back down beneath the sail.

Alexander silently agreed. Then once again his gaze strayed to the lady in the bow.

No, he was not like Ingar, or he would have done more than kiss her last night. He would have taken her there in the trees, sating the desire she roused with no thought beyond that. He would have teased and caressed and stroked with all the skill he possessed until she whimpered with need, anxious and desperate for him.

He would have been long in the loving, savoring every moment she was in his arms, lingering over every part of her. He would have made her moan with yearning and cry out for him to love her. When he finally entered her, he would have listened to her every word and sigh and breath, seeking to pleasure her to the utmost so that his would be all the finer. Only when he was sure she could wait no longer would he release the full power of his desire. Only then would he have given free rein to the ardor she inspired and thrust hard and deep, until he reached the pinnacle of excited bliss and release.

After, he would kiss her lightly, sweetly, like a lover should. He would whisper tender endearments, yet all the while he would touch and brush and fondle, until she was ready for him once more. Then he would love her again, fast or slow as the mood took him.

If he were like Ingar and thought only of himself.

Chapter 6

Later that day, after Ingar had successfully guided his ship around several tall, jagged rocks, Isabelle wrapped the blanket more tightly about her body as she stared at the bluffs surrounding a small bay. Perched on an outcropping, dark against a slate gray sky, were the remains of towers and crumbling walls. It was obvious that there was no village nearby, or there would be vessels in the bay.

Two roofless towers stood at the corners of the outer wall. She could make out two more beyond that, probably at the other corners, indicating that this castle had not been a large one. There was likely only the one outer wall, and perhaps a dry moat on the landward side. All the buildings would be inside that single barricade. Unfortunately, a small courtyard would be easy to watch from the surrounding wall walks.

She did not have to be told this was where they intended to imprison her. A more lonely, desolate and isolated place she could scarcely imagine. Gulls wheeled above the bluffs and the ruins, their mournful cries adding to her feeling that she would never be able to escape this place.

She might as well be a million miles away from home. She could not swim back, and a journey overland, even supposing she could escape and had any idea of the route back to Bellevoire, would surely take days.

How could Connor and his men ever find her here, even if they surmised she had been abducted? They would have no idea what had happened to her, and the thought of her sister's fear and misery added to her own.

And what if Allis was so upset and worried that she lost the baby?

Someone came up behind her. Steeling herself, she did not turn to see who it was, because she did not want to have anything to do with anyone on this ship, not even the Gascon.

DeFrouchette came around to face her, his warrior's body blocking out the sight of the ruins. He had something made of cloth in his hands, which he held out to her. "Put this on. You need to be wearing more than that shift and a blanket."

Once again controlling her fear, she curled her lip and regarded him with scorn. "How kind of you to think of my modesty."

"It is not your modesty that concerns me. It is your safety."

"If you were truly so concerned with my safety, you should have left me safely at home."

He took a step closer and glare met glare, his

bright blue gleaming like sapphires in torchlight. "Don't argue with me about this, my lady. The men who guard this place are not known for their restraint."

She refused to be cowed. "Unlike you?"

"I am as gentle as a sparrow compared to them."

"You are a lustful lout who could never have been a chivalrous knight."

"Even a knight has desires, my lady, as you should know. Did not desire for you compel your husband to forget his vow of chivalry? He wooed and loved another man's betrothed."

"I may have agreed to wed your father," she replied, answering as she was sure Allis would, "but he didn't care for me, except that I was to be the means for him to gain control of my family's estate and sate his base desires. So I chose another."

DeFrouchette's face reddened. "I think you are wrong, my lady. He did care for you. He didn't care for my mother or me, but you . . . why else did my father wait for your hand in marriage all those years?"

"It would have been better for me and my family if he had not," she retorted, flushing, "and whatever was between your father and me, that did not give you leave to kiss me."

DeFrouchette's face resumed its normal stoic calm, and he tilted his head in a mocking little bow. "I humbly beg your forgiveness."

"Humble is one of the last things I would ever call you."

His lips curved up into a little smile that filled her with annoyance. "What would be the first?"

"Tempting though it may be, I am too much of a

lady to use the words that would best express what I think of you."

Challenge flashed in his sapphire orbs. "Try."

Challenge was infinitely better than condescension, but she was in no humor to bandy insults. "I will not bring myself down to your level."

"Giving up?"

"You bloody bastard!" she hissed so that only he would hear.

His infuriating smile grew. "Oh, come, surely you can do better than that and call me worse. The boys of my village could, and they were much younger than you."

She snatched the tunic from him, then waited for him to leave. He didn't. "Do you intend to stand there and watch me dress?"

Again, their gazes met, stare for stare.

Then he ran a slow, measuring gaze over her. As he studied her, something strong and primitive began to throb through her body, something unwelcome but undeniable. It had to be a weakness caused by fatigue. Whatever it was, it was wrong and she would not acknowledge it.

She shifted the blanket so that it was wrapped around her breasts, leaving her shoulders and arms free, tucking in one end so that it would stay. She pulled on his tunic, which smelled of horse and leather and him, as she well recalled from when he had held her on the gelding. She would probably never forget how it felt to be clasped in his powerful arms then, or when he had embraced her and forced his hot kiss upon her.

Or when they had been on the ground, his body pressing against hers, his lips sliding across her mouth and his hands moving with slow, sure leisure over her. Her heart had pounded and her whole body had been hot with fear.

As he stood here now, her heart began to pound and her body to warm just the same, but she was not afraid. She could not name the feeling coursing through her as she inhaled his scent, the memory of his strength and passion coming to her whether she willed it or not.

She told herself to attend to her task, and forget that he was there.

The tunic fell to mid-thigh and the sleeves covered her hands. She tied the lacing at the neck, which nonetheless hung low enough to expose the tops of her breasts. She could roll up the sleeves, and as for the length. . . .

She reached up under the tunic and pulled the blanket loose, then retucked it about her waist, so that it became a long skirt. "Now that I am more decently attired, you may go."

He frowned and made no move to leave. "I should have guessed it wouldn't matter what you wear. Your beauty has nothing to do with the clothes on your back."

A strange feeling stole over Isabelle and, flushing, she looked away. Other men had told her she was beautiful, other men with rich, deep voices and warriors' bodies. Why was it, then, that this time—for the first time—she truly believed that in a man's eyes she was beautiful?

Perhaps it was his annoyance.

"I hope you're not intending to put me back in that sack," she said, determined to forget his compliment, such as it was.

The corner of his lips lifted. "There's a thought."

"I nearly suffocated."

"It wouldn't be for long."

She crossed her arms and prepared to denounce him, until she saw what looked suspiciously like mischief in his blue eyes. "You aren't, are you?"

"It's tempting, but I don't think I could make it up the bluff with you over my shoulder."

"Thank God! Now go away."

He bowed with a mocking—and unexpected—elegance. "As you command, my lady, I obey."

She sniffed and didn't look to see where he went or to whom he spoke; it was enough that he had left her alone.

She didn't want to be anywhere near him and his disconcerting eyes or full lips. She wanted to be as far away from him as possible.

She wanted to be home, where most men—except Connor—treated her like an overgrown child.

Ingar shouted, and the Norsemen who were awake roused their companions. Together, with the same unexpected brisk efficiency they had demonstrated before, the crew began to disassemble the yard and mast.

As the Norsemen went about their task, Isabelle kept her eyes on the shore, even when she heard De-Frouchette return. She tensed, ready to maintain her air of haughty defiance.

It wasn't DeFrouchette. Regardless of whether or not he was in the way, Osburn picked his way to the prow, nearly tripping over a large coil of thick rope before he turned to lean his back on the curving wooden decoration. His face was deathly pale, and tinged with green, whether from the effects of the wine or the rocking motion of the ship, she wasn't sure. His brown eyes were red-rimmed and blood-shot, his fine clothing wrinkled and his blond hair disheveled.

"The land is not much to look at, is it?" he asked over the orders and curses of the Norsemen, as if they were any two passengers on a journey.

"What land is it?" she asked, wondering how guarded he would be in his answers.

"Wales."

It was even farther from Bellevoire than she thought, and she fought to hide her dismay.

Obviously she was not successful, for Osburn smiled. "I share your distaste for the place, my lady. I've done my best to make it comfortable, and I hope my company will make up for any deprivations you might feel."

"Do you honestly believe I could ever be comfortable anywhere when I have been abducted?" she demanded incredulously. "Do you think I want to spend any time at all with you? If you were the only man left in England—Europe—the world!—I would not. Even if I were not here against my will, I would say the same."

His eyes flickered with annoyance, but he kept smiling his awful smile. "You had best have a care how you speak to me, my lady, and act toward me, too. We're not going to be alone there, you know. I have a garrison to guard you. The Brabancons won't be nearly as forgiving and patient as I."

New and even more consuming fear gripped her as she stared at him. She was going to be guarded by Brabancons, the most reviled, cruel, rapacious mercenaries in Europe?

Suddenly, DeFrouchette's words made sense, for he might indeed seem as gentle as a sparrow compared to the Brabancon. Her gaze flicked to the center of the ship. He wasn't there. She quickly scanned the vessel and saw him and his friend in the stern near Ingar.

No wonder now that DeFrouchette had offered her his tunic. He would want his prize better covered against the lustful eyes of the Brabancons so he wouldn't have to exert himself to fight them off.

"I see you've heard of the Brabancons," Osburn observed, coming closer. "If your husband doesn't pay the ransom, first I'll be repaid for all my trouble and having to live in such a dismal place by enjoying your favors, then I'll turn you over to the Brabancons to do with as they will." He smiled with genuine, sickening pleasure. "And after they've had their sport of you, I'll send you home. Will your doting husband love you so well when he hears what has happened to you, do you think?"

She gripped the gunwale, tempted to jump again. "You're a monster!"

While Osburn laughed at her epithet as if it both pleased and amused him, out of the corner of her eye, she saw DeFrouchette rise. If she did jump, he would be right behind her.

"There's no need for such harsh words, my lady," Osburn said. "If your husband pays, you'll be safe enough. I've already warned the Brabancons not to touch you, and I'll set DeFrouchette to guard you, like a big hound, for as long as he is here."

As long as he was there? He was leaving? He did seem the lesser of several evils, which no doubt explained her dismay.

"After your little escapade last night, I'm sure he'll keep a careful watch while he can. He'll not want to lose the five thousand marks he has been promised for his part in our scheme."

Five thousand marks? Connor could not possibly raise such a sum!

Osburn's smile grew, and he sidled a little closer. "Perhaps I shouldn't upset you more by saying this is merely a quarter of what we will demand to guarantee your safe return."

Oh, God! Connor was not wealthy enough to afford such a sum. If he managed to borrow it, he and Allis would be indebted for life.

"Why look so worried, my sweet? If your husband loves you as much as I hear, he'll find it somehow. Borrow some from Richard perhaps—oh!" Osburn's eyes gleamed with evil mischief as he covered his mouth with his fingertips. "I forgot. All Richard's money is going to his new fortress in France." The gleam crystallized into something hard and cold as he lowered his hand. "Your husband had better find it somehow, or you may find yourself very intimately acquainted with several Brabancons."

A wail of anguish rose up in Isabelle. Death sounded preferable to the fate Osburn described. Yet even then, her will told her she must live. If she died, there would be no one to give evidence against Osburn, and Lord Oswald, and all those involved in this despicable crime. If she gave in to despair, they might never be brought to justice. She had to believe that Connor would capture them all eventually. If she could survive whatever they did to her, she would see that they were punished.

So she must be strong and find some way to escape, no matter how hopeless it seemed.

"A very interesting plan to dispose of me, Osburn," she said, her decision giving new strength to her voice.

As she spoke, she noticed DeFrouchette approaching, skirting the Norsemen as they finished laying the mast down the keel of the ship.

Osburn threatened her; DeFrouchette claimed she was to be treated as an honored guest. It was obvious DeFrouchette did not have a very high opinion of Lord Oswald's son. Why not sow a little more dissent?

"You must have come up with this plan all by yourself," she said to Osburn, her tone mocking and loud enough for all to hear as they sat on their chests and prepared to out oars. "I know it cannot be your father's because, unfortunately, there is no denying that he is a clever man. A clever man would know that to rape the wife of any lord will turn all the nobility against him, even those few secret allies he may have left. A clever man would know that if he did that to me, my husband would hunt him—and all his band of outlaws—down like the dogs they are and gladly send them straight to hell. A clever man would know I would happily drown in a bog rather than spend a moment in his arms, no matter what fate he threatens me with."

His face growing purple with rage, Osburn's hand went to his jeweled dagger.

"Will you make some more useless threats, Osburn? Why not spare yourself the effort and go back to your wine?"

He yanked the dagger from his belt.

"Will you strike me dead, Osburn?" she jeered. "I will believe it when you do it."

As she had anticipated, DeFrouchette came around her and grabbed Osburn's wrist before he could strike. His gaze darted from Osburn's red and furious face to Isabelle's. A shrewd, appraising look appeared in the bright blue orbs as he regarded her, and then he loosened his grip on Osburn. "Will you let her goad you?"

"I wasn't going to kill her," Osburn mumbled as he shoved his dagger back in his belt.

"Good, because if you do, she is worth nothing."

Osburn straightened his tunic. "I know that."

"Nor was I goading him," Isabelle retorted, blithely lying through her teeth. "I was merely stating facts and asking questions."

"I can imagine," DeFrouchette muttered.

"I daresay, you and Ingar, his men and his ship do not come cheaply, DeFrouchette." She addressed the sulking Osburn. "I must say, Osburn, for a man stripped of all his goods and holdings, your father seems to have a lot of money. How is that, I wonder?"

"He has ways," Osburn sullenly replied.

"I have not heard of other women taken in ransom, and I surely would have over the course of three years. Am I the first, then? Or have you never been successful?"

"Osburn, can't you see what she's doing?" DeFrouchette demanded in a low, stern tone. "Tell the Norsemen they'll be paid."

Osburn blinked, as if he didn't understand at all, but he obeyed DeFrouchette's order anyway. "Pay no heed to her," he declared. "My father's very wealthy. He hid away his fortune before he had to forfeit his goods and property to the Crown."

"I had better be paid what was agreed," Ingar warned from the stern. He looked at Isabelle in a way that made her shiver. "I will have my money one way or another."

Perhaps her plan had not been a wise one, after all.

"Of course you'll be paid as we agreed," Osburn said. "My father keeps his word."

Isabelle sniffed at that. "The man is a traitor. Who can trust a traitor?"

DeFrouchette moved to stand in front of her, and his whole body seemed to burn with rage, his blue eyes most of all. "My lady, keep that lovely mouth of yours shut, or I will gag you again. I know what you are trying to do, if the rest of them do not, and I will not permit it."

Since she did not want to be gagged again, and was quite sure he would do as he said, she did not speak, not even to answer. Instead, she walked away and went to sit near his friend.

Denis grinned as she joined him, then sobered. "My lady, I would not be so quick to make my friend angry."

"Why not? He says he won't hurt me. I am worth too much to him."

"And he should be worth much to you, for he will protect you. If you anger him, you might make even Alexander think you are not worth the trouble to guard you from these others, and that would be a mistake."

Perhaps he was right. At least DeFrouchette was no Brabancon or Norseman.

"I do not say this to frighten you, my lady, for in truth, I have seen Alexander lose his patience only once—and it was unforgettable, I assure you—but it could happen. There is much about this business that has tried his patience already."

"There is much about 'this business,' as you call it, that has done much more than try my patience."

Despite her haughty response, as the ship neared the wharf built parallel to the shore, she considered what the Gascon had said. Perhaps DeFrouchette was the one man it would be foolish to further antagonize.

While they were still several feet away from the shore, Ingar ordered his men to pull in their oars. The momentum and Ingar's steering brought the vessel's left side close to the wharf.

One of the men nearest the bow grabbed the rope coiled there and leapt ashore. He tied the rope to a piling. Another two hastened to lay a plank from the ship to the wooden platform.

"Thus I bring you safely," Ingar announced as he strode down the rocking ship as easily as another did a village street.

He passed her by with only a glance before halting in front of Osburn. "When do I get the rest of my money?"

Osburn drew a purse out of his wrinkled tunic and put it in the Norseman's outstretched hand. "That is for this journey. There will be more after the next, and when my father arrives. Now that we are here, will you join us for a little celebration?"

"No. We must set up camp."

"Very well, if that's what you want to do," Osburn replied with a wave of his hand. "I won't insist."

That would mean more wine for him, no doubt.

Osburn headed for the plank, then glanced back at DeFrouchette. "Bring her," he ordered as he strolled off the ship. He nearly stumbled when he was on the wharf, but he quickly righted himself.

"He has got to get his land legs," Denis said to Isabelle as he reached down to pick up the leather pouch at his feet. "It will feel like you are still on the ship at first."

DeFrouchette joined them and gestured toward the plank. "After you, my lady," he said with an impertinent bow and shrewd gaze, as if daring her to try to run from him now.

She started forward, but Ingar blocked her way. "Not yet!" he said, grinning. "Not until I have made my farewell to your lady."

With that, he tugged Isabelle into his arms and kissed her full on the mouth.

For an instant, she was too shocked and immobilized by his bearlike grasp to respond. He tasted of ale and fish—nothing like DeFrouchette—and his beard scratched.

Recovering, she pulled away and slapped him hard across the face.

Ingar laughed as he let her go. "Ah, my lady, it is too bad that Osburn's father has powerful friends among the Norse of Dublin, or by Thor's thunder, I would risk his wrath, and DeFrouchette's, too, and keep you."

She wiped the back of her hand across her mouth. "And I would risk your wrath and try to kill you."

Ingar chuckled and shook his head. "I think not, my lady. No woman of mine has ever had cause to complain."

"To your face," she retorted. "Who can say what they mutter about you when you are not there?"

She had finally said something that took Ingar aback. God's blood, was there nothing she would not say, to anyone?

In spite of the frustration and annoyance the lady created in him with her tart tongue, Alexander nearly laughed out loud to see the Norseman's expression.

His shock was no more than he deserved for kissing her. Neither was the slap.

As he followed her down the plank, he also took a secret pleasure in noting that she had not struck him when he had kissed her. She had not enjoyed it, but she had not hit him.

She swayed on the wharf, and he was finding it difficult to get his balance, too.

"As I said to her," Denis remarked, coming up behind him, "we need to get our land legs."

"You don't seem to be having any trouble."

"When you have been tossed through the air as many times as I have, the difference between a ship and the land is nothing," he said cheerfully. He nodded at the lady. "Perhaps you should help her."

"I think that is one woman who does not require much assistance."

Denis laughed softly. "*Oui*, you may be right."

Sure enough, she managed to walk relatively normally as they left the wharf. They followed Osburn across the small pebbled beach and up narrow steps cut in the bluff leading to what had once been the postern gate. It was a difficult climb for all of them, made even worse by the worn steps.

Alexander stayed close to the lady. She slipped

once, but when he reached out to help her, she refused his offer with a look that would have curdled milk.

By the time they reached the top, even he was winded. Osburn complained bitterly between gasps for breath; Denis said nothing, his silence a more eloquent comment on his exhaustion.

The fortress did not improve upon closer inspection. Although Alexander would have been hard-pressed to describe what he had expected, he had not anticipated finding a castle that was little more than a ruin.

While attempts at repairs had been made to the crumbling outer wall, the workers had used a haphazard jumble of stone. It looked as if carts of rocks had been brought there and simply dumped. In other places, where the gaps were not so wide, barricades of pointed stakes filled in the spaces. Both these measures were meant to be temporary, or masons would have been called in to do a more thorough repair job.

Alexander could easily imagine that the lady, who seemed as slippery as an eel and just as hard to hold, was already plotting a way to get out of there. It would take more than a few pointed spikes or hastily repaired walls to keep her inside. He hoped the very notion of being caught by the Brabancons would make her think twice before she did anything foolish.

Even from this distance, he could make out several scruffy-looking men watching them. If the lady was smart, and it was obvious she wasn't stupid, she would not attempt to get past them.

Two more were standing guard at the postern gate as they approached. Both were large, stocky and unkempt, and their clothing was similar: the padded gambesons knights wore beneath their armor, leather jerkins over top, dark wool breeches, and boots. Their swordbelts were wide and their scabbards without adornment, like the metal hilts of the swords protruding from them. These were not weapons for decoration or show but were clearly intended to be used, and often. In addition to their swords, both had long daggers stuck through their belts. Alexander would not have been surprised to learn they had at least one more knife hidden in their belts or boots.

The shorter one, whose hair and beard were filthy blond, stood a pace behind the other, indicating he was subordinate to the man in front of him. This fellow was easily over six feet tall and looked like an ox on two legs as he waited with his hands on his hips. His lank mud brown hair hung past his wide shoulders, and it was as if all the evil things he had done had left their mark upon his scarred, ugly face.

"Hail, Heinrich!" Osburn declared as he reached the tall man, and they clasped arms in greeting.

The lady came to a stop before she got within ten feet of them. She clutched his tunic at the neck and held it tightly closed. He couldn't blame her for attempting to cover her chest as much as she could for the Brabancon was studying her with an openly lascivious leer on his ugly face.

"So, this is the woman," he said, his voice more like the growl of a bear than a man's, his accent Germanic. He switched to passable Norman French. "A beauty, as you said. Nice and ripe." A feral grin came to his beady black eyes. "Just the way I like my women."

Alexander put his hand on the hilt of his sword and moved closer to her. The sooner the Brabancons knew she was under his protection—and not the useless Osburn's—the better. And maybe fighting would quell that other excitement raging in his blood, the excitement that had been there ever since he had first laid eyes on her, and that he was not able to subdue.

"Allow me to introduce you," Osburn said, mockingly polite. "This is Heinrich, my lady, the commander of the garrison here."

Once again, this astonishing woman did not start to cry or cower. She regarded Heinrich with haughty dignity and said, "Since your garrison, as you choose to call it, is composed of thieves, murderers and cutthroats, he looks vile enough for that command."

Heinrich's heavy brows lowered ominously, and he took a step closer.

So did Alexander, drawing the man's attention to him even as his blood sang with the hope of battle.

Then the fool Osburn broke the tension simmering between them. "Take care, my lady. Heinrich is like a wolf on a lead, and I don't know how long I can keep him on it. It could be that if he's enraged, he'll bite you. I won't consider myself responsible if he does."

"Since you hold me here against my will, you most certainly are responsible for whatever happens to me," she said. She glanced at Alexander, then back at Osburn. "And obviously you are forgetting my watchdog DeFrouchette. He will not be happy if his prize is harmed."

"No, I will not," he seconded, watching the Brabancon study him.

He half smiled and waited, hoping the Brabancon would challenge him.

The Brabancon stayed frustratingly silent. Alexander was about to challenge the man himself when it began to rain, a slow, steady drizzle.

Osburn looked up at the dark sky. "This isn't the time or place to talk, and I want some wine."

He shoved his way past Heinrich. The lady hurried after him and so did Denis, his shoulders hunched against the wet.

Alexander took his time, strolling through the gate as if he had all the time in the world. As he did, he felt the Brabancons watching him from the gate and the wall walk. He rested his hand on the hilt of his sword, prepared for an ambush, or at least a confrontation.

None came, but he felt their hostile gazes and knew it was only a matter of time.

Chapter 7

Isabelle hurried after Osburn, as equally determined to get away from those two men as she was to get out of the rain.

Opposite the small postern gate through which they entered was a wider one, with two heavy oaken doors studded with iron. Inside the yard, the buildings seemed as hastily and haphazardly repaired as the walls, all save one. Obviously of newer construction, it was not stone, but half-timbered. Another smaller building, made of stone, was attached to it at the east end. Judging by the smoke coming out of the louvered hatch in the roof, she guessed it was the kitchen. The west end of the new building abutted a tower that seemed in relatively good repair.

In addition to the new building, which she thought must be a sort of hall, there was a long, low structure that had a stinking pile of straw and manure outside it. These must be the stables. Across from that was a storehouse or armory and what appeared to be the remains of a chapel, for there was a cross carved over the door. Of all the buildings, it was in the worst condition—not surprising, considering the sort of men who lived here.

Her gaze swept over the men on the wall walk, counting them. There were fifteen, including the two at the gate.

They all looked to be wearing the same sort of mismatched hodgepodge of garments of cloth and leather, and a few sported breastplates. It was as if they wore whatever they could find or steal, which was probably the case.

Trust Oswald to have hired Brabancons, and probably the worst of those he could find! And she should have guessed he would flee to the west, far from London and the king's court.

As for those two at the gate, what a pair of horrible reprobates they were! The one named Heinrich especially looked like something from a nightmare. She had been glad when DeFrouchette had drawn closer to her, and she'd actually taken comfort from his presence. She was grateful for DeFrouchette's tunic, too. She didn't want to think about what Heinrich might have said—or done—had she been clad only in her shift.

As Osburn drew near the new building, the door opened and a young woman with a shawl thrown over her head came rushing out. Clad in a simple gown of gold-colored wool that hugged her slender form, a plain leather girdle about her waist, she was very young and very pretty, with thick dark hair and bright brown eyes. Most surprising of all, for it seemed so incongruous in this place, her smile of welcome was glorious.

Isabelle halted as Osburn did, and so did Denis and DeFrouchette behind her.

"Osburn!" the girl cried as she threw herself into his arms and kissed him.

Her actions explained her place here, for that was no sisterly kiss. She was either Osburn's wife or his mistress.

Osburn put his hands on the young woman's upper arms and pushed her back. "Can't you see it's raining, Kiera?" he demanded, moving forward. "I hope you've got a good fire going."

"I 'ave, and I 'ad the serving women start preparing food as soon as I saw your ship," she quickly replied, pathetically eager and apparently not disturbed by his less than enthusiastic reception. Her manner of speaking belied a humble origin, telling Isabelle that she was probably not his wife.

The object of the girl's affection didn't reply as he continued on the way. Kiera hesitated a moment as she looked at Isabelle and the others, then hurried after him.

Isabelle, too, glanced at DeFrouchette, curious as to what he made of Kiera and her presence there.

What she saw shocked her, for on his stern visage was an expression of distaste amounting almost to revulsion.

Why? She was pretty, so it couldn't be because of her appearance. Because she was Osburn's mistress? He was hardly a model of virtue, to look at Kiera thus. Because she obviously liked Osburn? In truth, Isabelle found that somewhat disgusting herself—but then, she had not been born a peasant.

If she had, Isabelle thought as they continued toward the half-timbered building, and a lord's son who was not unattractive came along and offered her a finer life than she could ever know, might she not be tempted, too? Might she not even overlook his drunkenness and other faults?

Perhaps, and she would remember that if that were so, Kiera's first loyalty would be to the man she believed had saved her from a life of poverty and want.

They entered what was indeed a rudimentary hall. There was a large open area, with a central hearth that contained a fire. The smoke made its way upward and out through the thatched roof. The only other ventilation was the door, so the smoke lingered.

Bundles and bags beside benches along the wall told Isabelle that the Brabancons bedded down here. She suspected the area behind a screen at the far end of the room was where Osburn and Kiera slept. A few chairs, large and ornately carved, were near the hearth. She also noted that in addition to the entrance, two other doors opened out of this building, one to the east, to the kitchen, and the other to the west, which must lead into the tower.

Several hounds, as ugly as the Brabancons and probably just as fierce, looked up from the bones they were gnawing. One or two rose on their haunches and growled, the saliva dripping from their massive jaws, until one of the serving women setting up the trestle tables in preparation for a meal gave a command that silenced them.

Isabelle had never seen more slatternly, unsavory-looking serving women. Their garments bespoke some quality when they were first new, but they had not been well taken care of and were laced in such a manner that they exposed far more than they should. The ages of the women were difficult to discern, except that none of them were as young as Kiera. Also unlike Kiera, their hair was untidy and their brazen stares more than impertinent. They looked like the sort of women who would be more at home in a brothel than serving in a castle.

When Isabelle saw Heinrich boldly caress one as he passed her by and heard the woman laugh and mutter something in response, she realized she was probably right, and their duties here no doubt extended to more than serving food and cleaning.

She wondered if DeFrouchette had ever availed himself of their services, then dismissed that thought as unimportant.

Osburn tossed off his sodden cloak. Kiera grabbed it before it hit the rush-covered flagstones and hung it on a hook near the entrance. He threw himself into one of the chairs.

"Kiera," he barked as the young woman waited anxiously, "have one of these women bring wine. Then take my bedraggled lady to her chamber, where she may change into dry garments. She must not catch her death from a chill, and what she is wearing is hardly flattering."

"I do not dress to please you," Isabelle said, trying not to shiver or let her teeth chatter although the rain had soaked her to the skin.

"This way, if you please, my lady," Kiera said, both eager and deferential as she indicated the western door that led into the tower.

Since she wanted to get dry and into something

that was not DeFrouchette's tunic, Isabelle followed Kiera as she led the way out of the hall.

Raising the blanket that formed her skirt so that she wouldn't fall, Isabelle climbed the worn, curved steps lit by flickering torches. When they were nearly at the top, they reached a door of thick timber which, like the hall, looked relatively new.

It also looked very strong.

Kiera opened the door and waited with a servant's deference for Isabelle to precede her inside the chamber. "Osburn forgot to introduce me," she said as Isabelle passed her. "My name is Kiera."

"And I am—" Isabelle caught herself before she said her real name. "I am Lady Allis."

Then she silently surveyed the chamber, an unexpectedly well-furnished room, with a large bed of oak covered in fine linens dyed in an earthy green, a delicately carved chair, and a dark wooden chest embossed in brass. A metal candle stand was near the bed, containing ten white candles. The loopholes were shuttered with canvas to keep out the night air.

The narrow loopholes, apertures suitable for archers, were not, regrettably, nearly big enough for her to climb out of, and she wondered what was in the chest.

"I know this chamber is not as fine as what you're used to," Kiera said, seemingly as anxious for Isabelle's approval as she was for Osburn's. She hurried to the chest beside the bed and threw open the lid. "These are my gowns. We're nearly the same size, and Osburn told me before he went to get you that you're to take whatever you need. I'm also to serve as your maid, if you like, and this whole room is to be yours."

Isabelle walked toward her. "Did he not tell you that he was *abducting* me?"

Kiera's face reddened and, holding the lid up, she looked at the contents as if searching for something. "Yes, he did, and I am sorry about that." She glanced at Isabelle, then away, but not before Isabelle saw the anxiety in her brown eyes. "But it is his father's plan, not Osburn's. He's not a bad man."

Isabelle did not share her opinion. And while it was clear Kiera realized that what her lover had done was wrong, it would probably not be wise to criticize Osburn to her.

Kiera reached into the chest, set aside a brown garment on the top, then lifted out a gown of deep green wool with some simple embroidery in the shape of blue flowers around the rounded neckline. "This is my best gown. I hope it's not too rough and poor for you."

"I'm sure it will do."

"There is no need to be frightened," Kiera continued as she laid the gown on the bed. "Osburn says you're not to be harmed. Besides, you've got that man, that knight, to look out for you."

"DeFrouchette?"

"Is that his name?"

"Have you never seen him before?"

"No, he has never come here, nor his friend, neither."

"DeFrouchette is not a knight."

"Oh." Kiera smiled apologetically as she turned back to the chest. "He certainly looks like one."

"Compared to the men in this place and the Norsemen in the ship that brought me here, I suppose he does."

"He's very handsome, too," she said. "And those shoulders!"

Perhaps Kiera would not be completely loyal to Osburn after all, and if she preferred DeFrouchette to Osburn, she showed slightly better judgment. De-Frouchette did not imbibe overmuch, for one thing, or at least she hadn't seen him.

Kiera turned and held out a white garment. "Here's a shift, too. I suppose you're used to silk?"

This situation was getting stranger and stranger. They were not two young ladies at court. She was here against her will, brought here by this woman's paramour in a hateful scheme of revenge. "Whatever you have is good enough, as long as it is dry."

Isabelle unwrapped the blanket around her waist. She pulled off DeFrouchette's tunic and her mud-stained shift and put them on the bed, then quickly dressed in the dry clothing.

"I'll tie the laces, my lady," Kiera said. She came behind her and began to tie the laces of the woolen gown with brisk efficiency, which told Isabelle she must have been a ladies' maidservant before she ran afoul of Osburn.

"There are some slippers, too, if you like," she offered.

Isabelle sat on the bed and pulled off her soiled shoes. The sole was tearing away from the top of one, and the other had a hole in the toe. Considering all that she had been through, it was something of a miracle she still had them at all.

Kiera studied her. "I used to dress my mistress's hair. Would you like me to do yours?"

Why not? "Please."

Kiera produced a wide-toothed ivory comb from the chest and proceeded to work the knots out of Isabelle's hair. It was a painful and arduous process, and Isabelle decided to use this time and opportunity to learn more about where she was. "What is the name of this castle?"

"Osburn just calls it 'the Welsh ruin.'"

"Who owns the land?"

"I don't know. Osburn doesn't . . . he doesn't talk very much with me."

No doubt he had other things than talk on his mind when he was with Kiera, Isabelle thought. "Are you not curious, though?"

"No. As long as I am with Osburn, I'm happy."

Isabelle subdued a sigh. Kiera sounded moonstruck—or lovestruck—and was clearly not a font of knowledge.

"Will you have braids, my lady?"

"That would be fine."

"One or two? Or more? I could coil them about your head, if you like."

Again, Isabelle felt that odd disconnection between the reality of her situation and Kiera's cheerful chatter. "One braid will do."

"I'm sorry I have no scarf to cover your head."

"I never—" Once more, Isabelle caught herself. Maidens did not cover their hair, but married women did. "I never expected that you would."

When she was finished, Kiera went to the door, holding it open for her. "Come, my lady. Osburn will be waiting for us."

Isabelle wanted to remain where she was, away from the leering stares of the Brabancons and the disconcerting presence of DeFrouchette. She must always remember that he was not her protector, no matter what he said or did.

She must only think of him as a slightly tamer beast, and always be on her guard around him.

A few moments later, Isabelle entered the hall, Kiera behind her. Osburn, DeFrouchette and Heinrich sat at a table by the hearth. Other Brabancons were also seated at trestle tables. DeFrouchette's friend was between two Brabancons, looking as uncomfortable as she felt.

Some bread was already on the tables, and Heinrich shoved the heel of a loaf into his mouth as if he hadn't eaten in weeks.

Osburn surveyed her over the top of the bronze goblet he held loosely in his long fingers. "Well, that's better!" he drawled, slipping down in his chair. "Now you look like a lady. Please, join us."

DeFrouchette rose as she approached—a courteous gesture oddly out of place, and it excused nothing.

"Since you're already on your feet, DeFrouchette, Lady Allis may have your chair."

Without a word, his expression unreadable, DeFrouchette went to sit with his friend.

Telling herself she didn't care where he was, Isabelle walked around the table and swept her skirt out of the way as she sat. Regarding Osburn as she would a bedbug, she said, "I am a lady whether I look it or not, but you will never be a gentleman no matter how well you dress."

Heinrich laughed, his mouth full of half-chewed

bread, while Osburn scowled, then downed more wine.

As the meal progressed, Isabelle tried to keep her attention on the food, which was surprisingly good. There was a beef stew with dumplings made of eggs and bread crumbs, mutton in gravy, brown bread and a filling dish of beans cooked slowly in a fish broth until they were almost a porridge.

It was more and better than she had expected, but then, perhaps good food was part of the bargain Oswald had made with the Brabancons.

However fine the fare, though, Isabelle could not will herself to deafness as she ate, or completely ignore the banter the Brabancons exchanged with the other women. It was nearly enough to turn her stomach.

She also couldn't ignore the way the women lingered long as they served DeFrouchette—especially one of them, a woman who had probably been attractive in her youth. She obviously still considered herself a great beauty and was not taking kindly to DeFrouchette's continued, inattentive silence.

Later, when the Brabancons were so into their cups that the hall was like a raucous tavern, the woman obviously thought she saw a chance. She set down the jug of wine she carried and leaned forward with her elbows on the table. Her gown gaped open to reveal much of her heavy breasts and she smiled, exposing what was left of her teeth. "What's the matter?" she cooed to DeFrouchette. "Don't you like women?"

"In general?" he calmly replied. "Not particularly."

The woman straightened. "What, you're one of *them*?"

"If by that you mean do I prefer men or women in my bed, the answer is women."

"Ahhh," the wench sighed, leaning down again. "My name's Hielda."

"Well then, Hielda, why don't you fill the mug of that fellow over there who is staring at the backs of your ankles?" DeFrouchette suggested as he dipped his bread in some gravy.

"Because you're better looking. And I'm sure you know how to make a woman sigh. Aye, and scream, too, if that's your pleasure." She grinned, and her eyes sparkled.

DeFrouchette raised his eyes to look at the woman, and the expression in them was frosty. "*I* decide who I invite into my bed, Hielda, and if I am interested in a woman, she won't have any doubt about it. What I do with a woman, then, is my own business. Whether she sighs or moans with the pleasure of it is something you will never know."

Isabelle couldn't quite catch her breath.

Hielda closed her mouth with a snap, turned on her heel and marched off across the room, where she threw herself into the lap of a startled Brabancon. The man recovered quickly, and Isabelle turned away as he started to grope her.

Unfortunately, she found herself staring at De-Frouchette's lean and handsome face.

He raised one brow.

"I am going to retire," she announced, pushing back her chair.

Osburn's hand darted out and gripped her wrist so tightly that it hurt. "Not yet. *You* may be finished, but *I* am not."

"Osburn," DeFrouchette said in a warning tone as he rose slowly, like a god roused from slumber.

Kiera cowered in a corner as the other women watched with eager curiosity. The Brabancons watched with a very different kind of curiosity, hoping for a fight, perhaps, and the Gascon was also on his feet.

Osburn glanced at DeFrouchette, but he didn't let go of her. "Don't you think she should be present when we discuss your next task, DeFrouchette?"

"What task?" Isabelle demanded as she tried to pull her arm from Osburn's grasp.

Osburn grinned his gargoyle grin at her. "Why, taking the ransom demand to your husband, of course. You *do* want us to do that, don't you?"

Her throat suddenly dry, Isabelle didn't answer. Allis and Connor must be nearly frantic with worry about her, and she wanted them to know that she was alive and unharmed—but the sooner the demand was made, the sooner they would learn they had the wrong woman, and the worse her situation would be.

"As much as I want to confront her husband," DeFrouchette said grimly, interrupting her tumultuous thoughts, "I first want your promise that she will be safe while I am gone."

"Of course you have my promise."

"You know I mean more than that," DeFrouchette said sternly. "Unharmed and unviolated."

"Both, unless her husband refuses to pay. Then

any other promises need not be kept, for we must be
compensated for all our trouble. And when we're
done with her, I'm sure Ingar will still pay a considerable sum. He clearly finds her fetching."

DeFrouchette strode around Osburn's chair and
pulled him to his feet. "That was not agreed upon."

"Heinrich!" Osburn screeched, and the German
obeyed the summons.

Scowling, but no doubt aware that he was seriously outnumbered by the Brabancons, DeFrouchette
let Osburn go. "I never agreed to sell Lady Allis into
slavery if Sir Connor didn't pay the ransom."

With a sour expression, Osburn straightened his
tunic. "What did you think *was* going to happen to
her if he didn't? We'd just send her home again?"

DeFrouchette's face reddened. "Oswald assured
me Sir Connor would pay, so there is no need to consider alternatives."

"Yes, he will," Isabelle declared, determined to
keep herself safe as long as she could. "How long
will you give Connor to raise the money?"

"A month from the day Alexander delivers the
message. But there's no rush." He addressed De-
Frouchette. "Surely you won't mind waiting a few
days before you go back to Bellevoire."

"What of Ingar?" he demanded. "Will he wait?"

"Ingar's been offered a considerable sum. I'm
sure he won't mind lingering here a little."

Osburn pulled out his dagger as he continued to
address DeFrouchette. "Regardless of when you go,
we must have some proof that we have the lady, to
ensure that her husband will pay."

"What's it to be?" Heinrich asked as calmly as if

he were discussing the weather but with a savage glint in his eye. "An ear or a finger?"

Panicked, Isabelle instinctively stepped closer to DeFrouchette. Meanwhile, the women gasped and whispered among themselves, all except Kiera, who started to weep. The Gascon looked sick, and the Brabancons excited in a horrible way. Even the hounds stirred, roused by the noise.

"I am to be treated as a guest," Isabelle whispered, too terrified to speak louder.

DeFrouchette moved in front of her to shield her from Osburn and Heinrich. She clutched at his arm as if holding him could help. At that moment, she would have welcomed the intervention of the devil himself.

"Your father said nothing of any proof," he declared.

"My father may not have raised the issue of proof with you, but he did to me," Oswald replied with disgusting delight. "However, calm yourself, my dear DeFrouchette, and you, too, my lady. I don't intend to follow Heinrich's bloodthirsty—if fascinating—suggestions."

She loosened her hold on DeFrouchette but didn't let go of him completely. "Then why have you drawn your dagger?"

Osburn gave her another leering grin. "To cut off your hair."

Her hair. Only her hair. Her legs went weak with relief, until Heinrich spoke.

"Plenty of women have hair that color," he said, his disappointment all too apparent. "How will her husband know it is hers?"

Osburn's eyes gleamed with a terrible pleasure as he turned back to address the Brabancon, and her grip on DeFrouchette tightened again. "That's a good point, but the same could be said of an ear or a finger," he said, "and as DeFrouchette so continually points out, she's not to be harmed—*yet*. Besides, I've no qualms about letting her husband doubt if the hair belongs to her. She could be alive and in our hands, or not. The only way he'll ever be certain is to pay us and find out. Now then, DeFrouchette, be a good fellow and hold her arms for me. I fear the lady will squirm like a fish otherwise."

DeFrouchette regarded him steadily, his expression unreadable. "No."

Determined not to add to Osburn's fiendish delight, Isabelle came around DeFrouchette and faced him. "Go ahead," she said, without the slightest tremor in her voice to betray her fear. "Cut off my hair."

Osburn's eyes burned with the anger of disappointment, just like Heinrich's, and indeed, he was no different, except that he had finer clothes.

Osburn stepped up to her and waved the dagger in her face. "Be sure you don't move, my lady," he warned. "Otherwise, I might slip and accidentally cut your beautiful face."

Isabelle willed herself to show nothing, to *feel* nothing, so that she would not increase Osburn's sadistic pleasure. "I will not."

Reaching around her, Osburn snatched her braid, and she was sure it was no accident that his hand also brushed her breast. "This won't hurt a bit."

His eyes fairly flashing with ire, DeFrouchette stepped forward and wrapped his long, strong fingers around Osburn's wrist, making him drop the dagger. "Do that again and I'll break your fingers."

Heinrich drew out his sword, but DeFrouchette paid no heed as he cast Osburn off, sending the man stumbling back. He swooped down and grabbed the dagger. "I'll do it."

Again, Isabelle willed herself to show nothing—not relief that a steadier hand than Osburn's held a knife so close to her, or disappointment and anger that DeFrouchette would help in this.

He pulled her braid in front of her. She stood absolutely still, like a soldier being reviewed by his general.

His brow furrowed with concentration, he sliced through it quickly. Once done, it looked like a blond snake, or the pelt of some strange beast, while what was left of her hair fell about her neck and just above her shoulders, not even as long as his.

He wordlessly handed the braid, and the dagger, back to Osburn.

"Put that somewhere for safekeeping until the morrow, Kiera," Osburn commanded. He tossed the braid at her and returned the dagger to his belt. "Then fetch me some more wine. Barbering makes me thirsty!"

As Kiera scurried off toward the screened area, she looked as stricken as if it were her own hair that Osburn had cut off.

Isabelle glared at the gloating Osburn and Heinrich and DeFrouchette, too, before she turned on her heel and marched toward the tower.

Chapter 8

Three days later, as the sun fell below the rugged hills beyond the ruined castle, Isabelle stood alone on the wall walk near the tower that housed her chamber. For once, she had managed to leave the hall without being followed by DeFrouchette, who was indeed like a watchdog—a large, muscular and grimly silent watchdog, better looking than the hounds that roved the hall and the courtyard at night, but no doubt just as fierce.

For now, though, as she looked out over the Norse encampment below, he was not near, and neither were any of the Brabancon sentries who were further down the wall from her tower. Seagulls wheeled and cried, and the sea in the bay looked just as restless as the birds.

The damp wind, tasting of salt, tugged hard at her garments, and she wrapped Kiera's woolen cloak more tightly about herself. Her hair, or what was left of it, whipped about her face, and she had to squint to see the Norsemen moving about below.

Several tents had been set up to house Ingar and his men. The pieces of wood that supported the ridgepoles had been carved into the heads of dragons. Iron pots suspended on metal tripods hung over their fires, and the scent of the smoke came to her on the stiff breeze.

Ingar and his men were like a nest of dragons blocking any escape by water, even if she could have found a boat to take her away. Indeed, short of sprouting wings like a gull and flying off, she would never be able to escape by sea.

But she was determined to find another way. In her chamber she had already discovered that several stones around one of the loopholes were loose. After digging out the mortar as carefully and quietly as she could during the night, she could remove enough stones so that she could squeeze through the opening. She would still be several yards above the ground, so she would need a rope, but she had already started to make one using strips of fabric. She had stolen any rag she could find, and if Kiera ever changed the linen on her bed, she would discover that the bottom sheet was but half there. Her shift was several inches shorter, too.

If she could make the rope long enough to get down to the wall walk, then climb from there to the ground, she could get out of this fortress, and avoid the hounds that prowled the courtyard at night, too. It would be a difficult, dangerous and desperate chance, but she was willing to take it.

She had no faith that Osburn would continue to ignore her except to jeer or sneer at her, or that Heinrich and his Brabancons could be kept on their leash. Although the mercenaries did not approach her, they watched her with hungry eyes.

Not only was she in physical danger, she could not deny that the stress and anxiety were clearly upsetting her mind. She could hardly sleep, and when she did, it was troubled and far from restful. Last night had been the worst of all, for she had dreamt of being in DeFrouchette's arms.

Making love with him. Passionately.

In her dream he had come to her chamber at Bellevoire; how, she hadn't known or cared. At first, she had felt an overwhelming joy that she was safe, even when she had seen him standing at the foot of the bed, clothed all in black, his blue eyes bright and gleaming in the candlelight. She had been surprised, but not afraid. She had been . . . excited.

He'd slowly come around the bed toward her, his eyes and their piercing, seeking stare never leaving her face. Without saying a word, he'd started to disrobe—and she'd said nothing to stop him. She'd even wondered what was taking him so long. When the last of his clothing had dropped to the floor, she had held open the coverings. She had not merely allowed him into her bed; she had welcomed him there.

She flushed to think of all that she had dreamt after that, of his impassioned kisses and thrilling caresses, his hands on her naked body, gliding over her skin with a touch so light, it could have been the brush of soft fabric. Then, when he put his hands between her thighs, he had pressed a little harder, until she began to writhe, her whole body undulating with need. His lips had trailed slowly across her breasts, as if he would explore them until he'd memorized every minute inch.

Then he had moved between her legs and looked at her with sure purpose, as if he'd known how much she'd wanted him to love her.

Closing her eyes, the most vivid moments lived again, including the one right before she'd awakened, when he'd been about to take her maidenhead, and she had been joyfully ready to surrender it.

"Enjoying the view, my lady?"

A curse flew from her lips as she whirled around to face DeFrouchette. He stood limned against the setting sun, his long dark hair blown back from his angular face, his lips set in a grim line, clad in the tunic he had let her wear. Her nipples tightened as if they were again being brushed against the rough wool that carried his scent.

How had he come there so quietly . . . or had she been too immersed in the memory of her dream to hear him?

Trying to recover, she said, "I am enjoying the fresh air, such as it is. This whole place stinks of fish and filthy men."

"Most of the women are none too clean, either," he remarked as he looked out over the Norse encampment.

"If you will excuse me," she muttered, sidling toward the tower, and away from him.

He turned and looked at her. "I don't."

"I don't need your permission."

"Then why did you ask for it?"

"I was just . . . I was just being polite. Foolish of me, considering where I am."

He leaned back against the wall and crossed his arms. "I'm leaving with Ingar at dawn. I'm to take the ransom demand to your husband."

Her mouth went dry. He was the only thing keeping her safe from Osburn and the others, and he was leaving her.

He pushed himself off and closed the short distance between them. "Before I go, I have two things to say to you. The first is that Denis will protect you in my absence. He is a better fighter than he looks. Bigger men underestimate his speed and deftness. The second is to remind you that you gave me your word you would not try to escape again."

She made a sweeping gesture that encompassed the fortress and the Norse encampment. "How could I? It would be impossible."

"For most women, I would agree. But you, my lady, are not most women, as you have already demonstrated."

Her heart started to pound with something that was both fear and . . . and something else she would not acknowledge. She backed away from him. "I can't fly."

"No, so there is no need for you to look for the places where the sentries cannot see, blind spots and shadows and the like. Nor should you study the men themselves so carefully." He crossed his arms again as he regarded her. "I think that if I asked you, you could tell me to a man who is lax and who is not. Is that not so, my lady?"

Damn him. "Perhaps you are giving me ideas."

"I think not." Although his face was harder to see in the dim light as the sun disappeared, his tone revealed his exasperation. "Can you not see the use-lessness of your actions?"

"I am merely getting some fresh air, as I said. Would you have me stay cooped up in that hall with those disgusting men leering at me?"

"The plan is to return you to your husband, but if you persist in putting yourself at risk, I cannot en-sure your safety."

"Now you sound just like Osburn, only not so drunk."

"And that is another thing. Do not goad him. He may be a drunkard, but he is not the less dangerous for that."

"How kind of you to be so concerned, but I am too valuable to be killed, am I not?"

"It is not only of death I am thinking."

She would not admit that he sounded genuinely concerned for her well-being. "*You* are the one who put me at risk, DeFrouchette," she said, reminding herself as well as him, "by kidnapping me and bringing me to this place. No amount of warnings or apparent concern for my welfare can change that."

"I didn't know about the Brabancons when I agreed to take you. I also thought this business would be more swiftly concluded."

Once more in command of her emotions, and feeling as if his apparent remorse gave her the upper hand, if only for now, she said, "Poor DeFrouchette—it will take that much longer for you to get your money. As for the delays, is that not part of the plan, to torture my family? Do you not want Con-nor to suffer beyond leaving him impoverished?"

"I want to tell him to his face what he has done to me, and I want some portion of what should have been mine." He took hold of her by the shoulders. "What I do, I do because I have been wronged by your husband. I am *not* like the Brabancons, or Osburn."

As they stood in the shadow of the tower in the dusk, she heard remorse in his deep voice, as if he really had regrets.

If she could make him see that what he was doing was wrong, if she could convince him that his quarrel was not with her or even Connor, if there was indeed some vestige of honor and chivalry about him, maybe he would truly come to her aid. "My family has done nothing to deserve your wrath—nothing except suffer at your father's hands before he met the end he brought upon himself. If wrong has been done to you, it was by your evil, traitorous father who sired you and did not acknowledge it. If you feel cheated, blame that same father who gave you nothing except a name that makes me want to spit the bile from my mouth when I speak it. If it is vengeance you want, take it out upon Oswald, who conspired with your father and avoided the king's justice. You have done me a great wrong, yet there is still a way to make it right. Stop this now. Help me. Take me away from here."

She put her hands on his chest and looked up into his face, trying to see his expression, his eyes. "If there is any goodness or honor in you, take me home."

The memory of his fiery kiss flashed through her. If she could convince him to help her, in any way . . .

She slid her arms around his shoulders, raised herself on her toes and captured his mouth in a kiss as fierce and passionate as his had been.

For a moment, he was still—but only for a moment. Then he gathered her to him and lifted her off the ground as his mouth crushed hers with heated desire. Eager, she parted her lips and pushed her tongue between his teeth.

Still kissing her, he carried her to the tower wall and set her down, her back against the stones. One hand gently kneaded her breast while the other began to bunch her skirt, his knuckles grazing her thigh. His knee moved between her legs and she instinctively thrust against it, the sensation exquisite and mind-numbing.

Heady, savage excitement coursed through her body, and she could scarcely breathe.

Caught up in that same excitement, Alexander gave himself up to the pleasure of her embrace. The beautiful, spirited woman he had admired and craved from the first was in his arms, and kissing him willingly. Wonderfully. The sensation of her mouth and her lithe body against his, the taste and touch of her, set fires of passion burning in his blood.

A moan of surrender escaped his throat.

Why?

The word burst in upon him, unexpected and unwelcome, conquering the need coursing through him as the answer shot into his mind like an arrow from a bow.

With a savage twist of his head, he broke the kiss, then shoved her away from him. "You kiss very well, my lady, but if you think to bend me to your will, to have me like soft clay in your hands so I will do your bidding, you had best think again."

As she stared back at him, he cocked his head to study her pink cheeks and slightly swollen lips in the dim, dusky light. She looked lovely and flushed with passion, as he would want a woman who desired him to appear.

It was a deception. He would be a fool to think there was anything more behind her kisses than an attempt to win him to her side by any means and help her escape.

She would rob him of his chance to have even a portion of his birthright.

"Is this how you worked upon my father, promising him your love while taking another man to your bed?"

Her body quivering, she stepped back. "No! There was nothing of love between your father and—and the object of his desire. He wanted Montclair and so he wanted the lady of Montclair. He lurked about our home like a bird of prey, waiting for the chance to take both, one way or another. I was the means to an end for him. You would use me just the same, yet you presume to stand there and tell me you are different."

Alexander continued to regard her, his heart hard as granite because life had made it so. For an instant, it had cracked, but he would seal the rift.

He tugged her to him. "For the last time, my lady, I am not like my father, or Osburn and his mercenaries. If I were the kind of man you think I am, I would take what I want regardless of my promise not to touch you, like this." One arm around her neck, he fondled her breast roughly, a gross mockery of his tender caresses.

He saw the fear and disgust warring in her eyes and told himself he didn't care.

He pushed her hips against his hard arousal, the

evidence of the savage desire she had kindled. "I would force myself upon you before I go mad with desire, and no power on this earth would stop me. But I am not like my father, or Osburn or a Brabancon, and I will not take a woman against her will, no matter how she inflames me. I would rather bed that whore in the hall than you, my fine, deceitful lady."

She glared at him as if he were the most loathsome creature in the world. "Then get your hands off of me before I scream."

"And summon the Brabancons? I think not." He shoved her away. "Take care not to anger me too much, my lady, because thus far, and despite what you think of me, I have sworn to keep you safe while you are in my care. But if you do not want the protection I offer you, I will withdraw it, and you may fend for yourself with Osburn and his Brabancons. Is that what you wish, my lady?"

"Hardly a choice, DeFrouchette."

Still insolent, still defiant.

"It is your choice to make, my lady, and I will not ask you again. *Do you want my protection?*"

"Yes!" she hissed, the word drawn out of her seemingly against her will.

"Then you shall have it, until the ransom is paid and you go back to your husband.

"As for my vengeance and the form it takes, until you know what I have suffered, until you have lived the life I was forced to lead, you cannot understand all that your husband stole from me. It was more than a title and more than land and more than money. Yet if he must pay in coin because that is the only way I can have any recompense, that is how it shall be.

"And understand this, my lady. I will not be prey to your feminine wiles again. I have your measure now, and although you could probably tempt an archangel to sin, you will never again tempt *me*."

Breathing as hard as if he had run to Ingar's ship and back, trying to control the flurry of emotions she had roused, he turned on his heel and left her.

His head bare, his hair blowing in the breeze, Alexander strode along the road to Bellevoire. His cloak was thrown over his shoulder and his broadsword slapped his thigh with every swift stride. Yesterday, Ingar had set him ashore a little farther up the coast, as they had planned. Mercifully, the weather had been clear and the wind brisk, so they had made a swift passage over the sea.

After Bellevoire's lady had been taken, Sir Connor would surely have patrols and search parties all over his land. The plan was to either continue unhindered to Bellevoire, or allow himself to be found by a patrol. If that happened, he would tell them to take him to Sir Connor, and why.

Soon, it would be the moment he had dreamt of since Lord Oswald had found him and told him of his father's death. Soon, he would face Sir Connor and watch the man's expression as he told him why he had taken his wife and what he wanted in return.

He would not allow any worry about the lady to spoil that glorious moment for him. Denis could keep her safe until his return, and Osburn was too drunk most of the time to make good on his threats. Besides, the sot had his young mistress to distract him.

He would not wonder if his prize would try to escape in spite of what he had said. She was an intelligent woman, so surely she saw the merit in his warnings.

She was so intelligent that he had nearly been duped like any rustic at a village fair.

Head lowered, he quickened his pace. *Damn the woman*! How could he have been such a fool to have believed, even for an instant, that she'd kissed him because she'd felt desire for him?

But if you were in her shoes, would you not try any means to escape, too?

Hoofbeats sounded on the road, drowning out the nagging voice of his conscience. He raised his head to see a troop of mounted men riding toward him, their helmets and chain mail shining dully in the sunlight. He halted and waited as they approached. His heartbeat quickened the closer they came, but he would maintain an aura of calm. He had the upper hand, and he would act like it.

The gray-bearded man leading the patrol spotted Alexander, and he raised his hand to signal his men to rein in their horses. "Who are you?" he demanded, his voice gruff and his manner that of a man who had been a soldier all his life.

"Are you a soldier of Bellevoire?" Alexander replied.

The man frowned as he studied him. "I am Godwin, the commander of the garrison of Bellevoire. I ask you again, who are you?"

Alexander bowed. "I give you greetings, Godwin, and I demand that you take me to your lord."

"Demand?" Godwin retorted, glaring, while the men behind him began to whisper and mutter and nod at him.

"I have come with news of the lady of Bellevoire. I am sure your overlord will want to hear it. If you will be so good as to ask one of your men to loan me his horse, I believe we will get to Sir Connor all the faster."

Godwin's gaping mouth snapped shut. Then he twisted in his saddle and addressed his men. "Joss, double up with Robert and give this fellow your mount."

The man did as he was ordered, and soon Alexander was riding beside Godwin, who regarded him with both suspicion and disdain. "What's your name?" Godwin asked as they rode around the curve that skirted the wood where he had waited with Denis.

"I will tell Sir Connor, and until then, it is enough that you take me to him."

Godwin sniffed. "Maybe you know something and maybe you don't," he muttered, sliding Alexander another look.

"I assure you, I do."

Whether it was because of Alexander's firm tone or the fact that he was not getting the answers he wanted, Godwin said no more, even when they reached the village. It was not as crowded as on market day, so they did not have to slow their progress.

Other people did, and stopped and stared. A plump, well-dressed fellow halted in mid-bustle to watch them. His eyes wide as the moon, he made the sign of the cross, then darted into the tavern. Soon, other men came pouring out to join the whispering women.

Alexander wondered how many of them recognized his father's likeness in him, and what they made of it. Whatever they thought, this was much better than sneaking into Bellevoire dressed as a peasant. His only regret was that he was not wearing finer clothes.

Once he had his portion of the ransom money, he would buy himself some, as well as a better scabbard. And an embossed leather belt, and new boots.

The horses' hooves clattered over the wooden drawbridge. They rode through the outer gatehouse in the outer curtain wall, and into the ward. The second wall facing them now looked just as impressive and strong as the first. Both walls had towers at their corners, although the fortress was not an exact square. The wall facing the village was longer, no doubt to give the defenders more chance to maintain an advantage over foes attacking the town.

He had known Bellevoire was a large fortress, but he had not known the half of it, he thought with awe.

They continued beneath the massive portcullis of Bellevoire and into the inner ward.

He was finally here at last, in the castle that should have been his.

Godwin ordered his troop to halt. Alexander reined in his mount and surveyed the walls, the buildings and the people.

The inner ward was nearly as large as the village, and just as busy. The clang of hammer and anvil declared which building was the smithy; another with smoke rising from the louvered opening in the slate roof must be the kitchen. Across the yard was another tall building, and judging by the wide steps and ornate door, it was the lord's hall. Another building adjoining it, with windows on the second level, must be the private apartments of the household.

On his left, a long building two stories high, with wide doors and small windows, was the stables. Grooms and stable boys were leading saddled horses out for the group of soldiers waiting near the entrance.

A patrol, no doubt, or search party, obviously preparing to ride out.

Then, among the men outside the stable, Alexander spotted Sir Connor, formerly of Llanstephan, now of Bellevoire, standing beside a saddled horse. The man was older now, of course, and his face was more angular, creased with a few wrinkles, as if he had known some suffering since those merry days of his youth. His clothing, however, was made of excellent cloth and his scabbard of wonderfully worked leather. His sword was surely a masterpiece of craftsmanship, too—nothing like the inexpensive one he carried that had nevertheless cost his mother so much, in so many ways.

No matter what had happened in the years since he had last seen Sir Connor, though, the man was what he had always been: an example of the rewards of privilege and rank, considered worthy enough to earn the love of an amazingly bold and beautiful woman, and to possess Rennick DeFrouchette's estate. Sir Connor had been blessed from birth, while *he* had been cursed.

As Alexander took his time dismounting, noting that an older maidservant standing beside the well had dropped her bucket and was regarding him with openmouthed shock, Godwin hurried over to his overlord, who started and looked his way.

Their gazes met and held, and Alexander watched the flash of recognition, the look of shock, the comprehension dawn, just as he had imagined.

He had not imagined the way Sir Connor's expression hardened into outright revulsion.

Connor issued an order to his men to carry on, then he strode across the cobblestones toward him. He came to a halt and regarded Alexander with a scrutiny that was both intense and suspicious. "Godwin told me what you said."

Alexander inclined his head in acknowledgment. "Yes, I know where your wife is."

The man blinked, as if he couldn't believe it.

"She is unharmed."

"You have my wife?"

"Not with me at present, obviously, but I know where she is, and for a price, I will return her to you."

"Ah!" Understanding dawned. "You stole her for ransom." Sir Connor ran a long, slow, measuring stare over him. "I see. Godwin also told me that you wouldn't reveal your name, but he is new here since Rennick DeFrouchette's death. It is obvious to me by your looks that you are related to him, and if I had any doubt, your villainous act would have confirmed it."

Alexander wouldn't allow himself to be upset by this man. "Have a care, my lord. It is surely not wise to annoy the man who has your wife's safety in his hands." His gaze swept over the courtyard, taking in the soldiers milling about and the maidservants.

More had come to cluster about the well, and they stood watching.

"Is it your usual practice to discuss your business in the courtyard, my lord?" he inquired. "Or shall we go somewhere more private?"

Chapter 9

His eyes flaring with undisguised rage, Sir Connor started for the hall. "Follow me."

Alexander did as he commanded, but he was not pleased at being treated like one of the man's foot soldiers, especially not here and not now.

Once inside, the comfort of the great hall surpassed his expectations, adding to his envy and indignation. Colorful tapestries lined the lime-coated walls, and there was a huge hearth along one wall, an innovation that made for a much less smoky room. The furnishings were many and wonderfully carved and polished. Most were of new oak, as blond as the braid of Lady Allis's hair, which he carried in the pouch at his side.

A few servants were here, too, cleaning out the hearth. With a brisk order, Sir Connor sent them away, so that they were alone.

He sat in a chair cushioned with a scarlet pillow and gestured for Alexander to do the same. "So, you look like DeFrouchette, so I assume you are a relative. Judging by your age, I suppose you are a nephew, possibly a cousin, although I am not familiar with any of the man's family."

"Neither am I." Alexander waited a moment, trying to summon the joy of anticipation. "Although I am his son."

Sir Connor's eyes merely narrowed. There was no shock, no jolt of surprise—just that subtle, disappointing reaction. "It is well-known that Rennick DeFrouchette had no sons."

"That is what your charming and beautiful wife said, too. I am Rennick DeFrouchette's bastard, and you killed my father before he could acknowledge me as his issue. If he had, I would now be master here, not you."

Again the man's expression barely altered. "So you claim. How is it nobody has ever heard of you, especially here in Bellevoire?"

As Sir Connor could be calm, so could he. "My father abandoned my mother when she told him she was with child. I daresay he never spoke of me because he preferred to pretend I did not exist."

He had believed that since he was eight years old, and the pain of that realization still galled him like an open wound, but he would not reveal that, either.

"Now *that* I can believe." Sir Connor folded his arms. "However, as to your claim that Bellevoire would be yours—your father was a traitor to the Crown. It would have been forfeit to the Crown regardless of your acknowledged existence or not, even if you had been named the legal heir."

"There was no trial, so no legal proof offered that my father was a traitor."

Sir Connor sat up straighter and stared at him incredulously. "There did not need to be, man! Your father tried to assassinate the king in front of a courtyard full of people."

Shock struck Alexander like the blow of an ax, and he had to fight not to betray it. Lord Oswald had not told him that.

A woman appeared at another entrance, flushed and panting as if she had rushed there. Attired in a royal blue velvet gown of simple, yet elegant, cut, the bodice fit to perfection, while the skirt flared outward from her slender waist. A leather girdle sat low on her hips, the ends dangling down nearly to the ground, like the gown's cuffs. Her hair was a lighter blond than Lady Allis's, yet her features were similar enough to guess that this was Lady Allis's sister. She was nearly as beautiful, but not quite, for she lacked the spark of fierce vitality that her sister possessed.

Connor jumped to his feet, finally demonstrating that he was more tense than he acted. "He has news of Allis."

Her eyes wide, the woman's anxious gaze went from Connor to him and back again, and she turned so pale, Alexander thought she might swoon. "Allis?" she repeated in a whisper.

"She is well, he says. He also claims that he is Rennick DeFrouchette's son."

The woman glided toward them, her movements as graceful as Lady Allis's. "Rennick never told me he had a son."

"My father did not speak of me," Alexander said. "But seeing me, do you doubt it?"

It was immediately obvious she did not. Again, a

look of utter revulsion came to the face of the person regarding him.

Then he learned he was indeed looking at Lady Allis's sister, for her expression darkened and her eyes flashed with a familiar ire. The woman gathered her skirt in her hand and marched toward him, the tassels of her girdle swinging and her expression as determined as that of an armed opponent who was about to engage him in single combat. "I don't care if your father was the king. I want to know what's happened to my sister. Where is she? Have you hurt her?"

"She is unharmed and where you cannot find her. There she will stay until you have delivered twenty thousand marks into my hands."

Both of them gasped. "Twenty thousand marks?" the lady whispered incredulously. She exchanged a doubtful look with Sir Connor.

It troubled him, that look, both the uncertainty and the seeming ... intimacy ... of it. If *he* were Lady Allis's husband, he would pay anything to get her back, no matter what he had to do, or who he had to beg. "I am sure you can afford it, or have friends who can help you. You had better find the money somehow, for I will have a portion of it—a small recompense for what *you* have stolen from *me*."

Connor drew himself up and the look he gave Alexander was full of loathing and disgust. "You are indeed Rennick's son, for just like him, you would get what you want through a woman rather than your own merit."

"What do you know of my merit?" Alexander demanded, his fists curling as he struggled to restrain

his outraged pride, which had been battered count-
less times. "Thanks to you—and your duplicitous
wife—I may never be anything but some man's bastard, without hope of land or title or the means to
achieve them."

"What you have done tells me all I need to know
of your merit, or lack thereof," Connor retorted.

Alexander took a deep breath and forced his emotions back under control. "Think of me as you will. I
have been called all manner of things, and whatever
you say makes little difference. Just make certain that
when I come back in a month, you have the money."

"A month!" the woman cried.

"I assumed you did not have such a sum handy.
Of course, if you do—"

"We do not," Connor interrupted with grim reluctance.

"How can we be certain that you have her, as you
claim?" the woman demanded. "You could have
heard that she has been abducted and think to profit
from it."

She was as clever as her sister. "You are very like
her, you know, and not just in looks," he noted as he
reached into the pouch tied to his waist and pulled
out the braid. It was soft in his hands and seemed
like molten gold, and for a moment, he was loath to
part with it.

He tossed it to her.

She caught it, then dropped it as if it were a live
snake. "Oh, God, Connor, it's her hair!"

Sir Connor gathered her in his arms and held her
close as he addressed Alexander. "Now that you
have delivered your message, go."

Again, something was too intimate here, too close for a mere legal relationship.

Alexander tried to ignore his troubling suspicions. Whatever was between Sir Connor, his wife and his sister-in-law was no concern of his—except that it might prove that neither Sir Connor nor this woman had the right to look at him with such scornful disgust. "You two seem very . . . loving."

They broke apart. "Would you deny me the comfort of a brotherly embrace?" the woman charged as Sir Connor took another step back. "Considering how cold-blooded your sire was, perhaps you would."

Was that guilt in the man's eyes? Had Oswald been wrong about Sir Connor's devotion to his wife? Maybe, then, Sir Connor wouldn't pay.

Then he would not have to bring her back to Bellevoire.

But what then? his mind argued. *She will be sold, for Oswald, Osburn and Ingar will have their money.*

Therefore, regardless of what he might prefer, she must return. He must make them see that a terrible fate awaited her if they did not pay. "What shall I tell my companions when I return? Will you pay, or shall we sell her to the Norsemen?"

The woman blanched. "Of course we will pay."

Sir Connor came to stand behind her. "Lord Oswald is behind this," he said with sure and firm certainty.

How had he known?

"If you want to keep her safe, pay the ransom," Alexander said, not willing to discuss Oswald's part in this. "In the meantime, you will give me the loan of a horse so that I may return and tell her you will pay. Neither you nor your men will follow me from here, or the lady will suffer."

"The *loan* of a horse?" Sir Connor queried with open disdain.

"A horse is not part of the bargain. When I have gone far enough, I will set it free to return to you."

"A fine morality you have, DeFrouchette, that allows you to keep a woman but tells you to return a horse." Sir Connor came closer until he was nearly nose to nose with him. "Take the horse and send it back, if that enables you to think you are not a dishonorable rogue. And you will have your money, but know you this, you lout: a worthy opponent would have challenged me directly. A noble warrior would have offered to settle this matter man to man. A man worthy to be a knight and lord of an estate would not have sought his vengeance in a woman's pain." His lip curled with scorn, as if Alexander smelled of something foul. "Now get out of Bellevoire and take your convenient morality with you."

The confrontation Alexander had dreamt of, the meeting that was to be such a glorious triumph, was over—and he had never felt so petty and ashamed.

After DeFrouchette had gone, Connor took Allis gently in his arms. For a long moment, he simply held her, feeling her tremble, knowing how difficult these days had been for her.

They had been terrible for him, too. Guilt gnawed at him every waking moment, and he had thought a thousand times of all the things he might have done differently the day that Isabelle had disappeared.

Allis nestled her head against his chest. "At least we know she is well. You did believe him when he said he hadn't hurt her?"

Connor took her hand and led her to a chair. "Yes, I did."

"I have never heard so much as a whisper of Rennick's son."

"No, nor I," Connor replied as he sat opposite her. "Still, I don't think he was lying about that, either. He was too much like the man, in looks, and in evil."

Allis's eyes welled with tears. "And now he has Isabelle, but he thinks he has me."

Connor pushed himself out of his chair and knelt in front of her, taking her hands in his. "I was so glad you realized that he must continue to think that! Otherwise, who could say what he might do to her? He might very well sell her as he threatened."

A tear slipped down Allis's cheek, her pain adding to Connor's own. "I wish he *did* have me."

"I don't," Connor replied as he brushed the tear away with the pad of his thumb. "You're with child, Allis, and don't forget that Isabelle is clever and brave. Of all the women I can think of who could endure what has befallen her, it would be her—or you." He gave his wife a comforting smile. "Men always underestimate her. I did. I daresay this fellow has, too. Why, I wouldn't be surprised if she walked into the hall tomorrow, told us she'd clouted her jailer on the head and climbed down a tower wall."

Allis tried to smile. "She might."

Connor's warm grip tightened, and he spoke with even more assurance. "There is more to give us hope. Although he would not admit it, I saw the

truth in his eyes when I asked him about Oswald.
That miscreant *is* involved in this. We know more
now than we did before."

Gleda came out of the kitchen, a tray bearing two
goblets in her trembling hands. She handed one to
Allis and one to Connor. Her hands were shaking so
much that she spilled some of the red wine onto
Connor's fingers. "Oh, forgive me, my lord!" she
cried, wiping it off with her sleeve. "It's just that I'm
that upset. I thought I was seeing a ghost!"

"So did I," Allis said as she sipped her wine.

Tucking the tray under her arm, Gleda nodded
eagerly. "Aye, just like his father, wasn't he? With the
black hair and those blue eyes, and the height of
him."

"Tell me, Gleda," Connor said, as he toyed with
the bottom of his goblet, "you were here when Rennick DeFrouchette was master. Did you never hear
talk of a son?"

She shook her head. "Not a word, but then, it
wouldn't surprise me. A lustful man he was,
and . . ." A look passed over her face and she fell
silent a moment. "We wondered, some of the
women, why he never fathered any children here.
We thought, maybe, you know . . ." She gave them a
meaningful look.

"That he could not?" Allis asked.

Connor glanced at his wife. They knew that Rennick DeFrouchette could indeed father children, for
they had seen that coloring and that build and those
eyes in another man—Connor's own brother,
Caradoc, or half brother, if the story told by their old
nurse was true. She had said that Connor's mother
had been raped by a squire named Rennick De-

Frouchette and Caradoc was the result. Connor believed it, for the resemblance between the late baron
and his brother was too strong to be denied.

Nobody at Bellevoire, except Allis, knew of this
relationship—not even Isabelle.

After Gleda had gone, and before the servants returned to their tasks, Allis said, "What about his
mistake? What if he finds out he has Isabelle, and
not me?"

"I don't imagine he lingered to talk to anybody in
the village or castle, and when he returns, we will
have the money, so his error will not be of such grave
import, even if he does learn of it then."

"I can ask some friends of my father to lend us
what we need to pay the ransom."

"And we can ask Caradoc, too. Speaking of
Caradoc—" Connor fell silent and glanced at the
maidservants who were filing into the hall. They, in
turn, glanced at their lord and lady, then away.

"Come to the solar," he said, rising.

Allis nodded and followed him. The solar was on
the second level of one of the inner towers, a smaller,
much more private place in which to talk. After
taking possession of Bellevoire, Allis had set about
removing all evidence of the baron's former occupa-
tion, especially here. The walls had been plastered
with a mixture of lime, water and sand, and then
painted in a pale blue, like the sky. The furnishings
were of new oak, the light shade adding to the airy
feeling Allis had tried to impart to this chamber,
which also had a larger window than most of the
buildings in the castle. The chairs sported cushions
stuffed with goosedown covered in silk the color of

jewels: sapphire, emerald and amber. A large chest, painted in those same colors and holding the records of the estate, stood behind the trestle table where Connor sat to study the rolls and lists of tithes and services due. Now, in the afternoon, a mellow golden light filled the room and warmed it.

"I'll ask Caradoc to bring the money himself," Connor said the moment he closed the door behind his wife.

Too anxious to sit, twisting the ends of her girdle around her fingers, Allis asked, "Are you thinking Caradoc should meet this half brother of his?"

"Not exactly." Connor walked toward the table, then leaned his hip against it as he regarded her with grave concern. "Allis, are you truly well?"

"I have been better, but I am not ill."

His expression grew even more grave. "Then you will be able to manage if I leave for a little while?"

She dropped the tassels of her girdle and stared at him. "Leave?"

"If Oswald is involved, as I truly believe he is, there is one person who might know where he would hide a captive."

Allis's eyes widened with comprehension. "Auberan," she breathed, naming the other villain involved in the traitorous conspiracy with Rennick DeFrouchette and Lord Oswald. He had also been stripped of his titles and estates save one far to the north. He had been banished there rather than executed, a rare act of benevolence by King Richard, brought on in no small part by Isabelle's request for mercy.

For a time, Allis had feared there was some

deeper bond between them than charity on Isabelle's part; fortunately, Isabelle had made it very
clear that there was not. "For Isabelle's sake,
Auberan might tell you—if he is not involved in this,
too," she said.

"He may be. Either way, I think I should ride
north and seek him out."

Allis rose and put her arms about her husband,
pulling him into her embrace. "I would rather you
went at once. Whether this young DeFrouchette has
noble aspirations or not, I cannot and will not trust
him, and I will not believe Isabelle is safe until she's
here again. If there is a chance Auberan knows anything about where Isabelle may be, we must not delay."

Isabelle simply couldn't bear another moment in
that horrible hall, where she was the object of the
Brabancons' lustful glances, Osburn's drunken rants
and the serving wenches snickers and snide looks.
She was even weary of Denis's perpetually cheerful
banter.

She was determined to go out this morning, and
without Denis trailing after her like a faithful dog.
She would have to be careful, and she didn't expect
to get far, but she was going to do it.

She waited until Denis was talking to Kiera and
those Brabancons who were still in the hall were either arguing with each other, or teasing the hounds,
or flirting with the serving wenches. Then she
slipped out.

To find plenty of other Brabancons loitering in the
courtyard.

That could not be helped, and since she didn't really want to raise anyone's suspicions, it was probably just as well, she thought as she wandered toward the ruined chapel.

Ever since Alexander had departed, she had been afraid of what he would discover at Bellevoire. Allis and Connor would be delighted to hear she was safe, of course, and they would surely agree to pay any ransom Alexander DeFrouchette demanded, but what about when he returned, knowing he had abducted the wrong woman? She could envision his terrible wrath, and even though she didn't believe he would physically hurt her, she didn't want to be here to find out. Therefore, she must escape tonight. She *would* escape tonight.

She raised her head and looked at the wall walk nearest the tower. Yes, if she stayed in the shadows, it would be difficult for the sentries to see her from the opposite—

Somebody tapped her on the shoulder. She twisted, ready to tell Denis that she was just getting a breath of fresh air.

Heinrich grabbed her shoulders and backed her against the rough stone wall of the chapel, blocking her with his bulky body.

This close, he looked even uglier, and crueler, and his disgusting stench made her want to retch. She tried to sidestep him, but he got in front of her again.

Isabelle hid her fear behind her dignity. "Let me go."

Heinrich's lips curved up in a disgusting leer, and his eyes gleamed like a fevered wolf. "What, you prefer that scrawny little Frenchman's company to that of a real man?"

"My *preference* has nothing to do with it. He has been following me since DeFrouchette left, taking his master's place."

"Until now. Your guardian is gone, so now it is my turn to enjoy your company."

Denis appeared behind Heinrich.

The sight of him did little to lessen her fear. Heinrich outweighed him by eight stone at least, and the Brabancons were notoriously fierce, rough fighters. It was said they would even use their teeth.

"You are not to touch her, or Alexander will make you regret it," Denis declared.

Heinrich stepped away from Isabelle to face Denis. She saw her chance and started to sidle along the wall away from them.

Heinrich chuckled, a low, horrible sound like a troll laughing. "You may be DeFrouchette's slave, but I am not, and I fear no man. I have decided this woman should learn her place."

Even as he shrugged, Denis's hand went to the handle of the dagger shoved through his belt. "If you want to be a fool and risk my friend's anger, so be it. I do not think Osburn will be pleased if you accost this lady, either."

Heinrich's bushy brows lowered. "You think he can stop me any better than you can? Do you think you or any man can keep me from what I want?"

"I think you would not be wise to upset the son of the man who hired you."

"I'm not afraid of Oswald, either."

"Perhaps not, but you would risk not being paid for a woman? Or have I heard wrong, and you have been paid all you are owed by Lord Oswald?" When Heinrich didn't answer, Denis grinned. "I think not.

There are plenty of women, many more than there are rich men who can afford your price, I'm sure, so should you not think twice about upsetting a rich man?"

"You may be right, Gascon."

Then Heinrich's face contorted with anger and he lunged forward. He grabbed Denis's tunic by the collar. The garment twisted about Denis's throat and lifted his arms so that he couldn't get hold of his dagger. "Or maybe you are enjoying the lady's favors and do not want to share."

Isabelle stopped creeping away.

A swift glance showed that all eyes were on Heinrich and Denis. With no clear thought for what she was doing, she ran forward and took hold of the hilt of Heinrich's sword with both hands. As he felt her close by and twisted to see what was happening, she managed to draw the heavy weapon from its scabbard, grunting with the effort.

"Stop!" she cried as she lifted the dull gray blade and put the tip against Heinrich's spine.

In a single motion, Heinrich let go and spun around, knocking the sword from her hand with a blow as another man would swat away a fly. It skittered across the cobblestones to rest near another Brabancon's booted foot. The man reached down to grab it while Heinrich closed on her, his teeth bared with anger like the beast he was.

Gulping for air, Denis pulled out his dagger. "Leave her alone, or I shall kill you!" he cried, rushing the German.

He tried to strike, but the man was quick, despite his size. Heinrich whirled around and shouted to the Brabancon holding his sword. The man tossed it to

him, and he deftly caught it. The hulking mercenary
and lithe Gascon began circling, each watching the
other without so much as a blink.

Osburn and Kiera appeared at the entrance to the
hall, drawn by the commotion. From that vantage
point, Osburn saw the two men, but he made no
move to stop their fight, while Kiera turned away
and hurried back inside.

They were not the only spectators. Some of the
Brabancons laughed, clearly expecting Denis to lose.

Isabelle feared that, too, and the thought sickened
her as much as Heinrich's stench. She searched for
something—anything—to use as a weapon. She
would rip up a cobblestone if she had to.

She spotted a large stone that had fallen from the
wall of the chapel and sidled toward it, being careful
not to draw any attention away from the combatants
and praying to God to watch over Denis until she
could help him.

Heinrich charged, swinging his blade in a mighty
blow—that missed, for the agile Gascon jumped
nimbly out the way. Then he ran past the bigger
man, lashing out with his dagger.

Bellowing with rage, Heinrich looked at the tear
in his sleeve and the growing patch of blood. "Now
you *will* die, you maggot!"

Isabelle bent down and grabbed the rock. Tension
fairly hummed along her limbs as she waited for her
chance.

With another bellow like an enraged bull, Heinrich raised his sword and swung at Denis. Denis
cried out, blood staining his tunic from the wound
on his arm. The Brabancons grew silent, watching

with the bloodlust of carrion creatures waiting for the end.

There was no more time to waste. Isabelle sprinted forward and struck the back of Heinrich's head with all her might. The man groaned and staggered forward, then collapsed facedown on the cobblestones, blood oozing from the back of his head.

As Isabelle stood panting and the rock fell from her hand, Osburn shoved his way through the Brabancons. He nudged Heinrich with his foot, then used his toe to roll him over. He bent down to get a closer look at the man's staring eyes. "God's blood," he muttered with disbelief. "She's killed him."

Chapter 10

Ingar's ship rose and fell as it skimmed across the ocean. Alexander, standing at its stern, gripped the gunwale to steady himself. The wind-whipped sea churned and frothed, and the sail billowed taut, straining the single line of rigging. Clouds scudded across the gray sky as swiftly as a hawk diving for its prey.

Yet neither the wind nor the seething sea, nor the apparently imminent storm, dampened the spirits of the Norsemen. It was as if they relished the terrible weather, and Ingar especially fairly reveled in it.

When Alexander had returned to the ship, Ingar had been disappointed that he had not been followed, muttering something about his men needing a good fight before they grew as rusty as old rivets. That might explain his fiendish delight in the stormy weather.

Or perhaps he appreciated the speed the wind gave his vessel more than the danger, or saw this as an opportunity to demonstrate his skill. His men seemed relieved not to have to row, and it was obvious they had no fear that the wind would tear the sail asunder, as he did. He also feared that the shallow drafted vessel would be capsized by a wave.

Ingar laughed, shouted something, and then deliberately steered the ship so that it was broadsided by another wave. His men got soaked and they cursed, shook their fists and raged, but there was no real anger or malice in it. They seemed to be enjoying the tilting of the ship as much as Ingar, while Alexander felt like he was in a cart driven by a madman and pulled by a runaway horse.

"Is this some kind of Norse game?" Alexander cried above the wind.

"What, is a great big Norman like you afraid of a little salt water?" Ingar shouted in reply. A wide grin slashed his face, which was glistening with droplets from the spray. "This is nothing. We have sailed through worse a hundred times, and Olaf needed a bath. By Woden's beard, this is what we live for—a fine wind and a fast ship! Give me this rather than staying on shore, waiting for some spoiled nobleman to decide to sail."

Alexander squinted at him through the spray. "His father pays you well to wait and be at his command, does he not?"

"He has to, to make us waste the summer months on land and not on voyages of trade."

Pillage and plunder, Alexander silently amended as he wrapped his cloak around himself, although it was as damp with spray as Ingar's face.

Once more Ingar heeled the ship, and Alexander had to grab the gunwale to keep from going over the side. When he shot the Norseman a filthy look, Ingar threw back his head and laughed as he leaned on the tiller.

Enough was enough.

Alexander let go of the vessel's side and made his way across the heaving deck toward Ingar. Once there, he stood with his feet planted, an arm's length from the gunwale so that he would not be tempted to grab hold and show his fear. "Are you so bored you are trying to drown me for your amusement?"

"I am not trying to drown you," Ingar objected as he leaned on the tiller and soaked half his crew. "My men need waking up. So long on land has left them sleepy."

"Then it is for them you steer this vessel like a madman, and not to send me over the side to a watery grave?"

Ingar grinned. "Man to man, would you blame me if I did? Then I could have that woman for myself."

"Osburn won't sell her to you," Alexander replied with far more confidence than he felt. In truth, there was very little he would put past that spoiled, greedy drunkard.

"You don't think so? By Thor's hammer, you are a poor judge of men if you think not."

"His father would be angry."

"For enough gold, that one would risk a father's rage, and I would give him plenty for her." Again, Ingar steered toward a wave. Again his men shouted and cursed and laughed, the one who must be Olaf shaking his fist at Ingar.

"He's too afraid of his father."

"And I tell you, you don't know men, my friend. He will take the money and flee, for it would be enough to free him from his father forever. He is like a spoiled dog who will not hesitate to bite his master's hand if he thinks he will be able to run away afterward. If it were between him and me, that woman would already be mine."

"It is not. As I have told you, she is not for sale."

Ingar grinned. "Out of respect for you, I have not made another offer, nor will I."

Respect. That was something Alexander had craved his whole life, and now, apparently, he had it—from a Norse brigand who wouldn't hesitate to buy an abducted woman.

Ingar pointed, and Alexander made out landfall on the horizon. "We are nearly there."

Alexander had never been so happy to see distant hills in his life.

Keeping his gaze on the horizon, Ingar said, "If you wanted to take her, that fool Osburn couldn't stop you, or his Brabancons, either. You're too good a fighter, and those Brabancons are not."

Alexander didn't mask his surprise at this observation. "They are the scourge of Europe."

"Because they are ruthless, like Berserkers. But risk their lives for one woman? None of them will want to die for that, unless they are very well paid." Still holding the tiller in his powerful hands, Ingar regarded Alexander gravely. "*You* would die for that woman."

Alexander told himself to ignore Ingar's words. "The lady is going back to her husband. I want the ransom, not her."

Ingar turned his attention to the rocks guarding the entrance of the bay, now looming closer. "If you say so. But if the money is not enough to satisfy you, I offer you a place in my crew. We sail far to the south as well as to the north, and there are plenty of beautiful women between here and there."

Maybe there were, but it was not Lady Allis's beauty alone he admired. It had sparked his desire, yet what he felt for her now was far more than physical craving, although that burned strong, too. It was her spirit, her refusal to yield, even her defiance of his advice, that made him admire her.

They said no more as Ingar concentrated on getting past the rocks. As the ship rounded the farthest one and shot into the calmer waters of the bay, he shouted another order. His soaking men leapt to their feet to lower the sail, and then the mast.

Despite Ingar's confidence, Alexander heaved a sigh of relief that they had arrived safely. Through the commotion on deck, he spotted Denis waiting on the wharf. The Gascon was hard to miss, and not because his cloak was snapping behind him like a pennant.

"Your friend looks like a flea on the back of a burning dog," Ingar noted as he aimed his vessel toward the wharf. He gave Alexander a speculative look. "Or as if he's missed a lover."

Alexander was too concerned with Denis's agitated state to take any notice of the implication. "Something has happened. Can you dock any faster?"

"Be patient, Norman."

Alexander was in no mood to be patient. He strode toward the bow, shoving out of the way any Norseman who interfered with his progress. They muttered and grumbled, but he paid no heed to them.

Maybe Denis had been unable to protect Lady Allis. Maybe she had enraged Osburn or Heinrich so much that they had killed her. Maybe she had escaped. Maybe she had indeed sprouted wings like an angel and flown away. He could believe almost anything where that lady was concerned, and despite his stake in returning her for ransom, he would rather she had escaped than be hurt or raped or killed.

His gaze swept the shore and the ruined castle beyond. The Norse encampment looked as he had left it, save that there was no smoke from any fire. The heads of sentries moved above the battlements without haste or alarm. All was as he might have expected, except for Denis's excitement.

The instant the vessel drew up beside the wharf, Alexander jumped over the side. "What's amiss?" he demanded as Denis hurried toward him.

"I thought you would never get back!" Denis cried as he grabbed hold of Alexander's arm to drag him toward the shore.

Alexander shook him off. He didn't need any physical coercion to make haste; Denis's manner was quite enough. "Is she dead?" he asked as he strode toward the beach.

If she was, whoever had done it was as good as in his grave, including Osburn, despite his powerful father.

"Not yet," Denis replied, panting as he trotted beside Alexander across the slippery pebbles.

Thank God. The relief took the ferocity from the worst of his rage, until the other import of Denis's response hit him. "What do you mean, *not yet*?"

"Osburn has imprisoned her in the northeast tower, in a dungeon there. A dank, cold place, Kiera says."

"I *will* kill him," Alexander muttered. What Osburn had done sounded like a slow death.

Denis grabbed his arm. "Stop a moment, Alexander!"

Alexander whirled on him. "Why?"

"Because you do not know what happened, and until you do, it would not be wise to go off in such a temper."

Alexander put his fists on his hips. "What happened?"

"She killed Heinrich."

Dumbfounded, Alexander's hands fell limply to his side as he stared at Denis. *"What?"*

"She hit him on the head with a stone when he was—"

Alexander's ire returned tenfold. "Trying to rape her?" He pivoted on his heel to continue on his way. "By God, it's good she did!"

Denis ran in front of him and put his hands on Alexander's chest to make him stop again. He stared hard into his friend's furious face. "He was fighting *me*, Alexander. He had done no harm to her."

Alexander stared.

"Oui, I know—a woman defending me. It is nearly enough to make a man ashamed, and I could have taken him eventually if she had not interfered. But she did."

God save him, she had done more than *interfere.* To think any woman would take it upon herself to attack a Brabancon. "What exactly happened, Denis?" Alexander asked, a little calmer now.

"He accosted her, so I challenged him. We were fighting and he wounded me."

"Wounded?"

Denis nodded and pointed to his arm. "Not too bad, and Kiera did a good job of bandaging it."

He didn't want to hear about Kiera. "Go on."

"Then Lady Allis came up behind Heinrich and hit him with a rock. Whether she meant to kill him or not, she did. Osburn had her thrown in that dungeon, without food and only enough water to keep her alive. That was three days ago. She has been there ever since, untouched but surely suffering."

As furious as this news made him, there were more reactions than Osburn's to be considered. "And Heinrich's men?"

That query brought the ghost of a smile to Denis's face. "It seems there is not much love or loyalty among the Brabancons. They only cared about who would take his place as their leader."

Rain began to fall, huge drops that splattered on the pebbles at their feet. Without another word, Alexander started again for the fortress.

"What of Sir Connor?" Denis asked breathlessly as he hurried along behind him. "Will he pay?"

"Yes."

"What did he do when he saw who had brought him the ransom demand?"

"Very little."

"It does not sound as satisfying as you had hoped," Denis murmured as they came near the postern gate where two Brabancons stood on guard.

Alexander didn't answer.

The two guards at the postern gate moved out to

meet him. Both were as rough-looking as any other Brabancon. One of them had only one eye, with a terrible scar where the other ought to have been. The other, younger and leaner, looked as if he hadn't washed since childhood.

Alexander halted in front of them. "Let us pass."

"So you're back, eh?" the one-eyed man said with the accent of a Scot. His gaze flicked to Denis.

"Let . . . us . . . pass," Alexander repeated very slowly and deliberately.

The younger one came to stand beside his companion. He watched Alexander warily, but the one-eyed man stood his ground. "Maybe I will and maybe I won't."

Quick as a fox, Alexander knocked the younger one to the ground. In the next moment, he had the other up against the wall, his forearm across his neck.

Alexander glanced over his shoulder and was pleased to see Denis holding the younger one down with a knee on his chest, his dagger at the man's throat.

Alexander returned his attention to the man in front of him. "You should have let us pass," he growled, pressing his arm against the man's wide neck.

When he let him go, the man scowled and rubbed his throat.

Denis straightened. "You men will have to learn that it is best not to enrage my friend," he said with a satisfied grin as he sheathed his dagger. "He has a very savage temper."

Then he realized Alexander had gone ahead without him.

By the time Denis caught up to him, Alexander was already halfway to the northeast tower. Another guard was at the entrance. A ring with two heavy iron keys hung from his belt.

Expecting trouble, Alexander drew his sword.

The guard's expression betrayed only mild curiosity.

"Open it," Alexander ordered, his grip tightening on the hilt of his weapon as his blood sang with the urge to strike this man—any man—who was responsible for Lady Allis's imprisonment in that dungeon.

"On whose orders?"

"Mine."

The man looked from Alexander's face to his hand on the hilt of his sword and quickly opened the door. He took a torch out of a rusting sconce. He kindled it, then led the way down into the dank, fetid darkness. Water dripped down the walls as they made their way down the slick stairs.

Osburn had put Lady Allis in this hellhole? Alexander's anger surged and burned hotter than any rage he had ever felt in his life. If Osburn had suddenly appeared before him on the stairs, he would have squeezed the life out of him with his bare hands.

They reached the lowest level, where they all had to slouch or risk hitting their heads on the ceiling, even Denis. There was one door, of surprisingly stout oak.

After the guard unlocked it, Alexander snatched the torch and kicked the door open. He entered—and found a dirty, disheveled lady with a stool raised in her trembling hand, ready to bring it down on his head.

Leaning back against the wall as if her legs had

lost the strength to support her, her eyes widened, and she slowly lowered the stool.

She was pale, her full lips cracked from thirst, and he hoped the gleaming of her eyes was only from her usual spirit, and not the sign of disease.

Dismay overwhelmed his rage. Before he did another thing, he must remove her from this place and see that she was tended to. He reached out to take the stool from her. "Denis!"

His hand over his mouth and nose in a futile attempt to block the stench, his friend stuck his head in the chamber. *"Oui?"*

"Take this torch." Alexander shoved it at him, almost setting the Frenchman alight in the process.

Her eyes closed. Rushing forward, he caught her in his arms and lifted her up before she fell to the ground.

She had fainted. For the first time during all this, she had swooned.

Paying no attention to anyone else, he carried her out the door and up the steps. She was light in his arms, and as he went out into the courtyard, he studied her dirty face. She looked as if she slumbered peacefully, safe and secure in his embrace.

Oh, God, what he would not give to have it so! For a week. A day. An hour.

But she must hate him because of what he had done. And she was married to another, the destroyer of his future.

The old anger and injured pride did not rise up as he thought of Sir Connor. Now he felt only shame and remorse. If injustice had been done, he had chosen the wrong means to reparation, and this valiant woman had suffered for that mistake.

As he held her in his arms, it was not the title or the castle or even a father's love that he envied Sir Connor.

It was his wife.

He kicked open the door to the hall and saw Osburn sprawled in his chair before the hearth. Then ire returned, bright and hot and strong as he strode into the building. The serving wenches and Brabancons stared and whispered, yet none made any move to intervene or stop him.

Osburn lurched to his feet, paying no heed to the wineskin that fell off his lap, or the wine spilling out and staining the rushes red as blood. "You're . . . you've . . . what did Connor say?"

"He'll pay."

Osburn tried to focus on Alexander's burden.

"What are you doing? I gave orders that she was to stay—"

"To hell with your orders, Osburn."

Kiera came around the screen and gasped.

"Bring food and wine and hot water to her chamber," Alexander commanded, ignoring Osburn.

Kiera glanced at her drunken lover, then hurried to the kitchen to obey. Osburn fell back in his chair and, with a hint of wisdom, said no more as Alexander continued to the tower.

He took the steps two at a time, and when he reached her chamber door, he shoved it open with his shoulder.

He was surprised that this room was furnished in a manner suitable for a noble lady, as it was supposed to be. In this, at least, Lord Oswald had kept his word.

Alexander was at the bed in three strides, and he

gently laid her upon it. He spotted a basin on the table. Relieved to find clean water in it, he looked for a cloth, but saw none. He went to the chest and threw it open.

Nothing suitable to bathe her face.

He removed his cloak, then took out his dagger and used it to rip off a part of it. He threw the rest of the damp garment over the chest, then fetched the basin. Sitting beside her on the bed, he put one leg around the basin, so that it rested in the crook of his knee.

With swift, deft movements that came from much practice, he wet the cloth, wrung it out and began to wipe her face.

He began with her dry, cracked lips. Her lovely lips, that he had kissed. That Sir Connor had kissed often and while making love to her because as her husband, he had that right.

She had given *him* her kiss, the night before he'd left to take the ransom demand, yet only because of the same desperate, determined urge that drove her to try to escape over and over again.

What urge had driven her to attack Heinrich? Fear for Denis's safety?

He felt a terrible twinge of jealousy. Denis was merry and charming, and women always liked him. He was not merry, he had no charm, and while women found him attractive, he could not think of a one who would fight for him.

Not even his mother. She had not gone to his father and demanded that he provide for them. She had not railed against the man who had deserted them. Instead, she had waited for him to return and dreamt her hopeless dreams.

Forcing away the memories of his mother, he once again dipped the cloth in the water and cleaned Lady Allis's forehead, brushing her disheveled hair from her brow. He wiped her eyelids and shapely brows that helped illustrate all the emotions that flashed across her face.

He was as tempted to kiss her forehead as he was her lips.

He wiped her cheeks. Her skin was wonderful, pliant and soft. She had the most lovely complexion, and her skin looked as soft as rose petals. Unable to resist, he put the cloth in the basin and let his finger glide down the curve of her cheek with a long, slow stroke.

Her flesh *was* as soft as rose petals. He brushed his finger across her lips and nearly groaned aloud with the desire to kiss her.

He grabbed the cloth and briskly wrung it out, then began to wash her hands. Because she was a lady, they should be as soft as the skin of her face, the nails smooth and perfect. But her nails were short and broken and filthy, and the skin of her palms rough, as if she had scratched at the door, or tried to dig her way out.

Would she never surrender?

Overcome with admiration, he let the cloth fall into the basin, then raised her right hand and gently pressed his lips upon her palm. Guiding it gently, he let her hand rest a moment against his stubbled cheek.

Marveling at the way even that simple contact made him feel, he pressed another kiss to her cool palm. Closing his eyes, he trailed his mouth up her fingers to their tips, imagining that it was she dragging her hands over his lips, willingly allowing him this intimacy. He kissed the pad of each of her fingers, one by one.

He looked at her slender hand in his—where it did not belong, and never could.

Cursing himself for a besotted fool, he lowered her hand to rest upon her gently rising and falling chest. He must not forget who she was, and what they were—or were not—to one another. Had he not seen all too clearly the folly of a hopeless passion? Had his mother not shown him how that could dominate and destroy a life?

He picked up the cloth once more, twisted it deftly and prepared to wash her neck.

When he turned to his task, he found a pair of soft blue eyes open, and watching him intently.

Chapter 11

❝**W**hen did you return?" she asked, her voice a dry rasp, but a spark of vitality in her bright eyes. Even after all she had been through, it would clearly take more than three days in a dungeon to dim her spirit.

"Today," Alexander replied quietly. "Don't talk. Food and water will be here shortly."

She tried to sit up, shoving her heels against the featherbed for purchase and leaning back on her elbows. "The ransom—?"

"Your husband has agreed to pay. Now you should rest."

Relief flooding her face, she smiled and sank back. "My . . . husband."

Alexander beat back the stab of envy and despair at her tone. He did not need to hear her love for Sir Connor in her voice, especially when he had grave doubts the man deserved it.

"How long was I in that place?"

"Too long. Three days." Lifting the basin that had been in the crook of his knee, he rose and set it on the table. Facing her, he said, "I shall make certain Osburn does not do such a thing again."

She didn't reply, yet her wordless scrutiny was so unnerving that he would rather she berated him.

Then her expression softened in a way that went straight to the lonely core of his heart. "You brought me out of that terrible place. You washed my face, and my hands."

God's wounds, how long had she been awake? Perhaps only at the end, for surely she would have made her awareness known had she been awake when he'd kissed her fingertips. "They were filthy."

"You could have waited for Kiera."

"I sent her for food and wine."

Another silence stretched between them. He had no more to say; neither, apparently, did she, yet he did not move from his place as the tension grew. He could feel sweat on his back, and he wiped his hand across his forehead, in case beads of perspiration had formed there, too.

Then he wished he hadn't as he wondered if he had betrayed too much with his gesture. Things were as they were and could not be changed. Remorse and regret would avail him nothing.

It might make her like you better, his heart prompted.

He didn't need her affection. Or her desire. He needed the money from the ransom.

And what will you do with it when you have it? his heart demanded. *Spend it on drink trying to forget her and what you have done until you are as disgusting a drunkard as Osburn? Buy yourself women to warm your bed and try to imagine they are this one?*

Somebody rapped on the door, startling him. He threw it open to find Denis and Kiera on the threshold, each bearing trays. The odor of fresh bread emanated from beneath the linen cloth on Kiera's. Denis had the wine, and he had brought two goblets.

Kiera looked pale and ill, as if she had been the one imprisoned. Denis was simply, avidly curious.

Alexander held the door wider and motioned for them to enter. Kiera hurried toward the bed. Denis walked slower, and he slid Alexander a speculative glance that he did not appreciate. He was having enough difficulty with his turbulent emotions; he didn't need Denis wondering about them, too.

"Oh, my lady, I'm sorry!" Kiera murmured, her knuckles white as she gripped the tray.

As Alexander watched the lady sit up, he thought she was more interested in the bread than the condolences, and he couldn't blame her. He went around the bed to put one of the pillows behind her back. He tried not to notice her swift, grateful look.

Meanwhile, Denis poured wine into a goblet and offered it to her.

"Slowly, and not too much," Alexander cautioned.

"But I'm thirsty," she protested as she reached for it.

"You'll just throw it all back up if you take too much at first. Trust me, I know. Not too much bread, either. A little now, and a little more after a while. Slowly and steadily, to build up your strength."

She nodded, and he was relieved to think that for once, she was going to do as he suggested.

Hielda appeared at the entrance, a steaming

bucket in her hand. "Somebody wants hot water?" she demanded, her cavalier tone setting Alexander's teeth on edge. As he took the handle of the bucket, his expression full of disdain, he wondered how cheerful Hielda would be after some time in that dungeon.

Hielda apparently didn't notice, or didn't care. "Osburn says you're to report to him at once."

"I'll report to him when I'm ready," Alexander said, closing the door in her face.

"He says now!" she shouted.

"Perhaps you should go, Alexander," Denis said nervously. "He is ugly when he's drunk."

"Which would be all the time," Alexander muttered.

Kiera looked about to burst into tears. How much she was like his mother, slavishly devoted to a man who did not deserve it.

"My sister—did you see her?" the lady asked, taking his attention from Kiera. "How was she?"

"She is well. Worried about you, of course, but I assured both her and your husband that you will be returned unharmed once I have the money."

Closing her eyes as in prayer, she fervently murmured, "Thank God."

"Your husband is also well," he said, watching her reaction carefully.

"He is a strong man."

She smiled, but there was something—or rather, there was *not* something—in her eyes that he expected to see when she spoke of the man she supposedly loved. Before he had seen Sir Connor with the lady's sister, he might not have noticed, but now . . .

"Your sister did not strike me as weak, either."

"No, she isn't." He neither saw nor heard any rancor as she responded.

Maybe he was wrong, seeing trouble where there was none. Or maybe she herself was ignorant.

Again he reminded himself that the state of the lady's marriage was none of his concern. "Stay in bed and rest, lest you swoon again."

"I won't now that you . . . now that you have given me the news."

"Good. Denis, I am going to our quarters."

Before I betray my feelings or my suspicions about your husband and your sister.

Frowning, his friend hurried to him and, taking his arm, steered him out of the chamber. "Listen to me, Alexander. You must go to Osburn before he orders the Brabancons to do something else—against all three of us. He's been drunk ever since Heinrich was killed and muttering more and more about how he was not born to be a jailer. He's been saying terrible things to Kiera about women. I think he's been hitting her, too, although she never complains. A message came for him yesterday, and he's been even worse since."

"What message?"

"He has not said, to anyone, not even Kiera. Whatever it is, I tell you, you must do something to rein him in, even appease him if you must, or who can say what he will do?"

"He's a useless sot."

"Who the Brabancon will obey." Denis looked at his friend with grave and pleading eyes. "Is it not in his favor that he did not kill the lady when Heinrich died? And you say her husband will pay, so we will not have to endure him long. Nor will she. Although it goes against your nature, Alexander, you must do this. In the meantime, we will take care of her."

There was nothing more he could do here anyway, and Denis was no fool. If he thought it wise to mollify Osburn, he would—a little. "Very well."

Leaving his friend, Alexander marched down the steps and entered the hall.

Ignoring the Brabancons and slovenly serving wenches, Alexander walked up to Osburn and planted his feet, his arms akimbo. He glared into the man's bleary, bloodshot eyes. "What the devil did you think you were doing?"

The Brabancons took a collective step forward, but Alexander paid no heed.

"Punishing her," Osburn replied, whining like a child. "She killed Heinrich."

"He deserved it."

As the Brabancons began to mutter, Alexander whirled around. He would give them a reason for Heinrich's death that they would understand. "He was touching *my* property that *I* stole, so he deserved to die, whether at my hand or my friend's. Is there a man among you who would not do otherwise? Or do you all share what each of you plunder?"

Alexander's point hit home, and he pressed on. "If Heinrich could be killed by a mere woman, however it came about, he was not fit to lead you. Who has taken his place?"

A man dressed in a patched gambeson and leather breeches stepped forward. "I, Rawdon."

"Well, then, Rawdon, if any Brabancon touches the lady for any reason other than at my express command, I'll kill him. Do you understand?"

"Aye," Rawdon muttered.

"I command here!" Osburn protested, staggering to his feet. "A fact you seem to be forgetting, you arrogant bastard. I say what happens to her, until my father comes. And he won't be pleased to learn that Heinrich's dead at her hand. He didn't come cheap—a thousand marks, in addition to what he charged us for his men. All for nothing now, because of her."

Alexander didn't have to be looking at the Brabancons to feel their shock and their ire. No doubt they were each earning considerably less for this guard duty. The news of Heinrich's fee would spread to the rest of them, too, and when Lord Oswald arrived, he might well discover that his mercenaries, a band of men never known for their loyalty, were even less loyal to him than before.

Osburn was either too drunk or too stupid to realize his blunder. "She couldn't be allowed to get away with killing him, any more than Connor should be allowed to get away with stealing your birthright."

"My birthright has nothing to do with this. She is a woman and of noble birth. You should have locked her in her chamber, if you felt imprisonment necessary."

Osburn's eyes flared with a dim spark of protest. "You'd have me treat this woman like a delicate, innocent maiden? Good God, man, I've never met a woman *less* delicate *or* innocent! How many times has she tried to escape?" His brow furrowed as if he were trying to count, but he gave up in the next instant. "Anyway, she's no more delicate than Ingar, and as for innocent, you seem to be forgetting she was as responsible for your father's fate as Sir Connor. Isn't that also why she was taken?" The gleam in Osburn's eye grew malicious. "Or is it that she holds just as much of an attraction for you as she did for your father?"

Alexander ran his fingers through his hair. It was so easy to forget her culpability in his father's destruction. Seeing her in that state, he had also forgotten how she had used her own attractiveness to try to win him to her side with that incredibly passionate kiss.

"She is nothing to me but something to be ransomed," he lied, determined not to give Osburn pleasure or power by revealing his confused feelings. "If she fell ill, or died, she would be worth nothing. Sir Connor has said he will pay."

The feral gleam grew in Osburn's bloodshot eyes. "Perhaps Sir Connor need never know *what's* happened to his beloved wife. Wouldn't that torment be an even more fitting recompense for what you have lost?"

Alexander silently cursed the day he had met Lord Oswald, and his even more despicable son. "I made a bargain with the man, and I will keep it."

Osburn shrugged his shoulders. "As you wish— as long as you don't get any ideas about stealing her away." His gaze flicked over Alexander. "Don't think I don't see which way the wind is blowing, De-Frouchette. You may be a handsome enough fellow, bastard though you are and in a rough, uncouth sort of way, but she'll never—"

"Do you intend to keep her locked in her chamber?"

Osburn blinked, taken aback by the abrupt interruption. "I suppose she's learned her lesson, and besides, now you're here to watch over her, as I'm sure you will do with great attention." He smirked as he held up his wineskin. "Let's salute the lady and our plan, as well as my dear father, who's informed me that he plans to be here soon."

That must have been the message Denis had spoken of. It struck Alexander that he should not be surprised that Lord Oswald was coming after the danger was over and the risk nearly nil.

Otherwise, Alexander had no wish to see the man who had kept so much secret about this plan. If he must, he must, however; then he would take his money and head for Europe, away from England and the lady's husband. And away from the lady, too.

Osburn took a long pull at the wineskin and wiped his lips with the back of his hand. "He wants to see Lady Allis one last time, he says. Can't say I blame him. She *is* a beauty, even if she looks a little like a shorn sheep. Still, he won't be happy to hear about Heinrich."

Alexander had had enough of this man and this conversation. He turned on his heel.

"I give you leave to go, DeFrouchette," Osburn said as if Alexander were leaving by his command.

Barely resisting the urge to pummel the man until he screamed for mercy, Alexander strode out of the hall.

Lying in bed wearing a clean shift, warm and relatively safe now that DeFrouchette had returned, Isabelle watched Kiera gather up what had once been her best woolen gown. "I'm sorry that it's ruined."

Looking down at the filthy bundle in her hand, Kiera softly replied, "It'll wash."

Isabelle doubted washing could repair what three days in that hellhole had done to it, but she had no other compensation to offer except her apologies.

Kiera's cuffs had fallen back to reveal bruises on her right forearm, as if someone had held the girl in a hard grip.

"Did Osburn do that?" she demanded, aghast.

Kiera quickly shoved down her cuff. "It was an accident."

Isabelle was quite certain it was not. The way the bruising encircled the entire forearm was proof of that.

Stronger now after the bread and wine that Alexander DeFrouchette had gotten for her, she sat up and regarded the young woman not with pity but with compassion. "Perhaps it was," she conceded, "or perhaps it was not. Perhaps it only happens when Osburn is nearly insensible with drink."

"It was an accident," Kiera repeated, heading for the door.

"Was he so angry for what I had done that he took out his ire on you?"

Clutching the gown to her breasts, her lower lip trembling, Kiera faced her again. "He was very angry about Heinrich."

"If that anger caused you to be hurt, that would be the only reason I would be sorry for killing him."

Tears filled Kiera's eyes and spilled over onto her cheeks. "I-I wish you'd never come here," she stammered as she wiped them away with the gown. "W-we were happy before you come."

Isabelle got out of the bed. The stone floor was cold on her feet, and her legs were still weak, but she wanted to get closer to Kiera so that she could speak softly, in case there was a guard outside the door. "I would escape, if I could. All I need is someone to help me to get out of this castle."

The gown fell to the floor unheeded as Kiera held out her hands as if warding her off. "Oh, no!" she said, her voice trembling. "I won't!"

Isabelle reached out and took the girl's hands in hers, pleading with her. "Kiera, you could come with me. We could both get away from this place, and these men."

Kiera pulled her hands free. "I don't want to go. I-I love Osburn. You don't understand. He saved me."

"Kiera, he is a drunkard, and a mean one. He delights in my anguish, and I suspect he enjoyed your pain."

The truth flashed across the girl's face as she backed away, staring at Isabelle as if she were Satan sent to tempt her from the true path. "You don't know what it was like for me before Osburn took me away. You're a noble lady born into riches and rank."

Isabelle tried again. "Kiera, I know a servant's life can be difficult—"

Kiera's back hit the door, and the collision seemed to awaken something in her—an energy of resolve that Isabelle had not suspected she possessed. "I have heard about you, my lady, from Osburn," she said, her hands splayed against the door as if she were trying to hold it shut, or keep something out. "You don't know *nothing* about the miserable life I led. *You* never had a lustful master who thought you were there for his pleasure. Aye, or his sons, like we were there for them to learn on. Osburn took me away from that, and I'd die for him for doing it!"

"Or let him kill you?" Isabelle asked gently. She knew that some households were hell for the women who served there, yet she could not believe that Kiera was much better off with Osburn. He might have been good to her at first, but clearly those days were coming to an end.

Kiera's gaze faltered, and seeing her chance, Isabelle rushed on. "My life has not been without trouble. I daresay Osburn did not tell you of the anguish Rennick DeFrouchette put my family through. And do you think being taken from my home and held for ransom is pleasant? Or being imprisoned in a stinking dungeon? I have suffered, too, Kiera. Not as you have, but in other ways."

"At least you weren't raped as I was—more than once!"

Even as pity filled her, Isabelle continued to regard Kiera steadily. "I have not been raped *yet*, but that is the fate I face at your lover's hands, or those other men below, if I don't escape from here."

Kiera shook her head. "No, Osburn won't touch you. He has me to love him."

"You, of all women, should know that if he takes me against my will, there will be nothing of love about it. It will be to conquer and subdue me. He would do it to hurt me, and Connor. You must see that. Please, help me!"

Kiera slowly shook her head. "You're not to be harmed. And you've got DeFrouchette and Denis to protect you. You'll be safe enough, and soon the ransom will be paid, and you'll be gone. I had no one until Osburn and I won't leave him or betray him, neither!"

"Then one day, in a drunken rage, he will kill you."

With a cry that was both gasp and denial, Kiera opened the door and went out, slamming it behind her.

As exhaustion and disappointment overcame her, Isabelle made her way back to the bed and climbed in. Kiera might never see Osburn as anything but her savior, no matter what he did to her. In trying to enlist Kiera's aid, she might have made a terrible mistake—just as kissing DeFrouchette had been. Yet he had rescued her from that terrible place. She had been so glad to see him that she had almost told him as much before he'd left the chamber.

He had even washed her, as she had realized when she'd seen the basin cradled against his muscular leg. It had been his gentle ministrations that had awakened her.

For one blissful moment, she had believed she was home, safe at last, until she had felt his lips against her fingertips.

Nobody at home kissed her like that. No man at Bellevoire had ever roused such exquisite sensations with the touch of his lips. No other man had ever made her feel a need that awakened her from slumber and made her want to reach out and wrap her arms about him to draw him close to kiss. None of the men who sought her hand had created anything like the forbidden desire Alexander DeFrouchette inspired.

She shuddered, and not with a chill—with an excitement that she desperately tried to vanquish. He was, after all, still her enemy, even if the sight of his concerned face had stirred her far more than she wanted to admit to herself. He had looked down at her with an expression of such distress that it had seemed there was more to it than mere worry over an object to be traded.

And then his cheeks had reddened as if he were blushing.

Was that possible? Was it possible that he could be capable of any tender emotion? Or was it only from bending over the basin?

Whatever he felt, the relief of knowing he was back to protect her had been even more overwhelming than hearing that Connor and Allis had not betrayed her identity. Surely that wasn't right.

She drew the covers up to her chin and stared at the worm-eaten rafters in the water-stained ceiling as she tried to focus on her family. How had they discovered the mistake? Or had they guessed, as she had? If DeFrouchette had met Connor first and spoken of his wife, that would tell Connor of the man's error. Like her, Connor must have realized that her safety depended on maintaining the ruse, and somehow he had managed to communicate that to Allis, too.

Isabelle rolled on her side, worry for her sister and her condition gnawing at her. At least now, though, Allis would know she lived.

That was good, and so was Connor's agreement to pay the ransom.

She turned onto her back. It was so much money, much more than he had.

Would Osburn and the Brabancons return her, even then? They might decide to keep the money and sell her, too. DeFrouchette might object—

indeed, she could believe that his warped sense of chivalry would insist that she be returned to her husband—but the Brabancons could overpower him. So could Ingar and his crew, if the Norseman wanted to buy her.

At that thought, she shuddered again. There was only one person here she could truly rely on for her freedom. Herself.

Alexander marched across the courtyard and, with a guttural curse, kicked open the rickety door to the quarters he shared with Denis. It was a room at the bottom of a ruined tower lacking most of its roof. Some planks from an upper floor remained and Denis had found a piece of canvas somewhere to put across them.

Alexander snatched up the leather pouch that contained the few pieces of extra clothing he and Denis possessed. He dumped out their clothes, then shoved straw from the pile that was their bedding into it.

The door opened and Denis entered, halting in surprise when he saw Alexander crouched on the floor.

Alexander looked up, then continued his task. "What are you doing here?"

"Kiera is staying with her," Denis said. "I came to find you and see how you are faring."

"Me? I am well enough."

Assuming a casual air, Denis leaned back against the wall. "What are you doing?"

Alexander glanced up at his friend, then returned to his task. "Making a pillow. I will not be sleeping here tonight, or any night until the lady is on her way back to her husband."

"You will sleep in the stables? Me, too! They've got a new roof." Bending down, Denis gathered up the extra tunic they each possessed, and the second pair of breeches. "Why did you not say so?"

"Because I am not going to be sleeping in the stables. I will make my bed in the tower where the lady's chamber is."

Denis's jaw dropped. "*Mon Dieu*, I don't think she likes you enough for that."

Alexander barked a sardonic laugh. "Of course she doesn't. She hates me. I will not be sleeping in her chamber."

Still holding the clothes, Denis plopped down on his pile of straw. "What, you are going to sleep outside her door?"

"Yes."

"Pillow or not, you will catch your death!" Denis cried as he tossed the clothing aside.

Alexander pulled the pouch's drawstring closed, leaving several wisps of straw protruding from the opening. "If she can live for three days in that dungeon, I can survive sleeping in the tower."

"What will Osburn say?"

"I don't give a damn," Alexander replied as he threw the pouch over his shoulder like a peddler's pack. "I don't trust him, and I don't trust the Brabancons. I never should have left her before."

"Well, somebody had to take the ransom demand, and you wanted to see Sir Connor."

Alexander couldn't refute that, but it did little to assuage his feelings. "Now I've done it, and now I will protect her."

Denis picked up a piece of straw and started to chew on it, as meditative as a scholar. "She is an amazing woman. Too bad she is already married, and to your enemy, too."

"I just want to make sure my prize is safe until I trade her for the ransom."

"*Oui, je comprends.* It is only her value in trade that has you so concerned—not that she is a beautiful woman of spirit and determination. Not that she is your match in pride and courage. No, only her value in trade."

"Denis," Alexander warned. "You've spent too much time with troubadours."

"Perhaps," he agreed. "Still, it would make a fine tale, would it not? How the Black Knight takes his enemy's wife and falls in love with her and then . . . dies of a broken heart?"

"Nobody is going to die, of a broken heart or anything else."

"Except Heinrich."

Alexander gave him a sour look. "Very well, except Heinrich. As for the Black Knight, there will be plenty of money for other women when this is over and we are back in France."

"Of course, *mon ami,*" Denis said with an airy wave of his straw. "Indeed, there are other women here, for that matter." He saw the expression of distaste cross Alexander's grim face. "Not that you are desperate enough for one of them."

"No, I am not." Alexander went to the door, then paused. He knew his friend had his best interest at heart. "Good night, Denis. Take care."

With a merry grin, Denis pulled out his dagger. "I sleep with this under my pillow, in case any of those

Brabancons attack or one of the wenches crawls into my bed." He mused a moment. "I think I would prefer that a Brabancon try to murder me."

With a more genuine chuckle, Alexander took his makeshift pillow and departed, leaving his friend staring thoughtfully at the door.

Chapter 12

❧

In a bone-chilling drizzle, Connor reined in his mount and looked at the cluster of gray stone cottages barely distinguishable from everything around them. The water in the loch below was gray, the sky was gray, the rocky hills were green . . . and gray.

Sir Auberan de Beaumartre had certainly come down in the world. Before his fall from grace, he had been one of the richest young noblemen in England. He had also been one of the most vain, weak-willed men Connor had ever met.

As he raised his hand to signal his small troop of soldiers to head down into the valley, Connor wondered if he should reveal that Isabelle had been abducted, or indeed, anything at all about what had happened. He could not be sure that Auberan was not still in contact with Oswald, even if Oswald seemed to have disappeared off the face of the earth.

On the other hand, if Auberan did communicate

with Oswald, he would already know about the abduction of "Lady Allis." Either way, Connor decided, he would have to be cautious of what he revealed.

When they rode into the settlement, for the collection of ramshackle buildings could not even be called a village, a boy came to the door of one of the hovels to watch them. His hair was an unkempt mess, his clothing little more than rags, and he was gnawing on the heel of a loaf of coarse brown bread.

Connor reached into the pouch at his belt and pulled out a penny. He tossed it at the lad, who let his bread drop into the mud to catch it. "We seek Sir Auberan de Beaumartre."

The boy pointed toward the furthest low stone building.

Connor nodded his thanks as somebody behind the door put his hand on the lad's shoulder and yanked him back inside. The door slammed shut.

Either because of the weather or—more likely—out of fear and suspicion, no one else appeared as they continued toward the far side of the settlement.

"Stay here unless I call or do not come out soon," Connor commanded his men when they reached the cottage. The windows were shuttered, and no smoke rose from the roof. It looked deserted, and he wondered if the boy had purposefully lied for the sake of the penny. There was but one way to find out.

Fearing that Oswald might have decided to silence his former comrade permanently, Connor went to the simple wooden door held in place by a latch and leather hinges, and pounded on it. "Auberan!"

When there was no answer, he pounded again, and this time, the simple latch gave way.

Connor didn't hesitate to enter. The building was divided into two parts, one for living quarters and the other, judging by the smell, for a barn. The scent of burning peat added to the pungent odor, although the fire had burned down to a mere glow in the hearth.

A table scarred and covered with crumbs stood near the smoke-blackened hearth heaped with ash. There were also the obvious remains of more than one meal on the table. There were no chairs, only stools and a bench, and a bed in the corner. Connor was relieved that there didn't appear to be any blood.

The mound in the middle of the bed moved. "I told you, I'll pay her next month," a sleepy—and familiar—voice muttered.

"Greetings, Auberan. It's been a long time."

A woman with flaming red hair and freckles and a nose that, when she became old, would be described as sharp, sat up abruptly. With a little shriek, she covered her naked breasts, then dove back under the covers. After a flurry of Gaelic, she shoved the man in the bed beside her out onto the floor.

"What the devil—?" Auberan cried, still half asleep as he staggered to his feet, as naked as a new-born babe and as pale as the moon. His long hair was as unkempt as the boy's had been.

To think that Auberan de Beaumartre had once been the jackadandy of the king's court.

Turning, Auberan tugged the moth-eaten brown woolen blanket from the bed, exposing his female companion. Paying no heed to her squeals of alarm, he wrapped it about his waist like a long skirt.

Obviously cursing him, the girl threw on her simple gown of black wool and scurried into the part of the building that housed the animals.

As Auberan made an elegant bow Connor noticed that his face was much thinner and his eyes harder. It was as if the weakling youth had become a man through his suffering. But was he still loyal to Oswald?

"Sir Connor of Llanstephan," Auberan said with the vestige of his former noble bearing. "To what do I owe the pleasure of this unexpected visit?"

"I need some information. About Oswald."

He watched the man's reaction and was pleased to see anger darken Auberan's brow as he sat on the bed. "That creature? I don't know anything about him, except that he escaped the king's wrath and I did not."

"Then I trust you do not maintain any sense of loyalty to the man?"

Auberan snorted. "I have seen the error of being a trusting fool."

Disappointment washed over Connor. "Then if you did know anything about him, such as where he might have sought refuge, or any secret sanctuary he might possess—"

"I would have told the king's men. Indeed, it would have gone much easier for me if Oswald and DeFrouchette *had* told me something so I could reveal it."

Connor stared in shock as Auberan held up his right hand. The man regarded his bent and gnarled fingers as a lady might to see if there was dirt beneath the nails.

"The king's men didn't believe me, either," he continued evenly as he clasped his right hand in his undamaged left one, hiding it from view. "They broke my fingers to make me tell them what I knew. When I told them I knew no more than they already did, they broke them again, one at a time. And again after that."

"But you were sent north!"

Auberan's lips curved up in a smile, as if Connor were an innocent, ignorant child. "So, I was not the only trusting fool. Richard said he would banish me to the north, and so he did—in his own good time, after his torturers had first ensured that I took no secrets with me."

In one fluid motion, Auberan got to his feet, pulling a sword from beneath the straw mattress with his left hand. He had it at Connor's throat before Connor could unsheathe his own.

Auberan's face fairly glowed with satisfaction. "I have learned to wield my sword with my left hand, you see, and I have had little to do here but practice. Oh, and bed the local wenches who think it a privilege to lie with a nobleman, even a disgraced and dispossessed one." He lowered his weapon, and his eyes filled with despair. "Now go, Sir Connor. I have nothing to tell you, and I do not think you will enjoy the meager hospitality I can offer."

Connor didn't move. "Do you still care about Isabelle?"

"What, do I still love her? No. That died in me about the time they broke my thumb for the third time." His gaze clouded. "She meant well. She did not know it would have been more merciful to let them kill me." He drew in a ragged breath and gestured toward the door with his sword. "Do as I say, Sir Connor, and go."

Still Connor made no move to leave. "Did you know Rennick DeFrouchette had a son?"

Auberan shook his head.

"He did, and the man has abducted Isabelle."

Auberan's shoulders slumped as he sat on the nearest bench and laid his sword across his knees. "So, another repercussion of that day. It is a pity none of us foresaw what would come of what we did, isn't it, Sir Connor?"

"Yes," he admitted. "But we are none of us seers and Rennick never spoke of him, so I was as shocked as you when he came to demand the ransom. But there can be no doubt he is what he claims. He is the living image of his father."

"A bastard, then?" Auberan guessed, sitting straighter.

"Aye, and he thinks I stole Bellevoire from him by killing his father."

Auberan laughed bitterly. "Then he's a greater fool than I was. Any traitor's land and property are forfeit to the Crown, to do with as the Crown pleases."

"Whatever reason he gives to us, or himself, he is bent on seeking vengeance. I am sure Oswald is preying upon that weakness, just as he tried to enlist me in your conspiracy because of my anger toward Richard for what he had done to me and my family."

Auberan nodded. "Of course. He is an expert at exploiting men's weakness."

"Alexander DeFrouchette neither confirmed nor

denied Oswald's involvement, but his refusal to deny it is significant."

Auberan's hand tightened on the hilt of his sword.

Connor regarded him intently. "That is why I have come here. Did Oswald ever speak of any place that might be suitable for imprisoning a captive?"

Auberan shook his head. "Regrettably, no."

"Then I shall leave you." Connor turned to go, then hesitated. He reached for the purse at his belt.

Auberan was on his feet and had his sword against Connor's chest before Connor could pull the purse free. "Don't even think it! I will not take charity from you."

Connor spread his hands, and Auberan lowered his sword.

"I have everything I need, Sir Connor," he said. "An estate, although this godforsaken valley might not be terribly impressive." He gestured at his surroundings. "A hall." He nodded at the bed. "A woman to warm me in the night." His lips curved into a sardonic smile as he looked down at the blanket wrapped around his waist. "Fine clothes. The men wear such things here, you know."

Connor had always believed Auberan a fool, as DeFrouchette and Oswald had, but now, as Auberan stood before him, Connor was sorry things had gone as they had. If Auberan had found the right path early on, he might have been a worthy ally and possibly a friend. He might even have won Isabelle's heart.

"I will save Isabelle," Connor vowed.

Auberan's smile faded. "If there is a man in England who could, it would be you."

"When I see her—"

"Say nothing of me, I beg you." Auberan's gaze faltered, and he bowed his head as if the weight of his anguish was a great burden. "Let her forget that I live."

A proud man himself, Connor understood Auberan's request and sympathized with it. "As you wish. God be with you, Auberan."

"The same to you, Sir Connor."

Dressed in a simple brown wool gown of Kiera's, Isabelle made her way down the steps and peered into the hall. The day had dawned fair and mild. She had been in her chamber ever since her imprisonment, and was desperate to breathe the fresh air blowing in off the sea, stretch her legs and reassure herself that she was strong enough to try to escape.

She was relieved to discover that the hall was empty save for a few of the women sweeping out the filthy rushes that were full of decaying food, damp with ale and no doubt home to fleas. As they worked, they roughly nudged the sleeping hounds that got in their way, and the sleeping Brabancons who did, too.

Tense with anticipation that someone might question her, Isabelle straightened her shoulders and marched toward the door. There was, after all, no way she could sneak past the men, the women and the dogs.

None of the women said a thing. One of the hounds raised his head and growled, low in his throat. The men didn't move.

She wondered where Osburn and Kiera were, until a sound made her look over her shoulder at the screened area. It was, she realized, the feet of a bed thumping against the floor.

Blushing, she hurried on. Of course she knew that Kiera was Osburn's mistress, but she didn't like this explicit reminder, just as she didn't like becoming more and more certain that Osburn took out his temper on Kiera by beating her. He never hit Kiera's face, apparently, but she could not disguise the bruises on her arms, and new ones appeared daily.

Kiera never spoke of them, and whenever she caught Isabelle looking at her arms, she abruptly left the chamber.

Wishing there was *something* she could do to help Kiera, Isabelle sighed as she left the hall. The sun was warm and quickly drying the remaining puddles in the courtyard. A couple of the hounds had come out to lie in the sun, and so had a few of the Brabancons. There were more on the wall walk, apparently keeping guard by leaning against the battlements and chatting.

If she tried to flee right now, she might be able to catch them unaware. She glanced at the gate. The guards there were just as lax. If she could get into the stable and take a horse, maybe she could ride out . . . but in the daylight, they would see her too easily for her to get far.

"A beautiful day, is it not, my lady?"

She jumped, and discovered Denis at her elbow. "Yes. Yes, it is. That's why I came outside."

She realized the Brabancons were starting to pay attention to her presence. "I was just taking a walk."

"*Oui*, as was I. May I join you?"

His sly grin told her he did not completely believe her innocent explanation any more than she believed his. He had probably been on watch, as he had been during Alexander's absence. She had underestimated Denis before he fought Heinrich; she wouldn't do that again.

"There is something of a garden over this way," Denis said, moving toward the kitchen. "Much neglected, of course, but there are herbs. It smells quite pleasant—a delightful change after that hall and those Brabancons, I assure you." His dimples deepened. "If you like, I can tell you the exciting tale of how I came to be saved by Alexander from a mob of villagers."

The *garden* sounded delightful. "Very well."

They started ambling toward the kitchen, and Denis slid her a shrewd glance. "And the wall there is very strong and easily seen by the men nearest the gate on the wall walk, so you will not be able to escape me."

"Oh, I wouldn't do that."

"Of course you would," he replied without rancor. "I think Alexander has considered tying you to a chair because that is the only way he can be completely sure you will not try to run away again."

"I have given him my word."

"Have you, indeed? Well, well, perhaps we are wrong and you will be content to wait until the ransom is paid."

She said no more, and she was relieved when he did not, either.

They reached the remnants of the kitchen garden, and she discovered Denis was right. The air was scented with rosemary, thyme and lavender, a very welcome change. She also spotted what appeared to be boneset and ladies' bedstraw. However, it was difficult to tell exactly what was growing there, for the beds were a mess and the paths virtually nonexistent. A wooden bench stood near the middle of the garden. Rain had smoothed the edges, and it no longer looked strong enough for anyone to sit on. Despite that, this place was easily the most pleasant spot in the fortress, especially in the warmth of the sun.

Even better, she did not find walking tiring at all. Of course, she had not gone far and she was not being chased.

"Where is Alexander?" she asked as they wandered down the side closest to the kitchen. "I did not see him in the courtyard."

"He has other business."

Such as? she wanted to ask, but she didn't want to reveal any interest in him. "So you are to be my protector against the Brabancons again?"

"Or you are to protect me," Denis replied with a chuckle as he bent down and picked a spray of lavender. He presented it to her with a gentlemanly bow. "If there is trouble, he can be here quickly."

As the scent of the lavender filled her nostrils, Isabelle wondered if Alexander was with one of those disgusting women whose most important purpose was obviously to accommodate the mercenaries whenever and wherever they wanted.

The Gascon chuckled softly as he picked another spray and tucked it behind his ear. "*Non,* my lady, he is not with a woman."

She started and flushed with embarrassment. "I was thinking no such thing!"

"Of course you were, and why not? Those women

slaver after him like dogs after a haunch of venison. I assure you, he does not return the feeling."

She began walking along the edge of the garden again. "I wouldn't care if he did."

They turned the corner and made their way down what was left of a path. She tried not to ask, but her curiosity got the better of her. "So, where is he then?"

"Teaching a lesson."

Of all things, she did believe Alexander De-Frouchette was a scholar. "What sort of lesson?"

"He is showing one of the Brabancons what can happen if he speaks disparagingly of an honorable woman."

Isabelle came to an abrupt halt and stared at Denis. "Do you mean to tell me he's defending my honor?"

Denis shrugged. "He has his notions of honor, too, my lady."

She jabbed the lavender at Denis. "So *now* he decides to be honorable?" She let loose a curse that made Denis's eyes widen. "It would have been better if he had had such scruples when he came to Bellevoire."

"He *does* have scruples," Denis protested. "I thought you would be pleased—"

She didn't want to hear what he thought. "Where is this battle over my honor taking place? Not in the courtyard, obviously."

Denis looked truly distressed. "He will be angry with me if I tell you."

"*I* will be if you don't!"

"Why are you haranguing my friend?"

She whirled around, to see Alexander standing at the far end of the garden, his hair an untidy mess and his tunic slung over his shoulder. Sweat glistened on his naked chest and trickled down the sides of his face. His snug breeches clung to his muscular legs, and she could see a bruise forming on his taut torso.

He had a magnificent body, even better than Connor's. Her blood, already hot with anger, grew hotter yet with something else, something that made the memory of his embrace explode in her consciousness.

She forced that away as she marched toward him straight through the tangled mess of plants. "Where have you been?"

She silently cursed again. God help her, she sounded for all the world like an anxious wife.

Alexander wiped his face with his tunic. "It seems Denis has already told you."

"Yes. And there was no reason for you to do that. As if I care what a Brabancon says about me! They are all louts and for you to risk your life—"

"If you will both excuse me," Denis murmured, "I will take my leave of you."

"No!" Isabelle cried.

She wished she had kept quiet as both of them looked at her with some surprise—but she certainly didn't want to be alone with a half-naked Alexander DeFrouchette.

"I do not wish to interfere in your little . . . spat," Denis said innocently.

"We are not having a spat!" Isabelle retorted, not for a moment taken in by his feigned innocence. "I just want him to know there is no need to put himself at risk over such a thing." She glared at Alexander. "After all, you are the person who is supposed to take me home. What if you are killed? Do you think Osburn will abide by the agreement with Connor?"

Alexander finally put on his tunic. "There was little chance of my demise."

She crossed her arms. "Your arrogance astonishes me—*again*."

"Oh, but it is not arrogance, my lady!" Denis said. "He is so excellent a fighter, he will never be defeated." Denis took hold of her arm and led her toward the very rickety-looking bench. "Now come, why do we not forget this unpleasantness and enjoy the day? You are well, my lady, Alexander has only a few bruises . . . and I suppose the other fellow—?" He looked pointedly at Alexander.

"A broken leg, a few gashes. Nothing overly serious."

Denis's smile beamed. "There—little harm done and they will all think twice before they say such things again." Denis made a sweepingly gallant bow when they got to the bench. "Sit, please, my lady, and I will tell you the story I promised."

She did, delicately. She slid further back when it seemed the bench would not collapse beneath her. Denis wisely did not risk adding to its burden; he sat cross-legged at her feet.

Alexander stood a short distance away. "What story is this?"

"How we met."

Her eyes widened with surprise when Alexander rolled his eyes. Then he, too, sat on the ground and calmly and deliberately removed his swordbelt and laid it beside him. "I had better stay, or who knows what embellishments you'll add."

Apparently not at all disturbed by Alexander's

implications about his honesty, Denis shrugged. "As you wish," he said brightly. "Before I met Alexander, I was traveling with a small troupe of entertainers—jugglers, troubadours, a fortune-teller and tumblers. *I* was a tumbler. We were the best troupe in Europe and performed at many feasts and festivals. When we were not employed by a nobleman at such times, we traveled from village to village bringing sunshine and laughter into the dreary lives of the villagers."

Alexander snorted.

Denis looked mightily affronted at both the interruption and the implication. "Well, we did!"

"There were five of you, three men and two women, and you were terrible. I swear you fell down every time."

"That is because Alphonse was an idiot! He was never in the right place to catch me."

Alexander gave Isabelle a skeptical look, and she had to smile.

"I tell you, it is a miracle I am not dead from landing on my head!"

"That's true," Alexander solemnly agreed. "They were the most pathetic group of performers I have ever seen."

"Enough about my troupe. She wants to hear about how you saved my life."

"Yes, I do," Isabelle concurred.

"In that case, perhaps *I* should tell the story," Alexander said. "Otherwise, we will probably be here until the middle of the night."

"Very well," Denis said with a wave of his hand. "You tell it—and if you don't bore her to sleep, I will be most impressed."

As Isabelle looked at Alexander DeFrouchette sitting so casually on the ground before her, his hair wild and the memory of his virile body so close to the surface of her mind, she doubted she would ever find him boring.

"Denis and his fellows were in a village performing on the green," Alexander began, "when a baker suddenly noticed several loaves of his bread were missing. At nearly the same time, he spotted one of the women from the troupe stuffing a loaf down her dress."

"That was part of her costume," Denis protested, as if Isabelle was about to accuse him of theft right then and there. "Giselle is small there and always wants to look bigger."

"You must admit, Denis," Alexander said, "that looked very suspicious. And you shouldn't have called the villagers those colorful names when they accused you all of theft. Still, I thought you were going to talk your way out of the mess, especially after you offered to pay the baker."

He addressed Isabelle. "Unfortunately, the butcher and a few others who kept calling them Gypsies were not inclined to be merciful, so they ran. There was very nearly a riot as the whole village started after them."

Unable to resist, Denis picked up the story. "The others managed to get to the wagons and away, but I was on foot and I fell. They left me, and I was the best tumbler they had. Can you imagine? Then the crowd fell upon me, beating me with sticks and their fists. I was certain I was about to meet God face to face, when suddenly, the crowd parts like the Red Sea and there is Alexander. He reaches down, pulls me up and says,"—Denis lowered his voice to a very dramatic and stentorian tone—" 'Whoever next lays a hand on this man will have to answer to *me*!' "

"I *said*, 'Let him alone.' "

Denis ignored Alexander's correction. "But the butcher, he is not willing to let me go. He grabs my shoulder. Alexander grabs the other. For a moment, I am in danger of being torn in two, when Alexander sees that the butcher has—*Mon Dieu!*—a cleaver in his hand. The next thing I know, the butcher is on the ground, holding his hand, and Alexander has the cleaver. 'You see what happens to those who challenge me?' he says. 'Who else will take me on?' "

"I never said that."

"You did!"

"I did not. I said, 'Now will you let him go?' "

"Your version would be boring."

"That doesn't give you leave to make things up."

"What, is it not true the butcher had a cleaver?"

"Yes, the butcher had a cleaver," Alexander reluctantly admitted, but his eyes were bright with a gaiety Isabelle had never seen there before, as if a burden had been momentarily lifted.

And suddenly, there in the tangled garden of a ruined fortress that was her prison, she saw Alexander DeFrouchette as the knight he could—and should—have been, and for the first time she truly understood all that he had lost.

"Whatever Alexander says, he saved my life," Denis said, interrupting her thoughts, "and for that, I will be forever grateful."

Alexander shifted as if he didn't like being thanked, or perhaps it was just from sitting on the unyielding ground. Then he hoisted himself to his feet and held out his hand to help Denis stand. "I have sat here long enough. My lady?"

Denis scrambled to his feet without assistance. "I have other things I should be doing, too."

"Such as?" Alexander charged as Denis hurried away.

"Making Kiera smile." Grinning, he dashed out of the garden, leaving them alone.

Isabelle slowly turned to face Alexander, her heartbeat racing, and she couldn't meet his steadfast gaze. "It was good of you to help him."

"He has repaid me many times over with his friendship."

"He seems a lively companion."

Alexander laughed softly. "Indeed, he is that."

She raised her eyes and took a step closer, as if drawn to him like a cold woman to the warmth of a hearth. The memory of his tender care and passionate embraces filled her mind and her heart.

If he had had the chance, this man could have been a knight, respectable and worthy of high regard. He could have been a welcome addition to any lord's retinue, or even the king's.

If his life had been different, if they had met under other circumstances and he stirred her heart as he did now despite what he had done, she would surely have welcomed his attentions and his kisses. She would have wanted more. She would have wanted him to take her to his bed and make love with her all night.

She wanted that now, and the passionate certainty hit her like a blow.

She wanted to be in her enemy's bed. She yearned to be his lover, to feel his powerful warrior's body taking hers with hot and anxious need. To have him thrust inside her until she cried out in ecstasy and completion.

The expression in his blue eyes shifted, and it was like a shutter closing on a window. "If you will excuse me, my lady, I need to wash."

He grabbed his sword and hurried out of the garden.

Breathing hard, feeling as if she had had a very narrow escape from something more fraught with danger than the Brabancons, Isabelle sank down on the bench.

Chapter 13

Alexander moved the sharpening stone up and down his blade, the smooth rasping sound the only noise in the roofless tower. He did this the first thing every morning, ever since the day his mother had presented it to him. She had been so pleased, seeing this as the first real step on his way to making his father proud of him, and her, too, he supposed.

In one way, he hated what his sword represented, for he had seen what it had cost her to get the money to buy it. Yet because of his mother's sacrifice, he loved the weapon, too, and took great care of it. The blade was not a fine one, but it was always honed sharp enough to pierce chain mail and the padded gambeson beneath.

This much in his life had not changed.

Other things had, especially after being in the garden with Lady Allis two days ago. He had allowed himself the pleasure of her company, as if he had a right to it. He had loosened the strictures he placed upon himself in her presence, and he had even enjoyed telling the story of how he had met Denis.

But then he had looked at her, their gazes holding, and he thought he had seen something that was surely impossible. She could not like him, not after what he had done, and yet the expression in her eyes . . .

Was that not why you went into the garden, to be more yourself in the hope that she might at least cease to hate you? Why then do you deny what you saw? What you felt?

Because it was useless. There could never be anything between them once she was returned to her husband.

Who might be betraying her with her own sister.

That is not your concern. When this is finished and she has gone back to Bellevoire, take the money and go far away and try—try!—to forget her.

He was not the only one who was going to have a woman to forget. He had seen the way Denis watched Kiera, and the look that crossed his face every time she went around the screen with Osburn. If *he* hated Osburn, it was nothing compared to the animosity that fairly shot from Denis's eyes every time the man even spoke to his mistress.

But that was a hopeless yearning, too. A woman like that, blindly devoted to a man, would probably stay until he killed her.

The door to the tower crashed open.

The woman who haunted his restless dreams stood there, staring at him, closer to panic than he had ever seen her, even when she thought Osburn was going to cut off her finger. "Come!"

His sword clutched in his hand, the sharpening stone fell to the ground as he scrambled to his feet. "What—?"

"He's going to kill Kiera! I tried to stop him, but he drew his sword and—"

A curse flew from Alexander's lips. "Did he hurt you?"

"No, but—"

Since she was unharmed, he lingered no more. He sprinted across the courtyard as the sound of a woman's screams reached his ears.

Fury rose up, hot and strong and powerful, as he barged through the door. The serving wenches, who were clustered around the door to the kitchens, fell silent as he charged forward. The Brabancons in the hall made no move to interfere; Alexander would have struck them down without hesitation if they had.

Rounding the screen, he saw a half-naked Osburn, his sword in his hand, and swaying drunkenly, in the midst of disarray. The bed linens were a heap of torn cloth. A dented silver carafe rocked on the floor in a puddle of wine. A goblet lay at the base of the wall, its contents splattered like blood over the stones above. Pieces of the bedpost had been hacked out, as if a mad woodsman had thought they were trees to be cut down.

Covering her head with her arms, Kiera cowered near the tousled bed. A huge tear in her gown exposed a red welt on her shoulder and an older bruise, purple and yellow and ugly. Her eye was blackening and her lip was cut.

The urge to run the man through pounded

through Alexander, demanding that he punish Osburn and assuage the fierce anger shooting through him.

He raised his arm, ready to strike the fatal blow, when Kiera saw him and screamed, "No!"

Her cry alerted Osburn, who whirled around to face Alexander, his bleary eyes trying desperately to focus. He raised his sword.

Stupid fool. He was drunk nearly to senselessness and he thought he could prevail? The joy of certain victory sang in Alexander's veins, even as he tossed aside his sword. "Come on, Osburn," he said, smiling. "Fight me. Show me what you can do against an unarmed *man*."

"No! You'll kill him!" Kiera wailed. "It's my fault. I didn't want—"

"Don't excuse him, Kiera," Alexander growled. "He doesn't deserve it."

"Get out of here," Osburn slurred, waving his sword. "Kiera is my woman to do with as I please—"

In the next moment, he was flat on his back on the floor, struck down by a single blow from Alexander's fist.

"You've killed him!" Kiera wailed.

His chest heaving, Alexander rubbed his knuckles as he stared down at his unconscious enemy. "No, I have not."

"Don't hurt him anymore!"

"Take her away from here," he said to Isabelle, who had come around the screen. He spoke to Kiera. "I won't hurt him anymore."

Isabelle hurried to the beaten, terrified girl. She put her arms around Kiera. "Can you stand? Can you walk?"

At that moment, Denis came careening around the screen. He took in the sight before him, especially Kiera's battered face, and his own reddened with rage. If Osburn was not already lying on the ground, Alexander was sure Denis would have attacked him.

He might give him a few kicks as it was, and if he did, Alexander wouldn't stop him.

Isabelle led the sobbing Kiera away, probably intending to take her to her chamber, where the girl could weep in private.

He watched them go, one a shivering, weeping mass of cowardice and insecurity, and the other the sort of woman he would have all women be. "Go after them, Denis. See if they need anything."

Denis nodded, then hesitated, his gaze going from the man on the floor to his friend. "What will you do?"

"Put his lordship to bed."

"Lord Oswald may not be pleased that you struck his son."

"Lord Oswald has much to answer for himself," Alexander grimly replied.

Ignoring the curious looks of the others in the hall, Isabelle led Kiera across the room, up the stairs and into her chamber. The girl sobbed the whole way, tears falling down her face, her choking, gasping breaths wracking her slender frame.

"Here, lie down," Isabelle said softly as she helped Kiera to the bed. Removing the torn gown could wait; for now, it was more important that Kiera feel safe and cared for.

While Isabelle pulled the coverlet around her and

tucked the free end beneath her, so she was swaddled like a baby, Kiera turned her head to sob into the pillow. Isabelle quickly filled the basin on the table with fresh water from the ewer and took the only scrap of linen left in the room to clean Kiera's face.

She sat on the bed and cradled the basin in the crook of her knee, just as Alexander had done when he had tended to her with such gentleness. She touched Kiera on the shoulder. "Let me bathe your face."

The girl obediently rolled over, and Isabelle's eyes filled with tears when she saw the wounds Osburn's blows had inflicted.

Not meeting her gaze, Kiera flushed and stammered, "I-it was the wine and I wouldn't . . . he wanted me to . . ."

"You don't have to explain to me, Kiera," she said as she dabbed at Kiera's cut lip. Other than cleaning this wound and wiping away the blood, there wasn't much to be done. The bruises would heal by themselves, and there was no way to bandage her lip. Fortunately, a scab was already forming, so the cut was not as deep as she had feared. "Alexander was right. Don't make any excuses for Osburn. Only a coward strikes a woman."

Kiera's expression shifted, and it was like a wall had come between them. "Osburn has been kind to me. He still is, most of the time. He's upset and anxious because his father is coming any day now, so he loses his temper quickly."

Isabelle's hand hovered over the basin. Oswald was coming here *any day now*? He would recognize her and reveal who she was, and what would they do to her then? Would Alexander still continue to protect her, or would he be angry that she had deceived him? Would whatever . . . kindness . . . that had developed between them be destroyed?

She could not risk that.

"If I were more obedient, he would not have to hit me."

Kiera's plaintive remark brought Isabelle forcefully back to the here and now. "If you were any more obedient," she said gently, "you would be no more than a dumb beast. I've seen how he treats you, and it's not right, Kiera."

Someone scratched at the door, sounding more like a mouse than a person, and Denis poked his head into the room. "I am to make certain Kiera is all right and to fetch you anything you need."

Kiera curled into a little ball with her back to him.

Denis sidled into the room. "Alexander is putting his lordship to bed."

He closed the door. "Forgive me for intruding," he said as if he feared speaking louder might increase Kiera's pain, "and Alexander will have my head if he finds out what I am doing, but I think I should tell you something about my friend, and why you should listen to him."

Although Isabelle was burning with curiosity to hear more about Alexander DeFrouchette, Denis had not been speaking to her. "I'll leave, if you would like."

Kiera quickly rolled over. Her hand shot out, and she grabbed Isabelle's wrist. "Please, stay with me," she pleaded, her eyes begging as well as her voice.

"Osburn is a jealous man, is he not, Kiera?" Denis asked as he pulled up the stool.

She nodded.

"Then you must stay, my lady, and I must be swift." He glanced around as if fearing spies, then leaned forward and regarded them, his brown eyes intense. "Alexander will be angry if he finds out that I've told you about his mother, so please, you must not let him know."

"I won't," Isabelle vowed.

"Nor I," Kiera whispered.

Denis gave a brisk nod of approval. "She was born a lady, into a wealthy family in France. When she was but fifteen, she was seduced by Alexander's father. He abandoned her, and when her family found out she was with child, she was thrown into the streets."

Kiera's hand gripped Isabelle's. As difficult as a servant's life could be, a maidservant bearing a child out of wedlock in a noble household was not unusual, or even particularly shameful. She would be compensated, and the child, especially if a boy, could hope to have some measure of worldly success and assistance from his father.

It was vastly different for a woman of noble birth, though. Her virginity had far more value when it came to marriage alliances. For a noblewoman to bear an illegitimate child was not just shameful; it devalued her completely.

"Alexander understands how a girl can be seduced by a handsome nobleman," Denis continued. "But she lived in hope that Alexander's father would come back to her. She was not a whore then, although they called her that. She earned her money working for a brewer, in a tavern, and all the time she told her son they must always be prepared for his father's return. They must always have fine things she could barely afford, just in case—wine and linens and a gown for her and clothes for him, awaiting the day they would be needed. Alexander had to learn to act like a nobleman's son, to sit and eat and walk and talk like one, although every day the other boys reminded him of his bastardy. But he was not slow to see that his father had left her with nothing except him—no money, no house, no name. He wondered why this was so, and why his mother continued to speak of his eventual return as some might the second coming of our Blessed Savior. Nor would she let him question the man's absence. *Non, non,* they must be prepared. He would come. They must be patient.

"Then one day, *voila*! He is there. The great man himself. Why he finally arrived, Alexander never did learn. All he can remember is his mother throwing herself at his father's feet, sobbing with joy to see this man who had left them alone, with nothing. A tall man, he towered over them both, and dressed all in black, so he was like a great crow. Handsome, and cold and without a hint of love for them."

"He looks just like his father now," Isabelle noted, her heart full of sorrow for the abandoned boy and his mother.

"It's easy to see how his mother was seduced, if he was as handsome," Kiera murmured. "And why she would wait."

"Do not tell Alexander that. He thinks his mother fooled herself for far too long. She was living in a dream, and even when his father came, so cold and aloof, she did not wake up. Instead, she humiliated herself. He told me once that she was like a dog whose master kicks it again and again and again, and still it comes sniveling back."

"But I thought he wanted to please his father," Isabelle said.

"He wanted what his father promised if his father was pleased," Denis clarified.

"The knighthood and estate and the chance to inherit," Isabelle explained for Kiera.

Denis nodded. "*Oui*. After his father left, staying for only that day and the night—in his mother's bed, and whatever you do, do not tell Alexander I revealed *that*!—she became more determined that he must be worthy. It was only after this that she sold herself, to earn the money for a sword and armor and a horse. That sword he carries now is the one she bought for him. He hated that she would do that, but what could he do, a little boy, except excel, and when he had his knighthood and his estate, look after her?" Denis sighed. "She died when he was twelve. All she had managed to purchase was the sword. The rest he earned the money for himself and he found an ancient knight willing to train him. Old Sir James could barely walk or breathe." Denis shrugged. "But when a man is keen to learn, he can learn from any teacher."

Denis rose and smiled down at Kiera. "So you see, *ma petite*, why he does not want you to excuse a man who will hurt you."

Kiera choked back a little sob and turned her face away. "Will you . . . will you thank him for helping me?" she whispered.

Denis came around the bed so that she had to see him, and a compassionate look softened his brown eyes as he squatted down so that he was face to face with her. "You are a beautiful, kind and loving woman," he whispered as he tucked a lock of hair behind her ear. He smiled tenderly, a different look from his usual merry grin. "You deserve a better man who will treat you well. And of course I shall pass your message on to my friend."

"Thank you."

He rose. "A word, if you please, my lady," he said to Isabelle.

She nodded. "I'll be right back, Kiera. You rest while I add my thanks to Denis's message for Alexander."

When they were outside the closed door, Denis regarded her with an intensity she found unnerving. "If Osburn had struck *you*, Alexander would have killed him. He cares for you more than you know."

"He has no feelings for me beyond what I am worth in trade," she replied, telling herself that was so.

"I would it were so, my lady," Denis said woefully, "for things would be simpler for him then. He has borne much and been disappointed many times. I would spare him pain if I could, because of the pain he spared me, so I ask you to be gentle with him."

"You are speaking of the man who abducted me," she reminded the Gascon, and herself. "Why should I have any mercy for the man who kidnapped me?"

"Because he deserves it, and because he cares for you more than he is willing to admit, even to himself. I would even say he loves you."

Oh God, this could not be! This must not be! Denis had to be wrong. Alexander DeFrouchette *couldn't* love her. Nor could she love him. It was improbable, impossible, unthinkable. Whatever she thought she felt for him, unless it was hate and anger, it had to be wrong.

She had to escape him and this place. Soon. Tonight. Before Oswald came and revealed who she really was. Before desire for her captor made her do something she would surely regret for the rest of her life.

Once she was away from here—and Alexander DeFrouchette—all would be as it was. She would be free in every way.

She abruptly opened the door and went back into the chamber where the weeping Kiera waited.

With a grunt, Isabelle removed the last of the loosened stones in her chamber wall late that night. The space thus created was small, but large enough for her to crawl through. Her arms and legs would be covered, so she would not be too badly scratched by the rough stones.

It had started to rain that evening, so she would be soaked before this night was through—but the rain meant clouds covered the moon. Between the rain and the darkness and the guards' desire to stay warm and dry by huddling in sheltered spots on the wall walk, there was less chance that she might be spotted climbing down the wall, or so she planned.

Whether the rain continued or not, she had to leave tonight.

Hoping her makeshift rope would hold, Isabelle knotted one end around the post of the bed, which she had slowly, carefully and quietly pushed close to the window. The other end she shoved through the loophole.

The rope disappeared into the darkness. If she

had guessed correctly, it would be nearly long
enough to reach the wall walk. If she had not . . .

She wouldn't think about that.

For her final preparation, she reached back and
pulled the back hem of her skirt through her legs,
then tucked it into her girdle, so that her skirt was
like a baggy pair of breeches. This way, her feet
would not get entangled in her skirt and her knees
would be covered as she crawled backward out of
the hole.

She took one quick look around the chamber. After this, if she was successful, she would never see
Alexander or Denis or Kiera again. She would never
see Osburn and those women and the Brabancons
again, either, she reminded herself, subduing any
hint of regret.

Pressing her lips together with grim determination, she grabbed hold of her rope, then, with repeated silent pleas to God for help and strength, she
began to crawl out.

Her feet dangled in the air until her waist was at
the edge of the wall and the window. She forced
down the bile of fear and inched further back until
she was able to get the soles of her feet against the
wall. She eased the rest of her body outside.

The rain pelted her bare head and soaked her
gown before she had gone another foot. The rope
was already hurting her hands.

If only she had gloves. And a hood. Water
dripped off her forehead and into her eyes.

How far above the wall walk was she? She didn't
know and didn't want to look down to find out, as
long as the rope didn't end too far above it and none
of the guards spotted her.

And she could hold on long enough. Her hands were chafed and her arms ached after only this little way.

She forced herself to ignore the discomfort. She had to escape. She had put it off too long as it was. What if Oswald came tomorrow? What if what she felt for Alexander was—

She would not think about Alexander as she crept slowly down the wall. She must think about Allis. And home.

The rope jerked, and one section of the braiding went slack, as if it had been cut or torn up above. She raised her head, but in the rain, she could see nothing.

The strand must have ripped on one of the stones. What if the others did, too? A swift, sickening glance showed that she was nowhere near the wall walk yet, and if the rope broke. . . .

She fought the panic surging through her. She must think.

But her arms felt like they were being pulled from their sockets. Her hands were raw.

Then, as suddenly as the strand had gone slack, somebody began hauling up on the rope.

Somebody strong, for he was pulling her with it.

She couldn't go down and she didn't want to go back. She wanted to go home.

She stifled a shriek as her rain-slicked hands slid further down the rope. It was only a few inches, but she foresaw her bloody death on the stones below. A sob choked her, for she knew she really had no choice. She had to go back, or she would surely fall. Gripping the rope, she began to walk slowly up the wall as whoever was in her chamber pulled her up.

Another section of the braiding slackened. Only one strand made of braided strips kept her from falling and dashing her brains out on the stones below.

"Oh, God," she cried, the words both prayer and plea, quickly lost in the driving rain. "Oh God, help me!"

She reached the bottom of the window. One hand holding the rope, she desperately reached in to get a grip on the inside edge.

A strong hand took hold of her and hauled her into the chamber.

Alexander enveloped her in a powerful embrace. He was warm and solid and strong, and she held on to him tightly.

"My love, my love, you could have killed yourself!" he murmured against her hair.

He kissed the top of her head. Then he drew back a little and lightly kissed her forehead. Her cheeks. Her eyelids. He brushed gentle, feathery kisses over her face.

Until he found her mouth.

Chapter 14

She returned his passionate kiss with fervent and desperate need. She wanted to share his strength, to feel his muscular body holding her, to know that she was safe.

His hands caressed her, stroking away the worst of her trembling. As he continued, his mouth still moving over hers, her panic dissipated, replaced by a yearning different from the need for comfort and protection. His body and his kiss promised so much more than that . . .

Unable to resist, not wanting to fight anymore, she gave herself up to the passion he inspired. Leaning into him, she, too, stroked and caressed, and parted her lips, opening herself to him as a flower opens to the summer sun.

His tongue slid inside her mouth, swirling about hers and enflaming her more, calling forth the torrid craving she had tried for so long to bury and deny.

No more. Not now. Now, she was aware only of

him, this man who had summoned forth all the longings of her woman's heart, who had become not her captor but her savior.

The man she wanted above all others.

As she moaned softly from the excitement he created, the blood throbbed through her, the rhythm primitive and vibrant and demanding. His hand moved to cup her breast, and her breath caught as his thumb brushed over her hardened nipple thrusting against the rough wool of her gown. With his other hand, he pressed her buttocks toward his hips, so that she was against him even more, feeling the length and strength of him through his clothing.

He aroused her in ways she had never dreamt. He was pure male, and in his arms, she was a woman to be desired. Passionately. Completely.

More, he made her feel absolutely necessary, like air and sun and food.

She slipped her hand beneath his wool tunic and up the bare skin of his back, the rises and valleys of his muscles a terrain she had to explore. His skin was hot and tight, and his muscles rippled with every move.

Leaning into him, she brought her hand forward and stroked his chest. Her fingertips discovered the hairs encircling his nipple, and she lightly brushed the pebbled nub.

He groaned. She leaned farther, grinding her hips against him. Responding, he pressed harder, so that it felt as if no clothing existed between them.

Clasped against his powerful body, tension built within her, a tension she had never felt before—a wonderful, tight anticipation that compelled her to thrust against him, while his long, lean and supple fingers continued to pleasure her breasts.

And then he stopped kissing her. He pushed her bodice aside, so that her breasts was free. Bending, he sucked her nipple into his mouth and swirled his tongue around the tip.

With a cry, the tension within her exploded. Her knees buckled as wave after wave of incredible release throbbed through her. In all her life, she had never felt anything like this. Never.

A thought skimmed across the surface of her pleasure-clouded mind. If he could do this clothed, what would she feel if they made love?

Alexander continued to hold her close as the waves of blissful ease receded and died.

"Oh, Allis," he murmured as his lips trailed across her cheek before capturing her earlobe.

He had said the name that was not hers, and she was called back to harsh reality.

She pushed him away, then backed up until she hit the side of the hole in the wall. She was not Allis. She was Isabelle—and he was the son of Rennick DeFrouchette. He had abducted her. She was his prisoner still. He was her jailer, her guard, the man responsible for her captivity and she must *not* forget that.

No matter what her heart desired, and even if she never again felt such intense, burning passion for another man, this could not be. She was Lady Isabelle of Montclair, and he was the son of their enemy.

She could not love him. She must not love him. She was wrong to love him and to be in his arms like this.

The cold, wet air brought her more to her senses, and she saw his tunic damp where she had pressed her shameless body against it as if she were one of the whores in the hall below. "What are you doing?"

He blinked, like a man dazed in brilliant sunlight after coming out of a dark building.

"Get out."

Lightning flashed, and she saw his face fully. He was shocked and uncertain, taken aback by her action and her words.

The thunder rolled up in the hills as he took a step toward her. "No."

She must and would conquer her traitorous body, her traitorous heart, and him. "You took advantage of my weakness."

"I would never call you weak."

"I nearly fell and was grateful that you saved me."

"So your response was mere gratitude—or was your embrace another attempt to win my assistance? Perhaps you will now ask me to find you a stouter rope."

Her hands splayed against the walls, she inched away from him. "No! I told you, I was overcome."

"As was I. Obviously."

With quick, agitated movements he gathered up what was left of her rope and untied the knot holding it to the bedpost. "My heart nearly stopped when I entered this room and saw that hole. I was sure you had plunged to your death, until I realized the bed had been moved and saw this. You are a very clever woman, but this would never have held your weight."

He surveyed the stones she had taken out of the wall and piled on the floor. "You are even stronger than I thought." He crouched down and pinched some dust on the side of one of them, then rubbed it between his fingers. "I should have guessed. This mortar was poorly mixed. This wall could have fallen in at any time, if the wind was very strong."

He straightened and dusted off his hands. "You gave me your word that you would not try to escape again. You could have broken your skull had you fallen onto the wall walk."

He came to stand in front of her. "There was no need for this desperate act, my lady," he said, his intense gaze searching her face, her eyes, as if he was trying to penetrate her mind. "Your husband will pay and you will be returned to him. Or is there some reason you think your husband may not pay the ransom?"

"Of course he will. He loves me."

Alexander took hold of her shoulders. "Say that again."

"That Connor loves me? Of course he does."

He shook his head. "No, he does not. You know it as well as I, for I hear your doubt in your voice. Your husband may have loved you once, but no longer. There is something between your sister and your husband, something far too intimate to be the love between a man and his sister-in-law. I saw it when I was there."

She had to maintain the ruse. Who could say what he might do if she told him the truth now? "He does love me!"

Alexander's lips jerked up in a sardonic smile as another bolt of lightning flashed. "I lived with a woman who deluded herself for too long not to recognize that same delusion in another. I thought you were an intelligent woman, but I see now you are all the same—blinded by love and devotion to men who do not deserve it."

"Of course there is nothing improper between them." She fled to the center of the room.

"Oh, yes, there is, my lady," he said, following her, his tread as soft and deliberate as a barn cat stalking a mouse. "So, this is the end of your great passion. This is the kind of man the wonderful, the marvelous Sir Connor turns out to be. Why, your husband is no better than Osburn. You would have done better, perhaps, to marry my father, after all."

"You know *nothing* of what is between Connor and my sister and me."

"So you trust him to ransom you?"

"Yes, I do!" she cried. "He loves me!"

"Then why did you embrace me with so much passion?" He circled her like a ship caught in a slow whirlpool, and she was the center. "Your marriage is a sham, and that is why there is such heat and desire in your lips when they meet mine. That's why you allowed me to pleasure you. How long has it been since he made you limp with release, my lady? How long since he heard you gasp like that? Perhaps he never has and that is why you were so eager for me to pleasure you. Perhaps you would like me to do it again."

"No!"

He halted in front of her, tall and powerful and certain. "I don't believe you."

"I hate you!"

His voice a purr, he ran his hand up her arm. "Do you, when this man you claim to love betrays you for another, and that your own sister? Does he desire you still, the great Sir Connor? Or does he come to your bed out of duty?"

His light touch stirred her as much as his kiss, and it must not—but she could not tell him to stop. He was right; she didn't love Connor, although he did not know the real reason why. She never had entertained more than a girlish admiration for her brother-in-law that was nothing like her feelings for Alexander DeFrouchette.

Still stroking her, he sidled closer. She closed her eyes, and she could feel his breath warm on her cheek.

Tell him to stop. Make him go.

I cannot. I want him too much.

So she stayed silent, while every part of her body tingled and quivered and waited . . . waited . . . waited.

"Perhaps he does not even visit your bedchamber at all anymore," he murmured. His hips brushed against hers, and her whole body wanted to melt against him. "Is that why there have been no children?"

His left arm encircled her waist and pulled her hard against him, while his right cupped the back of her head. His mouth captured hers, his lips moving with sure deliberation, demanding that she respond.

She did, her body firing like dry tinder to an open flame. Her blood sang and every muscle tensed, aching for the release only he, with his lips and hands and magnificent body, could give. "Allis, my Allis, you want me as much as I want you."

Allis. Not Isabelle. A reminder that no matter what she felt, this must not be.

"You don't know me! You don't know what I want!" she cried, pushing him away.

More lightning flashed, and she saw an expression that would haunt her forever—eyes full of accusation, of sorrow, of loss and pain, as if a trusted friend had stabbed him in the back.

Tell him the truth. Tell him who you are.

The thunder rolled, another bolt brightened the room, and in that short space, his sorrow had departed, replaced by something dead and cold in the blue depths of his eyes, which became as Rennick DeFrouchette's eyes had always been.

"Put back those stones, or Osburn may decide that cell is the only place that will hold you," he commanded as he picked up her rope and marched to the door. He whirled around to face her before he departed. "I hope you are happy in your delusion, my lady, and that your husband will pay."

"If you do not stop, you are going to wear away that blade until it is nothing more than a dagger," Denis noted the next morning as he warily watched his friend rub his sword blade with hard, brisk strokes of the sharpening stone.

Alexander's only response was to frown more deeply and keep polishing, even if his friend's remark was not without merit. But he had to do something other than think about last night and remember her passion. Her embrace. Her denials of what he knew was true.

His confusion. His pain. His soul-searing realization that he had deluded himself into thinking she was different from other women.

And most disturbing of all, the stunning, horrible conclusion that he had been in a dream as pleasant—and false—as the one his mother had harbored.

All love was a kind of delusion, he snarled to himself, a dream based on hope and desire. He had learned that hard lesson once and for all.

"You look exhausted, too," Denis noted. "Perhaps you should stop sleeping outside her door. The Brabancons are too afraid of you to go near her anyway."

Even after their confrontation last night, and although he was rightfully and furiously angry with her, he had still slept outside the lady's door. Despite what had happened, he wasn't willing to risk that some Brabancon or Osburn would try to rape her—and he wanted to be certain she put the stones back in place.

He had listened to her do it, the sounds like those that had first aroused his suspicion, the noises familiar from his days as a mason's helper. Many a time he had helped slowly push stones into place.

She would probably be as tired as he was this morning—a small punishment for what she had attempted to do.

Denis began to fold his blanket. "Well, it is dry there, at least. I tell you, I thought I was going to wake up drowned from the storm. Thank God it has passed."

Alexander nodded. The courtyard had been full of puddles in the dawn's light, and there were still clouds, but the sun would soon burn the moisture away.

"Are you going to eat this morning, my friend? If you don't go soon, there may be nothing left."

Alexander picked up a cloth and wiped down his blade, finished for now. He would find something else to do, and he wasn't hungry. "Later."

"She's probably eaten long ago and is back in her chamber."

"Who?" He did not want to talk about Sir Connor's wife, or admit that he was upset about her, or even thinking of her.

Denis put his blanket down on his pile of straw. "The lady—who else?"

Alexander sheathed his sword, stood up and stretched. "I don't care if she's eaten or not."

"*Non*, of course not. How silly of me to suggest that you care about anything the lady does." Denis sat down on his folded blanket and regarded Alexander gravely. "Before you run away from me—"

"I'm not running." To show that he was not, Alexander sat down again.

"Very well, you are not. Alexander, my friend, when we leave this place, I want to ask Kiera to come with us."

Alexander nearly groaned out loud. He had hoped he was wrong about Denis's growing affection, seeing emotions that were merely the inward reflection of his own for Lady Allis.

Perhaps he should have spoken of this sooner, to spare his friend the pain of the inevitable. "She won't. She'll stay with Osburn to the end, whatever it is."

From his expression, Denis obviously did not agree. "You cannot judge all women by your mother, Alexander. At present she may feel trapped, and as if she has no choice. If she is given one, I think she will come."

"If she persists in thinking that he loves her, she won't."

"I do not know if she believes that, or not."

Alexander studied his friend. He wasn't sure how to proceed without hurting Denis, but if Denis must be hurt, better he should do it fast and clean, like the cut from a sharp weapon compared to the tear of a dull one. "Denis, do you think she feels any affection for you in return?"

His friend flushed and did not meet his gaze. Instead, he picked at the frayed edge of his blanket. "The important thing is to get her away from that brute."

"I don't disagree," Alexander replied. "I just don't want you to get your hopes up, only to see them dashed if she doesn't care for you that way."

Denis stopped fiddling with the thread. "I know you mean well, my friend, but I cannot help how I feel any more than you can. If I am not successful, we can console one another, eh?"

Alexander got to his feet. "I don't know what you're talking about."

With lithe speed, Denis was at the door before Alexander, who couldn't believe the intent look on his friend's face. "If I have a hopeless passion, I am not the only one. You can lie to yourself all you want, Alexander, but I know that you care for that woman."

Angry at Denis for guessing his innermost feelings, and angrier at himself for still having them, Alexander shoved Denis, sending him staggering back. "What does it matter what I feel? She has to go back to her husband, and that's the end of it!"

As Alexander strode out of the tower, he heard the Brabancons crying out a challenge to a party on the road beyond the castle. He came to an abrupt halt.

Was it friend, or foe? Had Sir Connor hunted them down, after all?

He prepared to draw his sword, then he heard the answer to the guard's challenge. It was the voice that had talked him into this disastrous affair—that of the traitorous and deceitful Lord Oswald himself.

Alexander's blood burned with anger. At first he had been so thrilled to meet this man, who had offered him a form of justice; now Alexander wished he had never seen him. He wished he had commanded Oswald to take himself off the moment the man had spoken of his father.

A party of at least twenty soldiers heavily armed and clad in chain mail entered the courtyard through the large wooden gate. At the head of them, riding a fine mare that seemed a delicate creature to carry one of his girth, rode Lord Oswald.

One of the serving wenches who had been watching by the well rushed into the hall, no doubt to alert Osburn and the others that they had visitors. The Brabancons who had been lounging around the courtyard in the sun recognized a man of power and position, even if they might not know exactly who he was, and snapped to attention or tried to look busy. Some disappeared inside the closest building. The men on the wall walk suddenly peered out beyond the castle as if an attack were imminent and they were seeking the first sign of enemies moving closer.

Lord Oswald wore a cloak against the damp sea air. As his escort reined in their horses, he threw it over his beefy shoulder prior to dismounting. His men also dismounted, and the noise of the jingling bridles and mail filled the yard.

Ignoring the commotion, Oswald's gaze scanned the courtyard and lighted on Alexander. "Alexander, my friend!"

The man was here and that could not be helped, but Alexander was not pleased to see him, and he would not pretend otherwise. However, a summons was a summons, so Alexander went toward the former nobleman. As he did, he saw that Oswald's clothes, which had once been very fine, were showing definite signs of hard wear. The bright green cloak was mud stained, and the fur lining had come away in some places. His boots were scuffed, and his long tunic was frayed at the hem.

Perhaps Oswald needed the ransom money as much as he did, or even more. Alexander, after all, was used to living frugally.

He inclined his head. "My lord."

"You have the lady?"

"Yes, my lord."

Oswald's broad face, which was thinner than Alexander remembered, beamed with delight, while his eyes brightened with a greed that was very like his son's.

To think he had once believed Osburn to be a better man than his father.

"I hope she has not given you too much trouble," Oswald said, regarding Alexander as if he were truly concerned.

"It would have been beneficial if we had been told of her courage and spirit," Alexander replied. "She tried to escape more than once."

"Well, I knew you would be a match for her." Oswald clapped a plump hand on Alexander's shoulder, making him wince, and not with pain. He didn't want the man touching him, or even standing that close. When Oswald steered Alexander toward the hall, Alexander wordlessly pulled away.

"Your father would have been a match for her, too," Oswald said, "if he hadn't been so besotted by her. Where is she now?"

"In her chamber in the tower."

The man slid him a sly, yet searching, glance. "I trust you have been immune to her considerable charms."

"Yes."

"And my son?"

"He has other amusements to keep him occupied."

Oswald's chortle rumbled out of his barrel chest. "I daresay he does! But I am glad to hear it nonetheless. Lady Allis could probably charm Richard into making her his queen, if she wished it—and if Richard liked women." Oswald looked around the battlements, and not simply to see the gulls wheeling overhead. His beady-eyed gaze was far too shrewd for that. He was surely checking the fortifications as well as the men guarding them, as the lady had.

"Osburn should come out to greet me," he noted after a moment.

"It is early in the day, my lord," Alexander answered. "Perhaps he is not yet out of bed."

Oswald laughed again, but this time, beneath the apparently jovial acceptance, Alexander heard disgust. "He's probably drunk again. It's always wine and women with him."

"You might have warned me about that, too, my lord."

Oswald didn't seem to hear as they reached the door to the hall. He waited expectantly until Alexander opened it for him, then he led the way like a conquering hero, leaving Alexander to follow like a faithful acolyte.

Alexander had never been more tempted to stab a man in the back in his life.

Surprisingly, not a single Brabancon or serving wench was in sight, until Kiera peered around the screen. Her face was still bruised, and her cut lip looked sore.

Without a word, she ducked behind it again.

"Osburn!" Oswald shouted, and this time, there was nothing at all jovial in his tone.

His son came stumbling around the screen, and Alexander smirked at the sight of Osburn's cheek bruised by his blow. It was no more than Osburn deserved for his treatment of both Kiera and Lady Allis, and even considerably less. Still, it was some measure of retribution.

He watched with undisguised scorn as Osburn came to a tottering halt before his father, straightening and pulling down his tunic. Alexander suspected the only reason he was dressed at all was because of Kiera's efforts, for it was clear the man was still too dazed from sleep and drink to do much for himself.

"Father," he said, bowing. Then his pale face contorted with agony and he lurched to the hearth, where he threw up.

"My son." After his sardonic greeting, Oswald went to the nearest chair—furthest from the hearth—and sat. Alexander stayed near the door.

Wiping his mouth on his sleeve, Osburn faced his father. "I-I wasn't expecting you today."

"Obviously." Oswald nodded at the chair opposite him. "Sit before you fall down."

Osburn did, gratefully slumping into the chair.

"Aren't you going to offer me some wine?"

Alexander thought Osburn was going to be sick again at his father's suggestion, but he managed to control himself, or at least his stomach. "Kiera!" he bellowed, sounding very like his father. "Bring us some wine!"

The girl appeared and scurried toward the kitchen without raising her head, like a mouse frightened out of its hole. Oswald glanced at her but said nothing about her as he turned his cold, beady eyes back onto his son. "What news of Sir Connor and the ransom?"

"He'll pay."

Oswald smiled. "I thought he would." Then he sobered, and his heavy brows furrowed. "Where is Heinrich?"

Osburn's voice was very faint as he answered. "He is dead."

His father started, then stared. "*Dead?*"

Osburn nodded, and his voice was even softer when he said, "Lady Allis killed him."

Oswald fell back against the chair, making it creak dangerously. "*She* killed him? How?"

"With a rock. She hit him on the head, from behind. To protect *his* friend." Osburn pointed an accusing finger at Alexander, who kept his expression blank.

Oswald looked at Alexander and raised an inquisitive brow. "Is that so?"

"Denis was defending himself, and the lady came to his aid."

To Osburn's obvious chagrin, his father started to laugh until his prodigious belly shook. "Poor Heinrich! What a way for a Brabancon to die! The shame would have killed him if the blow hadn't." When he stopped laughing, he again regarded his son, and all trace of good humor disappeared. "Still, the man was a valuable asset."

"Y-you won't have to pay him the rest of his fee," Osburn said, his voice so high with anxiety that he sounded like a rat with its tail caught in a trap.

"That's true," his father answered, apparently somewhat mollified. "And I see the other Brabancons are still here. What of Ingar? I hope the Lady Allis didn't scuttle his ship and send him to a watery grave, or we'll have his whole family after us for denying him Valhalla."

"No, no, Father," Osburn answered. "He and his men are camped on the beach. He's not happy about staying on land during the summer season, but he's still here."

"Thank God for that, at least."

Kiera appeared with the wine. The dented silver carafe and two silver goblets rattled on the tray as she carried it in trembling hands and set it on a table. While she poured out wine for the two men, Oswald ran a measuring gaze over her. "So, this is how you've been spending your nights, is it, my son. She'd be pretty if not for the bruises."

Kiera blushed bright red, and Alexander was sure

he saw her eyes shine with unshed tears of humiliation. "That is your son's handiwork," Alexander
said.

As Kiera handed him a goblet, Oswald stopped
looking at her to glance at Alexander.

But he said nothing about Kiera's injuries to his
son. Instead, he spoke to Kiera. "Fetch Lady Allis."

Chapter 15

A lexander heard the lady's footsteps before he saw her. Steeling himself, he turned to see her scan the men gathered in the hall. For a brief moment, her shining gaze met his and held it until he looked away.

He wouldn't look at her again if he could help it, he vowed, as his feelings for her struggled back into his consciousness and demanded that he heed them.

Trying to subdue them, he focused on the nobleman and his son—and got the greatest shock of his life. Lord Oswald was staring at Lady Allis as if she were a ghost. Then his face reddened almost to purple, and he slowly got to his feet.

"Isabelle?"

She inclined her head with haughty dignity. "My lord."

Alexander could not believe his ears. Her name was *Isabelle*?

Oswald whirled on his son. "You fool, what have

you done? This is not Lady Allis! This is Isabelle, her sister, you dolt!"

Alexander felt as if a mace had crashed into his head. Yet if she was Lady Allis's sister, that would explain so much. The intimate looks back at Bellevoire.

And why he did not believe she loved Sir Connor.

Why hadn't she told him?

Because she was your prisoner. Because you stole her away. Because being an intelligent woman, she would fear what dishonest men would do if they realized they had erred.

To her, you are such a man.

Oswald grabbed Osburn's tunic and hauled him to his feet. The action jolted Alexander out of his stunned immobility, while Kiera squeaked with alarm, and shocked mutters arose from the Brabancons and serving wenches.

They did not need an audience. "Get out," Alexander ordered them, not waiting for Oswald or Osburn to do so.

"Yes, go," Oswald seconded, releasing his son.

The women and soldiers quickly obeyed as Osburn, coughing and spluttering, tried to regain his balance. Kiera scurried behind the screen. As for Lady Isabelle, she did nothing at all except stand there, resolute and dignified.

As distraught as a chastised child in the midst of a tantrum, Osburn jabbed his finger at Alexander. "It was *him*! *He* brought her! *He* made the mistake." He pointed to his chest. "*I* stayed at the ship."

"Yes, you did," Alexander agreed. "My friend and I took all the risk and went into Bellevoire. You stayed in the ship and drank."

"I was keeping watch!" Osburn screeched, flecks of spittle at the corner of his lips. "Don't you try to blame me!" He looked back at his father. "I've never seen Lady Allis. You always made us stay at home. You never let us travel or visit, or go to court. How could I know he'd got the wrong woman?"

Not bothering to answer his son, Oswald turned his stern visage toward Alexander. "Explain to me how this happened."

"Since this may take some time, my lord," the lady quite calmly interrupted, "I believe I shall sit down."

And so she did, without waiting for either approval or censure.

"Let us *all* sit down," Oswald said with some semblance of his normal, seemingly kindhearted manner, as if he was beginning to regain his self-restraint.

But now Alexander saw that manner for what it was: a mask.

Osburn sullenly threw himself into the chair beside his father. Alexander sat on the bench nearest him, by the wall, until Oswald imperiously pointed at the chair beside the lady. "There, Alexander, so that I can hear you."

I am part of a noble circle at last, Alexander thought as he did as he was commanded. It was a mockery of what he had dreamt of for so long, but he had brought this upon himself by aligning himself with such men.

He saw with a horrible clarity how Oswald had used him, working on his wounded pride and shame, luring him with what he most wanted. Preying on his weakness, until Oswald got what he wanted.

Was it any wonder that with such confederates, his grand plan to have vengeance on the man he believed had wronged him lay in ruins?

Even the lady wasn't who he thought she was—a jest of God, perhaps, or the ultimate proof that he was nothing but a blind fool, after all.

Oswald laced his fingers over his stomach. "Well, Alexander, explain."

He did, without emotion or inflection, like a child reciting a lesson he had learned by rote. "When I saw her in the market at Bellevoire, it was obvious by her dress and manner that she was a noble lady. Since she looked precisely as you described and was talking and laughing with Sir Connor in what seemed an intimate manner, I believed she was Lady Allis. You never told me the lady had a sister." He allowed more than a hint of disapproval to creep into his voice. "Indeed, my lord, there were *many* things you never told me. Nor did she say she was *not* Lady Allis before we sailed away."

"What would have happened if I had?" she demanded of Oswald, ignoring Alexander. "I doubt I would have been set free. Your son would probably have killed me or sold me to Ingar."

Alexander felt a small measure of gratitude that she charged Osburn with being capable of such things, not him.

"Then you might have gone after Allis again," she continued, "and that I could not risk."

Oswald slid Alexander a shrewd, searching look. "Tell me, Alexander, how was it that this grave error was not discovered when you took the ransom demand to Bellevoire?"

"Neither Sir Connor nor Lady Allis ever gave any indication that the woman I was speaking of was not Sir Connor's wife."

"You see?" Osburn cried, straightening. "I had nothing to do with it. I didn't know. I kept her here just as you told me to and—"

"Shut your mouth, Osburn," his father snapped as he rubbed his chin. "Your sniveling is making my head ache. An error has been made, and now I must consider what is to be done."

Sweat trickled down Alexander's back. He did not fear for what might happen to him if he incurred Oswald's displeasure; he didn't particularly care. His concern was for Allis—Isabelle.

He glanced at her, seemingly so calm and resolute, but he knew her well enough to note the extreme stiffness in her posture and the defiant thrust of her chin, which kept it from trembling. She was afraid and trying mightily to hide it.

I have given my word that I would keep you safe, my lady, he silently promised, determined to keep his word so he could retain some small measure of self-respect. *I will do so to my last breath. And I will get you home.*

"Why must anything be done?" he asked Oswald. "Sir Connor knew, if we did not, that we had his sister-in-law and not his wife, yet he has offered to pay the ransom nonetheless. Why change anything now? I shall take her back, collect the ransom and return here, where we will split it as we agreed and go our separate ways."

"Yes, why change anything?" Osburn cried eagerly, obviously forgetting his father's command to hold his tongue. "Of course he'll pay."

Once again Oswald looked at his son, but this time, his gaze was more speculative than annoyed as he ostensibly addressed Isabelle. "You are not yet married, are you, Isabelle? Or even betrothed? I'm sure your dowry will be considerable." Oswald steepled his fingers and rested them against his full lips as he mused aloud. "Ransom, dowry, what does it matter what it is called?"

Alexander couldn't breathe as the import of the man's words hit him like a slap across his face.

Her face flushed, Lady Isabelle shot to her feet. "I would rather die than marry your son!"

A rage and horror nearly blinding in its force filled Alexander, and he stood so abruptly his chair fell backward, crashing against the stones of the floor. "It was ransom that we planned," he reminded Oswald, his words fierce and full of the ire sweeping through him. "A temporary captivity—and she was not to be harmed!"

Oswald smiled indulgently, as if they were a pair of squabbling children. "Ah, the excitability of youth! And you, my lady, so quick to choose death! Really, my dear, you should think before you speak. There would be advantages to marrying my son." His expression hardened. "The first, of course, is that you would not die."

He looked at Alexander, and the expression in his eyes altered to one of greedy conspiracy. "As for you, my young DeFrouchette, what does it matter what happens to her as long as you get your money, and I arrange for your knighthood—as we agreed?"

"I did not agree to *this*, and I will not be party to this change of plan."

"It doesn't matter what you think," Osburn said, his father's new scheme having revived his bravado.

Oswald paid his son no heed as he ran a long, slow gaze over Alexander. "You claimed that you were immune to the lady's charms. I was referring to Lady Allis, but this young lady has obvious temptations of her own. Your father thought so, too. Did she tell you how she offered to marry him in her sister's stead?"

Stunned, Alexander faced her. "Is this true?"

Her eyes blazed as she straightened her shoulders. "Yes. I offered myself to your father so that my sister would be free to marry the man she loves. Oswald can twist it and make my offer sound sordid, but that is the reason and I am not ashamed of it. I would do it again."

So it was true—and yet after hearing her explanation he was no longer surprised. She had the strength to make that kind of sacrifice, or any that she felt necessary.

"I think you will see the wisdom of living and becoming Osburn's wife," Oswald replied, smiling a little smile that was monstrous in its callousness. "After all, this marriage will guarantee that I will leave your sister and her husband and even that brat of a brother of yours alone. You would have my word on it, because we would be family then."

"I am not a fool to trust the word of a man like you."

Alexander did not, either.

"I am glad to hear it. What man wants a fool for a

daughter-in-law, especially when his son is fool enough already?"

Osburn muttered something, but his father continued without pause. "However, you have no choice but to trust me, for if you do not become my son's wife, you will die, and I will most certainly go after the rest of your family."

"I could kill your son as he slept."

"Father!" Osburn whined.

"Osburn, leave us. Do something useful. Go to the kitchen and make sure they're not burning the meat."

"You can't send me away—"

"I can and I will. Go!"

As the father and son glared at each other, the one old and powerful, the other young and weak, Alexander's hand moved toward the hilt of his weapon, tempted to strike them both down—but then how would he get the lady from this place, as he must? Even if he succeeded in killing Osburn and Oswald both, there were still the Brabancons in the courtyard and at the gate.

He could not abandon Denis, either. The Brabancons might kill him out of revenge, or Ingar might take him to sell as a slave.

After a moment's useless glaring, Osburn slunk away, heading toward the kitchen as his father commanded.

"Now, where were we?" Oswald asked brightly, as if they were discussing an upcoming feast or festival. "Ah, yes. Why all this fuss, Isabelle? You were willing to marry Rennick for your family's sake. What is so different here?"

"It was *my* decision to make."

Oswald shook his head as if she were a little girl making silly demands. "That is the trouble with women. They want to make decisions, although we all know they act with their heart, not their head. So much trouble could have been avoided if your sister had not betrayed Rennick with that Welshman."

"She fell in love with Connor, and it was not wrong of her to listen to her heart."

Oswald *tsk*ed. "But it was very convenient for her, and her lover, too, when Rennick was accused of being a traitor by Sir Connor and they were rewarded with his estate. Isn't that right, Alexander?"

Alexander no longer cared what had happened in the past. All he could think of was Lady Allis's—Isabelle's—future, and he could not bear the thought of her being forced to be Osburn's wife. To be his chattel. To share his bed.

Once more his hand moved toward the hilt of his sword, and again his hand itched to strike a fatal blow. "I have nothing to say about matters of the heart, my lord. I do about honor, though, and if you force this marriage, you will have broken faith with me. Think carefully, my lord, before you do that."

Oswald didn't bat an eye or lose that disgusting smile. "I remind you, DeFrouchette, I am still a powerful man and you are still the unacknowledged bastard son of a traitor to the king of England. If you break with me, that is all you will ever be. Are you willing to accept that, and all for the sake of the sister of the couple who destroyed your chance before?"

Silently, fervently, praying that Alexander would break his allegiance to Oswald, Isabelle held her breath as she waited for him to answer. She saw the struggle in his eyes, the very way he stood.

"No, my lord. As you so wisely point out, I would be a fool to pass up the opportunity you offer, and I have been made a fool enough already."

She sank back in her chair as he marched from the room, leaving her alone with the wolves. In spite of everything, she had hoped he would stand with her against Oswald. A foolish hope, obviously, and yet . . .

And yet she had forgotten that she had always been a prisoner here, a thing to be bargained for.

Oswald laughed with malicious glee as the door to the courtyard banged shut. "Poor fellow—he is so like his father, whom he hates so very much even though the man is dead. But then, I think you know that better than I, my lady."

She crossed her arms. "I don't know what you're talking about."

"No? Then he has not been swayed by your charms after all? Amazing. I would have said that like his late, unlamented father, he wanted very much to love and be loved. The baron's great weakness was his love for your sister even though she spurned him." Oswald's beady black eyes gleamed with more malice and triumph, and only her courage and defiance kept her from fleeing the room.

"But I digress," Oswald continued, folding his hands over his belly and speaking with a placidity that showed just how cold-blooded a man he was. "This is how it shall be, my dear. You will marry my son or I shall take the ransom and kill you. Then I will move to have my vengeance of your sister and her husband. Not right away, perhaps. Later. Maybe

I shall even spare them—but not their children. This is your chance to save them such anguish. You see, my dear?" He feigned moving a piece across a board. "Checkmate." His hand returned to rest. "You are a clever chess player, I know—more clever than you've ever let on." The corners of his lips curled up even more. "But you are not better than I."

She sat up straighter. "This is not a game, my lord. Either way, Connor will hunt you down and kill you."

"He can try. It will take some time, this hunting down, and by then, you might be with child."

Which would mean Osburn in her bed, making love with her.

She nearly threw up.

"Oh, it won't be as bad as all that. Osburn will do his best there whatever else he does and he's had plenty of experience," Oswald said in a way that made her feel even sicker. "One could say he's spent years practicing."

"You're disgusting, the pair of you!"

"Come, come, my dear, that's no way to address your future father-in-law."

She gripped the arms of the chair so hard that her nails dug into the wood. "I won't let him touch me!"

"Your *permission* will not enter into it. I must confess my son has had plenty of experience with unwilling women, too, or so I hear, and I do not doubt it. Do you?"

Isabelle choked back a sob, because she did believe it. Osburn surely enjoyed having a woman helpless beneath him, beaten into submission.

"I must encourage the dear boy to give it his best effort," Oswald said, leaning forward as much as his bulk would allow, "because you see, my dear, if you have children, they will be my blood, and by them my family will be restored to its rightful place at court."

Isabelle's whole body quivered with disgust, with fear, with rage, with righteous indignation. "If you had been an honorable man, you would not have betrayed your king and lost your place at court, as you so richly deserve."

Oswald waved his fat fingers dismissively. "Let us leave the question of guilt, shall we? In the end, it doesn't matter."

He put his hands on the arms of the chair and heaved himself to his feet. "What does matter is that if you do not marry my son, there will be death and retribution. If you do, there will be life and hope that I will stay my hand."

Defeat and despair washed over her. He had beaten her. She had no real choice. She had to agree. If she refused to marry Osburn, she would be ensuring that Oswald would act against her family immediately. If she agreed, his actions—which she was sure he would take one day, no matter what he promised—would at least be delayed. During that time, she could hope that Connor would find them and save her, or that she could escape.

She might have to wait until she was Osburn's wife before she could get away at last, she realized with a shiver of revulsion, but she would not give up. Not yet. She had managed so far; she would find the strength to continue with the hope of rescue, or liberty. Until then, she must do whatever she could to stay Oswald's hand, in any way she could, all by herself. "Very well, my lord. You win."

Oswald came toward her, a lascivious look in his dark eyes that made her tremble anew. She shrank back in her chair.

"You know, my dear," he said in a smooth and oily voice, "I thought it a pity Allis was betrothed to Rennick, and always rather regretted I never offered for her myself. I begin to think you will indeed be wasted on Osburn." He took her hands in his fat, pale ones and tugged her to her feet. "Perhaps I should marry you myself."

As terrible as marriage to Osburn seemed, she discovered there was something worse. "You already have a wife."

"She could die."

Never had she felt such a disgusting loathing for anyone, not even Osburn. Was there nothing this man would not do to satisfy his lust, whether for gain, or power, or to satisfy his own desire?

Yet she said nothing, because this man truly terrified her, in a way Alexander DeFrouchette never had. Alexander had told her he would not hurt her, and deep in her heart, she had believed him. He had meant it when he'd said he would protect her, whether from Osburn or Ingar or all the Brabancons. She had felt free enough with him to say what she thought, to speak her mind, even to upbraid him, while maintaining her pride and dignity. Alexander had given her that. Oswald would not.

"But no," Oswald murmured.

He let go of her hands, and she breathed again.

"I fear I would find you too distracting and, like Rennick, forget what is most important, and that is not the fleeting pleasure to be found in a woman's arms, however tempting." He pulled her arm through his and patted it companionably. "Now come, my dear. Let us find the future groom and tell him of his good fortune."

Chapter 16

Humming to himself, Denis crossed the courtyard, heading toward his quarters in the
tower. He had been in the stables, tending to a sick
horse and trying to avoid the men of Lord Oswald's
entourage, who seemed to be a better-dressed version of the Brabancons. Alexander was probably still
in the hall with the nobles, discussing the ransom
and the return of the lady to her home, and trying to
convince himself that he felt nothing for her.

Of all the men he had ever met, Alexander was
the most willfully blind, stubborn—

"*Mon Dieu!*" Denis gasped, staring at the sight
that met his eyes when he entered the ruined tower.
He couldn't have been more surprised if he had
found Hielda naked in his bed.

Denis had never seen Alexander look so upset. Indeed, he had never seen Alexander look upset at all.
Angry, certainly, stern, forbidding—but never like
this, as if all he felt was an all-consuming anguish.

"What is it?" Denis demanded. "What has happened? Is it the lady?"

"Then you don't know?"

"She's not hurt or . . . or dead?" Denis asked fearfully, his voice quavering—but that would explain Alexander's eyes.

"No, not hurt or dead."

Denis let out his pent-up breath. "Thank God. But then, what is it?"

In a few short sentences, his face settling back into its usual grim demeanor, Alexander told him of the lady's true identity and Oswald's change of plan.

His eyes as large and round as the wheels of a cart, Denis lowered himself to sit cross-legged on the edge of the straw, looking as stunned as Alexander had been. "She is not Lady Allis?" he repeated in a whisper as if trying to get that thought lodged in his brain.

"No, she is the lady's sister."

"Not married to another?"

Alexander tried not to think about that part of the revelation. "No. That is why Oswald came up with this other despicable plan."

"And it *is* terrible. *Diabolique!* So what do we do about it?" Denis asked. He regarded his friend warily, as if expecting him to announce that they should attack all the Brabancons by themselves and spirit her away.

Alexander was grateful that Denis was not ready to abandon him yet, and he was ashamed that he had gotten his only friend involved in this.

"I should have made you stay in Dieppe. Then you would be out of this mess—and it's only going to get worse," Alexander muttered as he opened the

door and peered outside to make certain nobody
was within earshot. He wouldn't be surprised to
find Hielda listening at the door.

Denis's grin was the first thing Alexander saw
when he turned back into the dim room. "If you had
left me in Dieppe, I would not have met Kiera, so say
no more about 'this mess.' I would not have missed
it, or her."

Alexander sat beside his friend and regarded
him gravely. "I will not let Oswald's plan proceed.
That is not what I agreed to, and I promised her she
would not be harmed. I intend to get Lady Allis—
Isabelle—out of here tonight."

Denis's eyes lit up. "Of course, and Kiera must
come with us."

As he'd made his plan walking across the courtyard, Alexander had feared that Denis would suggest this. It was not going to be easy to tell Denis that
the girl was too dangerous. "I don't think we can
risk telling her our plans, Denis."

An unusually stubborn look appeared on his
friend's face. "I trust her."

"Involving her in our escape could put us all in
danger. She may tell Osburn."

"When he is going to marry another? I think not."

Alexander did not raise his voice; instead, he
spoke with firm command. "She may love him still
and be willing to do anything to prove it, Denis, to
show him that she's worthy of his love—and that in-
cludes betraying us. That's a risk we cannot take."

Denis regarded Alexander with equal intensity.
"Alexander, have I ever asked anything of you before? Even when you saved my life, did I ask you to
intervene?"

Alexander subdued a sigh. Perhaps everyone harbored hopeless dreams and yearnings that logic and rational thought were powerless to destroy. "No, you never have."

"Then I am going to ask her. It is as simple as that. I do not think she will betray us, whether she stays or goes."

"What if she decides to stay?"

"Then so will I. I have hope that one day, she will see that Osburn does not really care for her, and on that day, she will need a friend."

His words compelled Alexander to persist. "You've been as good a friend to me as any man could ever ask, Denis, and that's why I don't want you to risk your life. That's what you'll be doing if you don't come with me. If we get away and you're still here, do you think Oswald will believe you knew nothing about our escape?"

Denis's features became innocence itself, and he spread his hands. "If I knew, why would I remain, my lord? That bastard deserted me! I should have known he was not to be trusted." Denis grinned. "You see? I will make him believe I knew nothing of your plans. After all, that is how Lord Oswald does things, is it not, by keeping most of his plans to himself? Surely he will believe that another man would do the same."

Denis's words and actions did not assuage Alexander's dread for his friend's safety. "He may not believe you. That butcher didn't."

"When someone has a cleaver about to chop off your head, it is difficult to lie well. I do not expect Lord Oswald to have a cleaver."

Still agitated and far from convinced, Alexander got to his feet and started pacing. "He might have a sword, and he probably wouldn't hesitate to use it. I don't like this, Denis. I don't want you dead."

Denis joined him, keeping up with Alexander's strides by taking two steps for every one of his friend's. "I don't want to be dead, either, but as you will not leave the lady, I will not leave Kiera. Besides, I think you are wrong to believe she has not seen the light about that drunkard. If she is given a chance to go, she may take it and gladly, even if she is not taken with me. I think the more important worry is, does Oswald have any suspicions of your feelings and intentions?"

As Alexander checked the door again, he gave up trying to make Denis see reason. Nobody could have convinced him to leave Isabelle behind, either. Who was he to say that Denis's unrequited devotion and determination to do what he felt was right was any less deeply felt than his own? "No. As far as he knows, I am still willing to do anything for money and a knighthood."

Denis looked impressed. "Excellent! So, what is the plan? I assume you are not thinking of simply escorting the lady to the stable, saddling some horses and riding out the gate with a wave of farewell?"

"The Brabancons are used to me standing guard outside the lady's door, so they will not question my presence there after she retires, nor will they wonder about my cloak, because I sleep in it. I will go there as always, but this time I shall have a rope beneath my cloak, and we'll climb down the tower wall from her chamber and meet you on the wall walk below."

Denis looked at him as if he'd gone mad. "Are you planning on shrinking like wool in steam, Alexander? You cannot fit through that loophole."

"The stones around the loophole are loose. We can enlarge the window that way. In fact, she's already been halfway down the wall herself. Her rope broke and she would have fallen if I hadn't heard her."

Denis sat down again with a thump. "When was this?"

"The night of the storm."

"And she chose *that* night—?"

"She might have succeeded, except for the rope."

Denis waggled his finger at his friend. "Which is *another* strange thing. Where on earth did she get a rope? One of us was watching her all the time! Is she a witch, that she conjured one out of thin air?"

"She made it from rags and her sheet, I think."

Denis stared as if he'd been stabbed. "Out of cloth?"

"Yes."

"I had no idea noblewomen were so clever, even that one."

"Neither did I," Alexander admitted. "But now you see that it can be done. We'll meet you—"

"And Kiera."

"And Kiera," Alexander conceded, "on the wall walk and then climb down the outer wall."

"How? We are not spiders."

"We'll have another rope."

"Where are we to get all this rope?" Denis asked, looking dubiously at Alexander, as if he expected Alexander to suggest he start making one.

"I am going to ask Ingar. He has extra rigging for

the sail that he can surely spare, if the price is right."

Denis's eyes narrowed. "What excuse are you going to give him for needing rope? He knows you do not have a ship that requires rigging."

"I'll tell him the truth." As his friend stared, Alexander slid down the wall so that he sat with his back against it. "He has to know what we're doing because he has to take us from here."

Denis looked sickened by that thought.

"We will not have horses," Alexander explained, "and attempting to steal them is far riskier than climbing down the walls. The Brabancons will have horses, so we can't get away on foot."

Denis rubbed his chin, then his forehead, then his nose as he took in all that Alexander said. "*Oui*, I agree that to go on foot when they are mounted is too dangerous."

"So it has to be by ship. If Ingar agrees, we should be out to sea before the Brabancons realize we've gone. They have no vessels of their own to chase us."

Frowning, Denis got to his feet. "You are worried about Kiera, but you would use the Norsemen? They are in Oswald's pay."

Alexander rose to face him. "I'll offer Ingar compensation, and we have no other choice. Nor do I think it will take much to convince Ingar. You didn't hear him when he brought me back from Bellevoire, Denis. He loves being at sea, and staying on land at Oswald's or Osburn's beck and call is not how he wants to be spending the summer months. I also think he doesn't like Lord Oswald any more than I do, even if he will take the man's money."

Denis gave him a skeptical look. "So he is bored and hates the man who pays him. That does not mean he will sail off with us in his ship." Sudden understanding lit his face. "Ah! You will give him part of the ransom!"

Alexander shook his head. "I won't have it. I dare not risk going anywhere near Bellevoire on my own if I have the lady with me. I'll set her free when we are close enough for her to make her own way safely to Bellevoire. It's that, or be captured."

Denis's brow furrowed with puzzlement. "Then how will you pay Ingar? We don't have many coins."

"I'm going to offer to join his crew and give him a portion of whatever I earn."

"You would do that? You would stay with that brigand and be one yourself?"

Alexander didn't meet his friend's astonished gaze. He didn't want Denis to see how deeply ashamed he was. "Why not? I have made myself an outlaw. I must live somehow."

His friend took him by the arms and spoke fervently. "The Norsemen are *savages*, Alexander. There must be something else you can do, another way to live. You could be a hired soldier for a lord in Europe. You are so skilled, they will not ask many questions."

Alexander raised his hard eyes. "So I would be a mercenary—killing for money like the Brabancons. If I must be a sword for hire, I will offer myself to Ingar and at least get us away from here."

"And what of me? Will you abandon me?"

"You can make a living as you did before. Nobody saw your face at Bellevoire. You did not take the ransom demand. I did the greater harm. You can be free, as you were before."

"To join up with ruffians and dishonest oafs who cheat me out of the day's takings."

Alexander's heart tore a little more as he regarded his friend. "Denis, please. Do not put your fate in my hands after we escape. I'm not worthy of the charge, as all of this has proven."

"You are my friend, Alexander."

"Then as my friend, please, do as I ask. I feel guilty enough for what I've already done."

Denis's eyes softened with both sympathy and understanding as he let go. "Very well. But if it must be so, will you not be honest with me?"

The words cut Alexander to the quick. "I have always been honest with you, Denis."

"Will you still try to deny that you care for this woman, Alexander? Will you tell me you do not love her?"

Unable to speak of the deepest, most secret matters of the heart even to Denis and even now, Alexander turned away and went to the door. "Ask Kiera to come with us if you must. I am going to speak to Ingar."

Alexander strode out of the tower. The Brabancons had collected into little groups in the courtyard, like gossiping women at a fair. As he walked past one such gaggle, one of them whispered something and the others started to snicker. It was not surprising they thought him a fool for taking the wrong woman. He was, and for more than that.

Nevertheless, he gave them a sharp, dismissive glance that momentarily silenced them.

When he reached the postern gate, the same two guards were on duty there. This time, they wisely made no move to stop him, or even issue a challenge. He trotted down the steps carved in the bluff.

Denis was right that making this request of Ingar was risky, but it was their best and only chance to successfully escape from this place, and to get the lady swiftly home, back to her sister and brother-in-law—not her loving husband.

Had she ever loved any man? Was there a man she wanted to be betrothed to? What would he be like?

Not like you.

He forced his thoughts back to Ingar. If the man did not agree, he didn't know what he would do.

Yes, he did. He'd kill Osburn. He'd be killed in turn, of course, but he would accept that fate as just punishment for his hand in this business, and for not making more certain of the men with whom he allied himself.

Surely, though, Ingar would agree. He must.

Alexander spotted Hielda crossing the beach toward the steps. The sly and proud way she smiled and swayed her hips when she saw him told him that she had not been in the Norse camp to exchange pleasantries, and she had no basket as if she had taken them any supplies. It was easy enough to guess what she had been doing there, and he suspected that she was now several coins richer.

As Hielda started up the steps toward him, he tried to remember if she had been part of that gawking group in the hall when Isabelle had made her appearance before Lord Oswald. He couldn't remember. He had been too shocked by what had come after to recall exactly who had been present.

If she had been, she would surely have told the Norsemen the news of the lady's real name and the proposed marriage. No doubt Ingar would think him a fool, too, but as long as Ingar thought him a fool with skills that made him worthy enough to be part of his crew, he would endure the jibes and mocking looks.

He paused and pressed back against the bluff to let Hielda pass by.

" 'Scuse me," she said as she rubbed against him far more than necessary. "Bit narrow here, ain't it?"

He could hear the chink of coins from somewhere between her heavy breasts, where she probably kept her purse when she was not earning more.

"I think you've done enough of that today," he said, trying to keep his annoyance and disgust at bay. "You could wear yourself out."

With a low, throaty chuckle, she said, "Worse ways to do it. You should find out."

Denis was going to tell Kiera; he was going to tell Ingar. Both of them might alert Oswald to the plan to escape, so it might be wise to suggest he had no such ideas in case it came down to one person's word against another's.

Barely able to keep his nostril from curling at her stench, he hauled her closer still. "Maybe I will."

Her eyes gleamed like a ferret's. "Now?"

Smiling with false intent, he shook his head. "I have business at the Norse camp."

"Tonight?"

He chucked her under the chin. "At night, I guard the lady. Come to the Gascon's quarters after you finish serving Lord Oswald and the others in the morning. I'll be waiting."

She gave him the most lascivious smile he had ever seen, and then grabbed him in a way that made him jump. "Why not now? What's so important you can't take a little time?"

He fought the urge to shove her away. "I want more than a quick tumble in the sheets."

Her brown eyes sparkled with greed, and she raised her face as if she was going to kiss him.

"How much do you want?" he asked before she could.

The talk of money grabbed her attention. Thank God.

She slid him a calculating glance. She would know the amount of the ransom soon to be paid and was surely figuring her worth based on that. "I'm good."

"I trust you will be."

"I'll be worth it."

"I expect so."

They negotiated the final amount for her services, and once her price was settled to her satisfaction— and he was quite sure she considered herself a clever negotiator— she seemed content enough to wait until the next day and went on her way.

He wanted to brush off his clothes and wash his hands as he continued down the steps and across the beach toward the cluster of tents with their dragon poles. Instead, he looked up at the sky, checking the weather and breathing in great gulps of fresh air, a blessed relief after Hielda's proximity. The sky was clear except for some high, thin white clouds. The water in the bay was fairly calm, but he could see foam on the sea beyond, where the wind was greater. It was not the stormy weather Ingar apparently preferred, but it looked promising for a speedy journey.

Recognizing Alexander, none of the Norsemen issued any challenges as he strode into their camp past a large pile of driftwood. The whole camp reeked of smoke from damp wood, salted fish, seaweed and the wet canvas of their tents slowly drying in the sun.

Obviously gambling, several of Ingar's crew crouched in a circle, the sound of the wooden dice in the leather cup unmistakable. A few more were practicing throwing their battle-axes at a stump set up as a target, and they were very accurate. Another man was fixing the strap on his shield, and three more stood near a pot, arguing about whatever was in it. One man sat on a log while another sat behind him, calmly picking the nits out of his friend's hair.

It was a cozy domestic scene—for Norsemen. Such was going to be his home for the rest of his days, if Ingar agreed to his bargain.

He didn't see Ingar anywhere in the camp or on his ship. That confused him, for he had expected Ingar to be bellowing orders or drinking ale and singing some ancient saga about valiant deeds that sent men to Valhalla to feast with the gods. Then he remembered Hielda.

He headed for what had to be Ingar's tent, for it was easily the biggest one in the encampment, and the poles outside were the most ornately carved and colorfully painted. "Ingar!" he called as he waited outside.

"What?" the Norseman's groggy voice called back. "Can't a man get some sleep?"

"It is Alexander DeFrouchette, and I have come to speak to you of an important matter."

The tent flap parted, and a half naked Ingar peered out at him. To Alexander's surprise, a large gold crucifix dangled from a wonderfully worked chain around his neck. "Well then, enter."

Alexander stooped to go through the opening. He couldn't straighten inside. Neither could Ingar, who promptly flopped down on the wooden bed covered with what looked like a black bear's pelt. Like everything else in the camp, the furnishings in the tent had obviously been made to be taken apart and stowed on the ship, then put together when needed. A bronze lamp, not lit, hung from the ridgepole by a chain and was filled with what smelled like sheep's tallow. Ingar gestured at a three-legged stool, and Alexander sat.

The Norseman wore only his brown woolen breeches, and his chest bore several scars. His boots were near the wooden bed, and so was his sword, a damascened blade, made of different qualities of iron and steel that were wound around each other, then welded together and hammered flat. The technique made for a strong, supple blade, and an expensive one. That weapon alone would have cost more than most men made in a lifetime of trade or farming.

But that was not the only weapon the Norseman possessed. Lying across an iron-embossed wooden chest was a battle-ax whose head was delicately carved with swirling, curving lines—a lovely thing it was, for a weapon of destruction.

The rumpled linen beneath the pelt and the general state of the feather bed told Alexander that Ingar had not been napping. Ingar saw his speculative gaze and laughed as he fingered the crucifix. "A man gets lonely."

"I didn't realize you were a Christian," Alexander said, not speaking of his activity with Hielda even while wondering if Ingar would heed the church's teachings about charity.

"My father was baptized, and so was I." Chuckling, Ingar pulled his tunic out of the rumpled linens. "It's good for trade."

"Speaking of trade, I have come to make a bargain with you, Ingar."

"What kind of bargain?" Ingar reached under his bed and pulled out a wineskin that he had probably hidden from Hielda.

He offered the skin first to Alexander, who shook his head.

"You speak for Oswald?" Ingar asked before he put the opening to his mouth and drank deeply.

"No."

Ingar lowered the skin, wiped his mouth and belched. "No? This is a bargain for yourself?"

"Yes."

Ingar's expression grew very shrewd, and certain. "You want the woman."

Oh, God, how he did! But he could never, ever be anything more to her than the man who had abducted her and caused her so much misery. "I want to take her home and return her to her family. I have discovered that she is not the Lady Allis after all. I took the lady's sister by mistake."

He felt himself blush as Ingar's eyes widened like Denis's. Then the Norseman threw back his head and laughed fit to collapse the tent. "The wrong woman? You put up with her and ran after her and nearly drowned yourself—and she was the wrong woman?"

Alexander waited until the man calmed down. "Yes."

Another idea seemed to strike Ingar. "Then she is not the prize for ransom."

"Nor is she married, so Oswald plans to force her to marry Osburn."

Ingar frowned with disgust. "Waste her on that drunken rat? Bah! He would do better to sell her to me. She would surely think so, too."

"I gave the lady my word she would not be harmed, and I intend to keep it. Also, that was not the agreement I made with Oswald, and I will not permit him to change it. Nor will I allow him to sell her to you."

Instead of being offended, Ingar smiled slowly, one side of his mouth lifting with sardonic cunning. "This is not about your honor and word given or broken. You would rather take her home than see her wed to that fool or in my bed."

Alexander started to stand. He had made another mistake coming here. They would find a different way to escape, even if it meant stealing horses. "I told you, I gave—"

"I know, you gave your word." Ingar half rose and put his large hand on Alexander's shoulder, pushing him back down. "But that does not mean there need not be a ransom. Won't this Sir Connor pay to get her back just the same? He may not want to pay so much, of course, but surely he will give you something for her."

"I won't risk going close to Bellevoire, for I'm sure Sir Connor has many more patrols out now, searching for her or anybody trespassing on his land."

"You could take some of my men."

Although he would not say so to Ingar, he would trust the Norsemen about as much as he would the

Brabancons. "She goes back to her family, and the loss of the ransom is the cost of my error. I will not further dishonor myself by bargaining like a man hawking goods at a fair."

Ingar's gray eyes narrowed, and all trace of good humor vanished. "Then what have you to offer me in return for helping you? You have no money and nothing of any value."

"I have my sword arm. If you agree to take us from here, I will serve in your crew for the rest of my life and give you half of all the plunder I get."

He steeled himself to betray no uneasiness as he waited for Ingar to answer, but with Ingar stroking his beard and studying him, even he thought his offer seemed pathetic.

"What you offer is not without value," Ingar said at last, "but Oswald is a wealthy and powerful man, with powerful friends. You ask me to abandon such a man and the payment he offers now for the sake of what you may provide later?"

"Oswald was rich and powerful *once*, before he betrayed his king. Now he is an outlaw, and one who treats you and your crew like hirelings, not Norsemen to be respected. Or do you fear this formerly wealthy and powerful lord?"

"Not at all," Ingar answered with calm certainty and no rancor. "And it is true, he keeps us here like dogs on a leash."

He eyed Alexander as he might a horse he was thinking of buying—as *he* had treated Isabelle. She had known this humiliation, yet it had not defeated her, and he would endure it, too.

"You might not live long," Ingar noted.

"That's true."

The Norseman smiled. "You are an honest man. And I suspect you can fight like a Berserker when you must." His smile disappeared. "But when a man does not care if he lives or dies, he usually dies."

He would say what was necessary. "I wish to live as much as any man, and if I am in your crew, Lord Oswald will not be able to catch me."

"Ah! You will be *hiding* with us."

Like a coward. But if that helped convince Ingar to agree . . . "Yes."

His gaze shrewdly measuring, Ingar studied Alexander more. "So, you will not keep her for yourself?"

"I gave the lady my word she would not be harmed, as I will give you my word that I will sail with you if you help me. How can you trust me to keep my word with you if I'll break it with another?"

"Very true," Ingar mused aloud. "Besides, there are many women."

None like her.

"I have many myself, in many ports." Ingar turned over his left hand so that his palm was facing upward. "One here." He did the same with his right hand. "One there. It is a fine way to live. You will see."

Alexander doubted that he would find anything about Ingar's way of life enjoyable, except perhaps the copious amounts of ale and wine the Norsemen consumed. That might help him forget Lady Isabelle, Denis and what he had done. "So you'll help us?"

"Yes." Ingar thought a moment. "As you have no wish to be captured by patrols, neither have I, so we dare not sail far inland this time. I will set you ashore and put out to sea, then return in two days to pick you up. If you are not there, I will leave you."

"Then you won't have me in your crew, and you'll have lost Oswald's patronage, too."

"I will risk it." Ingar gave Alexander another sly grin. "You will come back. Your honor will demand it, and if you don't, I'll know you're dead. As for Oswald, I am no man's churl, and it is worth some coin to prove it."

Chapter 17

In the dim light of evening, Isabelle sat on the bed in her chamber, her head leaning limply against her hand. She had not gone below for the evening meal, and no one had come to check on her, or to bring her food. Maybe they planned on starving her into obedience.

She sighed wearily and wiped at her running nose with her free hand. She had cried her cry, and felt drained and empty of far more than food. Every time she thought things were terrible, they became worse. Every time she was pleased to have maintained her dignity in the face of her troubles, new ones arose to test her mettle.

Worst of all, when she had finally believed that Alexander DeFrouchette was not her enemy, she had discovered fully, completely, incontrovertibly, that he was. He had decided in the end to remain in Oswald's camp, abandoning her to a terrible fate.

The door to the room crashed open, and Isabelle shot to her feet.

Dressed in his fine clothes and shining boots, a smug smile on his face, and his wine-befuddled eyes fairly glowing with lust, Osburn sauntered in. "So here you are, my bride-to-be. I came to beard you in your den."

She moved around the bed, away from it and him. "Get out, Osburn. We are not married yet."

"As good as," he slurred as he reached back and closed the door. "Why wait for the formalities? You're here, so am I, and there's"—he gestured lazily and smiled with demonic pleasure—"a bed."

"Does your father know you're here?"

"See how she asks, like I am a child?" he demanded, looking around as if the chamber were full of spectators before his sneering gaze returned to her. "Rest assured, my lady, I am not a child, and my dear father has finally found that out, too. My dear *dead* father."

Isabelle gasped, disbelieving. "Dead?"

"Completely."

She backed away. "I heard no sound of a struggle."

Swaying as if he were again on the deck of Ingar's ship, Osburn grinned. "I'm too smart for that. I sent Kiera to sleep with the other women and told my father I wanted to discuss his plans in private. He came around the screen and sat in my chair. *My* chair, not his." Osburn shook his head as if to clear it, then regarded her with glistening, frightening eyes. "But I was ready for him. I went behind him and slit his throat. Easy, really. He burbled a bit and tried to get up, but he was too fat." Osburn laughed, a hideous giggle, then ended in an angry sob. "He thought I was stupid. Well, who's the stupid one now, eh? He's the one that's dead, not me!"

So one of her enemies was dead—but she was still in danger because Osburn was not.

"Now come, my dear, and kiss me. I've waited long enough to have you."

As Osburn stumbled toward her, she saw the dagger in his belt. She had gotten a weapon away from Heinrich; surely she could do that again and defend herself.

Osburn halted and shook his finger at her. "Don't get any ideas, my lady. I won't let you near my dagger—or at least, not that one." He giggled again at his own joke and shoved the knife further into his belt. "You really must learn to act more like a lady. As my wife, I'll expect no less."

"I was only marrying you to protect my family. Now that your father is dead, so is my reason."

He fingered the hilt of his dagger. "You think I don't have money to pay assassins? Besides, I have to marry you, because if I don't, there's nothing to prevent your family from coming after me." He nodded as he crept closer. "I told you I wasn't stupid, Isabelle. I don't want to die because of you."

She continued back toward the outer wall, near the loophole and the loose stones. If she could get him in front of them. . . .

"Oh, come, come, Isabelle," he cooed, sounding so eerily like his father that it made her flesh crawl. "I'm not so bad, really. I'm handsome, and if you cooperate, I'll treat you well."

"What about Kiera?" she charged, inching toward the loophole. "She loves you."

"She's nothing but a servant, a woman to warm

my bed and pleasure me when I desire it. I've taught her well, though, so I won't discard her just yet. After all, a man can have a mistress as well as a wife. Are you jealous?"

"That is the last thing I will ever be where you are concerned."

He stopped a few feet away and drew out his dagger with measured deliberation. The blade gleamed in the moonlight shining in through the loophole. "I told you to come here and kiss me."

She had to get him to come to her, one way or another. If he swung at her to hit her, he would be off balance, too.

Every muscle tense, ready for action, she planted her feet. "When I am your wife, you will have the right to command me. Until that time, I am free."

"Free?" he scoffed, gesturing at the chamber with his dagger. "You're not free at all." His expression changed to fierce anger as he pointed to his feet with the tip of his weapon. *Now come here and kiss me*, or I'll make you sorry you refused."

"No."

"Always proud, always stubborn," Osburn jeered. He shoved the knife into his belt. "Very well. This time—this *once*—I'll come to you."

He strode toward her and reached out for her. She deftly twisted away from him. He whirled around, his back now to the wall. She put her hands on his chest and with all her might, pushed him against the wall.

"What in the name—!" he cried, putting out his arms, his hands against the stones that were not loose. The stones shifted back a few inches. He lost his balance, but that was all.

She ran to the door. With a furious cry, he caught her by the arm and swung her around. Her shoulder ached as he tugged her close. "You stupid bitch!" he snarled, his whole body seeming to seethe with rage. "Can't you see you've lost? You're mine, and you will be for the rest of your life! If you don't want to suffer—and by God, I'll make you!—you'll do what I tell you. *Whatever* I tell you."

Cursing him for the loathsome, disgusting beast he was, she kicked and hit him as hard as she could, in any way she could. He could not draw his dagger if he had to fend her off.

"Let her go, Osburn."

Neither Isabelle nor Osburn had heard the chamber door open. They both stared at Alexander De-Frouchette, limned in the torchlight from the burning brand in the corridor outside. He looked huge. His cloak was thrown over his shoulder, his sword drawn, and on his face was an expression of such outrage that he looked like the very embodiment of a warrior heritage stretching back for centuries.

"Get out!" Osburn screeched, letting go of her to pull out his dagger. "You've no business here, De-Frouchette. I'll call the guards! Let's see how you fare against the Brabancons."

Alexander kicked the door closed behind him, shutting the three of them together in the room. "The Brabancons will not risk their lives for you, Osburn."

He tossed his sword onto the bed, and with slow, deliberate movements began to take off his cloak. He threw that on the bed, too. He had a length of rope slung around his shoulder.

What was that for? Osburn stared at it, obviously wondering, too.

"I have given this lady my word she will be safe, and I mean to keep it." His lips curved in a sneer as the rope followed his cloak and sword onto the bed. "I don't expect you to understand that. It's time we settled this matter, Osburn, man to man. If you want the lady, you must fight for her."

"I'll do no such thing!" Osburn cried, still waving his dagger at Alexander as Isabelle began sidling toward the door. With both of them occupied, she could get away. She didn't doubt that Alexander would triumph, but what then would her fate be?

Crouching, his fists raised to protect his face, Alexander closed on his armed opponent. "You may keep the dagger, Osburn. It won't make any difference."

"Get back!" Osburn cried, panic in his voice and tears starting in his eyes. "I'll kill you!"

"As I told a certain lady, you are most welcome to try."

Isabelle moved another foot toward the door, then halted as Osburn lunged at Alexander.

Alexander grabbed his wrist. Osburn's face contorted with pain but, desperate, he did not let go of his knife. He managed to twist away and free himself.

He ran at her. As she dove for the door, he got hold of the back of her gown and tugged her close. Wrapping his arm about her, he held his dagger at her throat. She stood perfectly still, certain Osburn would kill her as he had his father if he thought that was the only way to save himself. "What will you do now, DeFrouchette?" he said, gloating.

She stared at Alexander, knowing that he was her only hope.

Yet knowing that, her fear diminished, even as the blade of Osburn's dagger pricked her throat.

"We are fighting *for* the lady, not *with* the lady," Alexander noted with a cold, deliberate calm. "If you would prove yourself a man worthy of such a woman, Osburn, let her go and leave this between the two of us."

"You think I'm stupid, too! You're a trained fighter, DeFrouchette, like those Brabancons below. What chance have I against a man like you?"

Alexander's frosty blue eyes regarded Osburn with a warrior's intensity, and his whole body tensed with anticipation. "You should have thought of that before you attacked the lady."

Isabelle bit her lip as the dagger pressed more against her throat. "She is mine, DeFrouchette, not yours. You were but the soldier sent to fetch her."

"I will never be yours," Isabelle muttered through clenched teeth, determined to get away if he loosened his hold on her for a moment.

Alexander's eyes flared with admiration, and then he smiled a smile of such icy deliberation that it made Osburn tremble. "You hear her, Osburn? Do you think you could ever really conquer her?"

Osburn's grip tightened about her and she felt a trickle of blood as his knife scored her throat. "I mean it, DeFrouchette! I'll kill her if you come any closer."

"If you do, I'll gladly disembowel you. Slowly."

That gave her the moment. Osburn was so frightened, the dagger wavered, and in that instant, she shoved her left elbow hard into his belly and pushed his hand away with her right. Freed, she lunged forward.

With a screech, Osburn tried to grab her. His feet got tangled in her skirts and together they fell to the floor.

Ignoring Osburn, who lay moaning and unmoving, Alexander swiftly helped her to her feet. His gaze anxiously searched her face. "Are you hurt?"

She wiped the cut across her throat with the cuff of her gown. "It's not deep."

"Thank God! If I had come any later—!" He left the rest unsaid as he gathered her into his arms.

For a moment, she delighted in the comfort of his embrace, but only a moment, for she could not forget his earlier betrayal.

She stepped back. "Your confederate is wounded, I think."

His eyes flared with dismay, but he said nothing as he went to kneel beside the fallen Osburn and rolled him over.

Isabelle gasped. Osburn's dagger protruded from his chest. He had fallen on his own knife, the force thrusting it between his ribs. Blood trickled from the corner of his mouth, and he was not moaning anymore.

His eyes glassy, Osburn stared up at De-Frouchette. "Perhaps I am a fool after all," he said, gasping for every breath. "But you'll never have her, either."

A bubble of blood formed between his lips, and when it broke, he died.

Alexander rose and turned toward her. "I've come to take you back to Bellevoire."

Uncertain, doubtful, trying not to believe him or
have hope in him, she moved back toward the door.
"Below, you said—"

"I said what was necessary to avert suspicion."

"How can I trust you? You might be taking me
away to sell to the Norsemen."

"I might, but I'm not. I came to your chamber to
help you escape. That's why I brought the rope."

Oh, how she wanted to believe him! But how
could she, after all that he had done? What evidence
was there that she could put her faith in the son of
Rennick DeFrouchette?

"We must hurry, my lady, before Oswald or the
Brabancons wonder where Osburn is."

"Oswald is dead." She glanced at the body on the
floor. "Osburn killed him."

Alexander followed her gaze. "I should have seen
that coming. He is as his father made him, as I am."

Isabelle shook her head as she went toward him.
"I would have said so once, but if you are truly going to help me get home, you are a better man than
your father would have made you."

Gratitude crossed his face, but he said no more
before he bent and rolled Osburn's body into a corner of the room. When that was done, he faced her
and spoke with a soldier's brisk efficiency. "We are
going out the window, as you did before. Denis and
Kiera will be waiting for us on the wall walk, then
we will climb down from there."

"Kiera?"

"Denis would not leave her, and now I'm glad he
would not. A terrible fate would have awaited her
with the Brabancons, now that Osburn is dead."

"I'm glad she's coming, too," she said as she joined him at the window.

They worked silently, and as she slowly lifted down the stones, she marveled at the ease with which he did this task.

He caught her looking at him. "I worked for a mason, remember? I have carried heavier stones than these many a time."

She nodded and went back to work, thinking of his past, and her own.

When the last stone was on the floor, she straightened and arched her aching back. He was already lifting and dragging the bed across the floor toward the window, no doubt intending to anchor the rope to the post, as she had done.

In preparation, she hiked up her skirt and tucked it into her girdle. "I can't climb with my skirt around my ankles," she explained when she saw him looking at her legs.

"I see. Come here." His deep voice was low, and his eyes seemed to smolder in the moonlight like a tinder glowing in the dusk.

She moved toward him hesitantly, uncertain of what he wanted, yet unable to resist his entreaty.

"Stand still. I need to tie the rope around you."

She stood as stiffly as any soldier facing his commander while he took the free end of the rope and passed it around her waist.

His fingers skimmed over her bodice, the way his thumb had skimmed over her nipple. She felt them tighten and pucker. Her breathing quickened, and she tried to ignore the throbbing blossoming lower in her body.

Biting her lip, she raised her head so that she was

looking at the beams in the ceiling and not at him while he knotted the rope. They were about to flee, not make love.

When he finished and straightened, he was very, very close. She could see his chest rising and falling as rapidly as her own. She could almost feel his heartbeat against her breasts. She raised her eyes to his face, his lips, and then wished she hadn't. She must not trust him beyond getting away from here, and she must not believe that he cared for her.

His brow furrowed and his gaze intensified. "I gave you my word you would be safe. I do not break my pledges, my lady."

She regarded him steadily, her gaze searching his face, and especially his brilliant blue eyes. "And of course, you will still get the ransom."

His gaze hardened and he stepped back. "I'll lower you to the wall walk where Denis is waiting, then come down after you."

He braced his feet, ready to play out the rope as she made her way down.

She crawled backward through the space, and with the rope tied about her waist and Alexander to lower her, she was not nearly so afraid. There was still that horrible moment when she was half in and half out, but once she had purchase on the rough stones with the soles of her feet, that terror departed.

Although she held onto the rope tightly, it was merely to steady herself, so her hands did not suffer nearly as much.

Nor was it raining. The moonlight made it more dangerous, though, because they might be seen by the sentries on the wall walk. She was glad that Alexander lowered her quickly.

When she was a few feet above the wall walk, Denis grabbed her waist and wordlessly guided her down the rest of the way.

Once she was on the walk, she began untying the rope. Her fingers were slightly stiff, and Denis had to help her. "Well done, my lady," he whispered.

"Where are the sentries?"

"Still at their posts, but unable to see." She followed Denis's nod. One man leaned against the parapet, apparently looking out at the shore, but he was slumped over rather oddly. His cloak billowing around him, Alexander began to climb down the wall.

"Is he—?"

"Dead. There was no other way. What took so long?"

"Osburn came to my chamber."

Denis sucked in his breath and she told him briefly and quietly what had happened.

Denis glanced over his shoulder at Kiera, waiting huddled in the shadows. "Say nothing of this to her yet, my lady. I will tell her when we are safely away."

Isabelle nodded and went to join Kiera.

"I'm so glad you're coming with us," she murmured. If there was one thing she would have regretted about fleeing this place, it would have been leaving Kiera behind.

"Not nearly as glad as I am," Kiera replied softly. "What a fool I've been!"

The instant Alexander was safely on the wall walk, Denis picked up another length of rope Isabelle had not noticed near him.

"We can go over here," Denis whispered, pointing to a place where rocks had been haphazardly tumbled into the gap. Rather than a vertical wall, it was like the rocky side of a hill down to a narrow ledge of land between the castle and the bluff. From here, that bit of ground looked *very* narrow.

"I will go first, in case the stones are unsteady," Denis offered.

"No, I should—" Alexander began.

Denis held up his hand to silence him. "I am lighter on my feet than you. Let me test the way, Alexander." His gaze flicked to Kiera. "It is the least that I can do."

Isabelle caught Alexander's eye and knew he was thinking the same thing: that Denis wanted to prove himself in front of Kiera.

"Very well," Alexander said. "There's no time for argument."

Grinning, Denis tied the rope around his waist. "When I am down, I will shake it, like this." He flicked his wrist like a man with a whip, and the rope snapped. "Then you tie your end around that part of the merlon there and start after me."

He nodded at a portion of the remaining wall intended as cover for archers. Alexander inclined his head, silently agreeing.

With a final grin, Denis disappeared over the wall.

As they waited, every moment seemed to stretch into days; for Isabelle, it was like the slow passage of time when she'd been in that dank cell. Kiera's cold hand found hers, and Isabelle clasped it, feeling the girl's tension matching her own.

She did not envy Denis the task of telling Kiera of

Osburn's death. Although Kiera was leaving him, hearing of his death would surely upset her. The man had helped her once, and despite all that came after, she would remember that, just as she would remember that Alexander DeFrouchette had come to her aid.

Isabelle watched him waiting motionless by the merlon for Denis's signal. If there was anybody who could get her away from here, he could. She could even believe he would die trying.

Yet even with his help, she would not be safe until they were far away from here. If the Brabancons discovered them fleeing, they would surely kill Alexander and Denis and take her for their spoils. They would sell her to Ingar, at the very least. But first. . . .

She shuddered, trying not to think of what would happen to her—and Kiera—if the Brabancons discovered them trying to escape.

Her gaze went to Ingar's ship rocking on the waves and the Norse camp, like a blockade on the beach.

Then, like a lightning strike, she had a sudden horrible thought: once they got out of the fortress, how were they going to get back to Bellevoire? They had no horses. The Brabancons would chase them down on foot. Perhaps Alexander and Denis had stolen horses awaiting them below . . . except that they were climbing down the wall closest to the sea.

Leaving Kiera, she hurried to Alexander. "How are we getting away from here after we get down that wall?" she demanded in a whisper harsh with anxiety. "If we climb down here, we'll be between the fortress and the bluff."

"We will make our way along the edge to the

steps leading to the beach. Ingar has agreed to take us back to England."

"Ingar!" she gasped. "He's in the pay of—"

The rope in Alexander's hands jerked twice. "It's time to go."

"But Ingar—!"

"Has no loyalty in his heart save to the man who makes the best offer, and today, I did."

What could he have to . . . ? Of course. The ransom.

"Now come, my lady, go down. I have no idea how long before someone suspects all is not well. We must be on the ship and out of the bay before that."

Kiera started to weep. "I-I can't climb down," she said as she splayed her hands back against the wall. "I thought I could, but I can't. I'll slip and fall and the guards will hear and we'll all be caught."

Isabelle went over to her and spoke softly, tenderly, as she would to a frightened child. "It is a slope, not straight down. We'll be fine."

"I'll slip and the height. . . . I've never even been able to look over the wall."

Isabelle grabbed her shoulders and gave her a little shake. "Kiera, we have no choice!"

Alexander joined them. "You go first, my lady. Kiera and I will come down together after you." He regarded Kiera with a calm confidence. "I will make sure you don't fall." He slid Isabelle an urgent glance, a silent plea to lead the way. "Now, my lady, please."

She grabbed hold of the rope and began to make her way down the wall. The hemp was rough and cut her hands, but she would get down this wall if it killed her.

The stones held firm, and soon enough, she was on the strip of land. She didn't look beyond that; she already knew they were precariously perched and a few steps would send her straight down to the beach below.

"Mon Dieu!" Denis gasped, looking up.

She did, too, to see Alexander climbing down with Kiera on his back, her arms wrapped around his neck as she clung to him as a man sinking in quicksand would cling to a log.

Kiera must be nearly strangling him! How could he hold on with such a burden? And if her hands were raw, his would surely be worse.

"Why is he . . . ?" Denis murmured before he choked on his own words.

"She was afraid to climb down by herself," Isabelle explained, unable to take her eyes from them even though she feared she would see disaster.

If he lost his grip, if his foot slipped, if she let go. . . . A host of catastrophes ran through Isabelle's anxious mind until Alexander's feet finally touched the ground. Then she could breathe again, and her whole body relaxed.

Denis ran over to help Kiera, whose face was white in the moonlight. With a grimace, Alexander ran his finger around the neck of his cloak and tunic to loosen them.

Isabelle wanted to ask him if he was all right and praise him for the effort. She wanted to look at his hands, to check their state for herself, although she had no salve or medicine to offer.

But she did not. He was helping her for his own ends, as always, and she must not forget that.

Denis put his arm around Kiera's shoulder, and they started toward the steps leading to the beach.

Alexander came beside her, tall and powerful, and he held out his hand. "Come."

She looked down at his palm. It was raw and red, but not bleeding.

She should have realized his palms would not be the soft and tender flesh of a nobleman who spent his days at leisure. He had the callused hands of a soldier, or a common laborer.

He snatched back his hand, as if just as suddenly ashamed.

"Follow me," he barked, his voice quiet, but as fierce as a general on a battlefield ordering his men to advance.

Chapter 18

Alexander led them swiftly to the steps leading to the beach below. "Denis, you go first. Then Kiera, then you, my lady."

Although Kiera was still weeping, she didn't protest when Denis started down, then reached back to take her hand. Isabelle went as quickly as she could after them, with Alexander close behind.

They reached the beach, panting, and it seemed they had succeeded in escaping without being seen—until a cry of alarm shattered the night. Glancing over her shoulder, Isabelle saw torches appear above the walls, along with the heads of many Brabancons.

Kiera screamed.

Alexander drew his sword. "Denis, take the women and run for the ship."

"Alexander!" Denis cried, aghast. "You're not going to stand and try to hold them off alone?"

"Not unless I must. Now *run!*"

As long as Alexander didn't intend to stay behind and hold off their pursuers, which would surely mean death, Isabelle needed no more urging. She lifted up her skirts and sprinted for the ship, Denis and Kiera right behind.

Breathing hard, Isabelle could hear the heavier tread of Alexander's feet pounding across the pebbles behind them. Then she heard another sound, one that gave her new energy: the Brabancons were howling like wolves, and the sound was getting closer.

"Oh, God," Kiera moaned, stumbling. She would have fallen if Denis hadn't been supporting her.

"Keep going! We'll make the ship," Isabelle cried. She wouldn't care now if the devil himself owned the vessel. All that mattered was getting away from the horde of men chasing them.

They made it through the Norsemen's camp, or what was left of it. Several of the tents were missing. Looking ahead, Isabelle saw the Norsemen seated at their oars, save for the one man standing on the wharf with the rope holding the ship in place, and Ingar at the tiller.

Would they wait, or would the sight of the Brabancons bearing down upon them make them go without them?

Please, God, make them wait, she prayed over and over again as she ran. She, too, stumbled and nearly fell, but Alexander grabbed her arm and steadied her.

She was grateful for his help, and even more grateful to see the flash of his sword blade in the moonlight.

They clattered across the wharf.

"Kiera, go!" Denis ordered, handing her across

the plank to one of the Norsemen in the ship, who reached out to help her.

"Now you, my lady," Alexander commanded, and she obeyed, hurrying across to join Kiera, who stood in the center of the ship. Then Denis ran across the plank as nimbly as a cat.

The Brabancons reached the camp, and their angry cries echoed across the beach.

Sheathing his sword, Alexander dashed across the plank and helped the Norsemen swiftly haul it in as the man still on the wharf slipped off the rope, then leapt into the ship. At a barked order from Ingar, the men on the side closest to the wharf put the tips of the oars against the wharf to push off. By the time the first of the Brabancons reached the wharf, the ship was far enough out to allow all the Norsemen to have their oars in the water. They pulled swiftly for the mouth of the bay, leaving the Brabancons uselessly shouting curses from the shore.

Isabelle collapsed in the center of the ship and tried to catch her breath. Looking as shocked as if they'd been spirited to the ship by magic, Kiera, too, sat heavily. Denis joined them, too tired to speak.

Alexander did not. He went to the stern and stood at the gunwale, looking back at the Brabancons and the fortress on the bluffs.

Kiera began to cry. Denis put his arm about her shoulder and whispered to her, the tone gentle and soothing.

Kiera gave a shocked little gasp, then leaned against him, sobbing in earnest. As Denis put his arms around her, Isabelle didn't doubt that he had just told her that Osburn was dead.

Isabelle sighed and looked away, her gaze drifting back toward Alexander DeFrouchette, who stood so still, so silent, and so very alone.

As the noise from the shore faded, to be replaced by the grunts of the rapidly rowing Norsemen and the quiet sobbing of Kiera, Isabelle felt free to consider Alexander DeFrouchette, and all that had happened to her. He had abducted her; he had rescued her. He was her enemy; he was her savior. He deserved punishment; he deserved mercy.

She hated him. She did not.

She would be glad to see the last of him.

No, she would not. After all that he had done, the good as well as the bad, this was the one thing that shone clear and certain in her jumbled thoughts.

Alexander never went near her that night, or the next day. He only joined them to eat the food the Norsemen offered—salted fish and bread and cheese—but he sat as far away from them as it was possible to be in the small space. Otherwise he was either in the stern talking with Ingar or in the bow gazing at the sea.

Ingar had ordered the sail raised in the night, and now most of his crew slumbered or talked among themselves. The day was a fine one, with a good wind and no rain.

Denis and Kiera sat together closely, and it was all too plain that whatever Kiera had felt for Osburn, Denis was helping her to forget him with his jokes and banter. He even juggled for her and got her to laugh.

Isabelle wanted to share that laughter, but she couldn't. She still didn't feel completely safe; she wouldn't until she was at Bellevoire. Then, she hoped, all that had happened would fade from her mind. She would forget Alexander and her tumultuous, confused feelings. She would be as she was before.

No, you will not, her mind chided. *You will never be the same. You left Bellevoire a girl. You go back a woman, and a woman whose heart has been awakened to desire.*

But how could she desire a man who had put her in such danger, even if he had also rescued her? Could she trust anything she felt since that day in the market of Bellevoire? Surely once she was back with her family, she would see things differently.

Such thoughts were not the only ones to trouble her. She would be safe, she would be free, but her family would be poor because of the ransom.

Her legs were aching after sitting all morning, and Isabelle rose stiffly and stretched. Denis and Kiera glanced at her, then went back to talking. She looked at Alexander who stood in the bow, leaning against the dragon's prow, his hair and cloak blowing in the wind.

Needing to walk, she made her way to the stern. Surely Ingar would be too busy guiding his ship to pay much attention to her.

Unfortunately, when Ingar noticed her, he called another man to take the tiller and came to stand beside her—far too close beside her. She inched away.

He realized what she was doing, and laughed. "Have no fear, my lady. I won't kiss you again. I want to keep my head, and DeFrouchette will probably cut it off if I so much as touch you."

She slid him a skeptical glance.

"What, you don't believe me?" Ingar's beard moved as he smiled. "I could try it and then you would have the proof you need."

"Please don't."

Grinning, Ingar leaned back against the gunwale. "Still the bold woman, whoever you are. Tell me, did he kill Osburn for trying to wed and bed you, or does that fool still breathe?"

"Osburn's dead."

Ingar sighed with satisfaction. "The Norman killed him over you. I thought he would."

"Osburn fell on his knife after I pushed him away."

"He died as he lived, then—a fool." He shook his head. "I would wager my sword that DeFrouchette is sorry he didn't get to run the man through. I think he's wanted to do that from the first time he saw the way that little rat looked at you."

"Then you'd lose your sword."

Ingar's demeanor changed to one unexpectedly serious. "I thought you were clever, my lady. Can you not see how the Norman cares for you? Why, his feelings are as plain as the sail of my ship."

Not wanting to hear about Alexander's feelings— even supposing she believed Ingar—she turned away. "Only for the ransom."

"But there will be none. He is going to set you free without it."

Dumbfounded, Isabelle faced Ingar again. "What?" Then her eyes narrowed with suspicion, for she certainly wasn't about to trust a Norseman's words. "I assumed he was going to share the ransom with you, the price for our passage."

Ingar chortled. "It is what I would have done, but he has some odd notions of honor."

"Then why are you helping us? You aren't doing it out of the goodness of your heart, I'm sure."

"You're right," Ingar answered without offense, his gray eyes twinkling. "He has offered to sail with me for the rest of his life. Men like him are hard to find, so naturally, I agreed. He makes many sacrifices for you, my lady, and apparently for nothing in return except knowing you are safe."

She was not willing to accept that Alexander De-Frouchette did anything solely for her. "He will also get whatever he can pillaging with you."

"Yes, there is that," Ingar conceded.

"If he cares for me in any way other than as a thing to be bargained for, it is lust and nothing more."

"Is it? Well, you may think so if it is easier for you."

She briskly stepped away. "Easy? Nothing has been easy for me since the day DeFrouchette abducted me." She put her hands on her hips. "And since when has a Norseman concerned himself with anybody's *feelings*?"

Ingar didn't look upset by her question. "A captain has to know his crew, and a good captain learns to read men the way he reads the stars in the sky. Alexander DeFrouchette cares for you the way few men ever do for a woman. He is willing to risk his life for you, and he is willing to give you up. He says it is for honor, but there is another reason. He does it because he thinks that is what you want. Is it?"

She flushed beneath Ingar's steady gaze, then looked away. "Of course!"

"Good. He has given his word to return to my ship after he takes you back to your family, yet if there is anything on this earth that could make him break that vow, it would be his love for you. But if you do not want his love, then he will keep his word, and I will have a fine fighter in my crew."

She stared at the planks beneath her feet. *Love?* He thought Alexander *loved* her?

A word that was obviously a curse flew from Ingar's lips, startling her. "Olaf!" he shouted at the man holding the steering board. "What are you doing? You are going too far to the west!"

With that, he crossed the deck, clouted the unfortunate Olaf on his head and resumed his position at the steering board, leaving Isabelle looking unseeing at the waves rolling past the ship, thinking about all that Ingar had said and all that Alexander DeFrouchette had done.

Ingar guided his ship into the small, secluded bay. The water was calm, and there was no sign of any habitation. Indeed, it looked as if nobody had set foot there from time immemorial. The ground sloped up from the shore, and nothing could be seen beyond the grassy ridge.

Ingar ordered his men to hold their oars steady in the water, so that the ship was barely moving.

Isabelle, Kiera, Denis and Alexander stood near the mastfish, Alexander a little apart. He held a small bundle containing his extra tunic, some bread and cheese, a wineskin, and a flint and steel. Denis had a slightly larger bundle, and of course, Isabelle had brought nothing.

"You will have to jump, for I can't get closer to

shore," Ingar declared as he left the tiller to Olaf and strode toward them. "You should be safe enough here. No one lives nearby."

"You seem very familiar with this part of the country," Isabelle noted.

Ingar chuckled. "I have been here before, as you guess. But have no fear, my lady. After we return for Alexander, we will not venture this way again. I have no wish to encounter your brother-in-law. Alexander tells me he rode with King Richard on the Crusade, and then was a champion of tournaments. A good warrior learns to avoid another."

Isabelle darted a look at Alexander. She had wondered what they had been talking about, deciding it must be strategy or some such business.

Ingar grinned again. "And do not think to tell this Sir Connor where we will be, for this is not where we will return for Alexander. I doubt Sir Connor has enough men to watch miles of coast."

He didn't, but she wasn't about to admit that.

"So, farewell, my lady." Ingar reached out and pulled her to him. Fearing another kiss, she turned her head. He didn't. Instead, his beard tickled her cheek as he whispered, "Remember what this has cost him, my lady, and be kind."

He let her go. "A little kiss, DeFrouchette," he called out to Alexander, whose dark brows had lowered like the clouds gathering on the horizon. "Her payment for the voyage."

Taken aback by Ingar's actions and words, Isabelle rubbed her cheek and watched as Ingar bussed Kiera heartily. Denis didn't look any happier than Alexander at this particular form of farewell, or payment, but both said nothing.

"To the steering board side!" Ingar shouted, and suddenly all his men went to that side of the ship, making it heel so that the gunwale was mere inches above the water.

Denis looked back at the Norseman. "My thanks, and may you always have a fine breeze," he said before he lowered himself into the shallow water.

Kiera eagerly leapt from the ship into his arms.

As Isabelle prepared to go over the side, she looked back at Ingar. The breeze gently brushed her hair across her pink cheeks, which were ruddy from the voyage. In the simple blue gown she wore, and despite her short hair, she looked like a nymph risen from the sea.

For a moment, Alexander thought she was going to curse Ingar, but she didn't. Instead, she regarded him with a studious mien. "You've made a better bargain than you know, Ingar, and gotten far more than you ever would have if you had sold me." Then she smiled, a bold, brazen smile that made Ingar and every man on that ship stare at her. "It isn't only a captain who learns to read men, Ingar. If you had tried to take me against my will I would have lain there like a dead fish, and you would have been even limper."

As those in the crew who could understand laughed with glee and began translating for those who could not, Ingar stared at her, openmouthed. Then she jumped into the water.

"By Thor's hammer, what a woman," Ingar muttered as he turned to Alexander. "Enjoy your time alone with her, DeFrouchette, and I hope she will be generous in her gratitude."

Alexander flushed. "That's not—"

"As if you would fear an English patrol!" Ingar scoffed, grinning.

Alexander scowled as he went to the gunwale. "I will be at the rendezvous in two nights, Ingar, or I'll be dead."

Ingar nodded. "Two days, Norman, and then for as long as you live, your sword is mine to command." His eyes twinkled with merriment. "And may your night with her be worth it."

Ingar would reduce everything to a bargain or payment for services rendered, Alexander thought as he went over the side and began wading toward the shore.

Behind him, he could hear Ingar shouting orders and the splash of oars in the water as the ship turned and headed back out to sea. Ahead, Denis, Kiera and Isabelle waited for him on the sandy beach.

"Well, my friend," Denis said as he shook the hem of his tunic as if that would help it dry. "Here we are, alone in some desolate spot."

"And here we must part."

Denis stopped shaking his tunic and stared at him. "Here? Now?"

Alexander nodded.

"Well, of course I knew that we must go our separate ways," Denis said, his face as mournful as the statue of a dead saint. "But I did not think it had to be today."

"The sooner we part, the safer it will be for you." He stole a glance at Isabelle. "I'm sure Lady Isabelle's brother-in-law has as many patrols out as he can mount. We have shown him how vulnerable he was. You and Kiera must not be found with us."

"Alexander." Denis took him by the arm and led him a little way from the women, so that they couldn't hear him. "You *are* going to go with Ingar, aren't you? You aren't planning on letting yourself get caught out of some notion of justice, are you? Because if you are, I won't leave you."

Resting his hand on the hilt of his sword, Alexander gave his friend a weary smile. "No, I do not plan on getting caught. I promised Ingar I would return, so I will. Nor do I wish to die or spend my days rotting in a cell. I struggled too long to live to give up easily now. So have no fear, Denis, and leave me with a happy heart."

Denis looked appalled. "A happy heart? *Mon Dieu, non!* I leave you because I must, but I do it with a heart as heavy as a lead ball. Happy? How can you even say such a thing? I am devastated . . . horrified . . . shocked . . ."

"And talking too much," Alexander said with another sad, wistful smile. "Take Kiera and go. Ingar says there's an inn to the west. Make for that." He reached into his tunic and pulled out his thin purse. "There is enough here for a few nights' travel and passage to France."

His hand on his heart, Denis recoiled. "I cannot take your money!"

"I won't need any for awhile, and you will." Alexander pressed the purse into his friend's hand. "Take it for Kiera's sake, if not your own."

Denis looked down at the purse, and sighed. Then his hand wrapped around it, and he looked up at his friend. "If I had any money of my own . . ."

Alexander clasped the hand holding the purse. "I
know." He managed a smile. "And who knows? We
may meet again, in some southern clime, perhaps.
Ingar tells me they sail very far south, to Greece and
Italy sometimes."

Denis's dimples appeared, but his eyes were moist
with unshed tears. "*Oui*, it is possible. I shall live in
hope, my friend who saved the life of a stranger."

With a heavy heart, trying to conquer his sorrow,
Alexander watched his friend trudge toward the
women. Denis spoke briefly to Lady Isabelle, saying
good-bye, no doubt, as did Kiera. Then, arm in arm,
the couple slowly walked up the rise through the
scrubby grass and disappeared from sight.

It was time for them to be gone, too, Alexander
told himself. They had a long walk ahead of them,
and walking would warm them. He was not the
only one shivering in wet clothes. "Come, my lady.
We must be on our way."

She silently obeyed, and he led her east, the way
Ingar had told him. There would be a road soon, and
they could follow it.

By the time they reached the top of the hill, the
sun was warm, and he was no longer cold. He
glanced back at Lady Isabelle and was pleased to see
that her lips—her lovely, full lips—were not blue
any more.

A bracken-covered meadow ran toward a wood,
just as Ingar had said, and the road was along its
edge. He made for the road, wading through the
bracken as he had the water, glancing back occasionally to make sure Isabelle had not fallen behind.

Maybe she would run off. She might think he

didn't mean to keep his word and decide she should take matters into her own hands, as she had so many times before.

He dropped back so that he was beside her. She slid him a wary glance but said nothing.

By the time they reached the road, he was perspiring, and so was she, but she was smiling, too. "I think I know where we are," she said. "We are closer to Connor's lands than I expected. But I don't think we'll reach the border of his estate today."

"I'm sure there will be patrols on the neighboring estates, too. We should see one tomorrow, and when we are close enough for you to hail them, I will leave you."

"Oh."

"As I told Denis, I don't intend to be captured or killed."

"Oh."

She sounded neither pleased nor displeased. He had expected delight. But he would not puzzle over the difference, because in the end, it could make none.

They walked on. The road was dusty and edged with bramble bushes in bloom, their pink blossoms moving gently in the breeze. In other places, the bushes parted, revealing the shady trees of the forest: elm, oak, rowan, chestnut, alder. Beneath them, in the dappled sunlight, foxglove and violets grew, as well as gooseberry and elder and hazel. With an instinct born of long and hungry practice, Alexander instinctively recalled when each would bear nuts or berries suitable for augmenting meager meals—another potent reminder that his life had very little in common with that of the woman walking so stoically beside him. Yes, she had known trouble and dismay, but surely the only time she had ever lacked for food had been when Osburn had locked her in that cell. She had never had to wait for an overseer's permission before getting a drink.

As if she had been reading his mind, she broke the silence. "I'm very thirsty. I think there's a stream just through those trees."

He nodded his acquiescence, and together they left the road and headed into the cool and welcome shade. Ferns curled out of the soft, damp ground beneath their feet. The stream itself babbled and burbled over rocks worn smooth. Brown butterflies swooped and dipped, and the birdsong of wren and lark filled the air.

How wonderful it would have been if this had simply been a companionable ramble through a wood. How he would have enjoyed simply watching her walk, with her poise and grace, even when she was wading through bracken. He would have been comfortable with their silence, listening to the birds.

Instead, all he could think about was her discomfort and the fact that he was the cause of it. Tonight, they would be sleeping on the ground, without so much as a tent. He had done so many times, but surely she had not.

She deserved to be mounted on a fine and dainty mare, and dressed in fine clothing, not the plain woolen gown that had once been Kiera's. He would have been content to be a common soldier in her escort, watching over her.

No, he thought as they both crouched beside the running water. He would never be content when he was near her, knowing she was as far removed from him as the moon was from the earth.

With a hunger that had nothing to do with his belly, he watched Isabelle cup her hand to drink. As she lifted it to bring the water to her lips, the liquid trickled through her fingers, over her slender wrist and down the cuff of her gown. Her throat moved as if it was being stroked while she drank, and the water that spilled from her lips glistened on her smooth neck.

His own thirst for water was forgotten, and he began to wonder if Ingar might have been right about his reason for refusing a guard of Norsemen. Perhaps, deep in his heart, he did yearn to be alone with her, at least for a little while.

How great a fool was he, to torment himself this way?

She reached down and brought more cool water to the back of her neck, patting it.

Oh, God's wounds, how he wanted to press his lips there!

With a luxurious sigh, she turned toward him and gave him a bright smile. "I almost feel grateful to Osburn for cutting my hair. It's much cooler on . . . my . . . neck."

Her words trailed off as she met his gaze. The silence stretched, broken only by the babble of the stream and the birds above.

At that time and in that place, it was as if nothing else existed. Just them, alone. He was with the woman he admired more than any other. The

woman he wanted more than any other. The woman
he loved.

Who was looking at him with her lips parted, her
breathing quick, and in her eyes, a look that made
him wonder if she did feel . . .

He turned away abruptly and splashed the frigid
water on his face until he was once more master of
his roiling, tumultuous, hopeless feelings.

Or at least calm enough to act it.

.

Chapter 19

As they returned to the road, Isabelle knew she should have been happy, and getting happier with every step that took her closer to Bellevoire.

And if Alexander DeFrouchette was about to pay a heavy price for getting her there, if he lost some of his freedom with his obligation to Ingar, was that not small recompense for what he had done to her? After all, he was not going to be executed, or even imprisoned. He would be with Ingar, and soon enough, he would probably be getting drunk with that band of Norsemen, singing their mournful dirges about Woden and Thor and the glorious days of the past.

She tried to picture that, but she could not. All she could see in her mind's eye was Alexander standing by himself in the prow of Ingar's ship, looking utterly, miserably alone.

When their gazes had locked at the stream, it had not been the fierce warrior she had seen but the lonely, vulnerable man who wanted to be more than his birth had made him. Who wanted something else, something that seemed to tremble in the very air between them . . .

Something she could not give. He had chosen his path, and it had been the wrong one. That could not be changed.

But had he chosen his father? His mother, with her deluded passion? Had he asked for poverty, despair, or the hope that a sly man had offered him, playing upon his desire to rise above the lot to which his birth had consigned him?

That was not her fault, either, yet he had not hesitated to take her. Because he thought she was Allis, the woman who had jilted his father for another.

He had tried to undo what he had done, and he had kept his word that she would not be harmed. Yet did she owe him any gratitude for finally doing what was right, when he should have done it all along?

She slid him a glance, watching his grim face as he strode beside her. If she had been born in his place, what would she have done?

He caught her eye, and she quickly looked away. "It is going to be dusk soon," he said. "We should find a place to make camp."

He turned off the road again and waited for her to follow. They went toward the stream, which was wider here, and came upon a small clearing bordered by bellflowers and thistles and a few yellow primroses.

"This is a good place," he muttered. He put down the leather pouch and, crouching, pulled out a small brown loaf, which he handed to her. He also had cheese wrapped in a cloth and a small wineskin. "It is not much."

"It's enough," she said, sitting on a large rock and eagerly eating what he handed to her. The wine was welcome, too.

He joined her, sitting on another rock a few feet away, and they ate and drank in silence. Above them, a few birds sang, and a wren swooped from branch to branch nearby. It was as if they were two people making a leisurely journey together, like a pilgrimage to Canterbury that many people undertook in the warm weather.

When Isabelle was finished, she washed in the stream and drank some of the cool, clear water, too.

Refreshed, she turned around . . . and gasped with shock, for Alexander was on his feet, his sword drawn. Alert for danger, she scanned the trees.

"If I was going to kill you, my lady, I would have done so before now."

"I thought we were under attack."

His bright blue eyes flashed, and his lips curled in a little smile. "I was about to start building you some shelter from the dew. The low branch of that oak tree will make a fine ridgepole."

He nodded at the large, ancient tree to her left, then started to cut some branches from a nearby chestnut tree. "These will do for walls."

She watched him at his work and found herself enjoying the sight of his strong, easy strokes, and the way he moved with a grace that came from strength. His body was truly a warrior's, and in his arms she had felt that warrior's strength and power. When he had kissed her, she'd known his warrior's passion.

When he had held her, she had known what it was to be truly desired.

When she returned to Bellevoire, she would once again be only Isabelle, Allis's sister. Would there ever be another man who would kiss her with such heated need? Would any other man ever make her feel that she could reward him with only a smile?

Would any other man give up his freedom for her?

Such thoughts availed her nothing. She must return to Bellevoire, and he must return to Ingar, or wherever else he chose, once she was safe. They would never see each other again, and she should be glad of that.

She tried to put any other thoughts out of her mind as she gathered the cut branches.

"Sit, my lady. Leave this to me."

She kept gathering. "As you should know by now, I am not a helpless, mewling creature. It is my shelter, after all, and if I help you, the sooner it will be built. It doesn't take much skill to lay branches."

He shrugged his shoulders. "I should know better than to try to order you."

The matter settled, Isabelle took an armload of the leafy branches and began to lay them so that they leaned against the long, low oak branch, like the sides of one of the Norsemen's tents.

Alexander brought others and, with more methodical care than she had expected, began to fill in any spaces she had left.

"You've done this before."

"Many times."

It was another glimpse of a hard life that had made a hard man.

She watched his hands as he set the branches in place—strong hands that she had assumed had come from years of wielding weapons. Lean hands that had so gently washed her face. Amazing hands that had stroked and caressed her, arousing her in ways that were wondrous and more exciting than anything she had known.

He caught her looking at them. She flushed with embarrassment to think that she had been staring, until he held them out to show her. "I have worked at many tasks, my lady," he said without rancor. "Carpentry, masonry, fetching and carrying, even tossing rocks at birds to keep them from the seeds sown in springtime. I have worked from the time I was five years old. It is a peasant's lot, and I was a peasant long before I got my sword and learned to fight. My hands are callused from those days, and will likely be for the rest of my life."

She couldn't help it. She just couldn't. She had to touch him.

She took hold of his warm hand and examined it in the waning light. "Yet holding on to that rope was not easy, and it *did* hurt." She touched the bruised pad of his right thumb, making him wince.

He pulled his hands away. "Yes—a little."

"You men are all alike," she gently admonished. "Afraid to admit that you're hurt. Connor's pulled his shoulder from the socket twice, and to hear him tell it, each time hurt no worse than a splinter."

Without another word, Alexander went back to cutting branches.

She silently cursed herself for mentioning Connor at all.

"That can't be good for your blade," she said after they had worked for a while and the shelter was nearly finished.

"I'll sharpen it in the morning."

"I saw you doing that on the ship today. Denis said you do that every morning."

"Yes."

"You must cherish your sword."

"It was a gift from my mother, three months before she died."

Isabelle straightened, and held the branches against her chest. "I'm sorry."

Still swinging the blade, he barely glanced at her. "It was long ago."

"Denis told me about her."

He stopped and turned to look at her, his expression fierce but his eyes . . . his eyes looked like those of a wounded animal. "What did he tell you?"

"Enough."

She laid the last of the branches down on the ground beneath the shelter for her bed, then went to him. She had made the foray; she would carry on, even if that meant revealing a pain so secret and so deep that even Allis didn't know it. Since she would never be seeing him again, she would have him know that she understood more of his suffering than he could guess.

He sheathed his sword as she drew near.

"Alexander," she began, nervous but resolute, "I know what it is like to feel as if your existence is not important to a parent. My father was so distraught after my mother died, it was as if he walled himself in a cave of grief and could not—or would not—come out. As if I was not important enough for him to consider at all. Allis did her best to make up for that, but she had many concerns, and my brother to look after, too."

Alexander's expression altered, to one of such tormented guilt that his eyes seemed to burn with it. "But you did not take out your pain on someone innocent, as I have done. You did not, in callous selfishness, think only of your own misery and do what you thought would ease it, without regard for anyone else."

He bowed his head before her, like a criminal brought before one of the king's judges. "My lady, I am ashamed of what I've done, of the hell I've put you through. I know now that I alone am responsible for all that I have done. I am to blame for my fate—not Sir Connor, or my father. I could have chosen better, and more wisely. I could have sought employ as a soldier and been content. I could, perhaps, have made something more of myself than that, but instead I chose with selfish, bitter anger, and with no regard for who else might get hurt." He raised his anguished eyes to look at her. "I am sorry, Isabelle. More sorry than I can say, and I will never forgive myself for what I have done to you."

Hearing the sincerity and agony in his voice, she remembered him as he had been at the first—bitter and brooding and full of hate for those he believed had wronged him. She thought of him as he'd protected her, and rescued her from that horrible cell. She recalled his tender care, and the kisses they had shared, even those she had not believed she wanted.

He was no knight in shining armor coming to her rescue. He was the villain who had kidnapped her.

Yet he was not like Osburn, or Oswald, or his father. He was far better, even if he did not shine with virtue, like Connor. He was darker, more troubled, more full of pain and sorrow. His noble impulses, the true goodness that lived in him, had been pushed far below the surface. But like the diamonds that came from far inside the earth, those virtues were all the more precious and valuable when they finally came to light.

She had seen the worst of him, but here, now, she was seeing the best of him. He had seen her, too, as few ever had, including her family. In her duress, she had shown him the real Isabelle—the woman who was nothing like the demure sort most noblemen wanted for their wives. Yet she had seen admiration in his eyes even when she'd upbraided him and defied him and fought him. She had seen the tenderness there, too, as he had nursed her after he had carried her from that dungeon.

Her heart seemed to open and expand, and what had been a grudging admiration, gratitude and undeniable lust combined and melded into a new and powerful emotion that she could no longer hold back, or deny.

She loved him. She loved the bastard son of her family's enemy, the man who had stolen her away— and who had brought her back again. She loved him with a greater depth of feeling than she had even suspected she possessed.

Now she understood why Allis had done what she had done to be with Connor. Why her father had been so stricken with grief at her mother's death that it had drained the vibrancy from his own. Why a woman would leave her home and all its comforts to be with a man who stirred the embers of her heart into fierce and fiery flame. She could even understand, if not excuse, why Alexander's mother had pined for her unworthy lover long after he had abandoned her.

But despite her love, there could not be a future together for them. Even if she begged for mercy for Alexander, she doubted he would get it. He had committed a serious offense, and Connor and every other nobleman in England who feared for their family's safety from kidnap and ransom would demand that he be punished as an example. No doubt the safest place for him would be with Ingar and his men.

So they had no hope and no future together, except for this one night. After tomorrow, she would never see him again.

She would be home, she would be safe . . . and she would surely measure every man who came to ask for her hand against her memory of Alexander, and find him lacking.

But they had this one night.

As the sun sank below the trees on the other side of the stream, she took Alexander's face between her hands. "I forgive you, Alexander."

Then, as his eyes widened with astonishment, she pulled him to her and kissed him.

Deeply. Passionately.

She didn't care if it was right or wrong. She didn't wonder anymore how or why she could love him. She didn't care about anything other than being with him, if just this once. Her whole body cried out for him, and her heart yearned to be with him completely.

If only just this once.

With a low moan, he clasped her to him, gathering her into his arms as he returned her kiss, passion for passion, need for need. Reveling in his powerful embrace, her hands slid slowly through his tangled hair and pulled him closer still, so that her breasts pressed against the hard muscles of his chest. Deepening the kiss, she thrust her tongue into his willing mouth.

With a low moan of matching hunger, his broad, strong hands moved down her back with a leisure that belied the fire of his lips and tongue. She arched against him, the rough wool of her gown rubbing against her in a way that sent new tremors of excitement through her already excited body.

His mouth left hers to trail featherlight kisses along her neck down to her collarbone. She groaned softly, the sound voicing her wanton demands, encouraging him. Telling him in a way words never could how much she wanted him, and this.

For a long while they kissed, and caressed and touched, warmed by their embrace even as the sun disappeared and night slowly fell.

She slipped her hand beneath his tunic to feel his taut flesh, not visible now but so well remembered. He gasped as the pads of her fingertips tiptoed across his stomach. Arching against him, she silently invited him to touch her intimately, too, as he had before.

His eyes flew open, and he caught hold of her hand. His hot, eager gaze searched her face in the dusk and belied the words he spoke. "We must stop."

"Must we?"

"Yes." He shakily ran his hand through his disheveled hair. Hades, indeed, dark and brooding and wondrous. "I . . . I forgot myself, and what must be."

She faced him squarely, boldly, as an equal. As she always had. "If I didn't want to be with you this way, don't you think you would know it?" She took hold of his hand and led him toward the shelter they had built.

He stared at her incredulously as he grasped what she was offering. He halted outside the shelter and planted his feet, giving her the oddest sensation. It was as if he were playing the coy maiden and she the ravaging savage. The notion made her nearly as giddy as her desire, until he spoke in a grim and serious voice. "You could get with child."

It was as if a wave had come up from the sea to wash over her, for he was right.

"You're a virgin, too," he said.

"Yes."

"Do you understand all that you give up if you let me make love with you?"

She reached out to take his callused hands in hers, feeling the strength in them—and in him, that would allow him to refrain from taking what she was so obviously offering. "Does anyone, Alexander?" she mused. "Does any of us ever really know what we risk when we fall in love?"

He stiffened, his eyes wide with disbelief. "What are you saying, Isabelle?"

She looked up at him, willing to let him see her sincerity, and hear it in her voice. "I'm saying I have fallen in love with you."

He stepped back, as if she had shoved his dagger into his flesh. "You can't have."

She smiled wistfully, hearing her own doubts echoed in his words. "I thought I could not, too. I knew I *should* not. But I cannot lie to you about what I feel, any more than I can to myself anymore. Not now. Not when this will be our last chance to be together."

He took another step back. "I will not make love with you, Isabelle, and not just because of a possible child." His gaze faltered. "I dare not, for your sake. And my own." His hands curling into fists of tension, he raised his tortured eyes. "I already fear I will end up like my mother. I see myself forever mourning the love I lost. In my arrogance I thought I was strong and proof against such loving weakness, but God help me, I am not."

She took his hand and pressed it against her cheek. "Love is not weakness, Alexander. I thought it was, too, and secretly cursed my sister for her frailty, and my father, too. But we have been wrong. Love is strength, Alexander, for good or ill. It has the power to destroy, or the power to redeem, to fulfill, to make us more than we were. Even if we must part, Alexander, and forever mourn the parting, I will be stronger for having loved you. I will know what love is, if nothing else. No matter what else happens to me in this life, I will have loved once completely, wondrously, with all of my heart. I will not regret that."

He twisted away from her, as if the touch of her skin burned his flesh. "Isabelle, I love you as I never believed I could love anyone, but there can be no future for us. Please, do not tempt me to give in to my desire for you. I will not have another bastard child endure what I have."

She went close to him, but with great effort did not touch him. "And you think you are not a good man? Here is proof that you are, if I needed more." She gave him another wistful smile. "But Allis and Connor would not cast me out, even if I disgraced them."

"Isabelle," he pleaded, his willpower fast losing the struggle against his desire.

"I will respect your wishes, and your wisdom, Alexander. As you say, I do not fully understand what it is I crave."

He nearly groaned.

"Can we not simply be near one another?" she proposed. "I promise I will try not to touch you, although it will be difficult."

"No." He gestured at the shelter. "Go to sleep. We may have another long walk tomorrow. I'm going to build a fire, and I'll stay near it."

Isabelle nodded and knelt down, then disappeared beneath the leaves and branches.

Scarcely knowing what he did, Alexander set about gathering dry dead grass, twigs and branches to make a fire, although it was nearly pitch dark. He had to do something to take his mind from her, the woman who'd said she loved him. The woman who had been willing to make love with him. Aye, and more than willing, to offer her beautiful body along with her heart.

It was wonderful and terrible, and never had he been more wretched.

He felt around for the tinderbox in the leather pouch. His hand curled around it and he drew it out, then struck the flint and steel. The sparks were bright in the darkness as they flew onto the tinder.

He blew gently on the ones that began to smoke until flame appeared, then he added larger sticks. As the fire grew, the smoke rose up in the still air, and it cast a flickering light over their little clearing, and the sides of the shelter where Isabelle, who loved him, lay.

On her side in the little shelter that smelled of damp foliage, her arms wrapped around herself for both warmth and comfort, Isabelle was wide awake. The scent of the smoke drifted into her nostrils, and she could hear small sounds of animals held back by the fire.

And by the presence of Alexander, too, no doubt.

She rolled over onto her back. She wasn't going to fall asleep, although she was tired and the branches beneath her were relatively soft and springy. She couldn't. All she could think about was Alexander, and what he had said.

He was right that there could be serious consequences of giving in to her desires. She should guard her virginity and keep it for her future husband.

Who would not be Alexander.

She should not bear a child out of wedlock.

Not even his.

She should be thinking about seeing Allis, and making sure she was well, and Connor and all at Bellevoire who cherished her.

But who did not make her feel as beloved and necessary as Alexander could with just one glance from his intense blue eyes.

No one had ever loved her as he did. Not her family, not any of the young suitors who had paid her attention. Auberan—poor, foolish Auberan—

might have loved her in his poor, foolish way. She had cared for him as she would a kitten or a puppy that was incapable of caring for itself. There had been nothing of the passionate hunger that Alexander inspired.

As she expelled her breath in a sigh, she heard a new sound—the slight patter of raindrops on the leaves above her. Even as she identified it, the rain began to fall more heavily.

She sat up and scooted toward the entrance of the shelter. Alexander sat on the far side of the clearing, huddled miserably beneath a tree. Between them was the remains of the fire, a damp, smoking mess of twigs and ash.

"Come here where it is dry," she called out to him.

"I don't think that's wise," came his answer.

"Is it any wiser to sit in the rain when there is shelter here?" She thought of something more to say, and with a bittersweet sigh before speaking, she added, "I promise you'll be safe. I won't touch you. Alexander, don't be a fool."

She held her breath as she waited, wondering if he would truly rather be soaked through than share the shelter with her. If he did, she didn't know whether she would laugh or cry.

Suddenly he crouched at the entrance, his wet hair clinging to his head. She had not heard him approach.

"Since I would not have you think me any more of a fool than I already am, and I do not want to get sick, I accept your offer of hospitality, my lady."

He shoved his sword and scabbard in along the side, then crawled in. She could see him more clearly now that he was so close, and he made a rueful smile as he looked at her. "I also appreciate that you will respect my honor as I respected yours," he said, his voice low and soft and deep.

Her chest constricted and she suddenly wondered if this had been a good idea, after all. Still, she didn't want him to fall ill, either. "I'll . . . try."

"Try?" The word came softly. "Have I not your word that you will not touch me?"

"I will not give my word when I doubt that I can keep it. When I do not want to keep it."

He turned. "Perhaps I should go back out into the rain—"

She grabbed his arm. "No!"

For one moment when all seemed still, when she did not even hear the rain, he turned back and their gazes met, and held.

And then nothing else mattered except their love. Whatever thoughts and fears and doubts lingered were suddenly unimportant, immaterial, consumed by the fire of their love and desire, and the knowledge that they were alone.

With hot, fierce need Alexander gathered Isabelle into his arms and kissed her. As he did, passion and need combined and ripped through her willing body. She thrust her tongue between his lips, feverishly deepening the kiss.

Wanting far more, she lay on her back and pulled him down with her, so that his body covered hers, his weight gloriously welcome, the pressure of his hips against hers astonishing and arousing.

Her swift and eager hands tore off his tunic and shoved it aside. She caressed his glorious skin and taut muscles, feeling the scars of old wounds and injuries that told her he was no callow youth, no young man full of silly ideals of love or seeking someone to guide him. He was a man, with a man's desire and a man's heat. Kissing him still, she pushed him up, then broke the kiss. Wrapping her arm around his neck, one hand free to stroke and touch as she would, she raised herself to kiss his chest, to let her lips play where her fingertips had been.

With a groan, he clenched his teeth.

Then she found his nipple. Remembering well how his light touch had inflamed her, she licked and flicked her tongue across it. His breath caught and he made a low sound in his throat that thrilled her.

And then he was pressing her down into the branches that made their bed, his lips hot on hers as his hands found the lacing that held her bodice closed. With impatient fingers he broke them and pulled her bodice lower, exposing her breasts. Then, with a sound like a cross between a growl and a purr, he began to stroke and kiss and lick, his tongue like the most sinuous fingertip playing upon her flesh.

Gasping, she gripped his upper arms, the muscles as hard as granite beneath her palm. What she had done for him was as nothing. His mouth and hands teased, enticed, aroused. The tension within her grew and grew, and she panted as if she had run for miles. Moving instinctively beneath him, she undulated with an anxious yearning that seemed limitless.

She bent her legs and pushed her feet against the ground, raising her hips as he moved, trying to do something about the throbbing need blossoming between them. He kissed her again, and his hand splayed upon her thigh, pushing up her skirt.

Their lips still joined, their tongues still dancing together, she clawed at his breeches. She wanted to make love with him. She wanted him to take her. Now!

When he was free, she fell back, breathing hard. He loomed above her, the Hades who aroused her, the warrior she desired, the man she loved.

Yet he hesitated.

She put her hand about his neck and pulled him close. "Love me, Alexander," she whispered, taking him in her hand and guiding him to the place throbbing with excitement. "Please, Alexander, love me."

His control snapped. Even as he had been swept up in the incredible rush of excitement and desire she inspired, a small part of his mind had still urged caution. He knew too well the price a woman could pay for loving unwisely, without marriage.

But when Isabelle had said she would try not to touch him, the first of many barriers had shattered. When she had pulled him down on top of her, the second had crashed.

Then, as she had used her tongue on his body, most of the remaining walls of his self-control had crumbled into dust. And when she'd encircled him with her hand and brought him to her, the last of the obstacles between them melted away.

She wanted this. She wanted *him*.

He pushed inside her, tearing her maidenhead.

He heard her gasp with the pain of it and, despairing and cursing himself anew, he prepared to withdraw. But in the next moment, she thrust her hips against him, with a power that shocked him. She grabbed his head and brought him to her for another mind-numbing kiss—and he thought no more. He controlled nothing more. He surrendered to their passion and rode upon the waves of ecstasy as she met him, thrust for thrust.

With every motion, the exquisite tension grew, propelling him into a realm of heated bliss such as he had never known. With every push of his hips and answering response of hers, his body seemed to tighten more and more.

He cupped her breasts, firm and round, and brushed her nipple with his fingertip. She murmured and moaned, the sounds enflaming his desire as much as her touch. He bent his head and sucked the pebbled nub into his mouth.

She cried out and bucked and her muscles clenched, then throbbed. His whole body seemed to clench, down to his toes, and then, like a rope snapping, he climaxed. Wave after wave of release surged through him, taking him and leaving him spent.

Still inside her, he rested his head between her breasts as his ragged breathing returned to normal. He could hear her heartbeat as it, too, slowed, and her breathing eased.

He raised himself to look down at her beautiful face. "Oh, God, Isabelle, I love you."

"As I love you." Even in the darkness, he could tell her eyes were gleaming with the bold, defiant spirit he knew so well. "And whatever happens, Alexander, I am not the least bit sorry for what we have done. I never will be."

Chapter 20

Half-awake, Isabelle snuggled closer to Alexander's warm body. He had held her close all night, his arm about her, so although it had grown cool and the branches had not been the most comfortable of bedding, she had slept relatively well.

But now it was morning of their last day, and all the comfortable ease gave way to dismay.

A glance outside showed that although it was not night, the sun had not risen very high. The grass and rocks glittered with early morning dew, and at some time in the night, a spider had made a web between the V of the two sides of the shelter. Droplets of water hung on it, sparkling like diamonds.

Alexander stirred, and she looked up to find his blue eyes upon her. "Awake, my love?" he whispered as he brushed back a lock of her hair that had fallen across her cheek. A little wrinkle appeared between his dark brows. "One of the many things I'm sorry for is not stopping Osburn from cutting off your hair."

Raising herself on her elbow, she brushed a lock of his black hair back in turn. "Well, it *is* a little disconcerting to have shorter hair than you." She kissed the wrinkle. "Still, of all the things he might have done, that is not so bad."

With a sigh, he took her face between his palms and brought her close to kiss her. If he intended it to be a playful kiss, that intention did not last beyond the first moment their lips touched. As always, the passion they shared kindled into vibrant, undeniable life. Isabelle gave in to it, leaning upon his powerful chest and sliding her mouth over his slowly.

His hot, strong hand splayed upon the skin of her back exposed by the torn lacing of her bodice, and the sensation sent excited thrills down her spine to other places. Reacting to the need burning within her, she put her leg over his hips, then inched closer until she was half over him.

Last night, she had meant what she'd said. She had no regrets about making love with him. She would have regretted it more if they had not, and so she still believed. So now, when he rolled her onto her back and looked at her, his blue eyes dark with desire, she smiled to show him she would not regret making love again.

He needed no more encouragement than that this time, yet he did not rush their loving. With exquisite leisure, he began to caress her body, creating that wondrous tension and anxious yearning. She took her own time to explore his magnificent flesh, to learn all she could of it, to remember forever.

As she arched against him, rubbing her pelvis against him in a shameless but necessary way, his lips left hers. Her eyes closed, she drew in a deep breath, then gasped as he sucked her earlobe between his teeth. His tongue toyed with it as if it were her tongue and they were kissing.

She had never guessed . . .

As he continued teasing her ear, his hand stroked her gown lower, his touch as light as a silken scarf passing over her skin.

Impatient for what she wanted next, she clutched his shoulders and ground her hips against him. "Please, Alexander," she murmured, too excited to do much more as he continued to arouse her with his lips and his hands.

"Patience," he whispered in response, sliding his hand from her breasts to her waist and lower as he turned, so that both were on their sides. "I have to make certain you are ready."

He cupped her between her thighs, rubbing gently, sending the first ripples of release rushing through her. "Ready?" she said through clenched teeth. "I am more than ready, and I will not be patient."

She pushed him back and hiked up her skirt to straddle him. His eyes widened even as they gleamed with anticipation, and his breathing grew ragged and hoarse. With slow deliberation, she raised herself and used one hand to position him. Then she lowered herself, groaning softly with the sheer pleasure of having him inside her.

Whispering his delight, he raised his hips in time with her as she rocked forward. Her breath caught, and it was not merely with the sensation of his power and strength filling her, although that was a part of it. It was knowing that in one way, she was the master here.

Elated and excited, she grabbed his wrists and held them above his head. His eyes flew open.

"Here you are mine, Alexander DeFrouchette, to do with as I will." She leaned down to trail her lips along his cheek toward his mouth. "Until we must part, you are mine."

She rocked again, raising herself until he was nearly free, then pushing down so that he was deep within. Closing his eyes, another groan burst from his throat. She moved again before bending down to suck his nipple, as he had done.

Alexander squirmed and moaned as she kept his wrists pinned. He could overpower her at any time, if he chose to, and the fact that he did not excited her even more, for it meant he enjoyed ceding his power to her. She could do what she wanted to arouse him, and herself.

Spurred by that, she quickened her rhythm. His hoarse breathing soon matched her own, and she had to stop kissing him to draw in air. Then, caught up in the passion, nearing completion, she dragged her hands from his wrists along his arms to stroke his chest. His hands now free, he lifted them to knead her breasts.

With increasing anticipation, she quickened her thrusts and pressed down with more urgency. The sounds of his own harsh breathing, the sensation of his rough hands on her skin, the feel of him inside her, overpowered her and finally the tension burst and pulsed through her.

Alexander arched and moaned, the tendons in his neck taut as he grabbed her hips and bucked with his own release.

She collapsed against his sweat-slicked body, gloriously tired, blissfully complete.

He held her gently and kissed her forehead. In her drowsy haze, Isabelle tried not to think of what lay ahead. *Enjoy this present*, she told herself, her cheek upon his chest.

All too soon, he shifted and parted from her. "Isabelle?"

She tried not to notice, even as he pushed her skirt back over her legs. "Mmmmm?"

"The sun is up. We must rise."

"Not yet," she murmured, although she felt the cold fingers of What Must Be creeping down her back. "A little longer."

He cupped her chin so that she had to look at his sorrowful face. "I would have this moment last forever, but it will not. We knew last night that it must be so. We knew it this morning. Pretending otherwise will avail us nothing."

"Are you so anxious to be rid of me?" She kissed him quickly when she saw his expression alter. "Forgive me, Alexander. I just want to stay with you for as long as I can."

His face betrayed an anguish as deep and painful as her own. "I would be with you always, but we know that's impossible. This night has been a dream far better than any I have ever had before, but it is time to wake and face the day."

Reluctantly, she sat up and hugged her knees.

"And then you must go with Ingar. To what kind of life have you consigned yourself for my sake, Alexander?"

He sat up and tied his breeches. "It is the life I consigned myself to when I agreed to abduct you. It is my fault, and my choice." He darted her a questioning glance. "How did you learn of my bargain with Ingar? Denis?"

"No. Ingar told me." She reached out to caress his cheek. "Although he's not what I thought a Norseman would be like, it will be a brutal, lonely life." Her chin began to tremble, but she could not find the strength to hide her sorrow. "Worst of all, I may never know what happens to you. I will never know if you are alive, or dead."

Kneeling, he took her by the shoulders. His resolve had never been stronger. "When you are home again, Isabelle, you must forget me—"

"No! I never will, and I don't want to!"

"Then you must think of what happened as a nightmare that came to an end."

"You're not a nightmare!"

That lightened his grim visage. "Then the nightmare had some better moments." He became serious again. "But it will be over, and so it must be, in your mind and in your heart, too."

"Alexander, I—"

"It will be *over*," he repeated, allowing her no dissension, once more the hard commander. Then his expression softened, if only a little. "Let me think that is so, Isabelle. Let me envision you having a happy life, the kind you deserve."

"With another man? Bearing another man's children?"

For one brief moment, he looked as if she had delivered a mortal blow, then his features assumed a stoic calm. "Yes. I dearly hope I have not got you with child, and I will curse myself even more if I have. Now, come. We have a ways to walk yet."

He crawled out of the shelter.

Isabelle did not immediately follow. She understood why he said what he did, she could even understand how he could picture her living a life without him. And he was right, she supposed, as she felt for the broken lacing and did her best to tie them with her trembling fingers. There was no future for them, and it would make her life difficult if she bore his child. It would be better if she did not, and best if she could forget she had ever met Alexander DeFrouchette.

She finally felt defeated.

Suddenly Alexander cried out, and something crashed through the underbrush.

Grabbing his sword, she scrambled out of the tent—to see Alexander being held in the fierce grip of two soldiers. Another man clad in chain mail and armor held the tip of a sword at her beloved's throat, and several more soldiers clustered around them in the clearing. Alexander was disheveled, and so were the men holding him, one of whom was going to have a black eye. As for the one holding his sword at Alexander's throat—

"Connor!" Isabelle cried, still clutching Alexander's sword as she got to her feet. Her brother-in-law whirled around.

Knowing that it was Connor and his men who had found them, yet also realizing what that meant for Alexander, joy and fear, delight and panic warred in

Isabelle as Connor lowered his sword. A broad smile lit his face as he strode across the clearing and hugged her tightly. "Oh, thank God, thank God!"

Dropping Alexander's sword, she returned her brother-in-law's embrace, and for a moment, her tumultuous emotions overwhelmed her.

Connor drew back and ran an anxious gaze over her and her hair. "You are well? You are not hurt?"

Regaining her self-control, mindful that Alexander was in the custody of Connor's men, she picked up his sword and nodded. "I was not harmed, or attacked."

More relief flashed across Connor's face, and she knew that if Connor believed that Alexander had raped her, he would have died on the spot. Indeed, she knew that might be Alexander's fate unless she could convince Connor that he must be allowed to leave. "You have to let Alexander DeFrouchette go. He was bringing me back."

Connor clearly didn't know what to make of her statement, or her demand. "Let him go?"

"Yes. He was willing to forgo the ransom. That's why we are here alone."

Connor's sharp glance darted between her and Alexander. "You've been through a terrible ordeal, Isabelle, but it's over now. Let's get you back to Bellevoire."

She stood her ground. "You have to let him go."

"I will not walk away and let this man go free," Connor replied, his tone shifting to one of command. "You are tired and overwrought, Isabelle. We shall return to Bellevoire, and then I will decide what is to be done."

"*You* will decide? I was the one he abducted."

"Exactly," Connor retorted. "You were abducted, by this man and at least one other. I am not about to excuse him for that."

Her grip on Alexander's sword tightened. "Connor, you must listen to me."

Her brother-in-law swept her up in his strong arms. "Not now and not here."

Before she could voice any protest or struggle her way out of his arms, he set her on one of his soldier's mounts. "First, we return to Bellevoire, then . . ." His expression softened a little as he looked up at her. "Then I will listen to what you have to say, after you've had a chance to eat and rest."

As she gazed down at her lordly brother-in-law, Isabelle realized there was nothing she could say or do at present that would make him change his mind. In truth, it might be better if she marshaled arguments a man would understand: less to do with feelings and more to do with vows and agreements.

Connor reached up to take the sword from her, but she clasped it to her breast. "I will keep this."

His brow furrowed, but Connor said no more about it as he mounted. "Bring the prisoner to Bellevoire," he commanded his soldiers. He ran another scornful gaze over Alexander. "And let him walk."

From the moment Connor and Isabelle were spotted near the village, the news that Lady Isabelle had been found spread through Bellevoire like fire in dry grass. By the time they reached the green, a crowd had gathered, full of smiling and obviously curious people. Beaming as brightly as if he'd rescued her himself, Bartholomew led the villagers in a rousing cheer as they rode by.

Isabelle was grateful for such a reception and couldn't fault them for being curious, but she also knew that speculation as to what had happened to her would be the topic of conversation for months to come. She wondered what they would say if they knew *all* that had happened.

But she still had no regrets, and even now, her thoughts were with the bound Alexander, whose eventual arrival was sure to elicit a far different welcome.

When they arrived in the castle courtyard, the door to the hall flew open and Allis ran down the steps toward them, her arms wide, as if she wanted to embrace them horse and all. "Isabelle!"

At that moment, all Isabelle felt was an equal, overwhelming joy. She didn't wait for Connor to dismount but threw her leg over the horse and jumped down.

Allis immediately enveloped her in a crushing embrace. "You're here! You're safe! Thank God, thank God!"

Still gripping Alexander's sword, Isabelle held her sister tight. During the long days and longer nights of her captivity, when Alexander had still seemed her enemy, and especially when she had been in that dank cell, thoughts of being back with her family had been her greatest source of hope and strength.

"I'll take my horse to the stable," Connor murmured behind them.

Reminded they were not alone, Isabelle let go of Allis and wiped her eyes before regarding her sister with concern. "Are *you* well?" She lowered her voice. "And the baby?"

Her eyes alight with happiness, Allis smiled. "I'm fine—wonderful, now that you are here and safe." She briefly hugged Isabelle again, then drew back to scrutinize her. "You must rest, and eat, and I'll have a bath drawn up at once. Edmond is out on patrol, but he will want to see you as soon as he hears the good news."

"Edmond?" Isabelle cried with surprise.

"I sent for him at once after you were taken," Allis explained. "Caradoc brought him. He's out on patrol, too. Neither of them could stand being idle while you were . . . were . . ."

"Not here."

Allis nodded. "Yes."

The low murmur of many voices reached Isabelle's ears. She quickly scanned the yard and realized that several people were now watching them with smiles on their faces, except for Mildred, who stood on the steps weeping. Efe, Leoma and Gleda were near her, obviously and avidly curious.

It wasn't difficult to imagine what they would think if they learned how she felt about Alexander. Efe would assume she'd been bewitched, Leoma would say it must be because of his dark good looks, and Gleda . . . Gleda would see only the son of Rennick DeFrouchette, a man she loathed.

Allis followed her gaze and, with a tender smile, took Isabelle's arm. "Everyone in Bellevoire has been worried about you. Now come and let me look after you."

Isabelle made no move to go. "I need to speak with Connor right away. He has captured Alexander DeFrouchette and he must free him."

Allis frowned, and her pink cheeks flushed as her gaze flicked to Isabelle's shorn locks. "He caught DeFrouchette?"

"Yes, he was bringing me back and—"

"Inside," Allis said. Although there was sympathy and loving concern in her eyes, her maternal tone would brook no protest. "We will talk about that man in private."

Perhaps that would be better, Isabelle silently acquiesced, glancing at the growing crowd of onlookers.

As she walked beside Allis toward the hall, her sister glanced down at the weapon.

"I want to keep this," Isabelle said in answer to her silent query.

Allis looked puzzled, and far from pleased, but she did not object.

As they approached the hall, Mildred trotted down the steps to meet them. "Oh, my lady," she sobbed as she wiped her nose with the back of her hand, "I'm so happy!"

The other maidservants who were clustered on the stairs murmured similar sentiments, their voices like a breeze through the rushes by the river. Isabelle smiled at all of them, while the sniffling Mildred hurried on ahead. "I'll get some hot water," she said, anxious to be helpful.

Isabelle and Allis continued on into the hall that should have been Alexander's. Isabelle could so easily imagine him here, standing on the dais in fine clothes with her, his wife, by his side. A man of such humble origins, he would understand better than most noblemen the troubles his peasants faced—poverty, hunger, injustice.

"You don't have to talk about what happened, Isabelle," Allis said, softly interrupting her reverie as they began to go up the stairs toward Isabelle's chamber. "Not unless you want to. No matter what has happened, all I care about is that you are safely here again."

"I am here because of Alexander DeFrouchette."

The corners of Allis's lips turned down in a displeased expression Isabelle knew well. "You have been through a great deal," she said, "and it may take some time before you are yourself again. When you are—"

Isabelle halted in the relative privacy of the stairwell. "I'm not an infant, Allis."

"I know."

"Do you? Do you see me as a woman, or only your little sister?"

Allis regarded her warily, and with a hint of frustration. "You are tired and upset, Isabelle. Besides, it is not for us to decide Alexander DeFrouchette's fate. That will be for one of the assize justices to decide. He can be here in a few days."

Isabelle sucked in her breath, more worried than ever for Alexander. Judges who represented the Crown traveled on set routes, holding court on matters beyond the scope of the local overlord. Because she was a lady, her abduction would be one such matter.

She could guess how such a judge would rule, and it would not be in Alexander's favor. No matter what she said, a judge was not likely to listen to a woman, especially if Connor contradicted her.

She had to convince Connor to let Alexander go before the judge arrived. And if he would not . . .

She would think of something else.

His back against the stone wall of the dungeon below one of the many inner towers of Bellevoire, Alexander slumped on a rough wooden bed that had a thin straw mattress and no blanket. Straw covered the flagstones of the floor, and a bucket that was not too rank stood in one corner. He could hear rats scurrying nearby, but none were in the cell, thank God.

There was one small window high up in the wall, grilled, and far too high to look out of. A bit of light made its way into the room, enough to illuminate it a little, and to tell him that he had been here for a night and a day and a night.

So here he was at last, an inhabitant of Bellevoire, the castle that he had never deserved, in a far better cell than the one Isabelle had endured. She had not been to see him here, and he tried to accept that. Now that she was safely among her family, it must seem to her that all that had happened between them on the journey back to Bellevoire had been no more than a pleasant interlude in an otherwise unpleasant dream, best forgotten upon waking.

Sighing, he scanned the room again, although he had the dimensions and furnishings memorized. He had had little else to do but look at them, and think, and try not to wonder about his fate, for that always led to the same conclusion: death.

Voices and steps approached, the voices low and the thud of boots loud. He scrambled to his feet. He would not be found in an attitude of defeat and despair, no matter how he felt.

A key turned in the heavy iron lock in the thick wooden door. It creaked open and two soldiers entered, one carrying a torch. The other was a big, burly fellow whose helmet shone in the dim light. The one with the torch was thinner, and his eyes gleamed with a malevolence that would have done credit to a Brabancon.

"Sir Connor wants to see you," the burly one said in the low growl of a Cornishman.

Before Alexander could respond, the force of a blow from the burly man's fist split his lip. As Alexander tasted blood, the one with the torch drew his sword. He poked Alexander's chest to push him back against the wall. Holding his arms out in surrender, Alexander obeyed.

"That's good, Charlie," the burly one said. "I'll tie his hands."

"There's no need for that," Alexander said through his swollen lips. "I won't run and I won't fight. I give you my word."

"Oh, ho!" the one named Charlie scoffed. "D'ya hear him, Burt? His word! That's a good'un." He scowled at Alexander. "The word of a blackguard like you doesn't count for nothing."

Burt grabbed Alexander's wrist and wrenched his arm so that Alexander had to turn his back to him. "Make it tight, Burt," Charlie said.

"I am. I only wish it was irons." Burt took hold of Alexander's other arm and tied his wrists together with a rough hemp rope that started to cut Alexander's wrists before the knot was even tied. He leaned forward and growled in Alexander's ear. "Count yourself lucky you're still in one piece, you lump of dung. If it was up to Charlie and me, you'd be minus your balls by now."

Charlie nodded with an eagerness that made Alexander realize how close he was to that fate, and probably worse besides. "I brought your lady's sister back unharmed."

Burt shoved him hard against the wall, so that his cheek was pressed against the rough, cold stones. The man held him there with an elbow in his back, and Alexander could feel another trickle of blood from his cheekbone below his left eye. "Mighty big o' you, is that it?" Burt jeered. "By the saints, I'd hang you myself if Sir Connor gave the word."

"Is he? Is he about to give the word?" Alexander asked, his face still up against the wall, wondering if he was going to that end, and not really caring. His fate had been sealed from the moment Connor had held his sword at his throat in the clearing.

Burt grabbed his tunic and hauled him back, then pushed him toward the door. "Not him. He's got notions of doing things by law, so you won't die today. Not by his order anyway."

Unable to use his hands, the bindings cutting his flesh, Alexander stumbled out the door and up the steps. "Then what does he want?" He didn't think Sir Connor was the sort to go in for torture, but his life had shown him he was no fit judge of men.

"What do you care, as long as he ain't gonna kill

ya? Get going," Charlie ordered with a swift kick on Alexander's back.

"Now we're seeing just what sort of blackguard DeFrouchette bred, eh?" Burt sneered from further behind him. "Rotten apples the pair of you."

Alexander didn't dispute it.

When they reached the exit, Charlie doused his torch in a bucket of sand by the door. Then he grabbed hold of Alexander's tunic and pushed him through the door so hard that Alexander fell on his knees on the cobblestones.

Trying to ignore the pain, Alexander blinked in the brighter light. It wasn't the full light of day, for the sun was low, but after being confined in the dungeon, it seemed so.

Burt pulled him up by the bindings around his wrist, and Alexander had to clench his teeth to keep from crying out.

Once he was on his feet, the two soldiers began to push, prod and shove him across the courtyard. Three serving women—very different from Hielda and her ilk—stopped to watch.

"Look at him—not so high and mighty now, eh?" one muttered.

"Spittin' image of his father and just as bad!" the oldest of them declared, glaring at him.

"I wish I had the punishin' of 'im!" the prettiest of them said, with a bloodthirsty glint in her eye.

Then he heard another voice, from the vicinity of the gate. "But if there is to be a celebration, you *must* let me see the lord. I am the best tumbler in all of Europe."

Alexander nearly fell over as he recognized Denis's voice. Craning his neck, he saw his friend talking to the guards at the gate, and he thought he made out Kiera standing just behind him. What in the name of the saints were they doing here? They should have been miles away.

Surely Denis didn't harbor some mad notion that they could rescue him from this vast and well-manned fortress? He would get captured, and then they might both face death.

Denis caught sight of Alexander. Fearing that any sign of recognition would immediately put Denis in danger, Alexander quickly looked down at the cobblestones at his feet.

At last they reached the hall. There were more servants here, women mostly, and although they didn't speak, the way they looked at him was more than enough to tell him they agreed with Burt, Charlie and those in the courtyard.

His journey did not end there, for Burt and Charlie pushed him on toward what must be Sir Connor's solar. After they knocked, Sir Connor opened the door. He ran a quick gaze over Alexander, then regarded his men with disapproval. "What happened to him?"

"Gave us some trouble, sir," Burt said meekly. "Big fella like that . . . bound to, wasn't he?"

"What did he do? Attack you?" Sir Connor demanded, staring at Charlie in a way that made the fellow blanch. "From what I've heard of him, I doubt that. If he had, you wouldn't be standing here now, not without a few bruises and cuts, at least. You two are confined to your barracks when you're not on duty."

Burt and Charlie looked as stunned as Alexander

felt. "B-but sir—" Burt stammered, recovering first.

"Do as I say, or you won't be in my garrison another day!"

With that, Connor took hold of Alexander's shoulder, pulled him into the solar and slammed the door.

Chapter 21

As Alexander lurched to a halt in the finely furnished room, a movement caught his eye.

It was Isabelle, rising swiftly from a chair near a
large oak table.

She wore a beautiful gown of green that fell in soft
ripples to the floor, the cuffs long and lined with
gold. A gilded girdle rested on her slim hips, and her
short blond hair was held back at the sides by two
golden combs.

"You're hurt!" she cried, clasping her hands but
keeping her distance, either because she was not the
only person there or because what he had anticipated had come to pass. Once she was safe with her
family, her feelings for him had altered.

He thought he had prepared himself for that; he
had not.

As dismay washed over him, he took note of who
else was gathered there, no doubt to sit in judgment
upon him.

Lady Allis was seated beside Isabelle. A young man stood behind them, one hand on Isabelle's chair. To judge by his blond hair and eyes, he was their younger brother, Edmond.

"My men were overzealous," Connor said as he unexpectedly slit the ropes around Alexander's wrists with a dagger he returned to his belt. "Not surprising, given what you've done. However, I shall remind them that they are to obey orders, not take matters into their own hands."

Alexander rubbed his wrists, confused that he was no longer bound.

"Aye, they've overstepped the mark," another man said with a Welsh accent.

Alexander started as a stranger stepped out from the shadows on the opposite side of the room from Isabelle. "And you'll have to come down hard on them, or they'll get out of hand quickly."

With his dark hair and angular features, the fellow looked rather like Connor, enough to lead Alexander to suspect this was an older relative, and apparently one who liked to give advice.

Even more surprising, Alexander had the distinct sensation that he should know him, and it was not because of his resemblance to Sir Connor.

"I know how to handle my men," Connor replied, a hint of annoyance in his tone.

Connor went to the chair behind the table and gestured for Alexander to sit in the chair opposite—another unexpected action. Alexander waited for the older man to object, but the stranger merely leaned against the wall again, as if this matter were not of much concern to him. Meanwhile, Isabelle sank onto her seat.

"My sister-in-law seems to think I should be merciful and let you go," Connor began. "Indeed, she was quite eloquent in her pleas, and *very* persistent. In fact, she's barely given me a moment's peace since she's been back, practically harassing me until I agreed to listen to her."

Alexander looked at Isabelle and saw, in the depths of her shining eyes, the confirmation that he had been wrong to doubt the strength of her love and the fidelity of her devotion.

She loved him still, as he loved her.

"So I did listen," Connor continued. "Over and over again, until she convinced me that you put yourself at great risk to bring her here and that you never intended to collect the ransom when you did."

Once more, Alexander looked at Isabelle, loving her with all his heart. He should have guessed that she would be as fierce in his defense as she had been in her own. As Ingar had said, what a woman!

Best of all, what a woman who loved him!

"Lord Oswald was not the man I thought he was," Alexander said on his own behalf. "His decision to force Isabelle to marry Osburn was the last proof I needed that I had made a grievous error, and one that I had to correct."

"So Isabelle tells me. Yet surely you know I would have paid the ransom for her."

The younger man spoke. "DeFrouchette knew he couldn't get it without risking his neck," he said as scornfully as Burt or Charlie would, "so he gave it up. Better to forfeit some money than be dead, I daresay."

Isabelle twisted in her chair to look at him. "You shouldn't speak of what you don't understand, Edmond. He didn't have to risk his neck to bring me back at all. But if he hadn't, I'd be married to Osburn by now, which I assure you would have been a fate worse than death."

The young man's eyes fairly blazed with ire and determination, very like his sister's when she was enraged. "Are you forgetting the hell he's put us through?"

Isabelle jumped to her feet and glared at him. "I was put through hell, too. But he has brought me back, and if *I* can forgive him—"

"I can't and I won't!" Edmond cried, his face reddening as he gripped the back of her chair. "You women are all the same, with your emotions overruling common sense! If we let him go, what will people think, especially our enemies? That we are weak and—"

Connor brought his hand down on the table with a resounding bang, startling them all.

"Edmond, you are here by my leave," the overlord of Bellevoire said. "When I wish your opinion, I shall ask for it."

Edmond retreated into a smoldering silence, as if the fire that burned so vibrantly in Isabelle also lived in him—as a glowing, steady flame of discontent and anger.

Yet the young man was wrong. Connor was not weak, and woe betide the enemy who thought he was. He was everything Alexander had ever wished to be.

Isabelle returned to her seat. While the action may have been obedient, her expression declared how angry she still was.

Connor addressed Alexander. "Isabelle is adamant

that you be shown mercy for bringing her back to us. Since I have no doubt that she will find a way to make her case just as eloquently and persistently to any judge the king may send, I have decided to acquiesce to her wishes and set you free."

Relief and happiness poured through Alexander, but as always, now there was an undercurrent of sorrow. Yes, he would be free, but he must leave behind the woman who had secured that freedom despite all that he had done.

"You're going to let him *go*?" Edmond demanded.

"This is not your decision to make, Edmond. In some ways, it is not mine, either, but Isabelle's, for she has suffered the most from his actions."

"I don't believe it! After what he did—"

"Edmond, either be quiet, or go," Allis said, not raising her voice, but with a steely resolve he had often heard in Isabelle's. "Connor rules Bellevoire, not you."

Edmond stalked to the door, pausing to glare at them all. "When I come of age and Montclair is mine to rule, I will not allow blackguards and varlets to go free!"

He marched out, slamming the door behind him.

Alexander waited for someone else to agree with the angry young man, but nobody did. Instead, Isabelle turned to Allis. "I'm sorry."

Allis shook her head and patted Isabelle's hand, comforting her and inadvertently reminding Alexander that he could never offer comfort to Isabelle, of any kind, in any way, ever again.

"There are other reasons for this mercy," Allis said quietly. "You will find out in a moment. I will go speak to Edmond." She rose, as graceful as Isabelle as she swept from the chamber. "In the meantime, Connor, tell DeFrouchette as we decided."

What other reason for such mercy could exist? Or had Isabelle told them of their love? If so, what then?

Connor cleared his throat. "Alexander DeFrouchette, before I tell you anything more, I must say that even Isabelle couldn't persuade me into letting you go without some conditions."

Alexander bowed in acknowledgment and acceptance, for he had wronged them all very much.

"I will allow you to go free provided you tell us what you know of Oswald, his fortress and anything else we ask before you leave. I also want your word that you will never move against me or my family again."

His conditions were fair enough, and Alexander did not hesitate to respond. "I know nothing about the fortress, save that it is in Glamorgan, and even Prince Llewellyan has apparently forgotten its existence. It was little more than a ruin, as I'm sure Lady Isabelle has told you, temporarily repaired. I expect that after our escape, it will be abandoned once again. As for the other, you have my word that I will never cause any harm to you or your family for the rest of my life." His gaze faltered. "I hope my promise will be enough surety for you."

"Isabelle assures me it will be."

Alexander darted a grateful glance her way.

"Well, Caradoc, what say you?" Connor remarked, addressing the other man who had stayed in the shadows. "Shall we tell him all?"

All? What more could there be?

The other man ambled closer, studying Alexander in a way he found both disconcerting and familiar.

What *was* it about this stranger that tugged at the edges of his memory, that made him think he should know who he was?

His eyes. His brilliant blue eyes, studying him as his father had done on that day so long ago . . . sapphire blue eyes that were so like his own they could be mirror images. "Who *are* you?" Alexander demanded.

"I am Caradoc of Llanstephan, Connor's brother." Caradoc made a little smile. "Half brother, or so I've been told." He ran another gaze over Alexander. "And it seems I've got another half brother. *You.*"

Alexander gasped. This could not be . . . and yet his coloring, his eyes, even the very way he stood—different from Connor and so like his father's.

"My old nurse told me that my mother was raped by a young squire named Rennick DeFrouchette," Caradoc continued. "Apparently I am his son, not the son of the man who later sired Connor and our sister."

Alexander nodded slowly as he began to accept this possibility. "My father seduced and abandoned my mother and me, so I can see that he might not hesitate to rape if he thought he could get away unpunished," Alexander said. He could even hear how a man like his father would justify it.

"Seeing you, I am even more certain of that myself," Caradoc admitted. "Connor, Isabelle and Allis all agree you are the image of the man, and I see a resemblance between us that I cannot deny."

Alexander could not contradict it, either. "Then that means I am related to you."

"Aye, and so Connor, as well."

Alexander surveyed them all, lingering a moment

on Isabelle's sympathetic face before returning his gaze to Caradoc. "And that is also why you are being merciful," he concluded. "Because I am kin to you."

Isabelle stood and shoved her hands in the cuffs of her gown. "He is being merciful because you deserve it, Alexander."

As Alexander looked at Connor, he saw doubt in his face. Whatever Isabelle believed, Connor was not completely convinced he was doing the right thing. Nevertheless, Connor said, "Since you have agreed to my conditions, you may leave."

Alexander bowed low. "Thank you, my lord."

Connor stood. "I will escort you to the gate, so that all in Bellevoire will know you have my leave to go."

"Again, I thank you."

He was free. He could go.

There was one undeniably good thing about his release. There would be no need for Denis to rescue him. Denis and Kiera could leave without trouble.

Ingar would have sailed without him by now, which meant he was free of that obligation. It galled him to have gone back on his word. Still, it was not his fault he had not kept the rendezvous.

But he would never see Isabelle again.

He looked at her for the last time, drinking in the sight of her, determined to lock this memory of her in his mind for all time. At that moment, nobody else existed in the chamber for him. "Farewell, my lady."

She reached around for something behind the chair.

His sword.

Holding it out in front of her, she walked toward him, her eyes glowing with love and . . . and resolution, not sorrow. Fierce determination, not sadness.

Because Isabelle knew exactly what she had to do. It would mean leaving behind her family. It would mean beginning a new life of poverty and uncertainty, no longer a lady destined to marry a nobleman and be the chatelaine of a castle. She would have to give up that life forever.

She didn't care. If she did not do as her heart commanded, it would shrivel and die, destroyed, not merely broken, and her body might as well be dead along with it.

Strong in resolve, certain in her love, she said, "I'm going with you."

As Connor made a sound of protest and Caradoc stared, Alexander's gaze searched her resolute face. "You can't," he declared, once more the imperious warrior. "You cannot leave your home, your family. I won't let you."

"Surely you do not think you can order me in this, as well? Have you not learned the folly of that?" she queried with a little smile, unfazed by his words, her voice level, because she saw a different truth in his blue eyes. "Besides, if you don't let me go with you, I will follow you anyway. I love you, Alexander, and you love me. I will never love another as I do you, and I will be miserable without you. You would not condemn me to that, would you?"

She saw the moment he believed that she loved him. Happiness blossomed in his face and then he laughed—a great, joyous burst of delight that made her laugh, too.

"I have learned the folly of trying to command you," he said as he pulled her into his arms. He still smiled with joy, but she saw the deeper emotion in his blue eyes as he murmured, "And my heart would be dead without you, too."

Connor loudly—and fiercely—cleared his throat. "I didn't anticipate this when I agreed to set him free."

"Nor I," Caradoc rumbled, planting his feet and crossing his arms, and looking so like Alexander in his ire that despite Isabelle's shock at the revelation of their relationship, she knew they *must* be brothers. "It's one thing to be merciful, but we never thought—"

"It doesn't matter what you think," she said gently, knowing their objections were based on their concern for her. "I have decided. It is what I want to do."

"Allis will object," Connor protested. "She'll be upset, too."

"I think Allis will understand. There was much she was willing to do for love."

Connor flushed, and he wisely didn't try to deny it. "Then there is no more to be said," he conceded, albeit with obvious reluctance. "As we followed our hearts, I cannot tell you not to follow yours."

"*I* can," Caradoc said. "What's to become of her if she goes off with him?" he demanded of Connor, as if Alexander weren't there. "He has no trade, no skills, no home."

"He has a trade and skills," Isabelle retorted, not pleased that Caradoc was interfering. "He can be a soldier. Or a mason. Or a carpenter. He has worked all his life and I have no qualms. We will manage."

"But you're a noblewoman and he's . . . he's . . ."

"A knight's bastard. I know, and I don't care.

What good is a title if it means you must marry without love? I would rather be the poor wife of a knight's bastard than married to a wealthy man I didn't love. And it seems to me, Caradoc, that you are in no position to preach to me, since you married the daughter of a wool merchant."

"A rich one," he shot back.

"Yet you love her dearly, or so Allis says. Is that a lie?"

Caradoc colored. "No."

"And if she were a poor wool merchant's daughter, would you love her the less?"

"Well, no."

"There then!" Isabelle cried triumphantly, her hands on her hips.

"I told you there's no arguing with her," Connor noted as he regarded his brother with manly sympathy. "She'll outtalk you every time. And she's right. Neither one of *us* was practical when we fell in love."

Caradoc looked as if he wasn't willing to yield, but as he opened his mouth to speak, the sound of pounding feet and shouts of alarm sounded on the stairs. The door burst open, and Denis dashed into the chamber, brandishing a rusty sword in his right hand and his dagger in his left, a coil of rope slung around his chest.

"Stand back, all of you!" he cried, waving his weapons around like some sort of mad knight. "Alexander, I have come to rescue you!"

Charlie and Burt came charging in after him, swords drawn. "He give us the slip, my lord," Burt panted apologetically as they halted, their eyes on the Gascon.

"Denis, what the devil are you doing?" Alexander demanded.

"I told you!" Denis cried with great bravado, although his face was as pale as a sheep's clean fleece. "I have come to rescue you!"

"Denis," Alexander began in a more moderate tone. "There is no need to rescue me, although I appreciate the effort."

"But I heard you were captured and . . . and . . ."

"I was, but all is well now."

"Or it will be soon," Connor said to Charlie and Burt as he shooed them out the door like a mother hen with her chicks. "You two can go now. Leave this matter with me."

"But he run up here and—"

"So I gather. There's been a misunderstanding all 'round. It seems the despicable DeFrouchette who abducted Lady Isabelle has a twin, and he discovered what his brother had done and took it upon himself to rescue Isabelle. Amazing, isn't it? Like some kind of troubadour's tale, really, but strange things do happen in families. Now get back to your posts."

Still holding his weapons defensively, Denis sidled toward Alexander. "What is going on? Who is he talking about? You have no twin brother, have you?"

"Not a twin, but there is a half brother," Caradoc announced.

Denis really looked at Caradoc for the first time since bursting into the room like a bantam rooster who sees a hawk in the coop. He was so shocked that he dropped his sword. Before he could pick it up again, Caradoc grabbed it.

"By God, DeFrouchette," he remarked, "you seem to be a popular fellow. Isabelle in love with you, this skinny fellow trying to rescue you. Next thing I know, you'll tell me there's some band of Norsemen about to—"

They all froze as the cry arose from the battlements like a call to battle. "Viiiiikings!"

Isabelle and Alexander exchanged shocked looks while Connor and Caradoc made for the door. Unfortunately, they both tried to get through it at the same time. After a brief struggle, Connor got out first, but Caradoc was right behind him.

"Denis," Alexander growled, "what's going on?"

Isabelle realized Denis looked as surprised as they did. "I do not know. All I know is, when I heard in the tavern that you had been captured, I had to help you. I thought we could climb down the wall as we did before, and Kiera has horses waiting and . . ."

"Please tell me you haven't stolen any horses."

"Not exactly. Kiera stole some jewels from Osburn and we traded one for them."

"Thank God for that," Alexander said, sounding stern, but his eyes were gentle. "You loyal fool, you could have been killed, rushing in here like that!"

"Well, I am not dead, and you are free, so let us go and—"

"And find out what's going on," Alexander finished.

"But we can go—"

"Not if Bellevoire is under attack," Alexander declared as he headed toward the door, Isabelle right behind.

* * *

As they all, including Denis, entered the court-yard, they discovered that most of the other inhabi-tants of Bellevoire were already there.

So were Ingar and twenty of his men. Ingar had a grip on Bartholomew's tunic and a knife at his throat. In the center of the band of Norsemen was a group of people, obviously hostages: a thin, grizzled farmer, a plump woman and what looked to be their five children, another man and a gaunt woman, and three young men. Ingar and his men must have cap-tured them on the way to Bellevoire.

Bellevoire guards milled about, their weapons ready, but they were clearly afraid to attack the Norsemen lest the Norsemen kill their hostages.

Connor and Caradoc stood facing Ingar, fierce but also not willing to do anything that would put Bartholomew and the others at risk.

Isabelle realized that poor Bartholomew looked about to faint. The other captives were terrified, as she had been that first day when Alexander had ab-ducted her, and her heart went out to them.

Then she noticed that Alexander had his sword drawn.

"Go to your sister," he muttered, nodding at Allis, who was standing, pale and tight-lipped, with Ed-mond in the crowd. "I will deal with Ingar."

She didn't want to leave him, but she had no wish to be taken captive by Ingar, either. She could not help fearing that his arrival here had something to do with her, so she sidled away into the crowd.

"Alexander!" Ingar cried happily when he saw Alexander striding toward him. Then his pleasure dissipated, to be replaced with a frown. "You are not dead."

"Obviously not," Alexander replied. "I was imprisoned, though, until a short time ago, which is why I did not meet you."

"Ah. I thought perhaps you had decided to stay with the lady, after all."

"I would have kept my word. But if you thought me dead, what are you doing here?"

Ingar grinned. "Perhaps I thought to see your lady one last time. Where is—ah!"

Ingar spotted her in the crowd. Then he saw Allis, and his eyes widened. "By Woden's beard," he declared, "there are two of them!"

Connor's face went as red as an apple, and Caradoc's grim visage grew even grimmer.

Afraid they would draw their swords and start a melee, Isabelle stepped forward. "You must have been drinking too much wine, Ingar, to come to Bellevoire like this, threatening to kill people—"

Bartholomew's eyes widened, and he made a strangled sound.

"Have I said anything about killing anybody?" Ingar demanded, offended. He waved his dagger to make his point, but he did not loose his hold on the poor reeve, either.

"I come in peace, my lord," he said, addressing Caradoc, "and if I have the lord of Bellevoire's guarantee that I may leave in peace, I have some information to sell. These others are only to guarantee the safety of me and my men until I strike a bargain with you."

"*I* am the lord of Bellevoire," Connor said, "and I don't negotiate with brigands who hold knives at my peoples' throats."

"And *I* would not risk coming here if I didn't

think I had something of great value to sell to you."

"What is that?"

"Information. I can tell you where the lady was held. I'm sure DeFrouchette and his friend cannot—they know nothing of the sea and how to set a course. I can tell you where those Brabancons have fled." Ingar grinned with savage glee. "Of course, if you think this information worth nothing, we can kill your people and fight our way back to the ship."

The crowd began to whisper and murmur and mutter, and Bartholomew moaned piteously.

"I will allow you safe passage," Connor said brusquely. "You have my word. Now let them go."

With a bow and a smile, Ingar did. Bartholomew fell to his knees, gasping for breath. He was quickly surrounded by Gleda and the other servants, who helped him to his feet.

"Inside," Connor snapped, turning and heading toward the hall.

Ingar and his men followed him, and so did Isabelle, Allis, Alexander, Caradoc and Edmond, leaving the others milling about uncertainly. Connor went to the dais and sat, but he made no move to invite anybody else to do so. Isabelle and the rest stood to the side.

"What do you want in exchange for this information?" Connor demanded of Ingar and his men.

"One thousand marks."

"Agreed."

Ingar slid a sly glance at Isabelle, his gray eyes twinkling. "I would ask for the lady, too, but she does not like me, and although she is a beauty, I prefer my horses spirited and my women placid."

Appalled, Allis sucked in her breath, while Isabelle sighed with relief.

Then Ingar looked at Alexander. "And what of your promise to me, DeFrouchette? Since you are free to go from here, will you keep your word?"

Before anybody else could speak, Isabelle hurried forward and addressed the Norseman. "You may have my dowry if you release him from his pledge."

"Isabelle!" Alexander gasped.

"Well, if it's that or you," she smiled at him, then turned to face the Norseman, "I intend to marry him, and I do not want to be married to a brigand, so I will gladly give you the dowry to release him from his promise." She tilted her head and gave Ingar her coy and innocent look. "You yourself told me how much he cares for me. Surely you will not take him away, especially when I am willing to pay you to keep him."

After a moment's dumbfounded silence, Ingar threw back his head and laughed until the rafters rang with it. Then he shook his head. "By Thor's hammer, what a woman! I wish you joy of her, DeFrouchette, and many fine sons. I think it will take a pack of you to get the better of her, and for that, I don't envy you. But your nights . . . well, for that, I do. But now, my lady, as to your bargain—I agree."

He turned back to Connor. "There may be other bargains struck, lord of Bellevoire, of trade and alliance. Are you willing to discuss such matters with me?"

Connor, having likewise recovered from his surprise, inclined his head. "Since I would rather make treaties than battle, I am willing."

"Good—but I would speak of such matters with you alone," Ingar replied. "Otherwise, I'm afraid that woman will bargain me out of my ship."

Later that night, after Ingar and his men had taken their money and departed, a treaty for trade negotiated—without Isabelle's help—and Denis had entertained the company in the great hall with his tumbling before going back to sit with his devoted Kiera, Isabelle slipped into Allis's garden. Roses climbed upon the walls, and poppies, primroses and other flowers filled the beds, their scent light on the evening breeze. The moon rose bright and full, its silvery light illuminating the path, but leaving other areas deep in shadow.

"Alexander?"

A strong hand reached out and drew her into one such shadow, and then her lover's lips found hers. Happy to be alone with him at last, she relaxed into his embrace. His hands meandered over her body, stroking and caressing and exciting her as only he could.

Raucous laughter burst through the silence from the direction of the barracks, and a door banged. Bartholomew wandered past the gate, regaling somebody with the tale of his near death at a fierce Norseman's hands.

"This is not as private as I had hoped when I suggested it," Isabelle murmured, disappointed.

"No," Alexander agreed with both remorse and laughter in his voice. "But perhaps that is for the best. After all, if we are found making love in the garden, it would be a great scandal."

"As if I care anything for gossip," she chided

with a smile, inching closer. She found the thought of making love with him then and there incredibly exciting.

"No, it's clear to me that you don't," he whispered as he pressed light kisses over her cheeks and lips. "I daresay many tongues are going to wag as it is, and there will always be those here who will hate me for what I have done."

"They will hate your evil twin."

Alexander pulled back, and she could tell he had that little wrinkle of concern between his brows. "Ah, yes, my evil twin. Did you put that idea in your brother-in-law's head?"

"Not at all," she answered honestly. "I don't know where it came from, but if it means people won't set upon you like those two guards did, I don't care."

He chuckled softly. "Nor do I." He embraced her tenderly. "And it's very good of Connor to offer to send a message to his friend about being his garrison commander. I hope Sir Ralph de Valmont will agree."

"I don't think you have to fear that he will refuse Connor's request," she replied. "Connor is a friend of the king, and Sir Ralph wishes to be, so he will probably be glad to accept Connor's recommendation—as well he should. I also understand he's terrified of Caradoc. There was some kind of misunderstanding, and he seems to think Caradoc is always on the verge of going off on some kind of rampage, so he does not want to be considered my family's enemy." She toyed with a strand of Alexander's hair. "I can understand why he would wish to avoid that. Caradoc is very like you, and you're frightening when you're angry."

Alexander ran his fingertip down her cheek, making her shiver in a very pleasant way. "I never seemed to frighten *you*."

"Oh, I was very afraid at first, but I didn't want to show it."

"You certainly succeeded." He sighed, his lips against her hair. "I cannot believe all that you are willing to give up to be with me."

"I gain far more than I lose." She relaxed against him, then raised her head to look up at his angular face. "We've already made love and we are not married yet," she noted as she caressed him boldly. "How much of a scandal do you think it will be if, by chance, we are found here?"

His breathing quickening, he closed his eyes. "I don't know."

"Shall we risk it?"

"I think I have just realized something about you, my love. You *like* danger."

"It does lend a certain spice to things, I suppose—as long as this is as dangerous as we get. I have had enough of true danger to last me a lifetime. And I think *you* like women who stand up to you."

"I admire women who stand up for themselves," he amended, "although I must say, I don't think I've met any other woman so capable in that regard. Which is one reason I love you so much."

"Perhaps one reason I found you so seductive was your dark and brooding temperament."

"You think I brood?" he asked, as if genuinely surprised.

She undid the buckle of his sword belt, and it fell to the ground. "You used to. I shall simply have to keep you too busy to think deep, dark thoughts."

He gasped as she put her hand under his tunic,

then sighed as she ran her fingers over his chest. "I don't think I'll ever be unhappy or discontented again," he murmured as he gathered her into his arms. "Everything I shall ever want is here in my arms."

She raised herself on her toes to kiss him. "And everything I have ever dreamt of is in mine."

Four stars of romance soar this November!

WHEN IT'S PERFECT by Adele Ashworth
An Avon Romantic Treasure

Miss Mary Marsh's quiet world is sent spinning the moment dashing Marcus Longfellow comes striding into her life. The Earl of Renn believes the young miss is hiding something, and a sensuous seduction will surely reveal her secrets. But is his growing passion for her interfering with his perfect plan?

I'VE GOT YOU, BABE by Karen Kendall
An Avon Contemporary Romance

Vanessa Tower has never met anyone like Christopher "Crash" Dunmoor, the sexy adventurer who can ignite sparks in her with just a smile. Will the gorgeous bookworm convince the confirmed loner that love is the most tantalizing adventure of all?

HIGHLAND ROGUES: THE WARRIOR BRIDE
by Lois Greiman
An Avon Romance

Lachlan MacGowan is suspicious of the mysterious "Hunter"—and shocked to discover this warrior is really a woman! Beneath the soldier's garb, Rhona is a proud beauty . . . and she is determined to resist the striking rogue who has laid siege to her heart.

HIS BRIDE by Gayle Callen
An Avon Romance

Gwyneth Hall has heard the dark rumors about Sir Edmund Blackwell, the man she is betrothed to but has never seen. Yet burning kisses from the gorgeous "devil" may be more than she bargained for . . .

REL 1002

Don't Miss Any of the Fun and Sexy Novels from Avon Trade Paperback

For Better, For Worse
by Carole Matthews
0-380-82044-7 • $14.95 US
"Like real life, only funnier, with sharper dialogue and more cocktails."
Valerie Frankel

The Dominant Blonde
by Alisa Kwitney
0-06-008329-8 • $13.95 US • $22.00 Can
"Clever, smart, and sexy. Fast and funny."
Rachel Gibson, author of *Lola Carlyle Reveals All*

Filthy Rich
by Dorothy Samuels
0-06-008638-6 • $13.95 US • $22.95 Can
"Frothy and good-natured . . .
it's part *Bridget Jones Diary*, part *Who Wants to Be a Millionaire*."
New York Times Book Review

Ain't Nobody's Business If I Do
by Valerie Wilson Wesley
0-06-051592-9 • $13.95 US • $20.95 Can
"Outstanding . . .[a] warm, witty comedy of midlife manners."
Boston Herald

The Boy Next Door
by Meggin Cabot
0-06-009619-5 • $13.95 US • $20.95 Can

And Coming Soon

A Promising Man (and About Time, Too)
by Elizabeth Young
0-06-050784-5 • $13.95 US

Avon Romantic Treasures

*Unforgettable, enthralling love stories,
sparkling with passion and adventure
from Romance's bestselling authors*